ASCENSION

SUSAN NORDMAN

Blue Forge Press
Port Orchard ❁ Washington

Ascension
Copyright 2020
by Susan Nordman

First eBook Edition May 2020
First Print Edition May 2020

ISBN 978-1-59092-983-4

For information about film, reprint or other subsidiary rights, contact blueforgegroup@gmail.com

Blue Forge Press is the print division of the volunteer-run, federal 501(c)3 nonprofit company, Blue Forge Group, founded in 1989 and dedicated to bringing light to the shadows and voice to the silence. We strive to empower storytellers across all walks of life with our four divisions: Blue Forge Press, Blue Forge Films, Blue Forge Gaming, and Blue Forge Records. Find out more at www.BlueForgeGroup.org

Blue Forge Press
7419 Ebbert Drive Southeast
Port Orchard, Washington 98367
blueforgepress@gmail.com
360-550-2071 ph.txt

· DEDICATION ·

To my wonderful parents, Vern and Faye.

Dad, when I was sixteen, you encouraged me to write down my stories. It took a while, but I finally did it. Thank you.

Mom, you always pushed me to be the best person I could be, while always allowing me to be myself. As a fellow writer, artist, and friend, I miss sharing this with you. I love you always.

· ACKNOWLEDGEMENTS ·

To my friends Dave Martyn, Linda Olsen, and Kimmy Cushner from my writing group, thank you. I appreciate your input, encouragement, and honesty—especially when I wrote something dumb.

ASCENSION

SUSAN NORDMAN

· CHAPTER I ·

The fog that still hovered on the wide tidal flats glowed a luminescent gold as the sun bent its rays and dipped nearer the western horizon. At least, Ilaria assumed it was west; it was hard to tell direction on some of these worlds near the outer edges of Janus space. Even though much of the Wald grew thick with jungle and tangles of vines, she knew there was little dry land on the soggy world. Especially in this coastal swamp she had been called to.

Studying the muddy flats as she circled her shuttle around for the best landing site, Ilaria was momentarily blinded as the sunlight refracted off a stretch of mud devoid of the coils of mist. The collection of moisture told the young Empati these few miles of coast were not empty of water for long. The tide may be out now, but they would have to work quickly before the basin filled again.

The only viable place Ilaria found to land Rill was at the top of a fifty-foot cliff next to the three other ships that had carried the work crews. The busy Infantry Keepers were already at the base of the cliff laying down a mobi-path out to the center of the viscous flats where the dead body had been found. The high, rocky area was naturally clear of trees and the only ground in the area stable enough for even her small interstellar craft to set down.

"You should have told me I'd have to repel down," Ilaria sent telepathically to her mentor. She didn't have to add Thane's name to her mental sending as he was the only person on this remote jungle world who could hear it, an unusual ability for the middle-aged empath wasn't telepathic.

"What does it matter?" Thane sent back. *"Or have you forgotten your training already?"*

"What matters is the Gala tonight. Sarkin will be pissed if I crack a nail or have rope burns on my hands. He has a special mission for me and we're also meeting the new ambassadors of the V'reem."

Thane immediately regretted the poor timing of his call. He had been waiting for months for a legitimate reason to call his ward out into the field. Such opportunities didn't come up that often and he hadn't realized the annual Summit was tonight. In almost any other situation, the emperor would have excused her absence, but not this one. The V'reem held the space near the Janus Empire and, after several years of attempting communication with them, the aliens had finally responded. The Gala was to be their formal introduction to Emperor Sarkin.

"I forgot about that," Thane said contritely.

"Lucky you," Ilaria grumble while strapping herself into the harness. *"At least you warned me about the mud."*

"I do try to not add to your problems. I am very sorry I called you here now."

"I'm not," Ilaria sent back. *"Even though I'll be in for it if I'm late, you know I wouldn't have missed this."*

Proving that her skills hadn't been muted during her three years of being a mental emissary for the Emperor at his Palace, Ilaria expertly descended the sheer embankment. The mud sucked at her high, watertight boots and, though she wore a protective worker's jumpsuit, Ilaria realized there was no way she was going to leave this world as clean as she had arrived.

Though focused on the task at hand, she fretted about running out of time to make herself presentable for the important date with the arriving dignitaries.

As soon as her feet hit the ground, Ilaria studied the area from ground level while she unstrapped her harness. The exposed delta was nearly three miles of muddy flats to the west and was easily a mile wide. The near side where she was standing was backed by the high cliff, but on the opposite side grew the thick forest of sequoia-like trees the Wald was infamous for. The sunlight playing over the mud and haze made the expanse seem even wider than it really was. The golden illusion was suddenly over as a thick cloud obscured the muted sun and returned the fog to its steely grey. At the inland edge of the flats, tiny rivulets cut alluvial veins as they branched out through the mud from a larger arterial stream about another quarter mile inland.

The path where Ilaria now stood on was the kind of temporary, web-like mobile road used by the military on worlds when it was necessary to access the undeveloped or more unreachable places. Flexible enough to be rolled up and light enough to be carried by hand, the mobi-paths still had the sturdiness to transport even heavy equipment. In her history classes on the Janus Empire, Ilaria learned that six battalions of Infantry Peace Keepers as well as ground tanks had marched over the Vega Swamps during the Battle of Tyrius on nothing but mobi-paths.

Ilaria was glad the road's strength wouldn't be tested on this mission because, even though it had long been proven to be so, the path didn't appear to be very stable resting on the soupy tidal mud. It reminded her of the training she had endured at the Academy for conditioning Keepers to low-gravity worlds and she felt as if she were walking across the soft, matted floors back at the training rooms on Marasa Prime. With great care, Ilaria crossed the path out to where Thane was standing. Being the bitch that karma was, Ilaria had often wondered why she had been forced to endure so many hours of training in various offworld environments because, after twenty years of being a

12 ASCENSION

Peace Keeper Empati, this was the first time in her life she had ever actually needed to use the skill. But since the emperor had assigned her to the Palace, she considered most of her training useless.

Squeezing past the *normal* Keepers still working to finish laying down the remainder of the path, Ilaria turned more than a few heads, but it wasn't in appreciation of her natural, unassuming beauty or her lithe grace derived from two decades of hard training in weapons and martial arts. Holding her head high and defiant as she quickly passed the working soldiers, Ilaria couldn't help but sense the unguarded fear that made these Keepers balance on the edge as far away as the narrow path would let them, a foolish prejudice that made them believe that any Empati could read the mind of a Normal. Though she was strong for a telepath, not even she could pluck a thought from thin air.

She heard one of them whisper *peek* in a voice low enough to be discrete, but deliberately loud enough for her to hear the derogatory term. *Peek!*

It was a name those without psionic abilities labeled all the Empati as if every psychic could actually peek into the hidden reaches of the minds of Normals. With Ilaria, though, the slur wasn't completely without merit. She did have the ability to scan their minds, but not without touching them first and that was forbidden without a mandate from either Admiral Torquil or Emperor Sarkin himself. An illegal scan was the highest crime a touch-feel such as her could commit and if they were lucky, it would only be a capital offense. At worst, she could be sent to the Pushers. Ilaria shuddered at the thought of having a Sona "push" one of their mental punishments into her mind; any nightmare they gave you was your reality until the dreamer awoke.

Even though her hands were sticky with sweat on this humid world, Ilaria kept her gloves on lest one of these paranoid Keepers accuse her of an unregulated mind-scan. She didn't look at the workers as she hurried past them, but her empathic senses could still feel their fear, their bitterness. The cloying vestiges of their hatred rolled over her like a tidal bore rushing at her down the path. They would never believe that even as powerful a telepath as Ilaria was, their minds were safe from her peeking inside. The entire Janus Empire, and especially other Peace-Keepers knew this, but still the belief persisted that mind-speakers were also mind-readers.

The irony was that outside the Empati, only Thane knew of her telepathic abilities. Ilaria wore the Keeper uniform indicating her psionic abilities as an empath, but not the insignia of the telepaths. The Normals were right about her, but only by playing the odds their prejudice.

Though the Empati were a special unit within the Peace-Keepers, they operated separately under the direction of Admiral Torquil who oversaw their entire department, from the cyborg Niegan, who managed the Control Center down to the Academy training instructors. There were tens of thousands of Normal Peace Keepers stationed on the dozens of systems controlled by the Empire and over a thousand new recruits in the Peace-Keeper Academy at any given time. But only a hundred of these had any measurable psychic talent that separated them from the other Keepers and made them Empati.

Empathic abilities were usually discovered at eight years of age when children of the Empire were tested for any psionic abilities. If any Citizen were discovered to have them, they were brought to the Academy for training in order to better harness their powers. Most of the children who tested positive had varying levels of empathy and a few were even considered low-grade telepaths, but only a rare few like Ilaria had possessed both talents.

To Ilaria's knowledge, only three others in the history of the Empati had her ability of not only sensing emotion and thought, but as rare of a gift as that was, she was still unique in what she could do. Until she had been born, telepaths could only mind-speak with other telepaths. With a physical touch, Ilaria could establish a telepathic connection with anyone regardless of species or psychic ability. The longer she held the physical contact, the stronger the connection became and the more she was able to discern. It was her most valuable asset to Torquil, Sarkin and to the government. It was also one of the emperor's most closely guarded secrets.

And it was because of these telepathic, touch-feel powers Thane had summoned her to this swampy forest world and it was only because the Denobian had made the request that Ilaria had agreed to come. Though she loathed her duties at Sarkin's Galas, had it been any other Keeper, Normal or Empati, she would have used the annual summit as an excuse to refuse the request. Crossing the any of the royal houses was a very bad idea, but annoying the emperor could be paramount to suicide.

"Doctor," Thane greeted her even though Ilaria hadn't actually earned her degree. When Sarkin had her transferred to his palace, her medical career officially ended. Sobek, the emperor's younger brother had argued on her behalf, but Sarkin wouldn't budge. If the healer needed a telepath so badly, there were half a dozen others he could choose from; Sarkin had other plans for the contact telepath.

"Detective Inspector," Ilaria responded with Thane's unofficial title. If the two were Normals in the empire, they both would have enjoyed the careers of their choosing; however, their status as peeks nullified any rank or respect a granted to a Citizen with the same training and experience.

"Thank you again for coming," Thane sent telepathically as she approached. *"I realize it was inconvenient for you."*

"No problem," Ilaria lied as she smiled down at the diminutive man, his short stature derived from being native to the gravity-dense planet Denobia. Considered tall by most of his world's standards, at 4'8", Thane was the smallest of any Keeper, or at least any of the adults. *"Fortunately, the Gala isn't at the Sarkin's palace on Marasa Prime, but on the Celest, so I only have to make it back to the Gate."* Then out loud she said, "Now, what is so important that you needed me?"

"The Indigenous found a body washed into this tidal flat," Thane explained, gesturing to where the workers were laying down the last of the path.

"You called me here to investigate a dead body?" Ilaria

asked raising her eyebrow and putting her hands on her hips. "That's the Psi-cops' medical examiner's responsibility, not mine. You've got other people for that."

Being a much stronger empath than herself, Ilaria knew Thane hadn't been fooled by her mock severity. If she hadn't been so pressed for time, she would actually be enjoying this trip. It didn't matter that the Wald was dirty and the stagnant mud carried the odor of everything that had ever died within it. It was a moment away from the Palace and the duties to the Emperor Sarkin.

But a few moments of adventure exploring a world were only part of her decision to come. Having trained her literally since infancy, Thane was her closest associate at the Academy and her mentor. He wouldn't have asked her to come if he hadn't felt it was necessary and Ilaria would do anything within her power to help him if she could.

"Of course, I didn't," said Thane pointing to three trees standing not with the forest at the edge of the flats, but near them and the hastily constructed path. "It's the trees I need help with. These particular Indigenous are a sapient, flora-evolved species, but our translators don't seem to work with their language. I was hoping you'd be able to mind-speak with them."

At first, Ilaria wondered why she hadn't noticed the trio of trees standing about ten feet ahead of them, but then she reasoned why would anyone take notice a bunch of trees on a forest world? They were definitely humanoid with one head and the usual pair of arms and legs, but that was where the similarities ended. Their hands were more like branches ending in dozens of twig-like fingers and the roots on their feet splayed out, supporting their weight on the viscous mud. The two taller trees she estimated at almost ten feet tall while the third was only about six feet in height. Whether it was considered clothing or just adornment, Ilaria wasn't sure, but each of them had garlands of yellow-flowered vines draped through their branches.

To get to the them, Ilaria had to walk back past some of the workers who were still working on the path. In an effort to avoid touching her, one man fell off the makeshift path and sank up to his shins in the viscous sludge. This unfortunate incident began a round of whole-hearted cursing while he waited for two of his comrades to pull him out; much of the profanity was directed at Ilaria's direction and laced with *peek* references.

Ilaria was glad the Normals couldn't read her own emotions or they would have known her external calm was a farce. She hated being among these mundane people as much as they hated having her there. The Keeper unit sent to investigate the deceased already had Thane embedded with them as their required Empati and resented the Denobian calling in a second. Regardless of their true ability, all peeks were mind-rapers and tolerated only if absolutely necessary and only for as long as it took to get their information. After that, peeks should crawl back under the rock of the Empati Keep and stay there until needed again.

Of all the people Ilaria knew, Thane was the only exception to the mind-speak rule that only telepaths had the ability. As a child, she found that she could mentally send her thoughts to her training master and, much to the surprise of both of them, he was able to respond back. As Thane wasn't a telepath, the connection shouldn't have been there. Ilaria tried many times over the years with instructors and psychic classmates, but as yet, Thane was still the only non-telepath who seemed to have the ability. Considering it a fluke due to their close relationship, they had kept their private mental connection a secret.

When she reached the waiting Trees, Ilaria pushed out with her mind. When they didn't respond, she concluded that whatever their method of communication was, these creatures were not themselves telepathic. As usual, Thane was right and she would have to establish physical contact for the mind-speak.

Despite the heat of the stagnant tropics, Ilaria's sweating palm chilled as if she'd dunked it in ice water when she pulled off her glove. Wiping the wetness onto her tunic, Ilaria held up her palm to invite a physical connection. After a moment, the tallest of the trees responded by holding up his own hand. *Her* hand, Ilaria corrected herself as she touched palms with the tree's massive hand. Once the mental connection had been made, Ilaria sensed the matriarchal distinction. These tall Trees were a mated pair; the smallest one was their child.

"*We are the Akilli Baum, Voice of the Rebe for the Edu of the world you call the Wald.*"

Ilaria's mind tingled as the Mother Tree spoke with the telepathic communication. Along with the unspoken words came mental images of the vast forests of their planet Wald IV with its wide swaths of swampland and diverse ecosystems broken only by areas too rocky for the sapient Trees to take root. The meaning of the words also flowed as the language barriers dissolved with her psionic touch. The *Baum* were all the sentient Trees within the Forest of the Wald, but the *Akilli Baum* were like the ones standing before her—sentient Trees who could uproot themselves and walk among the *Edu,* who were the other in lifeforms of their world. The meaning of *Rebe* was more difficult for Ilaria to define, but she got the impression it was the ruling class entwining itself around all the others and whom the rest of the *Edu* followed.

"*I am Ilaria, Voice for the Janus Empire,*" the young woman mentally said, true only in the fact that she currently speaking. Ilaria wasn't really the voice for anything as the telepath held no real place of power within the Empire and was merely a servant for those who were, but she didn't feel the need to clarify that distinction at this time. Continuing, she asked, "*How did you discover this offworlder?*"

"*We crossed with our Anak for the Improva and the Edu told us,*" the Mother Tree answered as images flowed into Ilaria's mind, reinforcing the meaning of their words. "Anak" simply meant this smaller tree was their child. The three had come to the flat during an unusually low tide and decided to cross it as a shortcut to meet with other Akilli for this *impova.* The *Edu* they were referring to in this sense were tiny, crab-like creatures who lived under the mud and surfaced at low tide in order to feed. These crabs had warned them of an offworld body, so the Trees had responded by informing the alien Miner.

Or at least they had tried to. Leaving their intended journey, they had traveled to the Pit to tell them of the Dead One. The Mother didn't expand on what the Pit was, but Ilaria felt the bile rise in her throat as Ilaria sensed the Akilli's hatred of the vast scar in the ground where alien *Humans* mined for the gas. When the trees found that no one at the Pit would speak with them, they felt their only option to alert the humans to the body was to bring them to it. They had picked up the nearest miner they could and waited for the others to give chase so they could lead them here.

Ilaria suppressed an urge to laugh at the image of the man bouncing on the Father tree's shoulder like a sack of old root vegetables. She recovered quickly and asked the trees why they went to so much trouble in order to inform the *humans* of the deceased. The images she received were even more troubling than the ones of the Pit and full of the memory of *humans* carrying tongues of fire and burning everything in their path. Great swaths of their forest had been cleared to where nothing was left but the dead and blackened stumps of their brothers and sisters and the remaining soil salted with poison so nothing could grow there again. The Akilli were afraid that if they hadn't informed the offworlders of the one who was dead, they would be blamed and the Burning would begin again.

With great difficulty, Ilaria buried her own emotions deep down as she witnessed the forest's destruction. Touching their minds through the mental link, she felt as if she were walking where they stepped, smelling their air and feeling the cool mud as it covered her feet. Listening, she could hear the voices of the crustaceans under the muddy surface, tiny voices telling the trees of the lifeless stranger who had ridden the waters on the incoming tide. Through the contact, Ilaria sensed that she would not be able to speak with these mud-dwelling *Edu* without her connection to the Akilli. Though sentient, their minds were too primitive for the telepath to understand.

"Is there anything more you can tell me about this dead stranger?" Ilaria asked. *"Do the Edu know where it came from or how long it has been here?"*

"They do not know. The moons are in alignment now and the tides are both higher and lower than usual." This was followed by more images of the two moons of the Wald joining together to pull the waters of the inland sea into a very low minus tide. Because of this, the small crabs enjoying the feeding in areas rarely exposed by the rising and falling waters, had discovered the offworlder buried in their mud.

As Ilaria was locked in communication with the tallest Tree, Anak stepped forward and planted his own wooden hand on his mother and with the added connection, she was joined mentally with the sapling. She sensed he was just on the brink of adulthood, and though still young by Akilli standards, Anak had seen nearly fifty springs. Too young to remember the Burning, the child was more curious about the funny strangers sinking in the mud than afraid. In this forest world, death was a way of life and he knew that every death nourished the living, so it wasn't something to be feared. Ilaria heard, though she didn't understand that it was *the balance of Edu.* How she would love to speak with these Trees in depth if she had more time!

Anak's view of the humans wasn't the view his parents shared. In their experience, on their symbiotic world, humans were not Edu. Whatever the *Edu* took, they gave it back. The offworlders at the Mine were considered parasites who giving nothing back from what they took.

With Anak's additional touch, Ilaria also sensed great worry emanating from the child. While the activity on the mud was exciting to the youngster, it was also causing a serious delay. Ilaria noticed the beginning of tiny buds at the ends of their hair-like branches. With a flash of inspiration, Ilaria understood the young one's worry. This was his first flowering! The Akilli had mentioned they were going to an *improva.* She hadn't known what that was when they first mentioned it, but she realized that it was his coming of age ceremony. They were going to Anak's first mating, or pollination, or whatever it was that these trees did to reproduce. No wonder they were so anxious to leave. Creatures like these breathed with the seasons and didn't have time for long delays.

Since Ilaria had witnessed the discovery through their eyes, she knew there was little more information they could provide. Bidding them a good journey she released the three Trees who immediately disappeared into the nearby forest lest any more the offworlders wish to question them.

"Where are they going?" Thane asked when she joined him at the end of the freshly laid path.

"Currently, they have more important business to attend to. I have all their information." Ilaria answered. She offered Thane her still bare hand, inviting him to make the telepathic connection with her in the same way she had with the Akilli. The brief touch, deeper and more intimate than the mental conversations they usually shared, instantly gave Thane the conversation she had shared with the Trees.

While Ilaria gave her mentor the images from the Akilli, she couldn't suppress the surge of melancholy that swept over her as she read her mentor's deeper motivations for asking her to come. It had been more than just his need for telepathic communication with the Indigenous. They hadn't seen one another in over a year and this had been a wellness check. And she had failed.

Though she tried to hide her deepest emotions, Ilaria was certain that Thane had picked up her sense of dread for the Gala. She had gotten used to burying her emotions during her time at the Palace and it was a relief that Thane knew how she truly felt about her life; she was not eager to for the annual summit or the duties Sarkin would be required to perform.

Though she had only spoken to some Trees, Ilaria's spirits rose; it felt good to be doing something more meaningful that surreptitiously reading alien dignitaries. In an effort to delay the inevitable a little longer, Ilaria checked her watch and decided she still had a bit more time to spare. Shutting out thoughts of the coming evening, she turned her attention to the deceased.

Two thirds of the dead woman lay buried in the tidal sludge making her seem more reminiscent of a relief sculpture belonging in a museum rather than a crime scene. With only the raised portions of the front torso exposed, the woman's gender was easily identified, but with the rest of her so entrenched in the muck, Ilaria couldn't yet identify her species. She was probably human, but the telepath didn't want to jump to conclusions. There were many other humanoid species indigenous on the colonized worlds and some even had wings that would be hidden from her current view.

Ilaria's touch had already told Thane how symbiotic the life on this world was with each other so he didn't need to ask who the Edu or the Akilli were, though like Ilaria, he was stumped on the Rebe. When his unit had been dispatched to the Wald after the discovery of the body, he had used the time in transit to familiarize himself with the nearly eighty-year history the Empire had with this particular world and there had been no mention of them which was extremely odd if the Akilli considered them their leaders.

When the survey team had first prospected on the Wald, they had originally designated this planet as part of the No Man's Land portion of the Badlands, a place in the galaxy that very few wanted to settle. At first, the young world seemed like a paradise ripe for new colonization with thick dense forests and an oxygen rich atmosphere and few animal lifeforms to compete with; however, the survey team quickly came to realize that the lack of fauna didn't mean the Wald was uninhabited. Teeming with a sapient, flora-evolved species that didn't take kindly to offworlders, the Empire decided this world wasn't worth the effort for colonization. The Wald was considered too harsh for humans and too barren of natural resources to be worth the hassle of establishing a hold on the jungle world. There were easier worlds to conquer.

But then the M-Gas had been discovered. The fuel used to power the Empire's fleet through hyperspace was normally created by powdering and then vaporizing Mephitis crystals and the Company, operating through the Mining Guild, was in charge of harvesting any cache of the minerals they could find. But on this swampy world, Mephitis was discovered already in a gaseous state making it instantaneously available for use.

Overnight, the Wald had become the most valuable planet in the Empire.

And inhabited or not, the Empire was going to take every molecule of the M-Gas it could. Determined that the valuable gas would be theirs, war erupted between the flora-evolved life and the invading humans; flamethrowers prevailed, forcing the Indigenous to submit. It was no wonder these Akilli feared a return to the Burning Times they had referred to in Ilaria's vision.

Squatting down to one knee, Ilaria took a closer look at the body and silently asked, *"Do you who she is?"*

"Not yet," Thane answered. *"Daneb insists she isn't from the Mining Guild."*

Ilaria enjoyed a brief memory of her connection with the Akilli and Daneb's humiliating ride through the jungle over the Father Tree's shoulder. Daneb was the foreman and second in command at the Mine and held little regard for anything that didn't turn the Guild or himself a profit.

In Ilaria's opinion, Daneb could obtain lot more of the precious M-Gas if he worked with the Indigenous. She knew the gas was going to be mined one way or another, but much could be done to ease the tensions that constantly arose with the natives. In her brief mind-touch, Ilaria had learned that the Gas was toxic to the Edu. It pooled in vast underground pockets, but occasionally would seep through fissures to the surface. When this occurred, the surrounding air would stagnate, killing any life in the vicinity. By removing the Gas, the Company was actually benefiting the Edu and thereby acting as part of the symbiosis of the Wald. With the indigenous lifeforms on their side, even more Gas deposits could be found and extracted, but Daneb wasn't interested in maintaining the habitat or good relations with the locals. He let his bulldozers and extractors do that for him.

"And he can determine that from way over there?" Ilaria asked, nodding her head to where the miner was huddled with the rest of Thane's unit near the edge of the mobi-path and as far away from the two Empati as they could get. Most of the Keepers had an empath embedded with them when they went

offworld so Thane's presence was tolerated. It was Ilaria they resented and kept well away from. They were already forced to work with one peek; they wanted nothing to do with another.

Thane sent, *"He insists that no one from the Mine is missing. Whoever she was, she wasn't stationed here."*

"That could be problematic if the Edu find that out. They would think their world is being invaded... again. But I guess there's not much they can do against flamethrowers."

"You'd be surprised what lesser people can do against their masters once properly motivated," Thane mused before dropping to his own knees. Reaching out, he dug through the mud and pulled out the woman's right arm. *"Look,"* he sent while wiping away the sludge, *"a prison tattoo. This woman was incarcerated."*

"Maelstrom, if I'm reading it right," Ilaria added out loud. "That would make her an In-Valid. What would a psychic be doing on this planet?"

"Possibly hiding, but that doesn't answer how she got out of prison or how she ended up dead. Could she have crashed?"

"Maybe, but I didn't get any indications from the Indigenous that there had been a landing, intentional or otherwise. There's a lot of shuttle activity around the mine, but they didn't mention anything away farther away from it. I don't think she crashed because that would have harmed the life which would have been remembered even by the lesser forms."

"You're right," said Thane, looking around the muddy plain with a frown. "And if that were the case, where's the wreckage?"

As he spoke, the middle-aged Keeper gazed out to the mouth of the bay. The inland sea was small, but still large enough that the far shore was beyond the horizon. "I suppose it could be out there. Maybe she crashed in the sea and drifted in on the tide."

"Maybe," said Ilaria checking her watch again, "but speaking of tide, you'd better move. It's going to start coming in very soon. And I have to get going if I'm going to make it back on time."

"Thanks for coming," said Thane before barking orders to the waiting crew. The Keepers hung back as Ilaria passed before they began the tedious task of exhuming the body from the mud. She resisted the urge to walk closer to them even though it would have pleased her immensely to have one of them fall into the mud again.

With another glance at her watch, Ilaria sprinted towards the cliff with a cry of dismay at how much time had suddenly vanished. She didn't bother to put the harness around her, but grasped the end of the repelling rope while speaking into her com-link, "Rill, I need you."

Immediately, her shuttle responded by latching onto the rope at the top of the cliff and lifting off. The AI system in the small ship was so sophisticated, Ilaria sometimes thought it had a mind of its own. Rill didn't ask what its human pilot had meant, but simply grabbed onto the ropes with his grappling claws and hoisted Ilaria up to the flat landing area. The ship hovered briefly while Ilaria climbed on board and made haste to the Gate.

Ilaria and Rill were long gone before Thane and his unit were ready. The final hour had been hectic as they raced the incoming tide to extract the dead woman and hoist themselves back up the cliff to their own ships. With a roar, their engines finally fired and the remaining Peace Keepers lifted off from the Wald. Once they were back on Prime, the body would be examined in the Keepers' morgue where they could scan the prison tattoo which would tell them who the deceased was.

But it couldn't answer the bigger question of how the woman had died on a planet most offworlders were forbidden to land on.

· CHAPTER 2 ·

Ilaria was trembling with relief when she docked Rill in the flight bay of the *Celest* with nearly two hours to spare and grateful that Sarkin's annual Summit was being held on his starship this year. If it had been in his palace on Prime as it had been in most years, the distance would have been too great for her to travel to the Wald and make it back in time. Grateful the flagship drifted in a lazy orbit around the Prime Gate, Ilaria had been able to help Thane and still fulfill her duty.

The Janus Empire had five Gates which created an Einstein-Rosen Bridge between the most traveled portions of the realm, the newest orbiting the planet Pyrite. While hyperspace was still the most common form of travel, even at lightspeed, the distance between some portions of the empire were too great for quick travel. With the Gates, Ilaria had folded space between the Capital system to the one orbiting Pyrite in the Outer Reaches in seconds and only spent half an hour traveling the rest of the distance in hyperspace.

But now that she was back, Ilaria raced to her assigned quarters in order to get herself ready for the Gala. Despite the hot water, her relief turned to a cold panic when the stench of the tidal marsh refused to leave her hair even after several washings. Running out of time and options, Ilaria applied a musky perfume, hoping the stench was only lingering in her imagination.

After ensuring she was smelling as fresh as she could, Ilaria set about tackling the bane of her existence: her hair. On most days, there was little she could do to tame the frizz and keep it out of her face. Since cutting it was out of the question as Sarkin insisted gentlemen preferred ladies with long hair, Ilaria was forced to deal with her uncooperative tresses. In her experience, the preference for long hair wasn't the case with all men, but in *her* case, she was in agreement with her emperor. Short curls tended to bounce around her head in an unruly mop and, despite a popular misconception, they weren't easier to take care of. The time it took to force them to swirl in a direction that actually looked good wasn't worth the effort. On average days, Ilaria preferred hair that was wash and wear and her hair hadn't gotten the memo. She generally solved her problem by twisting it into a long braid that was still so long it swung to her hips like the pendulum of an ancient clock.

Unexpectedly rushed for time, Ilaria blessed her naturally curly tresses for the first time in her life. Using their natural tendency to coil on their own, all she had to do was pin portions of her dark locks up high and let the long curls fall down and frame her face. She smirked to herself at the irony that her every day braid took more time to achieve than the five-minute pin up for a diplomatic party. Deciding she was finally presentable, Ilaria ran as fast as her tight gown would allow her before adopting a refined and elegant gate into the Gala.

The ballroom was resplendent, but everything Emperor Sarkin did was measured to impress. The *Celest* crew must have been working around the clock since they received the message the Summit venue had been changed just a week ago. While it wasn't the first time the Gala had been held on the ship, the workers usually had more time to plan and prepare. As it was, they had outdone themselves with floral centerpieces accented with soft blue lights.

The crew had even managed to get a life-size ice sculpture of Sarkin carved and delivered. The features of the imperious statue, decidedly accurate as tendrils of condensation coolly radiated frigid auras which collected around the base, did nothing to alleviate Ilaria's tightening knots of cold anxiety.

Across the crowded room, most of the dignitaries were pretending to enjoy their conversations while trying to look more important than they really were while others were twirling their partners in exotic dances. As she watched them, Ilaria felt Torquil's displeasure mingled in the hazy veils of mist that drifted in icy ribbons from the crystalline statue. Her heart pounded so fiercely in her chest, Ilaria felt it would crack open her ribs when she sensed the Admiral step casually to her side, his pleasant smile obscuring his dissatisfaction to the oblivious Gala.

"Cutting it close today, weren't you?" Torquil asked in an easy tone.

"Closer than I had intended to, sir," Ilaria said trying to quell her growing panic as the Admiral's ire assaulted her mental defenses. Even though he was a Normal, the Admiral was so difficult to read, her empathy could only detect the strongest emotions from him and sometimes not even then. Ilaria suspected his guarded mental control had been honed from rising through the military ranks in Laran's fleet before he retired from the Stellar Navy in order to become director of the Empati.

Ilaria found it disconcerting that even so close, she could rarely read anything from him. Not that she ever tried; she felt random emotions and the occasional stray thoughts the same way Normals heard the buzz of conversations not their own. Generally, she was unaware of them and tuned it out like white noise until a strong emotion broke through the din. The only thing she found more disturbing were the few times she had been alone in deep space. With her senses constantly under assault by those around her, she found the emotional deprivation of solitude to be almost maddening.

This time, however, Ilaria sensed everything as if he were deliberately projecting his emotions. His fury singed the air around her like the radiation from a nuclear bomb site, silently poisoning everything in its radius years after the dust had settled. Ilaria's trepidation deepened when his steely eyes fixed on her, searing her soul with his toxic glare.

"You left the ship today." It was a statement of fact.

"Yes, sir," Ilaria acknowledged as her body shuddered when her heart resumed its pounding after skipping several beats. While she had cut her return to the *Celest* too close for comfort, she couldn't imagine how she could have erred this much with the commander. She had followed every protocol in her mandate as an Empati and had left word with the officer on duty to the reason she was traveling to the Wald. "I received an urgent message from Thane requesting his need for my help."

"Thane," Torquil said, dismissing the urgency that another empath would have need of her. "You are no longer in the service as a physician."

"No, sir. He needed my help as a translator to communicate with the Indigenous." Even though it was unlikely anyone was listening to their conversation, Ilaria said this last part carefully so only Torquil would understand his need was for a telepath. "They are a flora-evolved species of tree and unable to properly use our universal translators."

"Why did he request you so close to the Gala? Jax could have gone in your stead."

"I don't believe he was aware Jax was here," Ilaria said, as her heart skipped another beat. This time, at least, it was for joy at the prospect of seeing her long-time friend again. She had been surprised by a chance encounter with him only a few days ago and he hadn't mentioned he would be assigned to the *Celest* for the Gala.

Though he was a Normal, Torquil knew how to manipulate emotion as easily as if he were an empath. The commander waited, neither acknowledging Ilaria's presence nor dismissing her until she was finally forced to speak.

"It was very sudden, sir. While I did leave word with the duty master, I should have informed you personally before I left. As it was, I barely made it back in time, which I greatly regret."

"But you did make it back," Torquil smiled, icily. Though

his deep mental training didn't allow Ilaria to sense any emotions from him, his calm body language let her know he was well aware of why Thane had summoned her to the Wald and that he more than likely already knew about the body on its way to the morgue back at the Keep. Though she'd only just learned about the identification tattoo, it wouldn't have surprised her if Torquil already knew about that, too. Despite the Gala, investigating a Citizen might be excusable, but it would only add to her transgression if Torquil was aware she had been called away over a dead peek.

"I apologize again, sir, for being as late. I didn't realize how smelly a world it was or how closely the odor would linger. I think it took longer for me to shower than it did for me to get there."

To Ilaria's surprise, Torquil genuinely laughed at her comment. In all of her dealings with the surly man, she hadn't known him to have much of a sense of humor.

"Then all things considered, you did well. Try not to cut it so close next time."

Ilaria smiled in relief, hoping this would be the last he said on the matter. "I won't, sir, though I doubt very much a similar situation will arise."

"I'm sure it won't," Torquil said in a tone so pleasant any guests close enough to hear missed the underlying warning in their conversation. With that, he left her to play pleasantries with a group of senators.

Watching Torquil's grey eyes narrow as he surreptitiously watched her across the room, Ilaria's stomach tightened again at the magnitude of her error. Maybe he would have seen her absence differently if the dead woman had been a Normal. Of course, they hadn't known her In-Valid status at the time, but the commander would never see it that way. She had to take several deep breaths to control a growing knot of fear when it occurred to her that Sarkin may not see her reason as valid, either.

Internally rattled by Torquil's admonishment, Ilaria nearly jumped at Jax's mental comment.

"I said, 'nice dress.'"

"Thanks," Ilaria answered, the tone in her mental sending causing Jax to sharply glance in her direction. Sensing her trepidation and sudden need for companionship, he politely excused himself from the trio of politicians he was charming and wove his way through the growing crowd to where she stood alone in the swelling throng.

Jax was like the first breeze at the end of a hot, stagnant day. At his approach, the tightness in her chest eased and Ilaria was finally able to draw in a proper breath. His nearness brought the scent of fresh rain, making her feel more cleansed than her multiple showers and masking perfumes had. Her smile widened as every step brought him that much closer.

Acutely aware the ever-watchful Torquil was still eyeing her, Ilaria flushed and demurely dropped her gaze away from Jax only to be embarrassed anew as all she saw were her breasts pressed high up her chest due to her over-tight corset. She felt a new blush burn her cheeks and self-consciously brushed at the flowing skirts of her ebony gown as if she were trying to push away her chagrin.

In her mind, the dress was both elegant and obscene. Tiny gems glittered randomly down the pleats like flashes of lightning. It made Ilaria feel like she was a titan goddess rising above dark storm clouds; however, the long slit exposing her left leg from floor to hip and the corset tied so tight it caused her to lose two inches around her already svelte waist, reminded the telepath she was as far removed from the divine as a human could be.

"I feel like I'm going to a funeral, but Torquil insists black is a seductive color to the Arkellians."

"Black is a seductive color for anyone, but with the cut of that dress, no one would think you're headed to a funeral," Jax said, his winning smile again expressing his appreciation and sympathy.

His scrutiny made Ilaria reflexively tug awkwardly at the strapless bodice. It was a useless gesture; her dress was so tightly bound to her breasts she could hardly breathe so there was little chance of it revealing anything accidentally. Even so, it exposed far more than she would have preferred. If she were alone with Jax in private, maybe.

Aware she was projecting her emotions, Ilaria quickly suppressed herself. Torquil may not be a peek, but there were too many in the room who were and she had more than enough trouble for a day that was still very far from over.

"With any kind of luck, I'm dressed for my own funeral," sent Ilaria bitterly, morbidly expressing her silent anxiety. Immediately, she regretted taking out her onus on her friend and smiled an apology to let Jax know she was truly glad to see him. With his return smile, she relaxed, grateful she didn't need to express her contrition with either a verbal or mental apology; as another empath, Jax generally knew how other people felt. Even among other empaths, some were easier to read than others depending on how closely they kept their emotions in check, but her bond with Jax was so strong, there wasn't much she could hide and even less that she wanted to.

They had been close since the first day he had arrived at the Academy after his psychic tests had officially labeled him with psionic abilities. Older than most psychics, Jax had been twelve when Ilaria saw the scrawny youth stumble off the shuttle a full head taller and twenty pounds lighter than the other arriving initiates. But like the younger empathic children, his apprehension grew exponentially as they inched down the ramp from the passenger shuttle, emerging through the venting steam like ghosts taking corporeal form. Feeding from the fear of their shipmates, the terrified boy had kept his head down, carefully watching where he placed his oversized feet as if he fully expected himself to trip.

Watching him watch himself from the upper catwalks of the landing bay, Ilaria knew his fear wasn't that he had just left a family he would never see again and it wasn't that he had no idea what would happen to him now that he was here; he was petrified of making a fool of himself. He had been born different and had sensed the ridicule for as long as he could remember. One of the few psychics whose powers fully emerged at puberty rather than in their earlier childhood, Jax was finally among peers who might understand him. As an Empati initiate, he desperately wanted to fit in and not be different.

But the gawky boy was more different than he knew. Stepping through the vapor, his head suddenly snapped up, his eyes immediately seeking out Ilaria hiding near the ceiling.

And he smiled.

Though she herself was only eight at this time, Ilaria knew what *different* was having endured it in unspoken silence in all the years she'd been at the Academy. Different was her whole life. It was being the best in all the classes, not because she was smarter than the other students were, but because she had been there so long, she had taken the courses several times before. Different was having the Denobian as a guardian and tutor which came with years of private, non-stop lessons. Different was being a telepath in a world of empaths. There were a handful of other tellies in the Academy, but no other touch-feels and none who could hear, not just other telepaths, but Normals and aliens as well. Different was all Ilaria knew.

Until now. Ilaria didn't smile back at the young Jax, but she was transfixed with him. She held his gaze until he was forced to break it after he walked right into the back of the kid in front of him. With the force of the collision knocking him flat on his butt in front of his classmates, Jax did something else he'd never done after embarrassing himself... he laughed.

Then Ilaria did smile, not at the boy's foolishness or at his reaction, but at the boy himself. Though they hadn't even met yet or spoken a single word, Ilaria knew she no longer alone: this boy was just like her: an empath *and* a telepath.

The real surprise came the next morning when Thane suddenly canceled their regular classes and sent her to join the new initiates. The Denobian was many things, but he was no fool. While he had given Ilaria everything he could, the one thing he couldn't give her was a friend. He hadn't been aware how much she had needed one until Jax arrived. The boy hadn't been born with his abilities and was almost four years older than his ward, but their shared talents made the two in-separable.

Her placement with the new recruits hadn't made much sense to Ilaria at the time. Due to her extraordinarily strong telepathy, she wasn't even a toddler during her own initiation when Thane had been ordered to be her instructor. Having never had a student like Ilaria before, Thane wasn't sure where to begin her training and had taken her through the initiate courses several times before he found his footing and began teaching her what he knew best: police investigation.

After the repetition of the initiate classes had long since become boring, Ilaria now found the benefits in having peers and the camaraderie of others with psionic powers. As Jax was also a strong telepath, he was one of the few in the Academy who hadn't resented her talents. Occasionally, he had taken advantage of her skill and knowledge in order to excel in his studies, but for the most part, their friendship had been one of mutual understanding and Ilaria cherished the closeness she had with him.

As the Gala swirled around them, Jax brought Ilaria back to the present by tapping her finely carved crystal glass with his own. "Now, now, don't be depressing. Funerals are the last thing on people's minds tonight."

"No, I can't," said Ilaria, smiling apologetically as she refused the light-gold liquid. "I'm on duty tonight."

"As am I, but can have this; it's just a sparkling wine and non-alcoholic. Take it," he insisted when she refuse again, "you look silly standing in the middle of a party without a drink."

"Thanks, Jax," she smiled, but then made a face after tasting the tart drink. Ilaria much preferred sweet things, but at least with a drink in her hand, no one would try to offer her anything else. Alcohol was out of the question and forbidden to the Empati as it inhibits psionic abilities for mind-scans. Getting intoxicated would have been far worse for her than her tardiness had been. Ilaria had never been officially punished for disobedience by the Pushers before and had no desire to experience their nightmares. If Torquil was angry at her delinquency, there was no telling how far his displeasure might go. The commander had absolute control over the discipline within the Empati.

Long experienced at masking her own emotional turmoil, Ilaria pretended to take another drink. Jax wasn't fooled, but he wisely didn't comment on it. His finger had lightly caressed her hand when he passed her the wine, the touch reinforcing the inward turmoil they both felt. Neither of the telepaths were eager to perform what their duties required.

"We're a long way from the Keep," Jax said, gesturing with his glass at the gathering in an effort to change the topic, his reference causing Ilaria to grin. Officially, the facility where the instructors drilled their initiates on everything from Infantry to Intelligence and how to become true Citizens of the Empire was the Peace-Keeper Corps Training Academy. No one knew who had first called their fortress-like section of the Academy "the Keep", but the name had stuck as older recruits continually passed the nickname on to the new generation of initiates. After so long, even Sarkin and Torquil called the Empati Academy the Keep now.

Recruits, Ilaria thought bitterly. The two things Empati could never be were willing servants or Citizens. Once they took the test and were officially registered as psychics, they were drafted into the Academy, their path to Citizenship in the Janus Empire gone forever.

"Fancy parties. It's not the worst way to make a living," Jax commented with a smile. "Except, of course, that you don't like fancy parties."

"No, I really don't," Ilaria smiled, resisting another urge to pull up her dress. That futile movement would have done nothing to cover the shapely leg that tended to peek out from the long slit every time she shifted position or took a step. Ilaria felt as if she was falling out of her gown from top to bottom. With a sigh, she raised her glass in a mock toast. At least with Jax, she really didn't have to pretend to like the bitter drink. The artistry of looking like you were having a good time no matter the circumstances was also a lesson that had been drilled into the young students.

At the Keep, the young psychics had practiced

everything from the proper way of holding and firing laser weapons to how to handle knives and forks like the aristocracy and then how to turn said utensils into weapons. Though wise enough to never mention it to anyone except Thane, that was one thing that never made much sense to Ilaria. With their psionic abilities, the Empati could sense an imminent attack and as a result, were trained in everything from advanced weaponry to martial arts should they ever need to act as a bodyguard for a high-ranking official. The caveat was that no one trusted peeks enough to allow them to carry arms. They were the best protectors of the empire, trained to fight in order to defend, and yet were forbidden weaponry of any kind. Ilaria still hadn't come up with the logic for that one.

"What about you?" Ilaria asked. "Where are you assigned now?"

"Investigative forces. Thanks to you and Thane, I'm the third best trained detective in the psi-cops. I'm embedded with a unit on the Outer Reaches. We were the ones who made first contact with the V'reem."

"Lucky you," Ilaria didn't hide her envy. Unlike herself, Jax was able to do something worthwhile in between the Galas. She'd had two promising careers taken from her the moment Sarkin requested her presence as his personal liaison. Thane had trained her as an investigator, grooming his ward to be his partner once she graduated from the Academy. Of course, that had changed when her telepathic powers fully manifested and Sobek insisted her two talents combined would make her a superb doctor. Ilaria didn't know if it was Sarken's intention all along or if he changed his mind, but her life was forced to change again when he ordered her to his palace on Marasa Prime to be his "personal physician". Without a choice in the matter, Ilaria moved into the palace and had hardly practiced medicine in the three years since.

Both telepaths stiffened at the shift in mood as everyone became aware that the Arkellian dignitaries had arrived. Turning, they watched several richly dressed people enter the grand ballroom. While their dark uniforms were decorated with the same red piping as the rest of the entourage, the importance of the Arkellians leading the pompous group was plain. Floor-length cloaks draped over their shoulders billowed as the four men and two women strode commandingly into the room. Their entrance was clearly meant as an elaborate show of the importance of Arkell to the other dignitaries of the systems the Empire held. Each of the three cloaked representatives' uniforms were weighed down with rows of medals while silver filigreed epees encased in richly decorated scabbards swung from their hips.

Three booming raps echoed around the chamber to get the attention of the assembled as the Arkellians reached the center of the ballroom to be introduced in the silence following their pompous arrival. As each were named, they raised an arm to acknowledge the assembly, their cloaks rippling as they swung a pirouette to the room.

"Vale, crowned Prince of the Arkell," rang the announcer's voice as the central figure did his regal turn, "Commander Valeria of the Royal Guard; Captain Damien Rey, Prime Minister of Arkell."

Jax notice Ilaria physically jump as the Minister was introduced.

· CHAPTER 3 ·

nteresting," Ilaria said to Jax. *"I've never met the minister, but I know the Commander Valeria is Vale's sister."*

"She is also a soldier in their Army and from what I understand has earned her rank." Jax said as he and Ilaria bowed to welcome the newcomers.

Ilaria was about to ask if Jax knew anything about Rey when she got her first look at the V'reem. From the shock that rippled through the humans, no one had been prepared for the mantis-like creatures as they skittered into the ballroom—least of all Emperor Sarkin.

Entering behind the Arkellians, the six-limbed insects walked on four of their legs while their remaining two arms were raised high and held next to their triangular heads and bulbous compound eyes. Over their heads, delicate antennae danced in constant motion while their disjointed mandibles twitched as if they were tasting the air as the insectoids studied the room full of bipedal aliens.

"Welcome, representatives of V'reem!" Sarkin said, raising his hands in a way he intended to project his charm. They responded by chittering back to the emperor in a language the communication chips couldn't translate.

"My lord," Ilaria said stepping to the emperor's side, "they don't understand; they can't speak our language as they have no vocal cords and their mouths aren't the right configuration for the sounds that we make. They also don't have ears so our communication chips are useless to them."

Sarkin frowned at Ilaria's reminder. He'd been told about the insects' vocal limitations, but had conveniently forgotten. A few other species had trouble with the chips, but they had the decency to learn the common tongue of the empire. Damn! Ilaria could speak to them, of course, but he didn't want to expose her to his delegates as a telepath.

"Wait," Ilaria sent, reaching forward to briefly touch him before settling back in her chair.

Surprised by her touch and what almost sounded like a mental order, Ilaria felt the emperor's flash of anger before he checked himself. Of all his peeks, Ilaria knew her place. Glancing at his telepath, Sarkin saw her eyes weren't on him, but on the bugs whose only movement since creeping to the center of the ballroom was their twitching jaws and antennae.

Quicker than Ilaria had ever seen a human move, one of the Mantises rushed toward the edge of the emptied dance floor, stopping short at the collected gasp when the people pressed themselves further away from the insect alien.

The only one who stood his ground at the approaching V'reem was Jax. Ilaria sensed his rising fear, but the man bravely didn't move as the insect's giant eyes stared into his own, its disjointed mandibles chewing the air only inches from his face.

"Ilaria?" Sarkin asked, expecting his mentally sensitive psychic to know what was going on.

At his voice the second Mantis snapped his triangular head in the emperor's direction, before cocking it in several directions.

"You said they couldn't hear," Sarkin hissed.

"I said they didn't have ears, my lord," she clarified, keeping her voice low and even. "They are apparently very sensitive to vibrations like your voice in the air."

No one spoke; some didn't even dare breathe. The only human movement was Jax tilting his head as he silently studied the V'reem back. Sensing his agitation, Ilaria was amazed that her friend didn't so much as twitch when the large bug stepped even closer and began caressing the telepath's face with its delicate antennae. It was then she remembered he'd said he was part of the expedition who'd made first contact with the intelligent insects.

"Yes!" Jax gasped as he listened to the telepathic V'reem. "I can hear you; I can understand you!"

Leaning into Sarkin's ear, Ilaria whispered everything she was hearing from both Jax and the Array. Using their combined abilities as an amplifier, the four telepaths were able to hear Normals the way an individual telepath could not. Even as the strongest telepath on record, not even Ilaria could pick up the mundane thoughts of non-telepaths unless she physically touched them. It had taken Sarkin years to figure out how he could use what was proving to be a useless skill. Except for Ilaria, they were the only other readers could only hear the minds of non-paths. Sarkin found it useless when telepaths could only talk to each; kept on their tight leash, peeks rarely had any information the emperor wanted to know.

His Array at least served a purpose. Dressing them as guards and posting them around the ballroom, all of them together could usually hear *something* of interest to him. And when they did, he sent Ilaria to find out more.

Sensing his need for constant information, Ilaria again whispered to the emperor what was transpiring between Jax and the V'reem. "Through their mind-link with Jax, they have learned our language, but are still unable to speak it. Their species is telepathic and use their antennae to relay information to one another. They realize their form frightens us, but they are only curious as we are a strange people and very different from the themselves. These emissaries come in peace. You may speak aloud. The V'reem will understand you, but they will need to be in contact with one of us for us to hear them... anyone of us, apparently. The connection doesn't have to be with a telepath."

Sarkin was immensely please that it was the V'reem who touched Jax first. Now, any psychic reading could be placed on these bugs and not expose his telepath's abilities. With a huge smile, Sarkin beamed, "Then on behalf of my people and the Janus Empire, again I say welcome!"

And just like that, the party got underway again. Couples started dancing, people started drinking and Sarkin smugly sat back in his chair as if he were responsible for it all.

Ilaria thought that the V'reem were the most *alien* aliens she'd ever seen. Most of the non-humanoids she'd encountered had something in common with humans; even the Akilli had attributes she could comprehend. But as far as she could tell, there was little she could understand about the mantises who seemed completely devoid of all feeling. Born into a caste, neither one of them had any concept of individuality, but lived to serve their hive. Human sensations of happiness or fear were alien to them because of their absence of it. The ambassadors didn't even have genders that Ilaria could detect.

The bugs didn't seem to know what to do once the humans started dancing and mingling again. Only Jax had dared entered the embrace of their feeling antennae, so once he'd moved on, the V'reem stepped back into a corner as unmoving as statues while they silently observed the Gala.

Ilaria actually felt sorry for them as she contemplated how to understand this strange new species. Touching minds with Jax to get his impression of their mantis-like visitors showed her that this situation was more unique than any she'd yet encountered and that was including the Trees of the Wald. The V'reem's telepathy didn't project a language, only the meaning of their thoughts and was why the Array couldn't detect it. With verbal people, even their thoughts were transformed into the words of their language and Ilaria's gift was being able to telepathically translate that language. Not even she could translate a language that didn't exist.

Human psychic ability had only manifested in the last few centuries. With only a small portion of the population having any measurable talents, not even Ilaria fully comprehended how her own powers worked. Empaths were the most gifted and numerous among them, but not even they would be able to read an emotionless species. After Jax's contact with the mantises, it now seemed even the telepaths would be useless with these insects. As they didn't have a language among themselves, Ilaria thought it most likely the mantises never had one and had evolved their mental communication from the moment the first V'reem cracked its shell.

Just because they were insectoids didn't mean the alien race would function as other hive insects would, but Ilaria had little else to go on. Noticing that they could make sounds with their wings and mandibles, and they clearly understood the common language of the Janus Empire, Ilaria had a flash of inspiration.

And the one person she needed just happened to be present at the Gala.

"Excuse me, but are you Damien Rey?" she asked the Arkellian minister.

"I am," the man said, his warm smile freezing as his eyes took in the woman addressing him. "What do you want?"

"To speak with you, if I may."

"I'm not interested," he snorted, smiling at his two companions as they sniggered.

"On behalf of Emperor Sarkin," Ilaria added, enjoying the sensation as their dismissive attitudes evaporated along with their arrogant smiles. "Gentlemen," she smiled with a nod of her head, dismissing them. Power was fleeting and peeks had very little of it, but Ilaria did enjoy the rare moments when it was hers.

"How can I be of service to the emperor?" Rey asked cautiously as Ilaria linked her arm in his and led the man to a quiet corner where they could talk.

"Please correct me if I'm wrong, but you are from Arkell?"

"I am," he said, warily looking at Ilaria from the corner of his eyes.

Had this been a less formal occasion and if she'd

approached him in uniform, Ilaria sensed he might be more open to speaking with her, but dressed as one of the emperor's empathic courtesan, he wasn't sure if this was a path he should take.

"I'm Ilaria," she smiled, hoping introducing herself would put him more in mind to speak openly with her. It didn't.

"Yes, I know who you are," Rey said, his eyes narrowing dismissively again.

He really didn't, but that was what Sarkin wanted people to think. Smiling apologetically, Ilaria said, "Please correct me if I'm wrong again, but you are the Prime Minister on Arkell and in charge of its technical industries?"

That she would know that seemed to catch him by surprise. Her dress alone screamed that her only redeeming quality was being one of Sarkin's empathic whores. As his eyes fixed on her burgeoning corset, it never occurred to the Arkellian that she had brains enough to know his position and title. Ilaria wasn't an idiot, but Damien Rey appeared to be an arrogant one. Only moments ago, he'd been introduced to the entire assembly, so there were few on the ship who didn't know his position on his home planet and that he held a seat in the senate.

Nodding his affirmation at his rank, Ilaria was pleased that she sensed his sudden arousal as Rey's eyes snapped up from her bustline to her face. As the emperor himself had sent this woman to him, his interest in her was growing.

"Excellent!" she said, feigning relief. Let him think she was just Sarkin's silly messenger. The more he underestimated her, the easier her job was. "Lord Sarkin wanted me to speak with you regarding the V'reem."

"Those bugs?"

"Yes," Ilaria said, keeping her own emotions at his derogatory label in check. Damien wasn't an empath, but she knew that many Normals compensated by being experts at reading body language. There had been occasions when non-paths had been accused of being illegal Psychs simply because they'd gotten good at recognizing slight facial tics as lies or agreement. Rey was young for such a high position and Ilaria sensed he hadn't achieved it by playing nice.

Continuing, she explained how Jax had telepathically spoken with the insectoids, making sure Rey knew it was the V'reem who initiated the mind-speak. The minister shuddered at the thought of telepathically sharing his mind with a peek, but let Ilaria continue without interruption.

"For myself, I've always been able to learn languages easily and rarely need the communication chips myself, but from what I can tell, V'reem don't seem to have a language at all."

"So, how would that help with the chips?" Damien asked. "If there isn't a language for them to translate, they'd be useless."

"That's what I thought, too, until it occurred to me that language is really just a set of sounds that we all agree mean something."

Rey snorted as he considered her statement idiotic. "There's more to language than that."

"There is," Ilaria smiled her agreement, "but at its most basic level, it isn't really. As the Minister of Tech, your people are in charge of every form of our technology and have given the empire incredible breakthroughs from our translation chips to cybernetic limbs. I know several people personally who have hands and legs thanks to you."

Flattery works every time, Ilaria thought to herself when she felt Rey mentally preen at the compliment.

"I think I understand where you're going with this," the Minister said, suddenly taking control of the conversation. In his excitement, he began to ramble off all of Ilaria's talking points and coming to the conclusions as if they were his own. So long as the result was the same, Ilaria didn't care that he would present the solution to the emperor as the genius he thought he was.

"You say these insects can understand our own language, but they don't have a language of their own. They don't need the chips to understand us; we just need to understand them. They can make verbal sounds; it's just not a language. Yes! In its most basic form, communication is nothing more than a set of sounds. If the cyborgs work with the bugs on a set of sounds, it is possible to create a rudimentary language our communication chips will recognize and translate."

"That's wonderful!" Ilaria said, grasping his hand. "Lord Sarkin will be so pleased."

In his new enthusiasm, Minister Rey chatted on about his new pet project. Ilaria found the concept fascinating, but was only partially listening as she tried to catch Sarkin's eye across the room. When he finally looked in her direction, Ilaria tugged the earring dangling from her right lobe.

Even at that distance, she felt Sarkin turn to steel, his face a mask of hidden fury. At his slight nod, Ilaria turned her attention back to the oblivious Rey.

As she called over a waiter to serve them drinks, Ilaria sensed that her exchange with the emperor hadn't gone completely unnoticed. Knowing she was a prisoner to Sarkin's demands, she felt Jax's unhappy resignation to her precarious situation.

"Wait," Jax sent, *"you don't have to do this."*

"In the entire history of the dumb things you've ever said to me, that has to be the dumbest," Ilaria inwardly sighed, while giving Rey a smile as he continued his rambling, completely unaware of the silent exchange between the telepaths. *"It was wonderful to see you again, Jax, but you're going to have to get out of my mind."*

Reluctantly, Ilaria severed the contact with her friend as she turned her attention back to Rey. She'd already signaled Sarkin she was on to something; she was now committed to finding out what the Prime Minister of Tech knew. She'd felt his guard rise at the mere mention of cybernetics, something he wanted to be kept private. Ilaria didn't hold strongly to coincidence. Seducing Rey had been the main reason for her attendance to the Gala and he'd complicated matters by refusing an escort for the evening. She had needed to find another way to introduce herself to the minister when the situation with the V'reem landed almost directly in her lap. What were the odds that the one man she needed to speak with was the very man she'd been ordered to sleep with?

No, thought Ilaria, she didn't like coincidences. Not one bit.

A sudden crash starled the party guests. In the following silence, Ilaria and Rey turned with everyone else to watch the scene unfolding on the dance floor. A courtesan in a flowing red dress cut much like Ilaria's had been dancing when her partner stepped on her long gown. Off balance and unable to correct himself, they both fell, hitting a non-dancing bystander squarely in his back. Now off balance himself, the man fell forward, his full drink drenching Vale and causing the prince to jump back as if he could avoid the liquid already dripping down his face and onto his bright and shiny uniform. Momentarily blinded by the alcohol, Vale flayed his arms, hitting the tray of a passing server. With his drinks crashing to the floor, the poor waiter was propelled into the sculpture of Sarkin, his silver tray severing the icy arm of the Janus emperor.

In the stunned silence that followed, Damien said in an undertone, "That was oddly satisfying."

Thinking it unwise to add her own pleasure to the minister's assessment at his prince's predicament, Ilaria enjoyed the chaotic scene in silence as the couple gushed their embarrassed apologies as they tried to help mop up the damage to Vale's front. The incident was all she needed to understand that, while loyal to his prince, the newly elected minister wasn't overly fond of the arrogant youth.

The ridiculous scene buoyed Ilaria's spirits even further as she recognized the woman who had tripped. Her name was Treena and was one of the more experienced courtesans. Believing that Ilaria usurped all the best contacts, Treena had made her contempt with the telepath's presence at the Gala plain and was now attempting ingratiate herself into the prince's good graces by mopping up the lower portions of his trousers where very little liquid had fallen.

Watching Damien's amusement, Ilaria took even greater pleasure in reading that Treena's evening wasn't going to end with her giving the prince such a fantastic night he would want nothing more than to take her back to his castle on Arkell. There were half a dozen reasons that was never going to happen, the least of which being Sarkin giving up a one of his courtesans.

With the distraction over and everyone involved wallowing in various apologies, Ilaria and Damien turned their attention back to each other with big smiles.

Suddenly with embarrassment, Damien said, "I owe you an apology. I'm afraid I took you for a courtesan."

Ilaria raised her eyebrows in surprise before glancing down at her breasts all but threatening to escape over the top of her dress. "Now, why in the world would you have done that?"

Nodding his head back to Treena's overzealous attempts to win Vale over, Damien said, "I can see now that you're nothing like her."

It was Ilaria's turn to blush as she put an arm up to hide her chest before dropping it for the futile gesture it was. "Dressed in this thing… I forgive your assumption."

"If I may ask, why are you dressed like that?"

"Long story," she answered with a sigh, "but the short version is that I was on assignment to the Wald and stopped here to give my report to Commander Torquil. He insisted I attend since I was already here and… this… is what I was given to wear. Whoever owns it may be my height, but we are definitely not the same size."

When she looked woefully at her burgeoning bust once more, Damien laughed heartily.

"Well, it looks lovely on you, though I suspect at some point you'd like to remove it… if only for the opportunity to breathe."

"Breathing would be good," Ilaria agreed, sensing his aroused spike. Though his interest in more than just polite conversation was why she was here, Ilaria had to concentrate to repress her own darkening mood. Now wasn't the time to wallow in her dejection.

Rey's embarrassment lowered his guard, so Ilaria pushed out with her senses, sifting through his varied emotions... and there it was. He hadn't refused a courtesan out of lack of interest in sex, but out of interest in his partner. He was a man who preferred big minds over big tits and detested drunken whores who only knew how to sexually stimulate their companions even more. Damien was an intellect and liked women who also had a mind. Maybe this evening wouldn't turn out to be as dull as she anticipated. Damien's interest in her was growing, so she would more than likely still have to perform her duty later, but she could at least entertain the hope that for once, she might actually enjoy it.

Returning to their previous subject, Ilaria said, "Even though most people rely on the translators, I've always had an ear for languages and can learn them quickly. It came in handy today in speaking to the Indigenous of the Wald as they don't use the translation chips. Can't or don't; I actually wasn't sure which."

"Well, you're one up on me as I didn't even know the Wald had intelligent life."

Ilaria chose not to comment on her belief that all planets had intelligent life. Just because they didn't live it in a way that outsiders measured intelligence didn't make them less smart. Instead, she turned it back to why she'd spoken to the minister in the first place. Just the mention of creating a new technology for the V'reem sent Rey into another long monologue of how to adapt the cybernetics to the bug's physiology.

He was, however, so passionate about cybernetics that Ilaria occasionally had to push out with her empathy to see if he was still interested in her, even going as far as deliberately crossing her legs so the fine fabric slid down to expose her leg. It worked; in the briefest of glances, she noticed Damien admire her bare thigh. The man might be shrewd and guarded, but Ilaria was immensely relieved she still had his attention as a woman.

It was well into the early morning when Ilaria escorted Damien to her quarters. Gently, but firmly he pushed her through the door and was kissing her before they had finished sliding shut. Ilaria wasn't surprised. She had been ordered to sleep with many men over the years and no longer needed her empathy to sense their eagerness to experience one of Sarkin's empathic courtesans and Damien was no different. She might not be a meta-morph trained fulfill their partner's sexual fantasies as they sensed them, but she was an empath and knew how to satisfy.

Damien wouldn't have bed her if had thought she had been one of those tedious whores Sarkin liked to pawn off on people. Fortunately for her, she'd stimulated his intellect before she'd attempted other parts of his anatomy. Rey was certain sex wasn't the only reason she was with him, but he was at a loss as to what that reason might be besides pleasing a lover.

· CHAPTER 4 ·

Sarkin was in high spirits when he took his seat at the head of counsel table early the next morning, but he seemed to be the only one in a good mood. Just like Commander Torquil, Ilaria found most of the high counsel extremely hard to read. Well, she amended to herself, that wasn't entirely true. Seated to Sarkin's right, his sister Laran projected her usual anger, an emotion Ilaria wasn't sure she'd ever *not* sensed from the admiral of the Stellar Navy. The woman scowled so much; the thirty-year old already had a permanent crease between her eyebrows.

On the emperor's left was Healer Sobek, masking his ambiguous indifference with a pleasant smile. Just like Torquil, who was seated to Laran's right at the long table, Ilaria found the healer extremely hard to read. She supposed, with their positions in the government, it probably wasn't that unusual; the most powerful people in empire had spent most of their lives keeping their minds and emotions in check through domestic, foreign and natural disasters. A council meeting wouldn't be high on their list of catastrophes to get upset over, but the heads of the Janus Empire kept themselves guarded.

Around the table, other aides and advisors were less skilled at hiding their inner selves; most of them were not taking kindly that a peek was sitting at the council table with them. Ilaria sensed their resentment towards her grow when Sarkin openly began to sing her praises.

"Well done, Ilaria! I knew that Techno was trouble."

"I began conversing with him regarding creating a translation device that would work for the V'reem…"

"I'm not interested in those bugs!" Sarkin stormed. "What did you find out about Damien Rey?"

"Rather than being flattered, he became extremely agitated when I complimented his accomplishments in cybernetics."

At Ilaria's mention of cyborgs, everyone turned to Niegan as if the Controller alone was responsible for the Minister of Technology's actions. The Array, standing in their usual circle around the perimeter of the council chamber, confirmed that the half mechanical man was as surprised as everyone else.

"What else?" Sarkin asked, his measured fury extinguishing his good mood.

"Only that he is aware of a plan involving cyborgs. When it came down to reading him further, I'm afraid Rey was very quick and immediately fell asleep afterwards."

Sarkin wasn't as amused as the rest of his counsel's laughter at Ilaria's assessment of Rey's libido. "You will sleep with him again tonight. If you can't get everything, force it out of him."

"Yes, my lord. And the matter with communication devices for the V'reem?"

To Ilaria's surprise, Sobek answered for her, "My lord, even though Rey is the Minister, I doubt he is the only Arkellian who can create this translator. Shall I look into it for you?"

"You're a healer. What do you know about Tech?"

"Very little, brother," Sobek admitted, "but I believe I understand Ilaria's intentions with such a device. There have been several occasions with patients who've lost the ability to speak so we've in essence created new languages using any sounds they have been able to make. With your permission, Ilaria abilities of touch-telepathy would be invaluable in its creation."

Sarkin growled as he contemplated his brother's suggestion, the deep sounds echoed around the silent room while everyone waited for the emperor's decision. "No, I need Ilaria here and I've got another job for her with that Denobian empath, what was his name again?"

"Thantos Thane, my lord," Sobek answered.

As Denobians rarely left their homeworld and those who did tended to stand out amongst the taller members of the empire, it didn't surprise Ilaria that the healer knew who Thane was. What did surprise her was that Sobek knew his full name and used it correctly when addressing the emperor. Peeks were rarely afforded such courtesy from Normals and she hadn't expected it from the third in line to the throne.

"You disapprove?" the emperor said, looking down at his brother as Sobek was clearly censoring what he'd like to say.

"Only that Thane, as one of our strongest empaths, isn't as expendable as you think."

"Oh, for god's sake, Sobek! I've got better things for my Empati to do than comforting the dead or dying."

"Of course," Sobek said with a tight smile.

"Of course," Sarkin mimicked. "Where is Thane anyway?"

"He returned to Prime late last night," Niegan said quickly as if his willingness to relay that information would erase the suspicious look everyone had given him simply for being a cyborg. He'd worn his mechanical legs and arm for decades before Rey had even been born let alone had become the Minister. Whatever the Arkellian had planned, Ilaria didn't think it had anything to do with the Controller.

"Returned from where?" Sarkin asked, his eyes darkening when the cyborg knew something the emperor didn't.

"The Wald," Torquil answered, his sly smile widening as he took immense delight at informing Sarkin of her recent sin. "Ilaria left to meet him there."

"And what were you doing on the Wald?" Sarkin asked

Ilaria, his voice full of ice.

The lush gardens Sarkin maintained in his yacht's arboretum usually gave Ilaria a sense of peace, but not today. Though the environment was unquestionably artificial, she came to the humid tropical climate often when she was assigned to the *Celest.* The manicured beauty of the garden along with the songbirds diligently going about their business in complete ignorance that the edges of their cage were the only thing between them and the airless void, made Ilaria forget for a time that she was also adrift in space. But not even their dedicated trilling gave her comfort as she tucked her knees to her chest and waited for the emperor after he dismissed her from the council.

It hadn't mattered that she'd followed procedure by informing Niegan and Control of her intention to travel to the Wald at Thane's request for a contact-telepathic or her duties as a translator when she interrogated the Indigenous regarding the dead woman. Once Torquil smugly told the emperor the body had already been incarcerated on Maelstrom, nothing had seemed to matter to the council except that she had abandoned her station at the Gala at the request of a peek to investigate another dead peek. Not even the fact that she had accomplished that and more without dereliction of her duties had been relevant to them. Dead or alive, peeks didn't matter.

Suddenly aware that Sarkin had entered the arboretum, Ilaria stood to attention and waited for him to approach her.

"Show me," the emperor ordered, thrusting his hand out to her. This was the one distinction Sarkin had over his siblings and council, his willingness to not only touch the one peek who really could do what other Citizens feared all psychics could do, but to use it. Obediently, Ilaria placed her tiny hand in Sarkin's, his fierce grip crushed her fingers as she mentally relayed the events of the previous day. Images of her contact with the Trees flashed through Sarkin's own mind as quickly as Ilaria's thoughts could relay them. She ended the connection by showing the emperor the night she'd spent with Minister Rey and what she'd learned about the cyborgs. It wasn't much, but Sarkin fully knew everything she did.

"You're right," Sarkin huffed, "he was quick. And don't be so glum; I don't have you sleep with people for your own enjoyment."

"No, my lord," Ilaria hesitated, startled that his anger wasn't directed at her. From the reaction at the council, she'd expected... she didn't know what she expected, but it hadn't been good.

"I think you did very well yesterday, considering," Sarkin continued. Clasping his hands behind his back, he began walking the paths around the gardens. The birds didn't like him there; Ilaria was aware of the silence surrounding them as they stopped singing. Without their songs, the gardens felt quiet; the gravel crunching under Sarkin's heavy boots was agonizingly loud.

Stunned at receiving praise over condemnation, Ilaria followed Sarkin in silence as he paced aimlessly through the colorful landscape.

"I checked with Niegan and noticed the first thing you did was check your flight to see if you did have enough time; you did, though I do trust you'll take into account the terrain next time. The Wald is a swamp; swamps stink and there's nothing you can do about it."

"Yes, my lord."

"You hadn't been there before, so you couldn't have known—now you do. I've only been there once; nasty place. Won't go back if I have a choice. Wear a full environment suit if something like this does ever come up again. It'll keep the muck off you."

"I will, though I doubt it will happen again."

"It better not," Sarkin growled.

Relief that her own plight wasn't as dire with her master as she imagined, it took Ilaria a moment to realize Sarkin had been referring to the body they'd discovered and not to her own response. While he didn't really care about a dead peek, Sarkin despised unanswered questions and the one he wanted to know

now was how an In-Valid had gotten out of Maelstrom in the first place.

Sarkin continued. "I want you to telepathically join with those two bugs. Since they initiated the contact last night, no one will be suspicious of your own telepathic abilities. Let the bugs know our plans to adjust our translators to their species; can't do anything if we can't talk to them and I'm not talking to them with those damn antennae all over my face."

"I will, my lord. Is there anything else?"

"Yes," Sarkin said, turning to Ilaria with a smile. "After the bugs, scan Rey again. Fuck him if you have to, force the scan if he can't keep it up long enough."

"If I force the scan, he'll know I'm a telepath."

"I don't care. Whatever it takes, I want to know his intentions with the cyborgs. When you're done with him, I want you to go to Prime and work with Thane. Peek or not, I want to know how that body ended up on the Wald and you're the only one who can question those Trees."

Ilaria was so stunned at this turn of events, even the prospect of having to sleep with Rey again couldn't diminish her elation. After her duties here, she'd be free to work on an actual investigation... with Thane!

The emperor and telepath turned in unison as they heard footsteps running down the path and then stopped.

"My lord?" someone called, unable to find the emperor in the lavish gardens.

"Here!" Sarkin called, giving Ilaria an amused smile.

The footsteps resumed and a breathless aide came panting down the path. "I'm sorry, my lord... the V'reem. They're dead!"

· CHAPTER 5 ·

Thane realized how much he missed Rill as he traveled back from the Wald to Prime. He wanted to discuss the body with anyone who'd care that the dead woman had been a Psych—someone like him. With the high probability of the tattoo being from the Maelstrom prison, the rest of his unit of psi-cops had already dismissed the death and were complaining about the waste of time it had been extracting her from the cement-like mud.

With his own duties temporarily complete, Thane became a non-entity and was completely ignored by the other Keepers. Even his partner Seth, usually rather open and friendly with the empath, chatted with the Normals without even a word the Denobian.

Not wanting to talk to them, either, Thane didn't mind; however, he was grateful for the endured silence of the trip to Prime because he got very little of it once they were docked in the Capital planet's space port. The engine noise of ships rising and landing alone was bad enough, but the ground crews shouting to be heard over the roar of dozens of revving engines made the Denobian wish he was back in the oblivion of space. It didn't matter that, through the din, no one was talking to him.

Thane's troubles continued after he entered the Peace Keeper compound and discovered Seth had returned home almost the moment the rest of the Keepers had landed from the Wald. Thane couldn't blame him for wanting to get back to his new wife and child, but he wished the young man had waited to fill out the reports with him. Not that he blamed Seth for that, either, but after slogging through a tidal marsh, Thane would have followed Seth's lead if the empath had a home to go to.

Crossing planetary time zones didn't make it any easier. He'd spent most of a day on the Wald, several night-time hours in transit and, now that he was back on Prime, it was only mid-afternoon. Though he was thoroughly exhausted from everything that had happened, Thane decided to force himself to stay awake for the remainder of this current rotation or he'd never sleep during his rest cycle. It didn't matter; tired as he was, Thane was too wound up to sleep.

Showering off the Walden mud, Thane stepped into the recreation lounge in his uniform ready to work a few more hours before he could retire with an uninterrupted night's sleep.

"Missed you on the Wald," one of the infantrymen smiled.

"Yeah, heard you ducked out early, not that I blame you," someone else quipped.

Thane wondered if they thought their pleasant conversation was meant to fool him or if they had actually forgotten he was empathic. Thane had actually been one of the last Keepers to board the departing shuttle and had left at the same time they did. What they were bitter about was that the job of exhuming the body had fallen to them while Thane had questioned Daneb at length. Repressing his sigh, Thane knew it was wiser to let it go.

"I wouldn't have been much help to you," he said, extending his arms and glancing down to indicate his size as a liability.

"I thought you Denobians could jump twice your height."

"Three times, given the right planet and conditions," Thane admitted, "but not on the Wald. In that mud, if I'd missed my mark, you'd still be there trying to dig me out."

Laughing with them, Thane made no illusions to himself that if he had gotten himself buried in the muck, they only reason any of them would have rescued him was because they had to, the same way they tolerated his presence during investigations.

"Besides," Thane continued, "I was only there to sift the truth during the interrogation with the witnesses and I'm afraid I was even more useless there."

"Is that why you called in that other peek?"

"Ilaria," Thane nodded. "She's the emperor's personal translator and has an exceptional talent for understanding languages. Those Trees spoke in a way our communication chips couldn't interpret."

"After all that, it's too bad it was all for nothing," someone said. Thane knew his face, but had long ago stopped trying to remember names when he realized he didn't care.

"What do you mean?" he asked.

"Well, she was a peek, wasn't she? The tattoo scanned as Maelstrom. We spent all afternoon digging up a damn In-Valid. Didn't know she was one of your kind, did you?"

From their attitude, the woman's prison mark was all they needed for the investigation to be over: she'd managed to get herself out of Maelstrom and died in the attempt. Case closed. Even though he knew what he'd find, Thane checked in with the attending physician in the morgue and discovered the body had already been incinerated. After the tattoo had been scanned, the medical examiner wasn't going to waste his time on an autopsy for an illegal peek no one would care about.

Depressed, Thane went back to sit in an empty cockpit where no one would think to find him, but he wasn't thinking about the dead woman.

"Did you know?" Thane demanded of his ship.

"Did I know what?" Rill answered Thane's question.

"That Sarkin is using Ilaria as one of his whores!"

In the years she'd been assigned to Sarkin as his interpreter, Thane's mental connection with Ilaria had lessened. Without another empath ever mentally connecting with a telepath before, he didn't have another reference to compare his weakening bond with Ilaria. He'd assumed it was a natural part of his surrogate daughter growing up and leaving the nest. The only dampening he'd ever felt before in their psychic connection was when either of them was offworld and the distance between planets were too far for them to sense one another, but even then, there was *something*. Ever since he'd agreed to raise her as an infant, Thane had felt the spark of her mind, but meeting her again after being apart for so long, he understood now she'd been deliberately shutting him down.

At first, the Denobian thought the worst sensation he'd ever felt was when he realized Ilaria had been deliberately sealing him out of her mind; only death and losing her completely could be more horrible than that.

He couldn't have been more wrong. Thane never thought of himself as much of an idiot before now, but as Ilaria's agitation on the Wald grew, he realized how much of one he was. The emperor would have many uses for a touch-telepath at a party filled with all his emissaries, ministers and political rivals and Thane knew he was an idiot for not seeing it sooner.

"Of course, I knew," Rill answered as he made the jump into hyperspace. "Everyone knew except you."

"Why didn't she tell me?"

"Because the only thing you could do about it was get pissed off," the ship answered. "You couldn't help her then; you're not helping her now."

"I know," Thane said defeated as he slumped in his seat. "I know. She's just never blocked me out before."

"I know," Rill said making his tone sound humanly understanding.

That he couldn't share Thane's righteous indignation was the most irritating thing the empath had with the AI. Rill had been so skillfully programmed he could tell a joke with pauses and punchline that could have both himself and Ilaria in stitches for hours that Thane forgot that he was just wires and circuits.

After a few minutes of quiet, the ship suddenly asked, "Why didn't you know?"

With a sigh, Thane slumped even further in the pilot's seat. "Because I didn't want to."

"Because there was nothing you could do about it. What would you do if you could?"

Thane didn't even pause in his answer; it was something he'd thought about since the first day Sobek had placed the infant Ilaria in his arms and something he'd thought about in the quiet recesses of his mind every day since. "I'd take her away— far from the empire and Sarkin."

"Why haven't you?"

"Because there isn't such a place. Well, nowhere we wouldn't be found."

"No," Rill agreed, "there isn't such a place. Not yet, anyway. But before you go despondent again, I've not only identified the dead woman, but I also have cause of death."

"Does it matter?" Thane gloomily sighed again.

"Of course, it matters if you care that she was murdered."

Closing his eyes, Thane shook his head with a sigh, "It's not murder in the eyes of the empire to shoot down an escaped convict even if her only crime was refusing to comply as a Psych."

"Then tell me how she flew a shuttle with a four-inch hole in the back of her head?"

Thane shook his head again, only this time as if he were trying to comprehend what his ship had just told him. "What did you say?"

"I said that Zin Tram was murdered because it would have been impossible for her to pilot a ship with half her head missing. She was either killed somewhere else and her body dumped on the Wald or she was killed there. Still interested?"

Stunned, Thane asked, "How do you know this?"

"Because I hacked into Alton's records before he dismissed the case."

"You hacked into the Keeper's data files?"

"I did," the ship confirmed. "As you and I were already aware that Tram was incarcerated at Maelstrom, I suspected the investigation would end once the regular Keepers discovered it as well. My suspicions were confirmed after Alton's autopsy only went as far as a full external body scan before she had been identified and he ordered the body incinerated, but his examination was enough for me to confirm how she died. As she was lying face-up on the Wald, I wasn't unaware of the wound until I hacked his files."

"Have I told you lately that I love you?" Thane said, astounded. There wasn't another AI in the fleet, possibly in the entire empire who would have taken such an initiative without orders or quoting lists of regulations of what peeks could and couldn't do.

"Not in the last six weeks," Rill responded.

"Okay," Thane said, his new focus momentarily erasing his exhaustion and depression from his mind. "You said her name was Zim?"

"Zin," Rill corrected as he transferred the files over to Thane's consol. "Zin Tram, an empath from Arkell. She was training in the Tech field of transportation when she took her Psych tests and was sent to the Empati as an initiate."

"Age?"

"Ten; slightly older than the average age for an average empath. She was mentally stronger than most, but nothing exceptional. After her Empati training, she was sent to Haven to work in the hospitals. At twenty-three, she vanished after a shuttle crash and was presumed dead for nearly a decade before she was rediscovered in a camp on the outer edges of the empire. She refused to return to the Empati and was incarcerated at Maelstrom where she had been for the last eight years."

"Until she turned up on the Wald," Thane amended as he studied her holo-image. "She looks young for her age, especially after hard labor in Maelstrom. I'm surprised she still had a face after being shot in the back of the head."

"I didn't say she was shot," said Rill.

"You said she was killed and missing the back of her head."

"I did," the ship affirmed. "Without a full autopsy, it is just speculation, but have you ever known a plasma blast to be so precise as to leave a head intact?"

"Never," Thane agreed. "Alton's done far too many autopsies not to have recognized this wound as the cause of death. Murdered or not, no one cares about a dead Psych, so why go to all the trouble of bringing her to the Wald?"

"Except for the miners, there is very little human activity on the Wald so they either didn't expect the body to be discovered or they didn't care."

"So, do you think one of the miners did this?"

"Possibly, but unlikely. If one of them wanted an empath, there are easier ways to get one than from Maelstrom. Besides that, when you questioned Daneb, you sensed his honesty that she hadn't come from the mine. It would have taken someone very high in command to not only smuggle an In-Valid out of Maelstrom, but also into the mine. If that were the case, it could only be one of the officers and Daneb would surely have known."

"Living or already dead, someone brought her there. The only other reason I can think of would be to either hide or destroy evidence. But again, why go to all the trouble? If they were worried anyone would care, which they clearly don't, why not jettison her into deep space or, better yet, into a sun?"

Rill was silent as he processed the information. "The most reasonable explanation is that Zin Tram died on the Wald after she was transported there. For some reason we are as yet unaware of, they either didn't care if she were discovered beyond that or they were unable to dispose of her further."

"So, they had a way to get her onto the Wald, but not off and so just left her to the elements."

"Correct," Rill said, "and as we know she wasn't at the mine, it is also reasonable to assume there is someone else on the Wald who is unassociated with the Company."

Thane nodded in agreement, "And this someone has the ability get a Psych out of Maelstrom without anyone knowing. Rill, my friend, we have more questions than we started with."

"We do, indeed," the ship agreed, questions Rill continued to contemplate long after Thane had retired to his bed back on Prime.

· CHAPTER 6 ·

After the meeting with Sarkin, Ilaria took a few moments to shower and get some rest. Judging from Sarkin's eagerness for her to sift through Rey's mind for more information, it was going to be a long day. Though she'd only intended to only lay down for a few minutes, the moment she closed her eyes, she was sound asleep.

Ilaria's dream hadn't started with a storm, but hearing the faint rumble of thunder caused dark clouds to gather followed by cold rain. Initially, she had been walking through the corridors of the *Celest* while speaking with Thane about something she thought was important, but the meaning was nonsensical because it had something to do with the trees of the Wald making great chefs.

Even in her sleep she felt how hungry she was! Well, if the gown hadn't been so tight, she could have eaten more at dinner and the Akilli wouldn't be needed to cook her food. Looking down, Ilaria discovered she wasn't wearing her uniform, but was still in the filmy dress with the constricting corset. Her growl of dismay blended in with the distant groan of thunder. How could she be expected to eat while still wearing this stupid thing?

Suddenly in need of air, when the psychics arrived at what she knew was the galley door, it instead opened to reveal the outer hull of the ship. Grateful to go outside, Thane stepped with her through the door onto the exterior of the *Celest* in order to admire the distant nebula without giving a thought to the fact that gravity was still normal and they were still breathing even though neither wore an environment suit.

Turning to make the comment that they shouldn't be alive, Ilaria discovered in the illogical dreamscape, she was no longer walking with Thane, but with Jax.

"J'rey is an Arkellian name," Jax told her.

Before Ilaria could question what that meant, the telepaths heard a distant rumble of thunder echo closer to them through the vacuum. Ilaria expected it because the moment she had put the dress on, it had reminded her of a storm. Sure enough, when she looked down at herself, ribbons of lightning arced across the fabric between the glittering sequins.

Another peel of thunder reached her through the void, louder and more insistent than the first, but it hadn't come from the storm swirling in her dress. Alarmed, Ilaria noticed the colorful billowing gasses of the nebula had transformed into a massive shelf cloud hundreds of lightyears across. In seconds, the maelstrom grew in its intensity, the static charges flashing inside as if two armies were squaring off on a battlefield. The acrid smoke from their cannon fire grew so thick, the only indication to the soldiers' position were the flashes of fire igniting from inside of the storm.

The thunder from the ion cannons was so loud, Ilaria could feel it reverberating through her bones; the smell of singed air burned her nostrils.

The intensity of the dream was too much for her sleeping mind. Waking up feeling even less rested than when she laid down, Ilaria quickly forgot about the disturbing images as decided she'd better go find Damien Rey. Anticipation overrode her usual self-loathing of bedding whoever Sarkin ordered her to sleep with. The emperor had given her an actual investigative assignment… with Thane! The sooner she was finished, the sooner she could fly off in Rill and escape both Sarkin and Rey.

Questions abounded throughout the ship over how the V'reem ambassadors had died with poison being Rey's favorite theory. He reasoned that since their bodies had been found alone in their separate quarters without wounds or signs of a struggle, a toxin seemed the most likely culprit. The only thing he couldn't explain was how it had been administered since neither mantis had consumed food or drink since their arrival or why anyone would… or whom, he grumbled as he knocked holes in his own hypothesis.

"I guess it's possible they died of natural causes," Rey continued, looping Ilaria's arm through his as he walked her through the *Celest* corridors.

"How do you mean?" Ilaria asked. "They both couldn't just up and die at the same time, could they? I mean, something must have caused it."

"That's exactly what I mean," the minister said. "They are the most alien form we've ever encountered. It's possible we were more alien than they expected, too. I guess we'll never know for certain without further examination, but our very air could have killed them. The peeks are questioning everyone for motive and opportunity and we both know there isn't one. Security footage shows no one entered their quarters after they retired. What if they just couldn't process our environment?"

As usual, Rey didn't wait for Ilaria to answer as he immediately continued on his own train of thought, "Even so, I actually pity Sarkin when he tells their queen that her emissaries died on our front porch, right under our noses. How do you think that's going to look? It's going to look bad, that's what I think."

Ilaria had to agree. With the emotions running high on the ship after the discovery of the dead V'reem, it was difficult for much else to get through, but what she could read was right where she would expect it to be. People were angry, confused, even frightened, but she couldn't detect any murderous intentions and certainly not a plot against either Janus or the V'reem.

As they walked, Ilaria squeezed the minister's arm a little tighter while placing her free hand over his to make sure she had full physical contact before gently guiding him back in the direction she needed his thought to go. "Damien, I'm certain you would know more about this than I would, but with the V'reem's exoskeletons, I wonder if the communication units you're inventing for them could be incorporated into environment suits."

"What makes you say that?"

"Because in less than twelve hours of being in our environment, the only V'reem we've ever encountered died. Minister Rey, with your expertise in cybernetics, I believe this is a problem only you can solve. You've already had some fascinating ideas in creating a language that our communication implants could interpret; would it be possible to extend that into a suit designed specifically for their insectoid bodies?"

"My dear," Rey said, patting her hand condescendingly, "if it can be conceived, it can be achieved."

As he rattled on about his achievements in cybernetics and his ideas for Mantis suits, Ilaria didn't need to be an empath to sense Rey's disappointment when he realized he and Ilaria were in the arboretum. She rather enjoyed his confusion as he looked around the arboretum and then at his arm still linked with Ilaria's as they strolled leisurely through the gardens because they weren't anywhere near his own intended destination. Managing to keep him talking about how great his accomplishments were, Ilaria made sure they were as far from his quarters on the yacht as they could be.

Feigning ignorance at his bewilderment, Ilaria hugged the minister's arm a little closer. "That is so fascinating, Damien. You're saying you've already thought of an environment suit with cybernetic implants? Emperor Sarkin will be so pleased that you can create what he needs."

"Potentially," Rey corrected. "We will still need to work out a system with the V'reem to program the comm chips, which already work cybernetically to translate languages."

"Yes, I understand, but still. Lord Sarkin will be happy to

know you already have a solution."

"A potential solu…"

Still linked with Rey as she attempted to read his thoughts, Ilaria was oblivious to the shot until she experienced the stab of searing pain in his back. Their connection was broken as the minister fell forward onto the path, cutting a gash in his forehead when his face hit the gravel path. Stunned as his mind ripped away from her own, the telepath wasn't sure if he was dead or merely unconscious.

Stupidly, Ilaria stared at the red puddle being absorbed into the path until other sensations finally penetrated her paralyzed mind. She became aware of screams of pain and panic, both physical and mental, and the ground shaking. It couldn't be an earthquake, she reasoned. There aren't earthquakes in space.

As the ground trembled again, Ilaria finally recognized the tremors were from explosions ricocheting off the shields. The *Celest* was under attack!

Deciding there was nothing more she could for Rey, Ilaria's next impulse as a trained Empati was to protect the emperor, but she hesitated on racing to the flight deck. She wanted nothing more than to join the fighters in space, but with Laran on board the yacht for the Gala, there were more experienced pilots to protect the exterior.

Swallowing her disappointment of missing a flight battle, Ilaria knew she would be of more use at the emperor's side. Stretching out her mind to locate the Sarkin, she felt his presence one deck below her on the port side. If her mental map of the ship was correct, he was in his suite.

Leaving Rey's prone and bloody body, Ilaria raced out as another explosion threw her into the door frame as she exited the arboretum. Steadying herself, she headed for the nearest Access Tube used for maintenance and emergencies. The Tubes ran the length of the ship and linked the ship together when the lifts were either inaccessible or unwise.

"*Jax!*" Ilaria sent as she stepped into the Tube, "*What's happening?*"

It was a few moments before she heard his mental answer. *"At least a dozen fighters are attacking our port side. Shields were raised in time so there is minimal damage and currently no hull breaches. I've already launched; where are you?"*

"I'm about to enter A-T 12. Sarkin's one deck below me."

"Good! Our fighters are more than a match for these ships. You need to get the emperor to the bridge. What about Rey?"

"Shot," Ilaria answered as she stepped out of the Tube and into the increasing chaos of crew members racing to their stations and panicked dignitaries impeding their path. Reaching the suite, she found two guards struggling to open the emperor's sealed door after their repeated hails went without a response. On the other side, she heard rapid laser fire repelling off the external shields.

"Jax," Ilaria sent, *"What is your situation?"*

"Eighteen ships total; they're still focusing their firepower on the upper port decks."

"An assassination attempt," Ilaria reasoned as those decks were directly outside Sarkin's suite. There were plenty of ways to die on a ship other than being sucked into the vacuum of space and a hard-enough external hit could send debris flying across the room. *"Do you know who they are?"*

"Negative," Jax sent. *"These ships don't have recognizable ion signatures. Whoever they are, they aren't ours and they're not from the Alliance."*

"V'reem?"

"Possibly, but these aren't the same class of ship their emissaries arrived in. These are definitely fighters, though and not passenger shuttles."

"We're going to have to blast the doors," one of the guards said after the next attempt at opening the doors failed.

"We may lose containment if there's a hull breach," the second guard cautioned.

Ilaria didn't know much about the structural engineering of the stellar ships, but she did understand that he was referring to the emergency force fields. In the rare event that the integrity of a ship was damaged by rogue asteroids or space debris, internal shields would seal the breaches to prevent implosion. It was a terrible choice. If they broke the seal and damaged the circuits, a hull breach could cause a cascade failure and destroy the ship; if they did nothing, they would lose the emperor.

"Ilaria, I thought you were with the emperor! Why did you launch?"

The force of Jax's call made the telepath jump. *"I'm at his quarters now. The doors are jammed; we can't get him out."*

"Then who's flying Rill?"

"How the hell should I know?" Ilaria demanded. Though she was bursting with curiosity at who gained access to her ship, she didn't have time to think about that now. *"Can your ships break the concentration of fire on the port decks? We can't get in and if this portion is breached, we lose Sarkin."*

"On it," Jax answered, not bothering to mention that if that happened, Ilaria would also be lost. That was something he could not let happen.

Before Jax could angle his fighter to break up the bombardment, Rill broke through and hit the attackers on the underside of their ships. Two exploded as his concentrated fire broke through their shields while the rest broke formation.

Plowing through the debris of the destroyed ships so he could fire on another approaching fighter, Jax sent, *"You're clear for the moment, but get away from the port side as fast as you can. The structural damage is extensive enough that it could still implode,"*

"I can't leave yet; Sarkin's still trapped in his suite."

"Ilaria, get out of there or you're dead."

Ilaria didn't move as she watched the men continue trying to get through the door. They were all dead anyway if Sarkin did survive and found out they'd ran away.

"Did you try rewiring the locking mechanism to bypass the main power grid?" Ilaria asked.

"Of course!" the guard shouted back.

"Good! Do it again, only this time cross the ion streams to force a power surge. It will open the doors leaving the main section uncontaminated. Do it now, or I'll do it for you!"

Glancing between the Empati Keeper and his partner, the second guard stepped in and did as Ilaria commanded. The doors slid open just enough for the emperor to squeeze through and the emergency force shield was raised.

Only seconds later, the outer wall of his luxurious suite ripped away from the rest of the ship sending everything remaining in the room into the airless void.

· CHAPTER 7 ·

That was close," Sarkin whistled as he heard the contents of his quarters being sucked into the vacuum of space. For the moment, with his adrenaline overriding both his fear and his fury, he actually laughed.

"Too close," said the guard who had managed to break the seal on the door before turning to Ilaria. "That was good thinking on your part."

"We need to get the emperor to the bridge," the second guard said, more concerned for his own safety than Sarkin's.

"Good plan," Sarkin agreed. As the most secure area of the ship, the bridge had secondary power and defensive shields would hold even if the rest of the ship was destroyed. "We can't risk using lifepods as the attackers would pick us off the moment we launch."

"My lord," the guard said attempting to implicate that when they survived, it would be his doing, "if you would follow me."

"What are your names?" Sarkin asked as the guards led him down the corridor.

"Lieutenants Krieg," the one who had opened the door

answered, "and Sully."

"Ilaria," the Empati said, raising her hand. She decided immediately that she liked Krieg who turned just enough to give her an acknowledging nod as he protectively escorted Sarkin towards an Access Tube. She detected that the emperor hadn't been taken in by Sully's bluster of command, but now was hardly the time to pick and choose companions.

Just then, another explosion rocked the ship, the jolt sending them into the nearest wall. The guards, Ilaria and emperor looked at each other in horror as the first percussion was followed by a cascade of smaller pops echoing from deep within the ship. Low metallic groans of metal ripping itself apart reached them as the integrity of the ship stressed and buckled.

The four froze as they waited for what was coming next. Ilaria counted eight full heartbeats before the singular, massive explosion finally came. The breach must have originated on the launch deck, she reasoned as the force of the blast began to tilt the aft end of the ship up.

The vast ship began a slow-motion, end-on-end spin in space causing the escaping humans to slide down the corridor. At the mercy of the artificial gravity trying to right itself with the centrifugal forces, they slammed into the wall at the end of the passage and continued tumbling towards the ceiling as the *Celest* continued rolling. In space and without any friction to slow it, the spin would continue until the engine stabilizers engaged and halted their rotation.

"Grab onto something!" Krieg shouted as they landed on the ceiling. As the ship continued to turn, they held onto anything that would support their weight while the gravity pulled them in a slow arc across the gaping maw of the long corridor. Sully lost his grip and fell down the full length of the ship, his screams echoing even after he disappeared from their view and only ceased when the guard hit the wall at the opposite end of the ship.

As the turning ship briefly righted itself, Ilaria released her hold and dropped to the floor, ordering the others to do the same while she raced to the nearest Access Tube. This particular passage crossed the ship horizontally so, once inside, they were no longer fighting the centrifugal forces with a long and deadly fall at one end, but could step around the Tube with the ship as it turned.

"That was an internal explosion," Sarkin said. "I think a ship hit our launch deck."

Ilaria nodded her agreement as Krieg said, "We're entering a new rotation. It's vital now that we reach the bridge. If the crew has been injured or killed, we may be the only ones who can stabilize the ship."

With a telepathic view on the exterior of the ship, Ilaria asked Jax what had happened.

"A ship broke off and aimed itself directly for the launch bay. He deliberately sacrificed himself to breach our hull. Be careful; unless we can stop these bastards, the ship is about to be boarded."

"Understood," Ilaria sent as she relayed that information to the others.

"That wasn't a malfunction on my door, was it?" Sarkin said darkly.

"No, my lord, it wasn't," Krieg answered. "If it wasn't for Ilaria, we wouldn't have gotten you out in time and we all would have been blasted into space."

"That may still happen if we don't get the ship under control," Sarkin replied. "Clearly, the bridge crew either can't get the ship back under control due to damage or they are no longer able to. Krieg, until we locate the Captain or his first officer, you're in command. Can you get us to the bridge?"

Ilaria wasn't sure of the crewman's position on the *Celest,* but, despite his youth, Krieg definitely knew how handle himself in a crisis. Only her empathic senses caught his slight hesitation as he assured his emperor that he could.

"Yes, I know the way, but it will be dangerous. We'll have to climb up four decks and the intersecting ladders in these horizontal Access Tubes will put our rotation back to the length of the ship."

"What does that mean?" Sarkin asked.

"It means if we lose our grip, we'll have a long way to fall," Ilaria answered.

They set out running across the walls and ceiling as the ship continued into a new rotation. Quickly making their way forward and pausing only when they had to carefully cross the gaping chasms as intersecting Tubes impeded their way, the four finally stopped at a ladder.

The climb was a challenge. During each rotation, they first had to ascend going hand over hand, but when their sense of up shifted, they had to then descend the ladder to accommodate the constantly changing perspective.

Another cascade of explosions caused the Krieg to lose his grip, but Sarkin caught the lieutenant's flailing hands as he fell. The emperor waited for the rotation to be upright and for Krieg to have a good grip on the rungs before he let him go. Closing his eyes at the near fatal fall, the man nodded his gratitude to his emperor before following him to the bridge deck.

"I'll go first," Ilaria told them, waiting for the floor to become the floor once more before she exited the Tube. Quickly, she ran down the hall and pushed the sliding bridge door open so she could brace herself against the jamb as the *Celest* began yet another turn. It took one more spin for all four of them to make it onto the bridge and one more to learn they needed to dodge the bodies of several unsecured bridge crew tumbling by them. Only the captain had avoided this fate. Strapped onto his chair at the time the suicidal pilot had rammed into the docking bay, Commander Reed must have been hit by debris. With his arms dangling obscenely over his head, Ilaria wasn't sure if he was alive or dead.

Having no choice, Krieg unbuckled Reed from the chair before securing himself to the Command seat, his hands dancing over the panels as he accessed their situation. "A ship definitely crashed through our shields into the launch bay, clearly an attempt to stop any more of our ships from launching. Can any of you make it to the helm? We need to engage the stabilizing thrusters."

"On it," said Ilaria, dropping to the ceiling before running at an angle across the walls before making it to the indicated chair and buckling herself in. Thinking only of the crisis, she forced herself to remain calm as her hands accessed the computers.

"Is there power to the forward stabilizers?" Krieg asked.

"Negative," Ilaria answered, "but I do have sub-light thrusters."

Krieg's pause was so slight, Ilaria was sure no one else caught it, but his emotional flutter told the empath that it probably wasn't a good thing. If she didn't get it exactly right, she'd wind up pushing the ship into lightspeed causing the damaged hull to disintegrate and ripping the *Celest* apart.

"Very good," Krieg said, calmly masking his anxiety. "Set thrusters at .001."

".001, aye."

"Engage thrusters in a three second burst."

"Three second burst, aye," Ilaria repeated, holding her breath while doing so. The ship lurched as the force counteracted the rotation. Ilaria braced herself against the helm panel, the change in motion making her nauseous as her stomach tried to catch up.

"Once more; three seconds," Krieg ordered.

"Aye, sir; three seconds."

This time the push wasn't as great and Ilaria could feel the gravity return to expected normal as it reasserted itself to the floor. She thought they were actually vertical from their original position though that hardly mattered in space. Whatever position you were in was up on a starship.

"Emperor on the bridge," Krieg said in the silence that followed, belatedly acknowledging Sarkin's authority on the ship.

"As you were, Mr. Krieg," Sarkin said. "Please continue saving us."

"Aye, sir," the crewman responded before calling the decks for situation and damage reports.

"Well, that was exciting," Sarkin said with a grin and

Ilaria couldn't tell if he was serious or trying to ease his own nerves. She knew the emperor had an adventurous side, but her definition of exciting was at the opposite spectrum from abject terror.

Ilaria's grin suddenly faded. Without being locked in a mind-link, this time she did sense the kill shot. Though she was unable to identify the source emanating from anyone on the bridge, the target was all too clear. Spontaneously reacting, she leapt in front of the emperor just as the unknown assassin pulled the trigger. The photon blast hit her chest in midair, the force knocking her into Sarkin before passing through her and grazing Sarkin's own shoulder.

Ilaria was unconscious before she even landed on the floor, her shallow breaths the only sign she only had minutes left to live.

The moment before oblivion took her, three light years away on Prime, Thane's head snapped in the direction of where the remains of the *Celest* were breaking apart in silent explosions in the airless void. The terrifying chill that swallowed him was colder than space when the Denobian remembered her despondency on the Wald when Ilaria tried to hide her dread in attending the Gala. In his grief, Thane was the only one aware that his surrogate daughter hadn't been trying to save the emperor.

· CHAPTER 8 ·

Hearing the nurses coming into her room, Ilaria feigned sleep so she wouldn't have to pretend not to notice the hypocrisy in their lying faces. She didn't know how long she'd been unconscious, hours? Days? However long it had been, it hadn't been long enough.

She longed for the silent oblivion again. She had been dreaming of Jax, becoming angry as his voice continued to haunt her mind, refusing to let her sleep. That was all she wanted; to sleep, but he wouldn't let her. Jax had been irritatingly insistent until, defeated, she finally open her eyes.

The searing throb in her chest was nothing compared to the disappointment she felt. Ilaria longed for her silent mind to overtake her once again, but now that was awake, it was impossible to get back.

Someone was holding her hand. Wincing against the glare of the white room, Ilaria was surprised to see that it was Thane and not Jax sitting by her bed. Confused, she wondered what Thane was doing on the *Celest* until she realized that, paradoxically, it was too quiet for space. On a ship, she got used to the dull thrum of the engines until they faded into the deaf curtain in the void. When the droning of the background noise ceased, its absence almost seemed loud.

Looking around, Ilaria noticed the natural sunlight streaming in through the windows gave her room a slightly orange glow. The old light of a late autumn evening, she thought, unless they were on Tyr where the aging red giant sun always imbued the air with the colors of a dying fire.

As her mind continued to focus and rationalize, Ilaria knew that wherever she was in the Janus Empire, Tyr would be the last planet she could be on. Laran wouldn't allow a telepathic peek on the homeworld of her Stellar Navy.

Noticing that she was awake, Thane opened his mouth to say something, but then shook his head when he couldn't find the words. It was only the pain reflected in her mentor's eyes and the pleading dream she'd had of Jax begging her to wake up that caused Ilaria to regret her actions. She hadn't thought about hurting either of the men closest to her when she had jumped in front of the blast. She didn't been thinking at all and certainly hadn't intended on saving Sarkin's worthless life. Just for a single moment, all she'd wanted was to not feel anything from herself or anyone else.

For the first time in their lives, Ilaria and Thane couldn't find any words to speak to each other. All she could do was lay there as Thane silently stroked her hand as they empathically shared their separate remorse.

"What happened?" Ilaria finally asked when she couldn't bare the emotional silence any longer. *"And don't sugar coat it; I'm not dying here."*

Thane opened his mouth to protest her choice of words, then thought better about it. Instead, he candidly told her the sequence of events as best as he knew them. Three dozen ships of unknown configuration appeared from hyperspace. A third of them immediately began firing on the port side of the emperor's yacht while the remaining dozen engaged the defensive fighters exiting the *Celest's* launch bay.

From his brief conversation with Jax in the aftermath of the attack, Thane believed the pilots were gifted psychics and well-trained in mental blocking techniques as the telepath had mentioned he had difficulty reading them even in battle. The attackers, however, didn't seem to have any difficulty sensing the Imperial pilots and enacting counter offensives in anticipation of every move the Janus flyers made.

When Ilaria asked who was flying in Rill, Thane admitted he didn't know. It was an unknown pilot and not even Laran had been able to identify him. "He made all the difference, though. Rill punched through the swarm concentrating on breaching Sarkin's quarters which gave you and Krieg that extra time to get him out of his suite. While you were making your way to the bridge, the Gate activated and Laran's reinforcements arrived from Tyr. With the arrival of the Imperial Stellar Navy, the attackers gave up and jumped back into hyperspace."

Thane stopped talking. After their retreat and the *Celest* was stabilized from its uncontrolled turning, everyone had thought the attack was over. The empath's eyes burned against the tears that suddenly stung his eyes when he realized how wrong he'd been. Though her act to jump in front of Sarkin was impulsive and unplanned, the Thane was mortified he hadn't picked up on her mental state before. He'd been right next to her on the Wald, touched her in a mind-meld, but had missed everything and it had nearly cost his ward her life. Thane wasn't sure if it made things better or worse that he was the only one aware of her true motivations in saving the emperor's life.

Thane went on to explain that she'd been unconscious for the better part of two days. Fortunately, Master Healer Sobek had been onboard and had managed to stabilize Ilaria after she'd been shot and had then rushed her to his private hospital on Haven where he continued to treat her.

"I can't believe you're even alive let alone talking to me," Thane sniffed. "The rumors have been flying that Sobek is either a miracle worker or you only took a flesh wound like Sarkin."

In the following days since the attack on the *Celest*, both Thane and Ilaria heard every theory, both public and private, about Ilaria's role in the attack. To her face, the nurses who tended her injury were full of smiles and praise for the telepath who saved the life of the emperor, but the touch-feel psychic couldn't shut out the silent condemnation when the nurses' fingers brushed her skin as they changed her bandages or their unspoken accusations where she was no longer a patient, but a *peek*. In their private minds, the nurses wondered how a *peek* could have allowed anyone to get close enough to the emperor for an assassination attempt that nearly succeeded. It didn't matter to them that Ilaria had thwarted the attempt, almost at the cost of her own life; peeks were useless if they couldn't stop such a thing from happening in the first place.

The one Normal who didn't place the blame for the attack on Ilaria for psychically missing the attack or that she was sleeping with the enemy at the time, was Sobek. The physician seemed genuinely pleased that she survived and greeted both Psychs like they were old friends.

"Thane, how are you?" the healer asked, smiling down at the Denobian while he shook his hand.

"I've been better," the empath answered with a meaningful glance at Ilaria. Thane had only met Sobek a few times before, but he always liked the way the tall man treated him. Not quite like an equal, but that could hardly be expected from a member of the royal family. At least it was with the same respect Sobek gave full Citizens of the empire.

"So, have you," Sobek said to Ilaria. "I'm not going to ask what you were thinking; I'm just going to say 'thank you'. You saved my brother and nearly got yourself killed while doing it. Ilaria, there are no words to express my gratitude."

"There is no need," Ilaria said, keeping her tone even. "It was my duty."

Sobek snorted, "It was his bodyguard's duty, not yours."

Excusing himself, Sobek left Thane to catch Ilaria up on the rest of the news. Vale and his entourage had been allowed to return to Arkell during the investigation to determine the identities of the attackers, but Laran had insisted on a blockade around their planet, in effect, putting the entire world under house arrest. That wasn't going to sit well with the Arkellians, but Ilaria had other things to think about. She asked about Damien Rey, but Thane didn't know what had happened to the minister. So far as anyone knew, Ilaria was the last one to see him alive.

Though she still had some residual pain, to the astonishment of both Psychs Ilaria's injury looked as if it had been healing for a month rather than a few days. Deciding that saving the emperor had at least a few perks in allowing a mere peek to be attended by Sobek himself, Ilaria felt almost as good as new.

Though the physician protested that Ilaria needed more testing, word of Ilaria's rapid recovery had reached Sarkin. Eager to find the terrorists who attacked his ship, the emperor called a council meeting and not even Sobek could override his brother's demand that his telepath be present with the healer only relenting when Sarkin agreed to hold it at the Sobek's palace on Haven.

Since Ilaria only had to travel a few miles from the hospital to Sobek's palace, she arrived early and filled her time by admiring his manicured gardens. While the castle wasn't as intimidating as Sarkin's palace on Marasa Prime, it was still a formidable structure. Great stone walls eclipsed the setting sun while its lengthening shade crept over the sculpted lawns, darkening the multi-colored blossoms. Ilaria felt her own mood darken when a large shadow merged to erase her own.

"My Lord Sarkin," Ilaria said dipping her head reverently when she sensed the emperor behind her in the same way she had in the arboretum on the *Celest*. Unlike the lesser lords she had met, the emperor's size was from well-conditioned muscles and not from the overindulgence of high living. Dressed regally in an elaborately embroidered silk tunic meant to both intimidate and impress, Ilaria wasn't sure which emotion the emperor wanted her to feel at the moment.

"Ilaria," he said in way of greeting, "I didn't expect to see you so soon after your injury."

"I am healing quickly thanks to Lord Sobek," Ilaria answered. "I was fortunate such a skilled doctor was on hand."

"Indeed, though I'm surprised at the speed of your recovery. I would have hated to lose you."

"Thank you, sir," Ilaria said, choking down a sudden surge of melancholy when he meant losing her as a courtesan and not specifically her as a person.

Sarkin grunted, but his attention was no longer on Ilaria. Nor did it seem to be on the elaborate gardens as his eyes held the unfocused gaze of someone studying their internal thoughts. Ilaria was glad she didn't have to wait long for Sarkin to state what was on him mind. Usually an impatient man, the emperor rarely wasted time in idle banter and came to his point quickly.

"About you leaving the *Celest* to join Thane on the Wald," Sarkin began.

"Yes, my Lord," Ilaria said, wondering what she'd done wrong now. After everything that had happened since then, she had all but forgotten about her delinquency prior to the Gala and wondered again if she'd ever hear the end of it.

"Good," Sarkin grunted to her surprise as he turning to face the young Empati. "Thane is a good man and wouldn't have called you if he hadn't found it necessary. I was angry, of course, that you disappeared right before I needed you."

"As was Torquil," Ilaria said, struggling to keep her voice even. "I apologize again. I thought I had enough time, but failed to account for how long it would take to clean up afterwards. It won't happen again."

"I'm certain it won't," Sarkin gave her a meaningful stare, silently warning Ilaria of the consequences if it ever did. "Now I want you to tell me your opinion on the matter of the Wald."

"I found it most distressing," Ilaria said, suddenly forced to follow Sarkin as he abruptly descended the light brown stone steps onto the garden path.

"'Distressing' is not the word I would use," Sarkin scowled. "Murders have become rare since the Psi-cops were founded. I know the Empati can't always stop crime from happening, but people like Thane are excellent in halting most of them and those they can't stop, they usually manage to find whoever committed them. Punishment is an excellent deterrent in itself, don't you think?"

Though murders were rare, they sadly did still occur, but stopping a crime before it happened was the main reason Psi-cops existed. The Empati branch of the Keepers had been formed in order to seek out aggression before anything could turn to violence. Crimes of passion were harder to detect as they were rarely planned. When such atrocities did happen, they were usually left for the councils on the planet of occurrence to deal with. It was these more ambiguous crimes like the one on the Wald that Thane usually investigated.

Ilaria caught his inflection and didn't for a moment presume Sarkin's mention of punishment wasn't aimed at her. She shuddered to think how close she had come to being sent before the Pushers, psychics so rare there were only three in all of the Empati. Officially, called the Sona, these meta-paths were the only psions in known to exist who had the ability to project, or "push" thoughts into another's mind. Occasionally, someone was rewarded by a session that fulfilled fantasies or erotic obsessions, but that was rare. Most often, the Sona were ordered to punish, to force their victims to have nightmares so terrifying, hearts had been known to seize in fright and minds had splintered like shattered glass.

"She was murdered then?" Ilaria said, catching her breath and hoping to move Sarkin away from any talks of punishment. She realized that if the body she and Thane had discovered on the Wald had been murdered, it could only have been premeditated. Such a crime hadn't been committed in centuries, indeed, not since the Psi-cops had been established. She wondered if Sarkin knew the victim had been incarcerated on Maelstrom because he seemed more agitated than usual over the death of a peek, even if she had been murdered.

"No question. I've spoken with Alton and he has confirmed it, but we will speak of it more it in Council. When I spoke of the Wald, I actually wanted your opinion regarding the Indigenous. I didn't realize these Trees had such initiative and I don't want there to be any problems with mining the Gas."

Pausing in order to organize her thoughts, Ilaria studied the bright purple flowers for a moment before speaking. "I know they hate us being there. With every expansion of the Pit, more of their forest is destroyed. All the lifeforms on the Wald are incredibly symbiotic with one another and the damage to one species often harms another."

"Yes, but I didn't know these Trees could walk let alone think. I won't have anarchy on one of my planets. It's bad enough that someone was murdered there; I won't have disruption in the mine."

"With respect, sir, while the Wald has been in Janus territory for a millennium, it was only just over a century ago the Indigenous ever saw their first offworlder when we humans had no idea there was any kind of intelligent life there. They don't see themselves as your subjects; they see us as invaders."

"They'll see us as more than invaders if they hinder gas production," Sarkin snarled, unmoved by Ilaria's description of the Akilli. "No matter how smart they are, they will give way to flamethrowers. I'll burn every blade of grass from the planet if I have to."

Ilaria inwardly sighed. Even though Sarkin had asked her opinion, he was digging for affirmation to maintain his control on the world and she was in enough trouble as it was without antagonizing the emperor further. As much as she wanted to defend the gentle Akilli, Ilaria kept her mouth shut.

"Now," Sarkin said, changing the subject again. "I want to know your impressions of this Damien Rey. He's their Prime Minister, but he was dressed as a guard. What was their reasoning for that subterfuge? I assume it was so they could get close enough to get a shot in at me."

"You don't know," Ilaria said surprised, instantly regretting her surprised reaction as the emperor's anger morphed the flecks of blue in his eyes into splinters of steel.

"Know what?" Sarkin demanded.

"I apologize, my lord, but with my injury, I haven't been able to inform you of things properly. It wasn't subterfuge for Damien to be in uniform as he was a guard in their military before he was elected Prime Minister. The Arkellians keep their rank for life, so he was merely showing his rank as any Arkellian in his position would. More importantly, he himself was killed moments before the attack. I was in a mind-link with him when he was shot in the back."

"I'd forgotten about that," Sarkin sounded disappointed. "Were you able to find out anything before that?"

"While his duties were to Arkell, I sensed no direct disloyalty to you or the empire. He was fishing for information, but I believe that was because he was new to his position and that was his first Gala. What caught my attention with him was the emotional spike when I mentioned adapting his cybernetics to an environment suit for the V'reem. He was very careful about what he revealed to me, but he definitely knew something. Unfortunately, I wasn't able to find out more."

"Rey wasn't a telepath, was he?"

"No, sir," Ilaria said shocked that Sarkin would have asked such a thing. The minister would have been given the standard psychic tests when he was eight same as any other Citizen of Janus. "Even during my telepathic scan, I sensed no indication he had mental abilities of any kind. I can't say for sure if the Arkellians weren't involved in the attack on the *Celest*, but I do know that Damien Rey himself wasn't aware of it."

"Good," Sarkin grunted. "I won't have unregulated peeks running amok outside the Empati. Anything else?"

"Only a name and I don't know if it means anything," Ilaria answered. "I must have picked it up from his mind during our lovemaking since I am certain Rey never said it out loud. Have you heard of an Arkellian named J'rey?"

"No, never heard of him before. Former lover?"

"Possibly," Ilaria admitted. "The name is faint in my mind, but I feel that he is important."

Sarkin paused, lost in thought before turning to walk back to the palace.

"You know Thane well, I presume?"

"I do, sir," Ilaria said with a slight shake of her head. Conversations with Sarkin were hard to follow when he jumped subjects so quickly. "When I was first brought to the Empati, Thane was my primary trainer."

"That's a bit unusual, isn't it, for an empath to train a telepath?"

Ilaria couldn't help but laugh. "It is, sir, but I have been informed on many occasions I was an unusual case. As you know, the circumstances that brought me to the Empati made me the youngest Psych ever to be found. I was an infant and my training fell to Thane until I was old enough to join a peer group."

With an approving nod, Sarkin said again, "Thane is a good man; from Denobia if I remember correctly. Bit short, these Denobians, but that's to be expected with their dense gravity. At least they make up for it with their offworld jumping abilities. When he was on the Wald, there were other telepaths he could have contacted, but he called you and you responded despite the Gala."

"I did, sir," Ilaria answered. "He raised me and we worked together before I was transferred to Haven and then to you; he knows the strength and limitations of my abilities. Also, I don't think he was aware Jax was also on the *Celest* at the time he called and he certainly didn't realize how close the Gala was."

Sarkin was silent as he considered the situation, but then grunted again as he made a decision. "After this Council, your duties with me will be limited. I still want you to return to the Keep and help Thane with his investigation; he might need a telepath with him. Even if it's only a peek, a murder is a terrible thing and I can't punish those responsible unless I know who they are. And since it happened on the Wald, I don't want anything to interrupt the Gas mining. And while you're at it, I want you to find out more about this J'rey. He could just be who Rey would have preferred to be fucking at the time, but I want to know for sure."

As Sarkin and Ilaria walked back to the Palace, Ilaria was inwardly thrilled at the prospect of returning to the Keep. Beautiful dresses couldn't match her Peace-Keeper uniform and luxurious palaces could never be more comfortable than her home. Ilaria hadn't realized it until the emperor reaffirmed her orders just how stressed she was in the palace. It would only be until Sarkin needed her again, but until then, she wouldn't have to tiptoe around the emotionally volatile senators who delighted in blaming her when anything they thought was a secret became public. Peeks were the usual scapegoat for leaked information even though she hadn't slept with most of those pompous gasbags. If they wanted to keep their secrets, they might want to sample the normal brothels and not indulge with Sarkin's courtesans. Months of pillow talk with an empath could be just as detrimental to a senator's career as a single night with a telepath.

At the thought of her assignment, Ilaria felt as if a band wrapped around her heart had suddenly snapped and released its pressure. Without the constriction in her chest, she felt as if she could breathe for the first time in years. With the mental weight gone, Ilaria schooled her happy smile as she followed Sarkin into the Council chambers.

• CHAPTER 9 •

Inside the council chambers, Thane and Ilaria wanted to close their eyes so they could concentrate on blocking out the chaos, but the throng milling about the room loudly demanding answers from one another made it impossible. The emotional turmoil was so loud, Ilaria couldn't shut it out and was forced to feel it.

"How do you feel?" Thane asked, tilting his head up so he could look her in the eyes.

All he had to do was touch Ilaria to know the truth, but he trusted her not to give him a placid "fine". Telepathically bonded or not, Thane usually knew when she was hiding something which was why he felt so guilty for missing her depression. He had deep shadows around his eyes making him resemble the dead rather than the living. He hadn't slept much since the attack, but sleep was still a long way off. Like a machine, Thane seemed to have the capacity to go days without needing rest, sometimes pushing himself until exhaustion forced him into unconsciousness.

"Surprisingly good," Ilaria answered. *"It's still a little painful, but whatever Sobek did worked like magic. I feel fantastic,*

like I could run for days."

"*Well, since you did just get shot, maybe hold off on that for a while,*" Thane told her as he eyed her shrewdly. Something was different; she seemed almost... happy. She'd entered the chamber behind Sarkin. The emperor must have given her good news for a change. Thane was eager to know what it was, but with the council about to begin, he'd have to wait.

"*I will, sir.*" Ilaria looked down at him with a warm smile. She had hated the day when she suddenly noticed she was taller than he was, childishly afraid that it would alter the dynamic of their relationship. Her approaching maturity had made her feel as if they were drifting apart into separate worlds, but Thane had told her that was nonsense and he had mostly been right. Their training had continued as if nothing was changing except her increasing height and he continued to laugh or comfort her depending on her ever-shifting moods, but there had been subtle differences. She was growing into a woman and each member of the council had wanted her abilities. As the emperor, Sarkin had overruled Sobek over what Ilaria's telepathic duties should be, something neither had been happy about, but since the healer still borrowed her on occasion, he had kept his peace. Occasionally, Ilaria wondered what her life would have been like if she had been permanently transferred to Sobek's hospital on Haven, but it hardly mattered. She belonged to Sarkin and he wasn't about to give up his political advantage by turning a powerful telepath into a nurse.

As Sarkin took his seat at the high table beside his brother and sister, Laran and Sobek settled themselves in their own elaborately carved throne-like chairs.

To Sarkin's right, the petite Laran was a formidable woman and Ilaria was impressed that someone only a few inches taller than herself had the power to cause trained warriors to step back simply by walking near them. Of course, they did that to the telepath, but not for the same reason. Shorter than almost everyone at the Keep, Thane also garnered that same respect from those who knew him even though he was only an empathic peek.

Watching Laran, Ilaria understood the respect she was given. As the commander of the Imperial Fleet, the Admiral defended the realm's surface, air and space. Most of the planets had their own defense, but as Citizens, they only needed to call on the stellar navy should the need ever arise. Occasionally, they did, especially on the eastern edges of Janus where the outer colonies occasionally had trouble with the Vega Alliance when they pushed the boundaries of their empire. Vega had been quiet for a while so Ilaria guessed they'd finally figured the territories out.

In comparison to his sister Laran, Sobek didn't look nearly as impressive. If Ilaria didn't know better, she wouldn't have thought them related. Tall and skinny, Sobek's figure seemed to be swallowed by his high-backed chair, but he was blessed with what seemed to be perpetual youth. Ilaria had yet to see a single grey hair despite his years devoting himself to the health and well-being of the empire's Citizens. The hundreds of master healers before him might have cured more diseases than were known to currently exist, but Ilaria decided that was just because there weren't as many illnesses left to for Sobek to cure. The healer's dedication to his profession was without repute.

"Ilaria," Laran said.

Stepping forward, Ilaria gave Laran a low bow, "Yes, my Lady."

"It is my understanding that as a touch-feel telepath, you are called to whore for the emperor," Laran said, her statement telling the Senators just how unworthy Ilaria was in her eyes. The fact that she had no choice in the matter was irrelevant to the Admiral. It didn't even matter to her how heroic her actions had been in saving Sarkin, she'd never see Ilaria as anything but a peek.

"That is true, my Lady," Ilaria said, lowering her eyes so Laran couldn't see the flash of humiliated anger. She literally bit her tongue so she wouldn't point out that the Admiral was wrong on calling her a whore because they at least got paid for their service; Ilaria didn't. If anything, Ilaria saw herself as a loyal servant of the Empire. She hated reading the minds of people as they used her to gratify themselves, but her mind-scans told Sarkin everything her contacts were thinking and not just the political secrets the emperor was after. Thanks to her, the emperor knew who was truly loyal to Janus. She wondered where the Admiral's fealty would lay if she was ever scanned.

"And in fucking Damien Rey you discovered his plot against my brother," Laran continued in contempt for Ilaria and the near miss against the emperor.

"No, my Lady," answered Ilaria, raising her eyes to meet Laran's flash of anger at being contradicted by a peek. "While I can't tell you if the Arkellians were involved or not, I can only say that the Prime Minister wasn't. I sensed he knew nothing of the attack beforehand."

"And I'm to take a peek's word for it over the evidence?"

Ilaria quickly censored her original reply when she heard Thane send to her. *"Be careful."*

"I hope so, my Lady," Ilaria said. "My job for Emperor Sarkin is to mentally scan minds without them knowing they are being read. Damien Rey's mind was clear that there was no plot against our Lord. He was at the Gala as a Prime Minister."

"You are certain of this?" Niegan asked, fixing his one organic eye on Ilaria. The cyborg worked within the Empati Keep at Control. Ilaria had no idea how Niegan had become a cyborg, but as she watched the brass cogs frantically ticking away inside his transparent head casing, she decided she didn't need to know. It probably wasn't a happy-ending fairy tale.

"Absolutely certain, sir," Ilaria answered. "Even though he was dressed as a guard, to the Arkellians that is what he should have been wearing to represent both his current position and former rank."

"Enough, Laran," Sarkin said with a sly smile at the information his master spy had uncovered. "As Rey was killed moments before the attack began, I think it's clear he wasn't behind it. Ilaria also tells me she unearthed a plot from Damien Rey's mind regarding his cybernetics program. You wouldn't know anything about this, would you Niegan?"

"No, my lord," the cyborg said unperturbed that, with a simple question, the emperor had all but accused him of being involved. After the meeting on the *Celest,* Niegan had anticipated the accusations and openly projected his sincerity that he was blameless on all accounts. "All I am aware of regarding cybernetics is Tech's desire for advancement. My own parts have been continually upgraded since my implants were installed. It is a possibility what Ilaria sensed is a new design or program they aren't ready to make public yet."

Guilt by species, Ilaria thought as the room erupted in arguments about the reliability of cyborgs. If they were involved in the attempt on Sarkin, wouldn't that be just the sort of thing a Cybo would say to divert suspicion?

Cybo? Ilaria hadn't heard that term before, though the label couldn't be anything but derogatory. Just like those with psionic abilities, labels were given to make sure people knew cyborgs were less than human. Ilaria wondered how quickly mechanical people like Niegan would lose their Citizenship if it was determined they had anything to do with Damien Rey's plot. That would be an interesting day in the empire as, unlike Psychs, cyborgs had a Citizenship to lose. But no matter what happened to them, peeks would always be the lowest rung in Janus society.

While she waited for the argument to wind down, Ilaria continued to study the room. Niegan's presence was no surprise as his function in Control was monitoring the communication implants all of the Keepers used. As the population continued to spread out to distant star systems, understanding languages became more of a problem.

The citizens of the Empire spoke a common language, but time and distance caused lingual drifts. With the addition of cultural idioms and accents, even the same language was becoming more foreign with every passing year. Speaking with the alien populations on their advancing borders would be impossible without their translation implants and it was Niegan with his Arkellian cybernetic upgrades who deciphered and programmed the strange tongues into their com-chips.

Ilaria didn't think there was a better person suited for the job because, along with most of his body, portions of the cyborg's brain were also computerized. With Rey dead, maybe she should speak with Niegan about creating a language for the V'reem. Ilaria decided she'd suggest it, but not until she returned from her mission with Thane.

As the arguments both for and against cybernetics finally diminished, Ilaria thought it was sad that after serving for years, a single comment from the emperor had thrust the loyal Niegan into a position of mistrust.

In the quiet that followed, Thane stepped forward to give his report while mentally telling Ilaria to stay instead of taking her position against the wall. Though dwarfed by the petite woman standing next to him, Thane had never been intimidated by his stature and used it to his advantage. Normals tended to assume a smaller size meant less strength and Thane was neither weak physically nor mentally. He was one of the strongest empaths in the Empati, but also smart and could think circles around almost everyone else in the room. But his greatest strength was allowing others to underestimate him.

"Thane, your unit was on the Wald a few days ago recovering a body?" Sarkin stated.

"Yes, my Lord," Thane answered with a bow after the emperor acknowledged him.

"You were already on the Wald; why did you need another peek?" Sarkin's tone and his empathic senses told Thane the emperor already knew and just wanted his answer to appease his council.

"To communicate with the flora-evolved Indigenous, my Lord," Thane answered. "As a touch-feel, Ilaria was able to establish a telepathic communication with the witnesses."

"Yes, tell us about these *witnesses*," Laran said, her tone expressing how little she thought of non-human creatures.

"They are a humanoid-florae species, intelligent, but lack a recognizable vocal speech. They only found the body and to our knowledge, no one actually witnessed her death or how she got to the location where we found her. We are still investigating, but we assume she crashed in the inland sea and then washed ashore."

Laran continued, "It is my understanding that this dead woman had a prison tattoo. Was it still viable for scanning?"

"It was, my Lady. Her name was Zin Tram; the tattoo was from Maelstrom."

Niegan's cybernetics were forgotten over the demands of how an In-Valid got out of the prison designed to hold such vermin. The primal emotions of raw fear, anger and hatred boiled from the assembly at the mere mention of an illegal peek escaping from the secure facility.

"Escaped or let go?" Ilaria asked Thane.

Without an answer of his own, Thane didn't respond to her silent question.

Sarkin raised his arms for silence, but whatever he was going to say was interrupted as the large doors burst open. Ilaria shot Thane an alarmed look when Daneb entered roughly pulling the young Akilli they knew as Anak into the chamber. Heavy chains had been wrapped around his thin trunk-like body, pinning his wooden arms to his side.

Ilaria knew "Anak" wasn't his name and only meant child or son. She wasn't even sure if the intelligent trees used names the way humans did, but it had been what his parents had called the sapling and was the only name she knew him by.

"What is the meaning of this?" Sarkin demanded, infuriated at the interruption.

"My apologies, my Lords, Lady," Daneb said, Ilaria easily reading his detest of the young Akilli and his utter satisfaction at being able to bring him to the council meeting. "This tree-person has more information that wasn't disclosed to the Psi-Cops during their initial investigation."

Anak looked as awful as she thought an Akilli tree could. The hair-like twigs beginning to grow on his cranium were drooping, but though the young tree was clearly terrified, it wasn't entirely from his fear of being brought before the humans. Ilaria noticed the leaf buds that had been a fresh new green on the Wald were showing signs of wilt. In the short journey from his world to Marasa Prime, the sapling looked as if he were already dying.

"If I may, my Lords," Ilaria shouted above the new outburst, "the Akilli cannot live off their world for long. We must return him immediately."

"This *Akilli* withheld vital information and must be questioned," Daneb seethed.

Ilaria gave Daneb a dark stare before addressing the emperor in desperation, "I agree, Lord Sarkin, but if he is not given proper nourishment again soon, there will be no information to be had. My Lord Sobek, may we take him to your garden? He needs soil and water and he must have them quickly if he is to survive."

At the healer's nod, Ilaria rushed from the room stopping only to make sure Daneb was obeying her. With a growl, Daneb yanked the chain and hauled the bowed sapling from the room. Evening had fully swallowed the garden, but it was far from dark as bioluminescent plants began to glow in the fading light. Ilaria decided that the only place on the palace grounds that even slightly mimicked the tree's swampy homeworld were the water gardens where sculpted waterfalls and fountains cascaded down decorative rocks continuously keeping the rich, loamy soil moist.

No sooner had Ilaria removed Anak's chains and led the tree to a small island in the center, did the young Akilli burrow his root-like feet into soil and lower himself down to his knees, supporting his sagging body with the branches on his hands. Looking up at Ilaria with his terrified eyes, he nodded his thanks to the human woman.

The alien soil, full of acrid fertilizers that forced the out-of-season garden into an unnatural dark green tasted sour to the sapling, but for now, it was also life. To anyone dying of thirst in a desert, even a stagnant pool was a gift, and Anak drank deeply, momentarily grateful.

Ignoring her soaking clothes, Ilaria stepped up to Anak after Sarkin nodded his permission once again. This time, she didn't offer the tree the hand-to-hand contact like she had to his mother, but placed her palm onto his bark covered chest. Closing her eyes, she felt his fear, not through emotions, but through his heart pounding against his wooden frame. The joining contact washed over her and she felt his fear become terror. Burning; he was afraid of the burning, the alien tongues of fire setting his people ablaze. Because Ilaria was the only one who could speak directly with the Akilli and was no longer on the Wald, Daneb had made his intentions clear by aiming his flamethrowers at the forest. If the Trees didn't comply and let him take Anak, he would burn them all. His parents had no choice as their anak was wrapped in chains and forced from his planet home.

Ilaria wasn't sure if Daneb comprehended that he had kidnapped a child from his parents, but she realized the miner's actions had already erased the youthful curiosity she had so recently sensed from the young sapling. The child fully comprehended now what the Rebe had told him: humans were the enemy.

"Be at ease," Ilaria told him gently. *"I will see to it you are not be harmed further and I promise I will get you back home. Please show me what is it you know."*

Locked in her telepathic bond, Ilaria couldn't move as the terrifying images began to flow from Anak's mind. It might have been the intensity of the visions she was being shown, but the mental connection was the strongest she had ever made. In her mind, the language of the Wald flowed like liquid, crystal clear and filled with nuance and meaning. The telepathic bond was so pure and solid, Ilaria understood what the Mother Tree had meant about being the Voice of the Edu as their voice was now ingrained inside her.

Others felt it as well. Suddenly, every empath who had followed them from the council chamber looked uneasily at each other as they picked up on Ilaria's growing fear. Thane was the exception when he also plunged into the fountain, splashing through the water in order to place his hand over Ilaria's so he could share the telepathic nightmare. When it ended, the two

Empati looked at each other in horror as they stepped back from the images the tree had given them.

"What is it?" Sarkin demanded. "What did he say?"

"Bodies," Thane answered when words failed the young woman. "The Trees found dozens of human bodies in the deserts on the Wald."

· CHAPTER 10 ·

After excusing the council and ordering Thane and Ilaria to return immediately to the Wald so they could begin their investigation over the new deaths, Emperor Sarkin and his two siblings lingered in the garden.

Now alone, the three rulers watched as Anak slowly straightened his trunk and became immobile. Anyone passing by in the gardens would have thought the young Akilli was just another tree decorating the elaborate island of the water gardens.

"It is really sentient?" Laran commented as Anak's eyes closed and the child seemingly slept after his ordeal.

"Not just sentient, but sapient," Sobek said.

"What's the difference?" the admiral scoffed as she turned her back on Sobek's newest addition in his garden. Now that the excitement was over, she was no longer interested in a mere tree. Unlike Sobek, whose gardens were even more elaborate than Sarkin's, flowers couldn't hold her attention for long. Laran's own gardens were small in comparison, her botanical collection consisting of poisonous plants which she could turn into weapons. Laran only admired the beauty of flowers in how they lured in their pollinators... or their prey.

"A lot, actually, dear sister. In terms you would understand, it is the difference between a hound tracking a scent and the master using that ability for his own gains. It is the difference between thinking and reasoning."

Laran remained unimpressed. "It can't even live a few hours without its feet buried in the muck; hardly a higher species."

"Well said, Laran," Sarkin said still watching Anak. "But still, I don't think I like it here. Thinking or not, it ruins the layout of your gardens, Sobek."

"Why not just chop it down?" Laran asked.

Sarkin glowered, "I would, but these Trees can not only think, but move and they've caused enough problems over gas production over the years. Placating the Indigenous by taking it back will be easier than forcibly reminding them who's in charge. Sobek, I want you to get it out of here just as soon as it can be moved without dying."

"I will take care of it myself, Sarkin," Sobek said. "I have to admit, though, I am curious about this species; sapience is actually a rare thing in the universe."

"Just make sure you don't kill it and return it to the Wald when you're done."

"Certainly, brother," Sobek said with a slight bow.

"Can we discuss something besides smart trees and sculpted gardens?" Laran asked impatiently. "What of these Arkellians and their Prime Minister? I don't like them sending spies and assassins to the Empire."

"No more than I do," Sarkin agreed. "I'm not entirely convinced it was Rey."

"You don't believe he was innocent of this?"

"Not a chance; however, he's not the type to put himself in the crosshairs. Whatever he knows, someone else was afraid that Ilaria would discover it."

"I wonder how they would respond if they knew the lengths you went to for their information," Sobek commented.

"That's his problem. It's not like Rey was forced into to

bed with my telepath. What I need to know now is what he was up to and who ordered both our executions."

Laran scowled, "Pretty poor assassins if all they managed to do was kill a couple of bugs. Clearly, they were here to infiltrate our defenses and find out our weaknesses in order to exploit them."

"Better to get the information first hand rather than leave it to interpretation," Sobek said. "Or to determine if we are trustworthy. I take it you don't believe what Ilaria said that Rey didn't know of the attack?"

"Certainly not! He's Tech's Prime Minister. I want to know what his cybernetics division is up to and how he managed to keep that information from Ilaria."

"You do believe your peek, though?"

"She knows the consequences of withholding information from me," Sarkin glowered. Lost in thought, he clasped his hands behind his back, and began pacing, all the while keeping his eyes on Anak resting on his little island.

Sarkin suddenly turned to Laran. "What is the purpose of these headband things again? You always wear one now and I think it looks ridiculous."

"Ah, that," Sobek answered for his sister with a knowing smile. "It's called a halo and it's innovation from Arkell; they protect minds against any peeks reading us. Which reminds me: I figured since these halos can be used as mental shields, I should be able to reverse the process. If I can isolate the right signals, I might be able to create a halo that will allow us to scan minds just like the peeks."

"That would definitely be an advantage," Laran said, "but I have no intention to screw everyone for information. That's what Sarkin's metamorphs are for."

"No, dear sister. Only Ilaria screws people in order to read them; his metamorphs merely screw people. If I can perfect them, these new halos will be able to pick up any mental signals. You'd be like a telepath, able to hear thoughts without physical touch."

Laran shuddered, "I don't know if I want to hear

someone else in my head. What would be the purpose of it?"

Sarkin's eyes gleamed with interest at the prospect. "For one, I could interrogate the Arkellians without the aid of a peek. Find out the real reason they were trying to kill me."

"Were they?" Sobek asked. "I've thought a lot about that and have been wondering about the V'reem. I haven't been able to determine a cause of death; as far as we can tell, the bug ambassadors just... died."

"Have we been able to establish contact with their empire?" asked Sarkin.

"No," admitted Laran. "Truthfully, the V'reem are a mystery to us. We've informed them of the deaths, making it clear we don't know the cause. I've sent messages that we believe it may have been an unknown pathogen and we're working on an environment suit to protect any future meetings. They haven't responded to any of our communications."

"That doesn't make sense," Sarkin said. "You think they'd at least accept our apologies or respond in some fashion, even if it's in anger."

"We shouldn't jump to conclusions about them just yet," Sobek reasoned. "They're the most alien species we've ever encountered. Their silence might be their way of processing what happened."

"Or their way of blaming us," Laran said.

"Maybe," Sarkin frowned. "The problem with their silence is that we just don't know. The ships that attacked the *Celest* didn't match the bug technology we're aware of, but we were attacked shortly after they died. On top of that, none of our peeks could read the pilots.

"Laran, I want you to put the fleet on alert and run extra battle simulations. Use the attack on the *Celest* as a guide and be ready should the V'reem attack again."

"We're already working on it, Sarkin," the Admiral assured him.

Grunting his approval, Sarkin turned to Sobek. "These halos you've mentioned, can you adapt them into fighter helmets?"

"That shouldn't be hard," Sobek said. "It's a new technology, but I think it can be done."

"Work with Tech and make it happen; I don't want warriors who can be read by these bugs."

When Sobek also assured the emperor that he'd take care of it, Sarkin realized he was glad his brother had been on hand after Ilaria stepped in front of the blast meant for him. Any of his meta-whores knew how to please a partner and he frequently offered them, but his telepath would have been hard to replace which made him immensely relieved he wouldn't have to.

"Now, this brings up the question of who tried to kill me," Sarkin said, glaring at the motionless Tree in the water garden. "Laran, contact the Arkellians and question them about Rey's work in cybernetics. Use peeks if you have to, but get to the truth. Ilaria also told me Rey mentioned an Arkellian named J'rey. Find him and determine if he is at the center of this. If he is, I want your fleet to wipe Arkell off of the stellar maps."

· CHAPTER II ·

For the second time, Ilaria found herself in the unusual position of being offworld and again finding her enjoyment diminished by the grim nature of the circumstances. She had been furious at Daneb for taking the young Tree into custody only to tell the council of the new bodies discovered, clearly a move from the miner to extract revenge on the Akilli for his humiliation. The fool hadn't taken into account Anak couldn't survive away from the moist soil of the Wald and had nearly lost them not only a witness, but a potential ally. Ilaria wanted to insist they return Anak back to his world immediately, but the child was too weak. Leaving him in Sobek's garden was the best thing for him for now, but Ilaria worried how the rest of the Akilli would react when she and Thane returned without him.

Since Thane wasn't Rill's primary pilot as Ilaria also flew Rill on occasion, the Denobian had adjusted the main chair to accommodate his physical needs with an empty threat to the taller woman that if she ever changed it, he'd jettison her into a black hole. With a tolerant smile, Ilaria took her place in the ship's co-pilot's chair. Settling into her seat, she tugged at her uniform's tight midsection as Rill lifted off from Sobek's palace.

She frowned at yet another reminder of why she hated Sarkin's parties and Galas with all the rich food. The survival suit was designed for offworld planetary conditions rather than every day wear rather than aesthetics. It could keep her alive in extreme environments, but wasn't very forgiving when it came to weight gain. She hoped that the exercise through the Wald's untamed wilderness would help her shed a few pounds before she returned to the drudge of her normal life.

If that ever happened, she thought wryly. Sobek was beside himself when he learned Sarkin ordered Ilaria's immediate departure to investigate the new bodies on the Wald. Like the telepath, Sobek didn't have a choice when it came to the emperor's decisions, but the healer insisted she return to the hospital for more tests the moment she could. Sobek explained that in order to save her life, he'd given her an experimental drug and he couldn't guarantee there wouldn't be side effects which he wanted to monitor. Ilaria assured him that, except for a little nausea, she felt fine. The healer only dropped the matter when Ilaria said she was following Sarkin's orders and promised to check in for the tests when she returned.

"What was that all about?" Thane asked.

"Doctors," Ilaria shrugged dismissing Sobek's overprotectiveness. "Okay, what's our plan?"

"The plan is we're going back to the Wald," Thane explained. Turning in his seat to give Ilaria his full attention, the Denobian left the flying to Rill. "I've cleared all this with Sarkin, so you're in no trouble. Believe it or not, he was still a little concerned about your injury, but I told him that, despite how it looked on the bridge, it was merely a flesh wound and you're practically recovered. Since you've already gotten all the information you can from Rey, Sarkin agreed that you are to help me with the investigation on the Wald. For the moment, you're in very good standing with the emperor. Sobek... not so much."

"What do you mean?"

"He was furious with Sarkin and they got into a lovely spat about you being released before his treatment was complete. Sarkin said you were healed and doing well, what more healing could Sobek want? I slipped out before he could come up with an answer Sarkin could agree with."

Ilaria laughed as she recounted her own recent spat with the Healer. "Good! I'd probably be doing boring tests for a month before Sobek got everything he wanted. In leaving, I probably set his research back five years."

"Speaking of research, Ilaria," Rill interrupted, "I wouldn't mind scanning you myself to analyze his wonder drug. If you do develop side effects, I'll be able to treat them."

Having just put on her environment suit, Ilaria grumbled about having to take it off again in order to lay down on the bio-bed for the exam, but recognizing her good mood, her friends were well aware that her heart wasn't fully in her complaints. Being off on an adventure with both Rill and Thane, even if it was back to the Wald, had lifted her spirits tremendously.

"So, where are we in the investigation?" Ilaria asked, her eyes closed against the bright lights reading her biometrics. "Do we know how she died?"

"Yes," Thane said, describing the woman's head wound. "But that was as far as Alton's examination went. As we suspected, her prison tattoo was from Maelstrom, but as soon as he scanned it, Alton decided a peek wasn't worth his time or effort."

Ilaria was disgusted. "Let me guess: they incinerated the body and all our evidence with it."

"That's about the extent of it," said Thane, not even attempting to hide his own feeling on the matter. "Thanks to Rill taking his own readings, meaning he hacked into Alton's files, we know her name was Zin Tram and she was incarcerated for being an In-Valid. Hopefully, between you and the Trees, we can determine how she ended up on the Wald."

"Do we know where these new bodies are?" Ilaria asked when Rill broke through the heavy Walden atmosphere.

It was early morning and the tide was high, flooding the tidal flats where they'd first found Zin Tram. Without a place for himself to land or the psychics to walk, Rill bypassed the cliff he'd parked on during their first trip and instead hovered over the water. Disappointed that it would be hours before they could examine the area again, the ship flew out of the bay to the shallow sea.

"No idea," Thane said, not regretting for a moment they'd left Daneb behind on Haven. If the Trees had led the mining foreman to the graveyard, the empath was confident they could find it as well.

"I may have something," Rill said. "My scanners indicate there is a ship about thirty meters under that inland sea. It reads as a Janus passenger shuttle."

"That is something," Thane agreed. "Maybe she crashed here after all."

"You forget the head wound," Rill reminded him. "She couldn't have flown here with it, so she was either with someone or met someone. And my scans indicate that ship is too intact to have crashed."

"Look over there," Ilaria said suddenly pointing to the coastline.

Following her gaze, Thane saw the edge of the forest moving as dozens of the walking Akilli stepped onto the beach. "Is that good news or bad news?"

"Let's go with bad so we can be pleasantly surprised if they turn out to be friendly. We didn't bring Anak back with us and that's not going to go over very well."

The sliver of coastline wasn't big enough for Rill to land on. Deciding to use his time to get more reading from the submerged ship, Rill flew his passengers over to the shore and hovered just long enough for them to hop off before heading back out to sea. With the AI on his own mission, Thane and Ilaria went to greet the Trees once more.

"*You have returned,*" they stated.

"*We have,*" Ilaria answered, suddenly aware that she'd understood them without telepathically touching them first. Standing next to her, she sensed Thane's own shock that he could hear them, too.

"*I can understand them!*" he said to Ilaria and then repeated himself to the Akilli. "*I can understand you!*"

"Of course," the Trees said. *"We were joined and now we hear you."*

"How is this possible?" Thane wanted to know. *"I'm not telepathic; without Ilaria, I shouldn't be able to hear you."*

"We were joined," the Trees said again.

Apparently, that was all the answer Thane was going to get. They either didn't know or keeping a telepathic connection was so natural to them, it didn't warrant an answer. Looking at Ilaria, she shrugged indicating she didn't know, either.

"Why are you here?" the Trees asked. Before, it had been clear that the matriarchal mother Tree had been the one communicating with them; this time, neither psychic knew which one was speaking. It seemed to be a singular mind projected from all of the Akilli gathered on the shore.

These were a different group of Trees than the family they'd met on the mud flats. When they didn't ask why Anak wasn't brought back with them, she wondered if they were aware of that Daneb had taken him. Deciding not to mention him until they did, Ilaria said, *"We came to determine how the dead one came to your shores. We found a ship in the sea. Do you know if she came on it?"*

"All of your kind come on sky-ships," the Trees told them, *"but this one did not come from there."*

"She didn't come from a ship?" Thane clarified.

"She did not come from the sea but from where your kind are buried."

The humans clearly didn't understand their explanation, so without another word, the Akilli turned and walked down the coast, pausing only to see if the two offworlders were walking with them. Recognizing they were leading them to the rest of the bodies, Thane and Ilaria followed until they came to another river flowing into the shallow sea. Here, the Trees entered the forest, but the loose, steep banks were too much for the humans to easily climb.

Coming to their rescue, Rill picked them up and skimmed over the top of the forest while he followed the Trees inland. After several miles, the landscape leveled off onto a treeless meadow. Touching down, Rill powered down his engines while the psychics met the Akilli at the edge of the clearing where the lush grass stopped and the dense forest began.

"The dead one didn't come from the sea," Thane repeated. *"Are you saying she came from here?"*

"She came from your sky-ships; the sky-ships left her body here. The floods and tides took her to where we first met."

"How do you know this?"

"We followed the Edu."

Edu? Yes, Thane remembered, they were the smaller lifeforms on the Wald. *"So, by following the Edu, you were able to trace the body from where it washed into the tidal flats back to here? That's amazing! It would have taken a team of forensic investigators months to figure all that out."*

Ilaria had her own questions, *"Why were you unaware of the body before this? There's no telling how long it was laying here before the floods moved her."*

The explanation wasn't as straightforward as the humans would have liked. If they understood the Akilli correctly, this meadow covered the top of a monolithic boulder. Enough soil had gathered over the centuries for grass to take root and flourish, but the region was too barren for the walking Trees. They considered this area a desert and avoided it whenever possible. The life that did live here didn't understand the significance of a dead offworlder until they had been questioned by the Rebe.

There was that word again, but the Empati weren't sure which lifeform the Trees were describing as the Rebe. They were clearly not the Edu who seemed to be barely sentient, nor were they the Akilli. When asked, the Trees told them the Rebe were everywhere.

"A deity, maybe?" Ilaria asked.

It was Thane's turn to shrug. They both had equal experiences on the Wald and he didn't know any more about life here than she did.

From where she stood, Ilaria couldn't see why the Trees had brought them here. The only movement in the meadow was the wind coursing through the sea of grass in undulating waves. It was pristine, a region unspoiled by either natives or aliens.

"Thane, this is the location," Rill announced then waited for the Denobian to jump to him in several of his low-gravity leaps. "I've been scanning the area; there are definitely more bodies buried here."

The ship had located the first body, second if they counted Tram who had washed into the tidal flats, from skeletal fingertips growing like a macabre plant out of the ground. In the dense grass, the humans would never have noticed it without hours searching the area.

Anak had been right that there were dozens of dead, and all of them with the same hole in the back of their heads in the same way Zin Tram had been killed. Not taking any chances in losing more evidence, Thane and Ilaria secured one of the bodies in Rill's hold for their own examination before they called it in.

As the Keepers arrived in answer to Thane, Rill lifted off from the Graveyard to make room for the larger psi-cop cargo shuttle to land for the extraction of the bodies. Neither Thane nor Ilaria were pleased to see the smirking face of Daneb exit the shuttle and even less to watch him strut about in triumph as the team began extracting the dead.

"At least the Indigenous were smart enough to leave us alone," the foreman gloated as he looked around the knoll. "Not a tree in sight."

"And as usual, you can't see the forest for the trees," Thane told him. "You came back without the one you took; we are surrounded and they are angry."

It wasn't a bluff. Ilaria knew almost all the Trees near them were the walking Akilli. They had known the Keepers were on the way and had gathered to watch and wait. Though Ilaria couldn't detect any movement now, she heard the creaking of wooden limbs and a rustling of leaves as if a gust of wind had swept through the canopy. It worried her because the light breeze across the knoll barely had enough power to lift small strands of her hair. She wasn't sure if she was imagining it, but telepath thought she could make out words drifting lightly on the wind. The Trees were speaking, but not to her.

As the Keepers set to remove the bodies, a hundred and fifty-three at the last count, Ilaria finally got a chance to speak with Anak's parents when she noticed them at the edge of the burial grounds. She learned that it was they who had discovered the Graveyard. Once they realized its significance, they had brought Daneb the same way they had taken him to the tidal flats, infuriating the miner all over again.

Daneb insisted they inform the council in person, but as he couldn't communicate with the Akilli, he had taken the only witness he could the only way he knew how: at flamethrower point. The two adults had been waiting at the edge of the Graveyard petrified of their child traveling offworld with Daneb, but as the sapling was the only one small enough to fit into the offworlder's metal ship, they had no choice.

"*Your Anak is safe,*" Ilaria said, touching the trees as she mentally communicated with the family. "*He was weak from the travel and will be returned to you when he is strong again.*"

More rustling told her that message had been passed from Tree to Tree as far as her hearing could detect sound. It hadn't been her imagination as the natural sounds of knocking wood and swaying limbs took meaning. Ilaria removed her hand and realized she could still hear them; not telepathically, but in a language rich with nuance and full of loathing for the human invaders. They were not looking for trouble… yet, but Ilaria didn't need to be psychic to sense trouble wasn't far off. They were waiting, watching these new offworlders and a missing child was all the reason they needed to find a human weakness and exploit it.

Ilaria wondered how the Akilli found the bodies as they avoided this deserted place. Not wanting to misconstrue anything by speaking in a language she was only beginning to understand, Ilaria made a new mental connection with the Mother Tree. She was told that all the Edu had joined together to find the origin of the dead offworlder. Though they didn't know how the dead one had come to their world, they had managed to trace her back to the desert rock and she had been there when spring rains flooded the area, washing her body down the river and into the sea where the tides had eventually pushed her into the flats.

After the final count, a total of a hundred and eight-four bodies had been recovered from the Graveyard and, as the burial ground was practically on Daneb's doorstep, Ilaria suppressed her pleasure at the awkward position the miner was in as he tried to explain how he had no idea. There really wasn't any reason he should know unless he had somehow been involved, which Ilaria greatly doubted, but those aren't always the easiest excuses to pass the Psi-cops' mental examinations. People in Daneb's position usually had something to be guilty about and the young psych was disappointed she probably would never find out what it was.

"I don't think we need an autopsy to find out how these people died," Ilaria said to Thane. "Every single one of them has been practically scalped."

"But we still don't know why," Thane grunted as he looked about.

"I have an idea," Ilaria sent. *"Want to place a wager they were all Psychs?"*

Thane snorted, *"Not a chance. But how could this many be undocumented and go unnoticed?"*

"Maybe they aren't illegals, but druggies? Ones who have taken the dampeners in order to live like a Normal. What a horrible way to live."

"What a horrible way to die," Thane agreed before asking, *"What did you tell them about the young Tree Daneb took?"* As the flora-evolved didn't have emotions like other species, his empathy couldn't detect the hordes of Akilli blending into the forest around them, but that didn't make the empath less aware of them.

"The truth; that he was in physical distress from the journey and was planted in the royal gardens to recover. I assured them that Anak would be returned to them when he was strong enough to be able to make the journey safely. They weren't happy

about it, but they have accepted it for now."

While she spoke, Thane scanned the forest surrounding the base of the rock and stretched his senses out to the forest around them, but felt nothing; the extent of his powers limited to the emotions of the species. Ilaria had said they were angry, but he couldn't detect the flora-evolved Indigenous. Even so, he knew his ward was right; if Anak wasn't returned to these people soon, there would be trouble and all the Peace-Keepers combined wouldn't be able to stop it. The entire Empire had already dismissed their intelligence and now a single human had just given them another reason for a revolution. To Ilaria Thane sent, *"We need to make sure Anak is brought back. Can he fit inside Rill?"*

"It would be a tight squeeze, but yes."

"What about his condition? That first trip nearly killed him."

"I think that was more fright than anything else. Putting him in the garden definitely helped, but these Trees are hardier than I let on. Anak will be fine for a second trip especially when he knows we're taking him home."

"Good," Thane nodded. *"We'll bring him back here at our first opportunity, but there's something else we need to do first."*

Nodding, Ilaria reached out to tell Anak's parents of their plan. The Mother and Father tree didn't respond, but stood motionless at the edge of the forest to wait for the return of their child. Saddened that she couldn't help them further, Ilaria joined Thane in their shuttle after Rill returned for them and they launched into space.

· CHAPTER 12 ·

The very idea of Maelstrom conjured images of a dark world, roiling with malevolent storms with continuous flashes of lighting and peals of thunder that could be felt to the bone. Ilaria found the reality was even worse. Centuries of processing the crystal had turned the lush, green world to a sickly mustard yellow. Entering the atmosphere, Rill passed through clouds tainted from the byproducts of the crystalline gas.

Nearing the echelons of the tallest structures, Ilaria saw they were also coated in the toxic yellow smoke billowing from the smelting stacks. Only up in the clearest portions of the sky did the buildings have windows; these became fewer and finally nonexistent the further down towards the ground she looked. Yellow... the entire world was yellow and dead; killed for the need of hyperfuel.

The Maelstrom prison was massive. The tall complex on the surface of the planet Mephitis was only half of the penal labor camp, the rest carved miles below where the convicts painfully chiseled the precious crystal free from the hard, worthless rock.

"Raise your mental blocks as high as you can," Thane told Ilaria as Rill landed in a hanger that somewhat protected his outer shell from the poisonous air. "Misery is the only thing we will sense here."

Thane couldn't be righter, Ilaria thought as she took in the condition of the man coming to greet them on the platform. She knew instantly that if this emaciated and jaundiced human was the warden, the prisoners would be even worse. The warden was a dead man walking. It seemed that on Maelstrom, it wasn't just the prisoners serving a life sentence.

Along with being nearly a hundred pounds underweight, the toxins had corroded his body from the inside out. After years of peering through the noxious gasses, his eyes had been replaced with cybernetic orbs; half his face pockmarked, melted from rain after being caught outside unprotected in an acidic downpour; and he coughed constantly as his damaged lungs futilely attempted to clear away the yellow air.

"Warden Drell," Thane said courteously, shaking Drell's hand, "thank you so much for taking the time to see us on such short notice. I apologize for the inconvenience."

"Nonsense," the warden said, quite warmly, Ilaria thought considering he was meeting peeks. "Most days my work here is rather monotonous, so I'm happy for the distraction. Now, how can I be of assistance to Keeper empaths?"

That was new, Ilaria thought, beginning to like Drell despite herself. No one had ever addressed her this way before. Most people referred to their kind as peeks or Empati, but by calling them Keepers, the warden wasn't making a distinction between their official status or their minority one.

"Well, we're unfortunately investigating a body recently discovered on the Wald and our only real clue was her prison tattoo."

"Released to the Wald, you say?" the warden's metallic eyes shifted between the two empaths. "It wouldn't have been Zin Tram, would it?"

His guests' startled looks were all Drell needed to confirm his suspicion. "Follow me to my office where we can talk and your eyes won't burn as much. You can't get away from it entirely here unless you go up to the top." As he spoke, Drell pointed skyward where the buildings still had windows.

"What's up there?" Ilaria asked as they followed the warden into his windowless interior.

"The bosses," Drell responded, ushering them into a sparsely decorated room. Considering his position in the prison, Ilaria was surprised that nothing in the warden's office had been replaced in decades. His desk may have once been top of the line, but the polished wood had long since lost the varnished shine as the toxic air gnawed across the aging surface. Not entirely certain the chair Drell offered would support even her slight weight, Ilaria gingerly lowered herself into it, sitting on the forward edge just in case the seat failed later.

Drell's own chair protested against his meager frame as he settled back to explain the workings of Maelstrom with the Psychs, "This whole place is run by the Mining Guild for the production of hyperfuel and only secondary as a prison. The bosses don't have to pay their workers if they're prison labor. They run the place from up top where the air is still relatively clear and only come down here if there's a problem. My job is to make sure they never come down. So far, so good; I've only had three visits from up top and not because of something I did."

As the warden rattled on about the prison, Ilaria realized he rarely spoke with anyone who had nothing to do with his job. The holo-cube on the desk displayed a younger, healthier Drell with his wife and two daughters. The family portrait was the only thing new in the room and had been carefully cleaned of the accumulating yellow filth leeching through the office walls. She noticed other cubes, all polished from the polluting residue, which showed the girls aging from their youth through their teens, but only the one closest to Drell on his desk had him posed with his family.

"How did you know the body was Tram's," Ilaria asked, bringing the lonely man back to the purpose of their visit.

"Just assumed it. I get requests from the Wald every now and then for psychic workers and she was the last one transferred over."

"Is that usual?" Thane asked.

"Been happening for about thirty years. I know the last two wardens had sent people over. Conditions there are hard, but they're better than here. I take it Tram didn't die in the mines or you wouldn't be here."

"What makes you ask that?"

Drell gave Thane a derisive snort as he poured himself a drink of a thick, dark liquid. Quaffing it in one swallow, Ilaria surmised it must be some kind of medicine as it eased the warden's hacking cough. "Mining is tough work; ages you, makes you sick. Even normal contracted miners don't last long. If they're smart, they move on to other things before their lungs rot. So, what happened to Tram?"

"We don't know exactly," Thane admitted. "She washed up on in a tidal flat some thirty miles away from the Wald mine."

"And the emperor doesn't like his *peeks* to go missing without knowing why."

Ilaria almost took umbrage at Drell's use of the derogatory term until she noticed his inflection was in disdain at the word itself. "Forgive me, sir," she said, "but for a warden in charge of a psychic prison, you seem very sympathetic to In-Valids"

"In-Valids," he sneered. "The only thing that makes them In-Valid to the rest of the empire is that they weren't born like the rest of us. Most of the poor souls working themselves to death below us didn't have a choice in what they are and their only crime is they wanted to choose the direction of their lives. That doesn't make them criminals; it makes them human."

Stunned at a Normal defending their kind, Thane and Ilaria didn't respond to the warden's sudden outburst. After a moment, Drell continued. "My niece was an empath, if you must know. I still remember how she cried when she failed her Psych tests and they took her away. I'll give you the same advice I gave her, girl: do what they tell you, when they tell you no matter what it is because you don't want to end up here."

As Drell didn't know what happened to the prisoners

once they were released from his custody, they thanked him for his time. Before the Keepers left, the warden gave them a data chip on all the information he had on Zin Tram, only saying he was sorry for her. While he never gave a thought to the prisoners after they left Maelstrom, he was certain her fate was better than what she would have endured here.

"I suggest you talk to Daneb," Drell told them. "He is in charge of the Wald mine and would have signed for their arrival. Now, I'm going back inside before I start coughing again."

Once they were back in space and Rill ran through a cycle of the air filtration to expel the toxins from the cabin, Thane asked Ilaria her opinions on the warden.

"I'm not sure," she admitted. "He was sincere in his consideration of our kind, but we didn't learn anything we didn't already know. All he did was confirm that over the years, he's transferred many prisoners to the Wald."

"Anything else?" Thane pressed.

"What did I miss?" Ilaria asked, suspicious at how pleased Thane was.

"This time, it wasn't in his feeling, but in what he actually said," Thane smiled. "Drell knew right away we were empaths, both by our uniforms and that he was forewarned of our visit. He shook my hand, but didn't even offer to shake yours. If you sensed misogyny, you were wrong."

"Drell knew I was a telepath."

Thane nodded his confirmation, "He knew you were a contact telepath. As the true nature of your abilities is one of Sarkin's biggest secrets, the only way he could have known that is if someone told him."

"But there's more," Ilaria said, fighting the chill as her mind raced through every person who knew of her touching powers. Only a handful of people in Sarkin's inner circle was aware of the full extent of her abilities, but if she included everyone she'd ever trained with at the Academy, the list became dauntingly long.

"There is. In defending our kind, Drell said something I thought rather interesting. Did you catch it when he said that most of the prisoners shouldn't be there because they hadn't committed a crime?"

"Yes, I caught that, but wasn't he referring to the In-Valids?"

"He was, while also taking offense to the term. Rill?"

As always, the ship was one step ahead of his pilots. "Oscar Drell, a professor at the Arcadian University until his fourteen-year old niece, Marda Drell, was classified as an empath and sent to the Empati Academy. She disappeared after six months of training and was later found in hiding with her family on their homeworld of Tyr. The entire family was convicted of harboring an illegal psychic; her uncle Oscar Drell was then transferred to Maelstrom where he eventually became warden."

Giving Ilaria a smile that told her he'd already worked out the answer, Thane asked how a man like Drell ended up running a prison for In-Valid psychics while his own direct family escaped punishment as the holo-cubes clearly showed.

"By making a deal," Ilaria answered, hoping she could one day piece together puzzles as easily as her mentor. If she hadn't been transferred herself to Sarkin's palace, she might not have missed it. "Rill, how much of a bonus does Drell get for every Psych he transfers to the Wald?"

"It's substantial," the ship answered, "and all of it held in trust to be paid to his family upon his death."

"So, the warden's sympathy of Psychs doesn't transcend exploiting them," Ilaria mused.

"It doesn't," Rill said. "But while you were interviewing Oscar Drell, I did some digging on my own. I was able to fully scan five tattoos from the new bodies uncovered on the Wald. No surprise, all of them were Maelstrom transfers, but I hacked into their system while I was waiting and have names and profiles for each of them."

As he spoke, Rill flipped through images of the dead. Ilaria gasped as he came to Tram's.

"This can't be the same woman we uncovered on the mudflats!" she exclaimed

"What do you see?" Thane asked.

"She's, well… old."

"According to her files, Tram was in her forties and mining the gas adds additional signs of aging to a body."

"No," Ilaria said, shaking her head. "The body we exhumed on the Wald was in her mid-twenties at least."

"Tattoo scan confirms the prisoner transferred from Maelstrom and the body on the Wald are the same person," Rill confirmed after rerunning the data.

"This is not possible," Ilaria insisted.

"I have a theory," Rill said as new information appeared on his monitors. "While I was waiting, I ran the bio-scan on the second body. His name was Domnik Turell, a Valid telepathic Arkellian who worked in the cybernetics industry. Though it is difficult to tell with the rate of decay, his scans indicate he was also in his early twenties, while his data files indicate he should be in his late thirties. Turell was labeled as an In-Valid and sentenced to Maelstrom after the newly elected Minister of Tech, one Damien Rey, accused him of industrial theft."

"That can't be a coincidence that both Turell and Rey were in cybernetics," quipped Ilaria.

"Certainly not," the ship agreed, "but there's more. This was six months ago, but Turell was only on Maelstrom three days before the warden released him to the Wald. The person handling the transfer of the prisoners was Torquil."

"And that explains his attitude at the Gala," Ilaria scowled remembering how terrified she'd been. "It wasn't because I left the ship, but because I went to the Wald. I bet he had something to do with Tram's incineration, too. There's nothing illegal about transferring prisoners to another labor camp, but he's done it with threats and bonuses. What could he possibly be hiding?"

"Thane, I've also been wondering why Sarkin sent us to investigate Tram in the first place," Ilaria said. "He only cares about how he can use us. All of these bodies had Maelstrom tattoos. As In-Valid peeks, they are of no use to him."

Thane had to admit she had a valid point; Sarkin wouldn't care. "True, but he only knew about the first one, that

Tram was a Psych. And even In-Valids are useful to him in their way. Maelstrom prisoners mine the Mephitis Crystals which they turn into the hyperfuel for the stellar fleet. It's not as lucrative an industry since the Gas was discovered on the Wald, but they still produce quite a bit for the private sector."

"If Sarkin doesn't care what happens to us, do you think he's the one killing us?"

"Sarkin?" Thane scoffed. "Not even! If the emperor was behind this, he wouldn't skulk on third-rate planets. Sarkin only hides what you can do so no one knows what you're up to when he orders you to sleep with them. As Tram's fate has already shown us, no one cares what happens to us when the Normals are done with us."

"Then why would Sarkin have us investigate them?"

Rill took this moment to answer Ilaria's question. "Because Sarkin, for all his faults, is smart. He's not behind it, but he would like to know who is and why. A deranged killer getting off by murdering Maelstrom In-Valids doesn't matter to him, but it would matter a great deal if psychics like you and Thane began piling up. Thane is a psi-cop and has helped bring to justice a number of criminals, many of whom were Normals; you have value to him by scanning the minds of his political enemies. Telepaths can usually only read the minds of others with the same ability, but Sarkin has even found a way around that by pooling the minds of those he calls his Array."

"Rill's right," Thane agreed. "A single dead peek is nothing, but I think the emperor will be very interested in what we found on the Wald. And speaking of the Wald, let's keep it to ourselves that I can also understand the Indigenous, though how that happened, I have no idea. You said those Trees weren't telepathic, didn't you?"

Ilaria shook her head, "No, they weren't, but we know very little about them."

"I have a theory," Rill said, which caused the two psychics to smile. Just as Thane always had a plan, the ship almost always had a theory. "Your own connection with Ilaria shouldn't be possible, but it is due to the familial bond she made with you when she was a small child. Having joined with you once through Ilaria, the Akilli were able to make a similar, permanent bond. It is possible that, with Ilaria establishing the initial physical connection, other people might also be able to establish such a continuous connection with the sentient Trees.”

"Maybe,” Ilaria was doubtful, “but I was present during both meetings with the Akilli. Even though we weren’t touching, they were able to speak to Thane, either because of me, because he’s also a Psych or through some means of their own. Would they be able to speak with another Normal if I made a telepathic connection first?”

"I have no idea,” Thane said. “Maybe one day we can find out.”

"More likely, we’ll never know.”

"We’re here,” Rill said as he exited hyperspace.

Ilaria groaned when she realized they were in orbit around Haven. Expecting that Rill had brought her here for more of Sobek’s test on his experimental wonder drug, both psychics were surprised when the ship landed on the pad of a large complex three hundred miles to the south of the Hospital.

"This is the Alesium Corporation,” the ship explained. “I have already informed the CEO of your arrival at the direction of Emperor Sarkin in regards to his advancement on the Juventas youth serum.”

· CHAPTER 13 ·

The Alesium Complex, nestled on the crest of a low rising hill, was one of the most beautiful places Ilaria had ever seen. Surrounded by sculpted hedges, the immaculate gardens exploded with a wide variety of colorful flowers. As it was late autumn in this hemisphere of Haven, the botanical species had been carefully chosen so something would be in bloom regardless of the season. At the base of the complex where the hill leveled out, green lawns stretched down to a series of water gardens gently rippling with artificial waterfalls designed blend in with a natural topography.

Ilaria couldn't help contrast Alesium with the sickly yellow plants in Drell's office in the dingy yellow buildings on Maelstrom. Her mouth dropped in awe when the two Psychs entered the main structure of the Alesium headquarters and saw the gardens weren't segregated to the exterior, but grew lavishly throughout the lobby. The thick vines entwining around the interior columns reminded her of ancient civilizations left abandoned and then reclaimed by the untamed wilderness. Unhindered by walls, Ilaria couldn't help but smile in delight as she watched a small, multicolored bird swoop into the open arboretum to pull a seed from the center of a bright yellow flower and then fly its nourishing prize back to the paradise outside.

"Where is Alesium in relationship to Sobek's palace?" Thane wanted to know.

"We are about three hundred miles southwest," she answered as another bird claimed a meal from the same flower. *"The Hospital is another two hundred miles north of that."*

"Good," Thane said, but didn't get a chance to expand as they noticed a young man in his late twenties walking purposely across the lobby towards them.

"Welcome!" he greeted them cheerfully, his well-trimmed hair and immaculately manicured nails seeming at odds with his casual, everyday clothes. As he eagerly shook both their hands, the contact was too brief for Ilaria to read anything except his surface thoughts, most of which revolved around smug pride for his accomplishments and the thrill that important people had taken notice.

His smile widened as he continued, "Rillian Fischer informed me of your unexpected arrival. I am Vanth Alesium and CEO here."

With Rill's ability for independent thought, Ilaria was momentarily grateful their ship was on their side because that computer's genius could be scary sometimes. She decided that if the cybernetics department on Tech ever designed an android that could pass for a real person and transferred Rill's CPU into it, not even she would suspect their AI was anything but another human.

"I'm Thane and this is Ilaria," Thane was saying, unperturbed by Rill's free-thinking.

"Welcome again," Vanth said. "Mr. Fischer explained that Emperor Sarkin sent you here to learn about my serum."

"Yes," Thane smiled as he gestured appreciatively at the healthy arboretum. "I must say, this place is amazing!"

"Isn't it?" said Vanth with no small sense of pride. "Come, let me show you this as it's part of what you came to see."

Waving them to follow, Vanth led them to a massive plant in the center of the room. While the flowers weren't the prettiest Ilaria had ever seen, they still had their own oddly exotic beauty. Each magnificent blossom was fully open with each teal petal nearly as long as a fully-grown man.

"This is the Amaranthine plant," Vanth explained. "It's native to Callis 4 and the inspiration for my Serum," Vanth explained. "These blossoms are beginning to fade now, but you should have seen it a week ago when it was in full bloom. It was truly spectacular!"

"It is still quite lovely," Ilaria said intrigued. She adored flowers and privately would have loved to study more botany if time would ever allow it. Though the Amaranthine wasn't one, some species were even sentient enough for her to make a telepathic connection with them, though they were quite different from the sapient species like the Akilli on the Wald. Ilaria found that plants had a unique outlook on life that fascinated her. "This is an annual?"

"Technically, yes," Vanth smiled. "though the conditions between Callis and Haven cause it to bloom once every seven years. With proper care, it can live for centuries and this particular one is over two hundred years old."

"That is impressive," she smiled appreciatively and then frowned. "Forgive me, but I just caught the inflection of your statement. You said *this* plant was your inspiration for your Serum; you did mean this particular plant and not just its species, didn't you?"

"Oh, yes," and Ilaria thought that if his pride could expand anymore, Vanth would literally explode. "As I was studying this particular Amaranthine, it occurred to me that many species are able to regenerate their cells, even humans up to a point, but when ours reach the peak of maturity, they begin to decay and die. I noticed that if this plant is ever damaged, within just a few days the injured leaves will actually repair themselves. This rejuvenation process will continue throughout the plant's entire lifespan. So, I wondered why should it be that a human's regenerative abilities shut down but can continue in the flora and other species of fauna?"

Thane said, "And through that you were able to discover what causes cell degeneration and halt human aging?"

"Not only halt it, but reverse it. I made this discovery when I was in my sixties," Vanth said squaring his shoulders with pride. "And that was nearly two hundred years ago."

"He's taken his own product at least twice, maybe three times," Thane sent privately to Ilaria. *"Assuming he waited until he was in his sixties each time."*

"That is astounding," said Thane out loud. "Are there any side effects?"

"None," Vanth smiled confidently.

"He's lying!" Ilaria sent as she caught an emotional spike.

"I felt it, too." Thane answered while he asked Vanth, "What is your process? How do you make your Serum?"

"I'm afraid that exact process is a trade secret and at the discretion of Lord Sobek, but I'll be happy to show you what I can."

With another easy smile, the old man with a young face led them to an elevator that descended several floors underground until the lift opened into a wide lab. Nearly two dozen men and women wearing long white coats were studying samples under microscopes or filtering liquids into test tubes.

"Talk about your mad scientist's lab," Ilaria quipped.

Ignoring her, Thane asked, "Is this where you create your Serum?"

"No," Vanth answered, "these people are working on perfecting it."

"It can already reverse the aging process, what more needs to be perfected?"

"Two things," Vanth explained. "Right now, the Juventas must be injected so we are experimenting with an oral dosage. It will make our happy customers even happier when they don't have to get stuck with a needle every time."

"I can understand that," said Ilaria. "And the other?"

"Once we have the oral perfected, we wish to create a diluted formula for our patrons. As you know, the Serum reverts the aging, but then the process begins again as our cells once again age and break down. Once my Serum is available in a diluted dose, it can be taken on an annual basis so no one ever need age again!"

"But only if one can afford it," Thane commented.

"Ah, the fly in our ointment," Vanth said, giving the Keepers a toothy grin. "Creating the Serum is both a time consuming and costly process, but it is my wish that oral dosages will bring costs down. Shouldn't this be a right to everyone and not just the wealthy?"

"*He is sincere, though it might be more for profitability than charity,*" Ilaria sent. "*At a lower cost more people would have access to it and it would double or triple his fortune.*"

"*I agree,*" Thane commented silently. "*I don't know if you can sense it, but Vanth is hiding something even deeper, though his confidence in his Serum is absolute.*"

"*I felt it,*" Ilaria confirmed.

"Vanth, this is amazing," Thane said out loud while gesturing to the room. "Thank you for your time; we won't take up any more of it."

"*What are you doing?*" Ilaria asked her mentor as Vanth led them back to the main floor. "*We haven't found out about what his Serum has to do with the Wald.*"

"*And we won't,*" Thane silently responded. Out loud, he thanked Vanth again for his time and turned to casually stroll out of the lobby.

"We are here following Lord Sarkin's orders to learn more about the serum," said Ilaria said once they were clear of the Complex and following the beautiful path back toward the landing pads.

"A grey area, to be sure," Thane amended, "and one not likely to hold up under much scrutiny. Our main directive was to investigate the dead psychics…"

"Which is precisely what we're doing," Ilaria countered.

"We are, but with this Juventas in their systems, I doubt even Sarkin expected us to question Vanth Alesium. Ilaria, think about it. Sarkin was concerned the bodies on the Wald might somehow disrupt the M-Gas production. It wouldn't sit well with the emperor if this Juventas production was put in jeopardy as well and certainly not because of the loss of a few low-ability peeks."

"So Sarkin is behind the deaths."

"Certainly not, but someone close to him most definitely is."

"Torquil then."

"Torquil doesn't hold as much command as he would like everyone to believe he does. He's clearly involved as he's ferrying the prisoners out of Maelstrom, but he's acting on the direction of someone else."

Simultaneously, the Keepers sensed the attack and dove to opposite sides of the manicured path just as a laser blast burned the air where they had both been standing. Rolling to one side, Ilaria looked behind her just as another shot sizzled through the bush she had been using for cover.

"*To your left!*" she sent to Thane as he narrowly avoided a third blast.

"*Hand pistols,*" Thane said, poking his head up to scan the area. "*Two men in field suits; their helmets are on, so they are probably detecting us thermally.*"

"*Fantastic!*" Ilaria mentally snarled. While the Psychs also wore their environmental suits, both of their helmets were on their ship. That would make it easy for them to be tracked with their warm, glowing heads bobbing disjointed among the cool foliage.

"*Take it high,*" Thane ordered. Few planets capable of supporting human life were as gravity dense as Thane's homeworld and, with Haven's pull almost half of his native Denobia, the empath jumped onto a high branch of the nearest tree in a single leap. Using the canopy for cover, he ran down the thick limb and leapt into the branches of the adjacent tree, hiding himself in the dense foliage.

Ilaria also took to the branches; however, as a prisoner to the human-normal gravity of Haven, she had to climb.

Or not, Ilaria thought, smiling to herself. Launching

herself off a decorative boulder and grabbing hold a low hanging branch, the lithe woman swung herself up to a wide sturdy branch before free-running the rest of the way up the trunk and into the hidden safety of the leafy canopy.

"*We need separate them,*" she said as Thane jumped into another tree.

Agreeing, Thane sent, "*Try leading yours to the pond; the water will mask your heat signature.*"

It took Ilaria a moment to locate the fountain Thane had seen from his higher advantage point. It wasn't close and it would be difficult to reach as she would have to cross an open lawn without any shrubbery for cover. Looking down, she saw that their attackers had indeed separated and hers was studying the rock she had stepped from. She cursed because Thane had warned her that they were equipped with thermal imagery and her footprint on the rock would still be visible to that kind of enhanced vision. She wouldn't be able to remain hidden once he tracked her into the treetops.

Thane went even higher into the trees. His own pursuer was having difficulty keeping him in sight through the dense branches. Waiting until his attacker was directly below him, the Denobian jumped, but even with his offworld abilities, it was a long way down. Though his fall was cushioned by the man's body, Thane felt his ankle twist. His leg exploded in pain, but he still didn't hesitate in his own attack. As the man crumple under his weight, Thane jumped up and brought his elbow down hard onto the man's sternum and heard the satisfying crunch of cracking ribs. While his assailant struggled to gasp in a painful breath, Thane wrested the pistol from his grasp before the man could regain his senses and then wisely froze when he felt the cold gun barrel directly under his chin.

Still in the branches of her own tree, Ilaria also didn't hesitate. Seeing only one path to escape she bolted across the tree limb before leaping onto the Alesium roof just as her attacker saw her and raised his weapon to fire.

Momentarily safe on the top of the building, Ilaria realized she hadn't gone unscathed in the attack. The blast had grazed her shoulder and her right arm had gone slightly numb. Not completely, she noticed in relief when she still had use of her fingers, but her hand tingled as if she had slept on it all night without turning over.

"*Thane, they aren't trying to kill us! The blasters are set for stun!*"

"*Is that a fact?*" Thane answered with a smile to his captive. Even on stun, he was sure a shot to the head at close range would more than likely be fatal. From the look in his captive's eyes, that thought had crossed his mind, too. "*My leg is injured; I can't make it to you.*"

"*I don't think much of Vanth's security if they haven't been alerted to all this commotion,*" Ilaria sent as she shook her hand trying to get the feeling back.

"*Agreed,*" Thane responded. "*I doubt his security is this oblivious, so he's either in on it or has been ordered to stay out of it.*"

"*Just give the word and I'll go back inside and get everything from Vanth.*"

"*Not without a warrant you won't!*" Thane warned, and even then, he'd make sure she didn't. Even if Sarkin ordered this attack himself, a mind-scan on a prominent Citizen such as Vanth would cause an uproar across the Empire so loud, there would be riots against peeks in every colonized system. Thane had no illusions that if word got out that a telepath scanned the head of Alethium, the emperor himself would publicly execute Ilaria to keep the peace with the aristocracy and to hell with how useful she was to him.

On the roof, Ilaria heard a whooshing sound. She turned just as a grappling hook embedded itself into the eaves, the gears of the machine grinding as her pursuer began hoisting himself to her level. She wouldn't be alone on the roof for long. Grateful that Vanth liked his plants, Ilaria sprinted to the far side of the roof and launched herself into another tree. Free-running down the gnarled trunk, she was quickly back on the ground, but then she hesitated. Furious that after a lifetime of training, these men had managed to ambush two of the strongest Psychs in the

Empati, she was torn on whether to aim for the pond as Thane had directed her to, or return to the gardens and try to help her mentor.

Forcing emotion down, Ilaria's rational mind returned as she reminded herself, they had been caught unaware and unarmed. Quickly, she analyzed the situation. Whoever these men were, she couldn't sense them. The only thing about them Ilaria had felt with certainty was the decision to fire on them. Stretching out her mind, even now, the only other presence she could feel out on the path was Thane, injured but alive.

Choking back the cold dread in order to keep her mind clear and in the present, Ilaria made her decision and bolted across the lawn towards the fountain pond. Ever since her discussion with Torquil on the *Celest* and then discovering his involvement with transporting Psychs to the Wald, it had been bothering her that there seemed to be a growing number of people able to block empathic probing. The only people she was aware of who could do it consistently were other psychics which could only mean they were being attacked by their own kind.

Ilaria resisted the urge to contact Thane about her suspicions. It may only be paranoia, but if even one of these men were a telepath, they just might be able to pick her sending out of the air. No one ever had before, but she didn't trust that she couldn't get a reading from them. It was ironic that she was worried these Psychs could do what Normals had accused them of doing for generations: plucking her thoughts from midair.

A blast near her feet caused her leg to tingle; it made her jump, but she didn't lose feeling. The near miss spurred her on and once she reached the pond, Ilaria dove under the shallow surface without breaking her stride. At least the pond afforded her some protection, but it wasn't deep enough to hide her heat signature completely. And she would also need to breathe eventually.

Gliding under the water, Ilaria surfaced on the far side of the fountain. Glancing around, she took another breath before submerging once more. The area she entered had a low, grassy edge beside the lawn, but the opposite side had been left more natural. Reeds and water lilies grew thick by its bank so she swam underwater to use the plants as cover.

When the lush undergrowth of the shallow water reeds began to entangle her, Ilaria carefully pulled her head up for another breath of air and a look around. Either by his own senses or the thermal goggles, he had followed her. The man was close, standing on the grass side of the pond while he scanned the water for any indication of a warm body. Filling her lungs, Ilaria dipped below the surface without causing a ripple and made her way to the pond's edge, following the bank until his distorted shadow told her he was directly above her. His head was raised up as he scanned the marsh grasses on the far side, so he hadn't noticed her approach directly below him.

In a sudden lunge, Ilaria sprang out of the water and grabbed the man's ankles, pulling him into the pond with her. Still unsure if he could read her, Ilaria hadn't tried to hide her thoughts, but had projected them, mentally announcing her intention to attack several times. If he was telepathic, he would never know which thought would be the real one.

Surprised by either her skill or her subterfuge, Ilaria's ambush had been successful and he had been taken completely unaware. Having spent far too many years at the Academy training for moments such as this, Ilaria now had the advantage. She didn't immediately try to disarm him as she grabbed the pistol, but twisted his hand backwards, not stopping until she heard his trigger finger break with an audible snap. A quick punch to his throat left him gasping so Ilaria sent another to his face, breaking his nose and rendering him unconscious.

Hauling her attacker out of the water, Ilaria left him on the bank as her thoughts turned to helping Thane. At least she was now armed with a pistol. As she started to run back across the trimmed lawn, Rill landed directly in front of her.

"A little late!" she scolded the ship.

"The comm lines are down," the ship answered. "I heard it crackle and became concerned when I couldn't raise you."

"That's because I got hit with an energy wave. Have you heard from Thane?"

"No," Rill said, his circuitry managing to sound concerned, "he didn't answer my hail."

"Guard that man," Ilaria said pointing to the pond and retraced her steps back to the garden path.

Remembering the second assailant also had thermal detectors, Ilaria ducked behind a tree as soon as she was back in the garden thickets. It was so quiet now, even the birds decided the commotion was over and had begun singing again. Silently, Ilaria darted between hiding places and made her way towards Thane.

Ilaria nearly laughed out loud at the sight when she finally found her mentor. Using vines and leaf fronds, he had hog-tied his attacker and now was sitting on the helpless man's back while he rubbed his own injured ankle.

"I see you didn't leave his nose intact," Ilaria commented.

"It's not my fault his nose tried to escape," Thane responded as he tugged the arms of his captive to make sure he hadn't wriggled free. As the man was still trying to gasp in a breath around his broken ribs, Thane was certain he wasn't going anywhere.

"Now," Ilaria said, "tell me again why we Empati are trained on every known weapon the Empire has to offer, but then they insist on putting us in the field unarmed?"

"Apparently, they think we don't need them," Thane answered. "Though if I had my own gun, it would have saved me from a twisted ankle."

"Mine's unconscious at the pond; Rill's guarding him," she informed.

"Good, we need to…"

"Look out!" Ilaria screamed as she belatedly sensed a third assailant as he stepped from behind a tree and aimed a rifle directly at Thane. This time, Ilaria knew the blast was set to kill.

Not even his Denobian jumping abilities could get the injured Thane out of the way of a laser blast. He barely had enough time to register a shot had been fired before Ilaria knocked him from the side and out of the way of the blast.

When Ilaria saw the rifle aimed at Thane, she reacted so quickly, she didn't even realize she'd moved across the clearing until the two of them were laying on the ground with the blast arching over their heads. Both Empati were stunned by how quickly she covered the distance between them and, though he was just as shocked as Ilaria, Thane recovered his senses more quickly than she did.

Grabbing his discarded weapon, the Denobian fired on their new attacker hitting him squarely in the chest. The force of the blast sent the man backwards into the bushes. Severely wounded, he gurgled as his damaged body struggled for another breath.

Recovered from her own paralysis, Ilaria raced into the bushes before it was too late. Clapping her hands over his face, she quickly reading the dying man's mind before the moment was gone.

With his sore ankle, Thane found his legs too unreliable to carry him the distance to join Ilaria in her telepathic scan, so he stretched out with his empathic senses.

The man knew he was dying, in shock that his life was actually ending he didn't feel the cauterized hole in his chest. As his broken body attempted to continue functioning, Thane couldn't help the surreal feeling of his own smug satisfaction when he felt his mind fade. After that, there was nothing to feel; the man was dead.

Thane didn't even have time to process his assassin's sudden death as Rill hovered over him, the ship's wide carriage crushing the carefully sculpted vegetation as he landed on the narrow path.

"Get in!" Rill ordered. "And bring the body."

Now that it was over, alarms suddenly began blaring inside the Alesium complex. As Vanth's security neared, the two Keepers sprang into action and together lifted the dead attacker into Rill's hold. As soon as his crew and cargo were onboard, the ship took off, only closing his hold door when they were off the ground.

But even with every security system across the planet

now on alert, Thane and Ilaria were grateful for their AI friend's memory when Rill set down in Sobek's water gardens. With everything that had happened, the Psychs had forgotten their wooden friend, but Rill hadn't. Anak was afraid when the ship landed just meters away from him, but quickly folded himself into the cramped interior when he saw the pilots were two of the only humans who'd tried to help him. Right or wrong, he decided to trust them as Rill engaged his hyper-engines while still in the atmosphere. A massive sonic boom which shattered the glass in nearby windows announced their departure from Haven.

But the ship wasn't finished. Exiting hyperspace closer to the Haven sun than any sane pilot had ever emerged before, Rill quickly changed directions and jumped back into hyperspace before his passengers could call out their heliocentric terror. The ship skipped through hyperspace three more times before he finally came to a dead stop in a vast region of the empire void of anything valuable… especially people.

"That's the good thing about space," Rill told them. "When you need it, there's generally a lot of it."

With her heart still pounding over the latest attack, Ilaria realized this was the second time she'd been mind-locked with someone when they died. It was unnerving to say the least. In order to focus on anything else, she turned to the poor Tree squashed in Rill's cabin.

"*Anak, you were frightened when the ship landed until you saw that it was us,*" Ilaria said. "*Why was that?*"

"*He said he had gardens on another planet and would plant me there,*" the tree answered as he tried to shift his cramped legs. Though Rill was smaller than Daneb's ship had been and Anak had to tuck himself into a near fetal position to fit inside the cargo area, he was still more comfortable than he had been on his first interstellar journey without the constant threats of being jettisoned into space should he misbehave.

"*Who is this person who said this?*"

"*Speak out loud so the ship can hear you,*" Anak told them. "*It was the thin one; the one who rules the flora.*"

"Sobek?" Ilaria clarified verbally. "You spoke to him?"

The leaves on the vines rustled as Anak shook his head as he spoke.

Interpreting Anak's portion for Rill, Ilaria said, "The Rebe wouldn't join with that one. Sobek didn't think I could hear him when you weren't there, but he came to watch me several times and once said he couldn't wait until I was strong enough to be moved."

"And you're sure this was Sobek?" Thane asked incredulous.

"It was the thin male of our three masters," Ilaria said. "The last time he came was shortly before we did when he said it was nearly time. Anak says that was why he hid, because he didn't want to leave without us. When we were joined in the mind-speak, we said we'd take him home. He believed us and so he waited."

"The mind can't lie," Thane said, reiterating the one telepathic truth he trusted. Though he didn't dwell on it, the empath had realized this truth did come with qualifiers. While a telepath couldn't lie, truth could be an ambiguous thing and what a person believed could weigh more than actual facts.

"Where are we?" Ilaria asked. She couldn't see even tiny pinpricks of stars in the black void outside the ship.

"Where no one can find us," the ship answered, "and I left a trail that no one could follow. Now, what happened?"

"Where would you like me to start?" Thane demanded as his numbing shock thawed only to spill out at his friends in anger.

"Start from when you questioned Vanth about the serum," Rill said logically. "But before you do, see if you can get around Anak and place your dead attacker onto my bio-bed so I can scan him."

As they worked to comply with the ship's unusual demands, Thane wondered if the shrewd AI was merely giving them a task to keep them focused on the here and now. The empath was grateful for the distraction because he had more on his mind than the recent ambush.

"What did you read from your mind-scan?" Thane asked Ilaria as she lifted the lifeless body onto the medical bed. Too short to be much help, the Denobian suddenly felt himself become much lighter than usual as Rill cut the cabin gravity in half so she could lift the dead man more easily on her own.

"It was strange," Ilaria admitted as she secured the body to the scanning bed. "He was there and then he was gone; this man just... faded."

"Sorry to be so blunt, but right now I don't care how he died. What did he say?"

"Only two words: he said 'our revolution'. He meant psychics, I'm sure of it. That his people are planning some kind of a revolution."

"I'm not surprised," Thane admitted. "There are many of us out there unhappy with our forced role in the empire."

"I'm not entirely sure that's what he meant," Ilaria said, turning her troubled eyes to her mentor. "He only said 'our revolution', but I saw visions as his mind died. Did you get any impressions from him?"

"I'm only an empath," Thane said, watching Ilaria closely as she continued to wrestle her thoughts into words. She was calm, but the experience had her. Thane could understand that; it had frightened him, too. Holding out his hand, he silently asked his ward to share the images with him.

Accepting his invitation, Ilaria grasped Thane's hand and mentally sent him the visions she had received from the dead man. As their minds connected, Thane learned his name was Goram Dram, but the rest of what she shared left the older Keeper even more confused. The experience had definitely unsettled her.

Through Ilaria's mind, Thane sensed Dram had been not only trained in warfare, but also in resisting psychic interrogation. Fully aware that he was dying, he had tried blocking the telepathic invasion by imagining a vast ocean.

The image had been a mistake. Ilaria had scanned the minds of too many people and knew how to combat defensive visions by imagining images of her own. Ships could ride the surface of the waves, the sun could evaporate the waters into a misty vapor, fish could breathe water... fish.

Dram had liked the image of the fish and his fading mind couldn't fight an image he himself had helped conjure. Ilaria mentally built up the imagery by thinking of individual fish rising and falling with the tides. When that brought her nothing, she pictured schools of them balling together to protect themselves from predators... and she was rewarded with an emotional spike. In his mind, she saw a single fish swimming towards the thousands; the vision shifted to small fish being eaten by larger fish being eaten by even larger fish. No matter how the vision shifted, Dram was the one fish swimming against the masses.

Those images were at the core of his thoughts. His people were the fish because they were the few who swam against the tides of many; they were the larger fish hunting the smaller bait.

"It's a telepathic technique used to resist mental probing," Ilaria explained when she'd finished sharing her experience with her mentor. "In order to hide the truth, reality is wrapped in illusion."

"So, these fish are real, just not to be taken literally," Thane wasn't sure he fully understood her concept that Dram had hidden the truth within obscure images that turned reality into riddles.

"Essentially," Ilaria said. "Dram gave us two images: a few fish swimming in the opposite direction of many others and larger fish preying on smaller ones. Actually, three images if we also account for the ocean. Did you get the impression that he felt superior; smug as if he knew he was better than us?"

"I did. Did you get any sense of why they attacked us on Haven?"

Shaking her head that she hadn't. "It doesn't make sense. If these fish of his are like us, why do they want to kill us? We're the same."

"Not quite," Thane said. "You were unique in that you were born with your abilities, but you had latent telepathic talents you discovered later. You've also embraced your abilities;

maybe Dram went the other way. Maybe he also discovered latent powers and hated us for them.”

"Maybe,” Ilaria said slowly, remembering that as a psychic, Dram's only options would be service or incarceration. Hardly the best choice if he'd been already living a life as a Citizen. "But since he was psychic, why was he after us? We're all on the same side.”

"As you and I are both Empati, technically we're not. We belong to the empire and in Dram's eyes, we are peeks working with the enemy.”

"With that in mind, I have a couple of theories,” said Rill, breaking into their conversation. "They've clearly been tracking you for some time and found an opportunity on Haven where you were caught off guard in a location without a Unit for back up.”

Thane agreed, "I think at least for the moment, we need to assume these Fish are the ones killing the psychics we found on the Wald. Perhaps they thought they found an opportunity to add us to the collection, but why try to stun us? Why not kill us out right?”

"Because they need you alive,” Rill answered. "Or at least they need Ilaria. Tell me what you discovered about the Serum from Vanth?”

"Only that it's an experimental youth drug,” Thane answered. "Oh!”

"Exactly,” the ship confirmed as Thane caught up with the AI's line of thought. "Excluding you, Ilaria, since you're not an In-Valid, all the bodies discovered on the Wald were Psych prisoners from Maelstrom. No one missed them when they went missing and it was initially covered up when the first body was found. Obviously, I haven't been able to examine all one hundred and eighty-six corpses, but the ones I was able to scan have three things in common: all were psychics incarcerated in Maelstrom, they had the same surgical wound in the back of their heads and they had this experimental youth drug in their systems.”

"Surgical?” Ilaria asked. "You mean they weren't shot?”

"Correct. With only one body to examine fully, I can still only speculate, but it did appear that all the ones I could scan have the same wound, it is a reasonable assumption. Any competent doctor, or forensic inspector, wouldn't have been able to miss the distinction between a shooting victim and laser surgery scoring."

"Which is why Zin Tram's body was incinerated before an autopsy could be completed. Everyone on the Wald was murdered, just not in the way we initially thought. Do you have a theory as to why?"

"I have several," Rill said. "The one that fits with all of the evidence is that these fish, or most likely the ones behind them, are using the Maelstrom psychics and Vanth's youth serum to create an augmented serum that can give normal humans advanced mental abilities."

At his crew's incredulous injections of such a notion, Rill explained his reasoning. They had to admit the AI's logic did align with the facts. In examining the second Wald body now stored in his hold, Rill not only discovered traces of the Alesium serum in his system, but also that brain cells had been removed via the surgically made head wound—specifically, cells which enable psychic abilities. By injecting the Psychs from Maelstrom with the youth serum, the fish were able to harvest psionic cells at the peak of their usefulness. Examining the soldier's body, a man able to block two of the strongest Psychs in the Empati, Rill found evidence of the serum. When Ilaria asked how the ship had found it, he responded that he had been looking for it.

"Only this serum was enhanced with psychic cells. This augmented serum not only reverted the users to their physical peak, it changed their psionic brain chemistry and gave them empathic or even telepathic abilities."

"They're creating an army!" Thane exclaimed. "A psionic army who can read us and block our own psychics from reading them. They were the ones who attacked the *Celest*. Jax said it was as if they were anticipating their every move. It wasn't until you broke through their ranks that they backed off."

"Because I have no mind to read," the ship confirmed.

"Could these fish also be behind the assassination attempt on Sarkin?" Thane wanted to know.

"As you both have been unable to detect these fish psychically except for the strongest of emotions such as a kill shot, I think it is most likely both attacks were orchestrated by the same group of people."

"Then we have to warn the emperor," Ilaria said.

"We'll do nothing of the kind," Thane countered flatly.

"Thane is correct if only in that would make the situation worse," Rill said. "It's you and your unique abilities they have been targeting, Ilaria. From the attack on the *Celest,* this has always been about Sobek trying to harvest your powers for his augmented serum. Unlike the prisoners on Maelstrom, your disappearance would have been noted and when he couldn't get Sarkin to transfer you to him, Sobek orchestrated the attack in order to specifically eliminate the emperor. Laran would have ascended to the throne as empress, but since she has little interest in psychics, Sobek's path to you would have been clear.

"When the ships were unable to break through the shielding in time to expel Sarkin into space, an augmented assassin already onboard tried again. This attempt, of course, failed spectacularly when you nearly died stepping in front of the blast. While he failed in acquiring you, he was successful in injecting you with his augmented serum."

Thane finished, "And when we went to Alesium rather than the Hospital, he sent his agents to take her by force."

Ilaria wasn't convinced. "If they wanted to capture me, why try to kill us?"

"They were only trying to kill me," Thane said quietly.

"Two soldiers with augmented abilities were no match for two fully trained Empati Keepers, one of them being an offworld Denobian. When you both overpowered their first two agents, a third attempted to eliminate Thane in order to capture you alone. They certainly didn't expect your own augmentation to manifest into teleportation."

"Wait," Ilaria said, stunned all over again, "what did you say? I didn't teleport!"

"You did," Thane said quietly. "I couldn't believe how quickly you cleared the distance between us, but Rill's right. You were there on the other side of the glen, then suddenly you were pushing me out of the way. It's the only explanation. Rill, you've seemed to have known about this for some time. You were the one who sent us to Haven to question Vanth."

"I only became certain of my theory when I medically scanned Ilaria," the ship admitted, "and, again, the facts align with the theory. Ilaria, you are without a doubt the most powerful Psych ever born in the empire, but your abilities aren't natural."

At her friends' suggestion that she'd developed new abilities, Ilaria now only had the power to shake her head in disbelief. It just wasn't possible!

Continuing his assessment, Rill said, "I first suspected psychic augmentation when you were born with empathic powers. As prodigies are occasionally born, I didn't give your abilities much consideration until Thane, as your surrogate father, developed a telepathic bond with you. Others may have been shocked when you became telepathic later, but I was expecting it.

"But it wasn't until I first learned of the Alesium serum that I began my research. It took several years to discover the truth, but in one of his experiments, Sobek used the youth serum on your mother. I'm sorry to say Jyn didn't survive your birth, but it was because of the serum she was given while pregnant with you that you were born empathic and later telepathic."

Through his reasoning, Rill explained that Ilaria had been augmented, not once, but twice. "The first was in vitro through the serum given to Jyn; the second was on the *Celest* when Sobek saved your life from a phaser blast that should have killed you. I've compared the serum Sobek gave you to that from both the Wald victim and your Haven attacker. I now know that there is the original youth serum, the one that Vanth has been developing, as well as an augmented version developed from psionic cells."

Thane was sorry for Ilaria. Still reeling from the ordeal on Haven, this new information about serum augmentation was overwhelming. Having been used for years by Sarkin, she now had to come to terms that her entire existence was one of Sobek's science experiments.

"I understand this serum is what saved her on the bridge," Thane said. "Is it also how she's developed a third and completely unrecorded ability?"

"Most likely," Rill said.

Thane wasn't sure he wanted to know what another possibility could be, but he couldn't help himself from rambling his theories to the others. "As we know, when Ilaria's mother was given the serum, it altered Ilaria's fetal development. What happens to the mother can have a profound effect on the child. The reverse can also happen; for example, a mother can develop, say a nut allergy while she is carrying if the infant is allergic."

Before Thane could finish his thought, a sudden explosion sent Ilaria flying out of her seat, her temple hitting the ceiling panels before she crashed back down to the deck while Anak braced himself against the walls of the hold. Before Ilaria could pick herself back up, Rill evaded the next blast which caused her to bruise her side as the force knocked her into the wall of the cockpit.

"Rill!" she cried, using his name to demand an explanation.

"A ship has just exited hyperspace and has fired on us," Rill said calmly as another shot nearly missed him.

"How did they find us?" Thane demanded, only to be ignored by the AI computer as the ship banked sharply, his phasers firing as the ship came back into view.

Ilaria rubbed her temple as Thane reached to help her back into her seat while mentally admonishing her to put her seat belt on. It had only been then when she realized the Denobian hadn't been the one managing the defense.

"How can you fire without us?" Ilaria demanded of the ship. She had never known a computer to be able to take the initiative against organics, but then she remembered Rill had launched without even a pilot during the battle around the *Celest.*

"My programming allows me to do what I need to in order to protect the life of my crew," the ship responded, sounding satisfied when the other ship's shields rippled at the damage. "Our own shields at fifty-percent; another direct hit to our starboard side will disable us."

"Can you still make the jump to hyperspace?" Thane asked Rill. "If he doubles back, he could come at us again from any direction. I don't think we should be here when he does."

They all knew it was still possible their engine signature could be tracked through hyperspace, but their opponent would have to act quickly if he had any chance of finding it.

"Yes, I can still enter hyperspace" Rill answered. "There is minor damage to my undercarriage, but hull integrity is still intact."

"Then go!" Ilaria cried, feeling the surge of speed as the accelerating Rill entered lightspeed.

"Any idea who that was?" Ilaria asked once they were inside the wormhole.

"Or how we were tracked?" Thane added.

"No," answered Rill, "but my guess would be your Fish. Who knew you were taking Anak back to the Wald?"

Ilaria didn't have to think about it. "Everyone at the meeting after Daneb first brought him in, but at this very moment, no one."

"Sobek," Thane accused. "Anak said he was waiting for him to be ready for transport."

"Why would Sobek send ships after this one tree when he could go to the Wald and have his pick? No offense meant to you, Anak," Ilaria added, looking back to the youngster who returned her gaze with wide eyes. From his expression, Ilaria decided he had been unharmed by the adventure, but would rather like to leave space travel in his past.

"He wasn't after Anak, but you," Rill stated. "Three times you have been attacked: on the *Celest,* on Haven and here in space."

Shaking her head, Ilaria disagreed. "You forget that on the *Celest*, Sarkin was the target. I was only injured when I protected him."

"That is the way the events played out," Rill said in his logical, most matter-of-fact way, "but Thane and I have been discussing another possibility. The attackers knew your training to protect the emperor or his heirs. An aim at Sarkin would hide their true intentions. If you were their target, it was successful as they did in fact hit you. Kill shots are masterfully hard to hide telepathically, so by aiming at the emperor, they could hide who they actually wanted to hit."

"That doesn't add up. Why try to kill me on the *Celest* only to stun me on Haven? And what about just now when they hit us in space? We were preparing for a hyper-jump and normally wouldn't have had raised shields."

Rill seemed unshaken from his reasoning, "A minor injury intended to disable and not destroy, which holds to our theory that you were the target. How is your chest, by the way?"

Ilaria was so amused that the AI would call his own phaser scalding an "injury" she didn't register his personal question for a moment.

"Oh, it's just fine," she said rubbing the score mark. "It's all but healed. It barely hurts and, to be honest, I'd almost forgotten about it."

"Isn't that fast for an organic to recover from a phaser blast?"

"I suppose so, but it's the first time I'd ever been shot. Sobek gave me something for the pain so I didn't think about it."

Rill didn't comment further, but he didn't have to as she saw where his argument was heading. If Sarkin had been killed, Sobek would have had unaccountable access to anyone with psionic powers as Laran didn't want anything to do with peeks. But since events played out differently, her near death was in his favor as it gave him a legitimate opportunity to inject Ilaria with his augmented serum. No wonder Sobek had been so frantic when Sarkin ordered her back to the Wald; with her out of his reach once again, Sobek hadn't been able to harvest his prize.

The entire notion made her feel sick again. Grasping hold of anything for a distraction, she voiced her observation of obvious facts. "Rill, you fired on organics without a pilot."

Unperturbed, the ship answered, "Like I said, I can protect my crew. And I didn't want you doing it because there is blood on your hands."

"I'm a trained Empati," Ilaria scoffed. "Sometimes it's part of my job to fight, even to kill if necessary. You're not getting on Thane's case for shooting that guy on your bio-bed. And it's not murder to defend yourself."

"Precisely," Rill said, "but I meant there is literally blood on your hands. Your head is bleeding from where you hit the ceiling. Stop touching things! You're getting it all over my console."

Naturally, now that he mentioned it, Ilaria's head began to dully throb. She gingerly touched the growing bump on her head and felt the sticky liquid matting her hair. It wasn't serious, but she found a piece of cloth to stem the flow of blood.

"Uh, oh," Rill said suddenly.

"What do you mean 'uh, oh'?" Ilaria asked. It was never good when a human said it, so she didn't want to imagine what could be wrong when an AI said it.

"Apparently, the damage is more extensive than I anticipated," Rill explained as his hull shuddered against the velocity of the wormhole. "Fortunately, we are nearing our exit point at the Wald; we should still be safe to land."

Ilaria liked the sound of "should" even less than "uh, oh" especially when ship's casing began a terrifying rattle when they broke free of the vortex. As Rill decelerated from lightspeed, the green world quickly grew from a small dot in their view port to a giant globe.

"Reverting all power to the forward shields," Rill informed them when the outer hull began to glow from the friction as they entered the atmosphere. The internal lights dimmed as the ship pulled every ounce of reserve energy available in order to keep his passengers from incineration during their reentry onto the Wald.

"I've lost directional control," Rill warned them. "Hold on to something; we're landing hard."

Looking back as she buckled herself into her seat, Ilaria saw Anak splay his limbs out in order to brace himself. As best as he could, Rill aimed for a large clearing devoid of trees, sentient or otherwise. The ship skidded to a halt, the hot outer hull melting a glassy swath across a once lush meadow.

· CHAPTER 14 ·

Though shaken from the rough landing, the three were unharmed. Looking at each other in fright, Ilaria and Thane began laughing as their agitated nerves relaxed now that the terror was over.

"*And you do this for a living?*" the tree asked them.

"Yes, but we don't usually crash," Ilaria chuckled. "Well done, Rill! Any landing we can walk away from is a good one."

Ilaria and Thane looked at each other in concern when the ship didn't respond. Only a few lights were blinking on his usually bright console, but the central orb that housed the AI's CPU remained dark.

"Rill?" Ilaria asked again, futilely pushing buttons trying to wake the ship up. Closing her eyes, she sighed. Even one of his acerbic I-told-you-so comments would have been welcome to the battered young woman, but the computer remained silent.

"Thank you, Rill," Ilaria whispered sadly before unbuckling herself from her seat.

"Don't worry about him," Thane said stepping over Anak's long legs to manually open the hatch. "He used all his reserve power in order to land us. He'll be fine once he recharges."

Giving the darkened panel another concerned look, Ilaria sighed again as she stepped out of the wrecked ship. She knew Rill was only an AI, but he had been her friend since she had first learned to pilot a shuttle. The advanced system always seemed to surprise her with both logic and advice and she often spoke to Rill about both her personal anxieties and problems with work. His advice had always been logical, but so humanly reasonable she wondered where it came from. It seemed to her the ship possessed the wisdom of the aged, full of the experience of someone who could only have lived it. Ilaria considered him a true friend and occasionally imagined she could sense an actual consciousness under all his circuitry.

Sighing his own relief at his release from the cramped quarters, Anak pushed himself out of the ship feet first and stood to his full height. Raising his arms to the green sky, the youngster gave a shout in his joy at being home.

"*Is Rill dead?*" Anak asked soberly.

"Offline, which is like sleep for someone like Rill," Ilaria said.

"Can you wake him up?"

"I'm not sure; not right now," Ilaria said shaking her head. *And certainly not here,* she admitted to herself as she looked around. It would be impossible to repair him on this desolate world. The only technology that could possibly achieve it was at the Pit where Daneb and his crew mined the Gas and thanks to their crash, she had no idea where that was.

"I'm sorry, Anak. I know this wasn't the homecoming you were expecting."

"*I am home,*" the tree answered happily. "*This is what I was expecting.*"

Shaking her head at his literalness, Ilaria smiled, "But it isn't where your parents are. I promised to get you back to your people."

Again, he seemed baffled by her answer. "*My people are everywhere; the Edu are all around us and the message is being sent that we are here. But I can get us back to my Mother and Father if that is what concerns you. The greater and lesser moons are still in conjunction and have only waxed nearly a half cycle since we first met.*"

"Which means?"

"*We must walk three day's in that direction,*" he answered while pointing to the northwest.

Ilaria was a bit daunted by how far they needed to go, but took solace in the fact that she had actually thought they had crashed much farther away from the Graveyard. It could have been much worse; they could have been several weeks from where they needed to be or even on another continent. Stepping back into Rill's darkened interior, she packed a shoulder bag full of supplies and emergency food rations for both herself and Thane.

Watching the young tree stretch himself back to his full height, Ilaria realized she didn't actually know if Anak needed food or if he absorbed his nutrients from the ground. For all she knew, he might even be able to photosynthesize everything he needed directly from the sun. Regardless, she and Thane would need sustenance, and soon, too, as it had been hours since either of them had eaten anything. Of course, if her nausea didn't abate, hungry or not, she wasn't going to hold anything down.

A loud rumble that sounded like a boulder crashing down a cliff face caused Anak to jump away from Rill, fearful that something even more catastrophic was about to happen to the damaged ship; however, Ilaria looked up to the sky as she recognized the reverberations of a sonic boom.

"Who the hell is this guy?" Ilaria demanded as she gestured to the landing ship.

"How should I know?" Thane retorted as he shielded his eyes against the glare of the sun. "One of our fish, probably. A single pilot," Thane said slowly, his eyes unfocused as he concentrated on reading the emotions emanating from the ship as it circled to land, "and... yeah, he's here to kill us... you," the empath amended, looking at his ward. "He's here to kill specifically you. I guess the fish have moved on from catch and release."

"Outstanding," Ilaria muttered darkly. Quickly sealing Rill's hull door shut, she bolted to the edge of the clearing, stopping only to tell Anak to stop watching the descending shuttle and follow her. Released from his own empathic paralysis, Thane ran after them, clearing the meadow in a couple of long, low-gravity Denobian leaps.

Once hidden in the thickets, they watched as the craft finally touched down and a human male exited. Drawing a long weapon from his hip holster, he slowly circled Rill, never once glancing in their direction.

"Good," Thane sent, *"he didn't see us, but I'm sure he'll pick up our trail."*

"Any idea on who he is and what I did to piss him off?" Ilaria asked. *"Since we seem to be able to sense him, he's neither Psych nor augment and even if Sarkin knows we're on the run, he couldn't have found us this soon."*

"You're right," agreed Thane. *"And I seriously doubt that even Sobek would go to all this trouble to recapture a single tree for his garden. But…"*

"But?"

"Anak is gone. Damn! We were so clever except for this. Only we would have taken Anak from the gardens and there's only one planet in the empire where we would have taken him."

Ilaria groaned, *"So much for clever, but in our defense, it's not like we planned to do any of this. What?"* she asked when Thane suddenly seemed to be more interested in something just above her head. It had better not be a bug because she suspected that on a jungle planet, bugs would be a nasty combination of both mean and large.

"Nothing," Thane sent in such a way that Ilaria knew it wasn't.

"It's a big-ass bug, isn't it?"

"It's not a bug."

"I don't believe you," Ilaria said, though she resisted the temptation to look. When it came to bugs, ignorance was better

than the confirmation of knowledge. "*If a bug jumps on me, I'm blaming you!*"

"*It's not a bug,*" Thane said again. "*I'm so glad you didn't have to meet the V'reem.*"

"*That's different. Alien ambassadors aren't creepy-crawlies.*" It actually wasn't insects that concerned her, but one more surprise after everything else she'd endured over the past several days. Her senses were overwhelmed and it seemed she hadn't had time to recover from one catastrophe before the next one began. With a sigh, she forced herself to focus. "*So, what's our move, master planner? Fight or flight?*"

By now the pilot had realized their ship was empty and was scanning the ground for evidence of where they went. Having been more concerned with getting under cover than erasing their tracks, the bent grass made by human-sized boots would be a dead giveaway to their direction.

"*Flight now; fight later,*" Thane answered, signaling Anak they should continue farther into the forest and away from the hunting human.

Reflexively, Ilaria rubbed her chest. Though her wound had healed, it wasn't an experience she wanted to repeat and it wasn't a great comfort for her to know that the man probably wasn't here to kill her outright. The fish wanted to harvest her first; however, she'd already seen what the end results would likely be if he captured her and she had no intention of ending up in the Graveyard with her brains scooped out. If it came down to that, she'd make sure there was nothing left of her for them to pick through.

Nodding his compliance at Thane's order, Anak lead the Empati deeper into the woods, the thick trees closing in behind them as they walked. For such a tall, gangly creature, the young Akilli could move surprisingly fast on his native world. With his heavy wooden frame supported by his wide root-like feet, Ilaria found herself jogging several times to just keep up. Whenever Thane lagged behind, he closed the distance with one of his moon-walking leaps that Ilaria envied. At one point, Anak paused as if listening and then informed Ilaria the stranger was indeed following them. The Psychs had expected no less.

"This human is the one who attacked us in space?" Anak wanted to know. *"If he is here for me, why is he tracking you?"*

"Because we are different from other humans and my people don't like others who are different." Anak was clearly confused by her explanation, so Ilaria continued. *"Thane can feel what others are feeling and I am able to read their thoughts when I touch them. Not many humans can do what we do and those who can't believe us to be a threat."*

"And are you?"

"Sometimes," she admitted.

"So, this man who now follows us is angry because you read his mind," the tree said sagely before he disengaged their connection and continued leading her deeper into the forest.

It wasn't a question and the truth of Anak's words stung Ilaria more than she wanted to admit. She had no idea who the man was or why he was after her specifically, but deep down, she always suspected there would be repercussions to her life as a courtesan. Sarkin had ordered her sleep with many men for their secrets, some of whom were powerful enough to send a tracker to make sure her threat to them had been eliminated. None of the ships or soldiers they had encountered had the markings from one of the Senate Houses, but there was every indication they could be from a private security fleet. Even the one man they had in custody had been eliminated before he could tell them anything useful which left the possibility open he wasn't a fish, but one of Ilaria's former lovers out for revenge.

As they walked, the terrain changed from the dryer woodlands into swampy wetlands and Ilaria found it challenging to keep up with her indigenous companion. Mud sucked greedily at her boots and the thick undergrowth that Anak and Thane could easily jump over blocked her own path. She was also assailed with clouds of little bugs who apparently thought her alien blood tasted delicious while they seemed to eschew the Denobian. Ilaria might have been drained dry by the little winged vampires had Anak not come to her rescue.

"Go away!" he commanded them, gently shooing the

tiny pests with his branches, his wooden joints groaning with the effort.

To her amazed relief, the swarms obeyed the young Tree and from then on, Ilaria was midge-free, though she noticed the thick swarms continued to hover several feet away as if they were waiting for the chance to attack again. She wondered how long Anak's command over the little insects would last if he ever decided to leave her to the mercy of the Wald.

"Thank you," she told him as she inspected a couple of bites on her hands. "Vicious little things."

"All life must eat to live," Anak told her sagely.

"Yes, but I don't particularly enjoy being the one eaten," Ilaria grumbled. She stopped when she noticed Anak watching her. Unable to read his wooden features, she thought she somehow might have offended him, so she added with a rueful smile, "But then I guess no one does."

The longer Anak studied Ilaria, the more uncomfortable she became. The emotions of the Akilli were rigid like the ancient and stoic forests stoic surrounding them. Although there were exceptions, with most humans there was always a slight buzz or pressure that told her if they were happy or annoyed. Anak, she found, was like a blank wall forcing Ilaria to guess his motives and she hated guessing. Having relied on her senses all her life, she was rubbish at interpreting voice inflection and body language. As Anak had very little of either, Ilaria was at a loss.

Anak finally said, "I find your species difficult to read; do you require rest?"

Nearly laughing at the similarity in their situation, Ilaria dropped her pack to the ground when Thane also looked relieved at the thought of a break. They were both exhausted. Mud and sweat clung to them like burrs and Ilaria's midge bites had begun to itch.

"I'm afraid I do," she told the child when Thane nodded his agreement.

"Not here," Anak said, picking her pack up. "That grouping of plants behind you is carnivorous to mammalian creatures and would devour you before morning. They are not of *the Rebe and I would not be able to stop them."*

"*Of the Rebe? Oh, right, the sentient life. Is that how you got the bugs to leave me alone? You can command them?*" Ilaria asked as she followed Anak into a clearing. She wondered if it was one of the Akilli deserts she had learned about on her previous visit to the Wald. The clearing was on a wide, low rising knoll. Knee-high grass danced in the gentle wind like waves softly caressing the surface of an amber pond. The setting sun backlit a single tree, its leaves shining an iridescent blue.

"*Only the Rebe can command the Edu,*" Anak said after giving her another one of his long stares. Now that he was back on his homeworld and among familiar surroundings, he seemed surer of himself. Ilaria got the distinct impression that with the return of his confidence, he was finding his association with his human charges more tedious as time went on. She couldn't blame him. She wondered privately that if Rill hadn't crashed and the other ship landed, Anak might have insisted the psychics return home immediately. Of course, if they hadn't crashed, they would have landed at the Graveyard and their mission would already be over without any reason to stay.

"*Does the Rebe command you?*" Ilaria asked, wishing he would stop staring at her. She didn't tell the tree it was making her uncomfortable as Thane had also been staring. The tree could just be following the cues of the humans and thought he was being polite.

"*The Rebe commands the Edu,*" he said again.

It wasn't an answer, but Ilaria reasoned it could be because he didn't quite understand her question. Or maybe it explained it perfectly if one was a tree. Ilaria was the alien here and she was at a disadvantage when it came to the order of life on this planet. If it wasn't for Anak, she and Thane would have tucked up and slept at the foot of a carnivorous plant and been fertilizer by morning.

Thinking of nearly being food reminded her of how hungry she was. Sitting down, she took an energy stick from her bag and began to nibble it. The food wasn't appetizing in either looks or taste, but it did provide enough sustenance to keep malnutrition and starvation at bay.

Anak watched her, so fascinated by her eating habits that she became self-conscious over the simple acts of chewing and swallowing.

"Is that good?" the tree sounded skeptical that it could be.

"Good for you, yes, but it tastes like shit," Thane answered instead, sniffing at his own food.

"Shit?"

"Excrement," Ilaria explained, wondering if that made it any clearer for the tree. His nod and look of distaste told her he did understand the concept of poop which made her realize he thought that was what they were actually eating. *"Thane only meant to describe that it tastes bad, not what it is actually made from."*

"Oh. What is it made from?"

Ilaria hesitated before answering, *"Um, I don't know. Maybe it is shit."*

Suddenly, Ilaria was no longer hungry and put the uneaten portion back in her pack while wishing the tree hadn't also regained his youthful curiosity for his offworld companions. They still had a long journey ahead of them and she knew her nasty rations would become appetizing again soon enough.

Now what? Ilaria asked herself when Anak abruptly turned and disappeared into the forest edge. He hadn't indicated either of them should go with him, but he suddenly returned before they could decide whether or not they should follow him. To their delight, Anak handed them some ugly, fist-sized fruit.

"It is the fala," the tree explained. *"Many creatures live off of this because this particular food grows flowers and fruit in every season. You may find it more appetizing than... shit."*

Laughing, Ilaria said, *"I just may. Thank you."*

Her offworld survival training had been extensive enough that, despite her hunger, Ilaria wasn't foolish enough to bite into the knobby gourd without scanning it first. A food that was life to a Walden creature could very well be death to a human. To her relief, the gnarled fruit registered safe, so she the split the thick skin and relished the sweet, juicy meat.

Licking the last of the juices from her fingers, Ilaria said, *"I can't sense our tracker; can you, Anak?"*

Closing his eyes, Anak began seemed to be listening. To what, Ilaria wasn't sure, but she assumed it was to the forest around them. At the Graveyard, they had been surrounded by the Akilli and she was certain the plants had been speaking even though she hadn't been able to detect a language.

"He is still following," Anak told them.

Thane nodded, saying he couldn't sense him empathically, either so they should have time to get some rest.

Grateful that they wouldn't have to press on into the woods just yet, Ilaria sat down to relax. Maybe her companions could walk for three days without a break, but she would eventually have to sleep. That thought made her wonder if Anak's timescale for their journey meant walking both day and night. Outstanding; at her pace they could be a week or more from the Graveyard.

"Anak, who are the Rebe? When we first met, you said that you were their voice."

"They are the oldest among us and it is from them that all life comes. The Akilli learned to understand your words so we were appointed their Voice."

"So, they are your masters; your rulers?"

"The Rebe do not master, but protect the balance of the Edu. We all serve that purpose using the abilities we are born with."

"I understand. It is the same with my job to find out information using my own abilities."

"You do not understand. The Edu are not slaves of the Rebe, but servants."

"We're not slaves," Ilaria said, *"We can come and go as we wish."*

Thane didn't join in the banter, but sat slowly chewing his protein rations as he watched Ilaria, lost in thought. There were a number of issues he would have debated with the young woman, such as with all of the benefits they did receive as Empati, they were not Citizens in the eyes of the empire. Point in fact, those who showed enough mental prowess to be initiated with psychic branch of Peace-Keepers lost any hope of becoming a Citizen. The terms "prisoner" or "slave" were never used, but should any one of them disobey an order or not have a verifiable reason to account for their actions, their society would quickly show them how low their status in the empire was. For the most part, the Empati lived a good life with many the benefits of the elite, but only as long as they obeyed. The Tree was right. For psychics such as them, it was slavery with the empire or slavery doing hard labor in Maelstrom.

"What is it, Thane?" Ilaria finally asked. *"You've been staring at me all evening. I swear, if I've got a bug on me…"*

"There's no bug," Thane said. Ilaria could handle almost anything, including bugs, but that didn't mean she liked them. Especially the big, creepy, hairy ones. *"I wanted to know how you're feeling?"*

His question caught her off guard. With a shrug, she answered, *"Good, I guess. Any particular reason you're asking?"*

"Just wondering," Thane said. *"How's your head?"*

"Oh, it was just a bump," Ilaria said rubbing her temple. *"Doesn't even hurt anymore. I forgot that I even hit it."*

"That's good. And the nausea?"

Ilaria groaned, *"It comes and goes."*

Giving Anak a glance to see if he was in hearing range, Ilaria lowered her voice to a whisper, "To be honest, that fala fruit is starting to turn my stomach. That's the problem with scanners; they can tell if a food is safe, but not if it will agree with you. That's all I need: to be tracked on an alien world with an irritable bowel from foreign food."

"I don't think it was the fala," Thane said. He was about to continue when he was interrupted by Anak.

"The man is no longer resting," the Tree said urgently. *"He has picked up our trail once more and is heading this way."*

"That's a relief," said Thane with an exaggerated sigh. *"For a moment there, I thought we had covered our tracks too*

well and he had lost us."

At both Anak's and Ilaria's look of astonishment, Thane grinned, *"I told you I have a plan. I always have a plan."*

· CHAPTER 15 ·

Thane wouldn't expand further on what his plan involved, but it apparently included hiking even farther through the ever-increasingly swampy jungle for several more hours until the Denobian finally called another rest. They were on another hill with another single blue-leafed tree. The scene was so much like their former camp, for a moment Ilaria wondered if they had gone in a circle until she realized this tree was much larger than the last one, its trunk more gnarled and twisted with nearly twice as many of the blue leaves in its swaying branches.

Gratefully, Ilaria dropped to the ground and propped her head on her pack while Thane scouted around the area asking Anak questions. Exhausted, she so wanted to sleep, but she was so wound up she couldn't drop off. Usually, she was full of energy and was becoming increasingly concerned about her bouts of lethargy and nausea. To add another log onto her shit-pile of worry, the pain in her stomach hadn't abated like a normal stomachache should, but was growing steadily worse. Even though the scanners would have detected any harmful bacteria or parasites on the fala fruit, once the thought her food had been contaminated had entered her mind, she couldn't get the idea out. Instead of eating dinner, she chewed on those misgivings until the sky darkened and her exhaustion finally forced her eyes closed.

Ilaria woke when her head thumped onto the ground, jarring her from uneasy dreams. The pack was still under her, so she tried to fluff it back up, irritably wondering what had shifted enough to cause her to wake up. Upon examining the bag, she gave an exclamation of dismay when she found the bag was partially empty and a hole torn through the side.

"No, no, no!" she cried. Dumping the remains of her supplies on the ground, she discovered almost half of her food supply was gone.

"*I thought you didn't like eating it,*" Anak said after she made the others aware of her dilemma.

"*I like starving even less,*" Ilaria growled as she examined her pack more closely. There was no evidence of the creatures who had accomplished the theft, but they must have been smaller than her closed fist. Whatever they were, they had gnawed right through the tough fabric and pulled her rations right out from under her. She would have been impressed with the little bastards if she hadn't been so angry.

"*Don't worry about it,*" Thane said sleepily. "*I doubt we'll be here long enough to starve. Besides, I'm sure Anak knows where there are plenty more fala fruits.*"

"*No thanks,*" said Ilaria, grimacing in disgust while putting her hand to her belly. Even the thought of the fruit made her queasy. Forcing herself to calm down, Ilaria told herself that panic wouldn't help anything. The worst-case scenario was that, while she might get very hungry, it wouldn't be a fatal fast. Thane was right; she wouldn't starve even if she did have to choke down a couple more falas. This was just another one of life's unpleasant kicks to the gut she would have to deal with. Besides that, there had to be other food here that met the criteria of both palatable and safe.

Fully awake now, Ilaria took a moment to do another inventory on her pack. The good news was the only thing missing was the portions of her food rations. The rest of her survival gear was still intact including her compass, water filtration and back up iodine tablets. She might get hungry, but clean drinking water wouldn't be a problem. The tablets were a last resort and she fervently hoped they wouldn't become necessary as she loathed the way the iodine made water taste, but they would be better than dying of thirst if something tragic happened to her filter. With the way her luck was running, that was probably next.

At that thought, Ilaria realized how moody she had been getting and sternly told herself adjust her attitude. She wasn't even sure where it was coming from because for as long as she could remember, she had yearned for an adventure on an alien planet. Now that she had one, she'd better enjoy it for there was no telling when she might get another. Well, maybe she would be having a better time if her bellyache went away. It felt like she had more gas than an herbivore at a cabbage buffet. Ilaria was sure her stomach was twice as big as it should be and she couldn't continue to blame the rich dinner at the gala for it. A single dinner wouldn't cause weight gain and that obscenely tight gown had ensured she hadn't eaten much of it.

After a few moments, Ilaria felt a little more grounded, so she looked over at her companions and felt even better because she was in very good company. Anak was a most unusual person as he continued to stand silently watching her, but he was, after all, a tree. He was in the same alert position from the night before when the two humans had fulfilled their requirement for sleep, so his own biological needs clearly differed from theirs.

Ilaria smiled at Thane as he yawned and began to pack up his own supplies. Even the best adventure would have been incomplete without him. Thane understood her in a way that went far beyond his empathy.

On the hill, the lone tree stood silhouetted against the sky and she admired the rustic beauty of its bare branches for several minutes before it dawned on her that its iridescent blue leaves were missing. On instinct, she walked out to the tree and quickly found the culprits responsible for the raid on her pack.

What she had thought were leaves were instead insects with teardrop shaped bodies. Hundreds of them were marching like ants in a line straight from their campsite towards naked tree in the clearing while carrying the remains of her protein bars in their jaws.

It hadn't once occurred to her that the leaves might be capable of leaving their host tree in search of food. Her dislike of bugs was momentarily overruled by her admiration for their ingenuity and gratitude that their appetites went towards energy bars and not human flesh. Feeling a tug on her pants, Ilaria found one of the little blue beasts climbing up her leg.

"I am not your tree," she told it, gently plucking it from her environment suit. Carefully, as not to step on any of the creatures, she walked to the center of the clearing where the rest of its swarm were beginning to disperse the remains of her food high in the branches.

"Here you go," she smiled, letting the bug climb from her hand onto the trunk. *"And for future reference, you have wings; you don't have to crawl on the ground."*

"What?" she asked the others when she returned to the camp. It was getting on her nerves the way Thane and Anak kept watching her as if she had sprouted a second head over night.

"Nothing," said Thane, "I just thought you didn't like bugs."

"They were just doing what they do," Ilaria shrugged, amused at her own conflicting attitude towards the creatures. She really didn't hate them or any other creature unless they were crawling on her. They were no more responsible for what they were than for what she was.

Ilaria sighed as it dawned on her that she really didn't want to run from the empire, but to coexist with them. That, of course, was now impossible. They had experimented on her before she was born; forced her into a life she never would have chosen for herself. Just like the blue bugs, she was now doing what she had to in order to survive.

Deciding she should probably eat something, Ilaria pulled a portion of one of her remaining bars from her damaged bag, but after sniffing it, she put it back. She knew she needed the nourishment, but just the thought of food made her lose what little appetite she had. Rationing food was easy when she didn't have any desire to consume what she had.

"Okay, man with the plan," Ilaria said to Thane with a resigned sigh. "What's our next move? Even I'm beginning to sense him now so he must be close."

"*What else do you sense?*" Thane asked telepathically.

"*Just that he's angry,*" the woman answered. "*Very angry which is probably why I can sense him.*"

"*Nothing else?*"

"*I'm not as strong of an empath as you, Thane,*" Ilaria answered, her thoughts tinged with annoyance. "*What is it I should be sensing?*"

"*Nothing,*" Thane sent, watching her intently. "*I was just wondering if you could.*"

Ilaria soured again at Thane's annoying habit of turning every moment into a training lesson, but she wasn't in the mood to argue, so she let the matter go. He'd tell her what she supposedly missed eventually and she wouldn't have to waste her time trying to figure it out.

"*This seems like a good place,*" Thane said as he reexamined their campsite.

"*A good place for what?*"

"*An ambush. Told you I had a plan.*"

"*And you couldn't tell me this earlier?*"

"*I didn't know about it earlier,*" Thane grinned. "*I always have a plan; I just have to wait for it to evolve until I know what it is.*"

Apparently, part of Thane's plan to ambush their tracker was to pack up and move out again, a move which made no sense to either Ilaria or Anak. With Thane now in the lead, the three set off and shortly the forest floor became muddier as the ground water increased. With every step, mud oozed around the soles of their boots. The viscous ground thickened the farther into the swamp they went and within minutes, every leg muscle Thane and Ilaria knew to be in existence, and others they had no idea were part of their anatomy, were burning with the effort of raising their feet in order to walk. Even Thane's jumping abilities became useless as the mud seemed to suck him back with every attempted leap. Both Empati were sweating from their exertions and the sticky, humid air. All the while, Ilaria kept up an internal mantra of how much she loved adventure, but her mind kept countering that this one wasn't living up to what adventures were cracked up to be. Next time, she wanted an adventure that included mai tais on the reef moon of Hale-akaloha.

"Oh, boy," Ilaria said as she panted for breath. "We're just not built for this terrain."

"I think it's time for that ride now, Anak," Thane said every bit as weary as Ilaria. "Anyway, I think we've given him enough to show that we crossed over. As determined as he is to get you, Ilaria, I have no doubt he'll follow us in."

At Thane's request, Anak began twisting his twig-like fingers together in his agitation. "Are you sure? The human at the mine who took me away was furious when he was carried. I do not mean to insult you."

With a short laugh, Thane shook his head, "We are not insulted and Daneb is a fool. He's the kind of person who can find a slight in a cheerful good morning."

Ilaria heartily agreed, "Anak, if you don't mind carrying us, we would be grateful."

Both Empati were far too used to the epitaphs many of the Normals in the empire hurled their way to be offended by an offer genuinely made so they couldn't possibly take offense at the young Akilli. With every reason to hate every human who occupied his world, Anak was able to separate friend from foe. Humans might be the enemy, but *these* humans had promised to bring him home. That return hadn't quite gone according to plan and had instead created even more problems for the sapling, but he didn't bemoan his situation or blame his companions for it. They realized the Tree could have easily abandoned them and returned to his own people, but instead he had stayed with them and willingly offered to help. On his homeworld, Anak was in his element and every bit as capable as the two Psychs were in their own environments.

"*Daneb was right; this is a little bit humiliating,*" Thane sent privately to Ilaria.

"*It could be worse,*" Ilaria countered. "*At least we weren't tossed over Anak's shoulder like a sack of turnips.*"

"*Ah, true enough.*" Thane chuckled. "*Between you and me, I did enjoy that image.*"

"*Thank you, Anak; this is much better,*" Ilaria told their friend while grabbing hold of his wooden shoulders to sway her body in time with his steps. As Anak walked, she tried to relax her cramped muscles as she rode, but it wasn't easy as she needed her legs to grip Anak's torso. Slowly, she figured out a way to shift her weight from side to side and give her protesting muscles some relief. Training at the Keep was strict and covered dozens of potential offworld scenarios, but no amount of conditioning could make up for real-life situations. Both Ilaria and Thane had crawled on their bellies through the mud on many highly imaginative obstacle courses at the Keep, but at the finish line there always had the promise of a hot meal and shower at the end of it.

"*Anak, what is this place?*" Thane asked, gesturing to a large copse of trees recognizing them as fala trees from the fruit hanging from the branches.

"*It is a garden place where many fala trees grow,*" Anak answered. "*We can stop here to gather some if you need more to eat. I am sorry about the loss of your shit food. The Rebe told the Edu to leave you in peace, but the Azula didn't realize that included your supplies.*"

The thought of food along with the motion of Anak's swaying gate set Ilaria's stomach rumbling and not in a pleasant way. To change the subject, she asked, "*The Azula were those blue bugs?*"

"*Yes. They are carrion eaters and were drawn to the scent.*"

"*Anak, you do know out food isn't made from shit.*"

"*We all must eat. Many of the Edu consume what would be unappetizing to others.*"

"Never mind," Ilaria said exchanging an amused smile with Thane as she said privately to him, *"He thinks we're nothing more than dung beetles!"* They had named the food and Anak was going to take it literally and that was fine so long as he didn't actually try to get them to eat dung.

"I still don't understand what the Rebe is you keep mentioning," Ilaria said in order to change the subject. She found Anak's description hard to grasp.

"The Rebe maintain the balance of the Edu. They entwine all life on the Wald."

Ilaria sighed. For all his explanations, she still didn't understand if they were an idea or actual beings on the Wald. Many species maintained a creed and the symbiotic nature of this planet would need a system of beliefs if they were all to live in harmony. She was impressed because the way Anak spoke of the Rebe made it seem as if the creed was planet-wide. Even the blue bugs had tried to obey the mandate to not interfere with Anak's guests. It made her think of the carnivorous plant she had nearly blundered into. Anak had said it wasn't a part of the Rebe and that meant it would have eaten them if given the chance. Ending up as plant poo wasn't a pleasant thought.

"Are we there yet?" Ilaria sent when she wasn't sure how much more her stomach could take. The thought she might hurl on her transportation was mortifying.

"Yes, we're just about there," Thane said every bit as weary as Ilaria. True to his word, about fifteen minutes later, the ground dried up and the mud became the firm and familiar forest once more.

Climbing down from Anak, it took Ilaria a few moments to realize why the place looked so familiar. They had sweated and slogged through muddy bogs only to end up at the very place they camped at the night before!

"Ah, thank you, Anak," Thane said cheerfully as he stretched his back.

Ilaria sputtered her indignation as she looked around at their old campsite. *"Why did we leave at all if we were only going to stay here?"*

"Because it's all part of the plan," Thane told her absently as he squatted down to examine the ground.

"Are you ever going to let me in on your plan?" Ilaria mentally snapped. *"What happened to team work?"*

"I'll tell you everything very soon. We needed to get some more distance between us and our pursuer first. No, keep your pack on," Thane said when Ilaria started to swing the bag from her shoulders. *"We're not staying."*

"Then why did we even come back here?" she demanded. *"I really hope there is a plan because all we seem to be doing is getting ahead of him only so we can stop to make sure he doesn't fall behind."*

"Trust me," Thane smiled before turning to Anak. *"Will you be alright here?"*

"Yes," the tree answered. *"You humans do not see us; he will not notice me."*

"Excellent! Now, which way do we need to go?"

Pointing, tree told them, *"Walk in that direction keeping sun up to your right and sun down to your left. The Rebe will meet you at the fala."*

Without another word, Thane headed into the woods. Confused and having no other choice, Ilaria followed. Fog swirled between stands of trees poking up through the thick matting and shaded the marsh in a constant, eerie twilight that played with her sense of space and distance. In the distorted atmosphere, plants and shrubs they thought were near them more often than not, turned out to be much farther away than they had first appeared.

Ilaria didn't understand how the trees calculated time, but to her, this dense portion of the Wald could have been either day or night; the subtle distinctions of morning, afternoon and evening were lost in what little light filtered down through the dense jungle. The direction Anak had indicated was currently clear enough, but that would change quickly if they ever lost their reference and her bearings.

"What is it?" Thane asked when Ilaria dropped her bag to the ground.

"*Ah ha!*" she cried triumphantly as she pulled out her compass. Growing up, Thane had always told her a compass was one of those items she might never need, but to always, *always* make sure she had one as getting lost was one of the quickest ways to die. Naturally, she always, *always* kept one packed in her emergency supplies.

"*I didn't say anything!*" exclaimed Thane when she scowled at him.

"*I'm not in school anymore,*" she admonished him. "*You don't have to test me on everything we do.*"

"*But I didn't say anything!*" Thane said again, trying to hide the pull of his mouth as he grinned.

"*Empath,*" she said, pointing to herself to reminded him of that portion of her psionic abilities. "*You don't have to say anything, but you also don't have to wait just to see if I'm doing everything right. You have your own compass.*"

"*Yeah, but I was okay with the 'sun up on our right' directions.*"

To that, Ilaria just rolled her eyes.

They filled their water bottles at the edge of a stream that seemed to have a very high mud to water ratio and waited for it to pass through the filters twice before they felt the liquid was worthy enough to be called water. After they scanned it, the two Empati were relieved the results came back green: no microscopic parasites and no harmful bacteria. If necessary, their Evi-suits could supply them with water, but both agreed that drinking water was one item they couldn't have too much of.

Closing her eyes, the way Thane had taught her, Ilaria did a mental inventory of her supplies. Most of her food was gone (not even sleeping on it had saved those rations), but they had potable water, blankets and a compass. Everything else they'd just have to do make do without or find along the way. With a nod to Thane, Ilaria indicated she was ready.

Prepared for another long hike, they realized they needn't have bothered when only after a half an hour they came across the fala grove. Just as Anak had said and they had witnessed in the smaller copse, these particular trees definitely grew both flowers and fruit and these twisting trees before them definitely fit that description. It was as if the trees couldn't seem to decide what time of year it was. Each branch held tiny clusters of purple flowers, larger clusters of young fruit and dozens of the huge, heavy ripe fala that Anak had first given them.

Thane and Ilaria took a moment to debate on whether the fala should be classified as a tree or a vine. The trunks were certainly tree-ish and nearly ten feet around with gnarled grey-green bark, but the branches splayed out in all directions, entwining the trunks of neighboring trees to continue skyward in order to latch onto the taller canopy above. Looking up, it was impossible to tell where one tree ended and another began.

"*This fala is apparently a favorite of something that lives in this swamp,*" Ilaria commented and pointed to the half-eaten fruit still hanging from the high branches.

"*Some variety of arboreal primate,*" Thane agreed. "*A big one if the bite radius is any indicator.*"

"*These are fresh, but I haven't seen or heard any living thing other than us... not counting the Azula, of course.*"

"And we won't," said Thane, dropping his pack. "*We've only been bothered by the midges and those blue leaf bugs since we got here.*"

"*So, I guess word got around that offworlders don't taste very good.*"

"*No, word got around that the Rebe has ordered the Edu to leave us alone.*"

"*Speaking of the Rebe, didn't Anak say they would meet us here? I don't see anything or even know what they look like.*"

"*I'm sure we'll find out soon enough,*" said Thane as he dropped his pack to the ground. "*In the meantime, welcome to ground zero.*"

· CHAPTER 16 ·

"Now are you going to tell me your plan?" Ilaria asked.

"I'll tell you part of the plan," Thane smiled as he studied the fala tree in front of them. Whatever he was looking for, he seemed to find it in the thick branches and without saying anything further, he free ran up the trunk and then jumped up the branches into the high canopy. "Yes, this will do nicely!" he shouted down to his ward.

"Nicely for what?" Ilaria sent back, amused that after twenty years Thane could still forget that he didn't have to scream himself hoarse when he needed to tell her something from a distance.

"Nicely for a net. Come up and see."

With a shrug of compliance, Ilaria also free ran up the trunk to the first, thick limb, but from there, she had to slowly climb. Envious of Thane's natural ability, she wondered if her height would allow her to jump up the tree the way the Denobian had. Deciding to attempt it while she still didn't have far to fall, Ilaria held her breath and was elated to find herself on the next branch up. Daring to press her luck again, she cautiously leapt up the tree until she was on the same level as her mentor.

"Ugh! I'm sweating in this climate. Look at me! I'm drenched!"

"I see that," Thane said, narrowing his eyes as he studied her. He'd been doing that so often lately that Ilaria had finally stopped asking about bugs.

"Now what?" she demanded when she noticed Thane was staring at her again.

"Nothing," he started to say when he saw the flash of anger in her eyes. "You just got up here quickly, that's all."

"Oh," Ilaria smiled. "I did, didn't I? I thought I'd try climbing like a Denobian. It seemed to work."

"Yes, it did." Thane said thoughtfully. "How do you feel?"

"Not as nauseous as before, but I still have a stomachache."

"Tired?" he asked.

"No," Ilaria shook her head with a shrug. "Only what's to be expected from not getting much sleep because we're in a bog and a tree's leaves stole my food, but, other than that, I feel okay."

"Minus the stomachache."

Ignoring him, Ilaria said, "So why did you want me up here?"

"These vines will make a perfect net if we can gather enough. They're a type of creeper and are already linked together as they have grown and latched onto other plants for support."

"I see where you're going with this, but we shouldn't cut anything living."

"No, you're right. With the way everything is symbiotic here, we don't want to harm any of the Edu. You're taller; see what you can harvest up in those branches. There should be plenty of flexible dead vines we can use."

Plenty was an understatement as multiple lengths of the vines came lose with the slightest tug. Ilaria was grateful the entwining plants didn't have thorns, but she quickly discovered why they hadn't needed to evolve such sharp defenses. Even the loose vines that had detached from their main stalks retained their grip and still had the capacity to wrap around her wrists and hands if she kept them still for too long. The first time it happened, Ilaria had to pry her hand out of the ensnaring cluster, nearly losing her grip in the process. The second time the vines grabbed her, she understood the dangers and potentials of their properties and it didn't take her long to dub them "strangle vines".

"Be careful with these," she sent while dropping a load of vines down to the ground. *"They continue to grip even after they've died. No wonder this upper canopy is so thick with them."*

"Oh, this is great!" Thane said in delight once Ilaria had made it back down to the ground, in record time, the Denobian noted. He was going to have to have a long talk to her soon, he only hoped it could wait until after they had dispatched their tail. "Look, the ends continue to ensnare anything they come close to. All we have to do is guide them to what we want them to hold."

As Ilaria watched, Thane carefully held an end of one strangler next to the length of another. Immediately, the flexible branch latched on with such a grip that Ilaria thought both branches might break if they tried to remove them.

"Nice!" she said approvingly while trying her own hand at putting them together.

"This is going to go faster than I thought," said Thane. "I've got this so there's something else I need you to do."

"Sure," Ilaria said enthusiastically.

Thane watched her eyes brightened with the excitement of the adventure only to dim when he told her what he wanted.

"That's not a good plan," she said disappointed.

"Maybe not, but it's the one I've got."

"Fine," Ilaria growled. Grabbing several of the vines, she headed out alone into the swamp, backtracking along their previous path.

Thane had been concerned that neither of them had sensed their pursuer in a while. He didn't think the man had given up the chase after following them through the swamps of the Wald, but he had to make sure he was still on their trail. It wouldn't do to set a trap if their prey never showed up.

Keeping off their original trail so she wouldn't leave prints that forewarned anyone she was backtracking, Ilaria followed their path back to their campsite. At least part of Thane's plan was clear: that fish was human and would have just as much trouble walking over the mud as they had, but he wouldn't have a friendly native on which to hitch a ride on. It would take him much longer to cross it and that would give Thane more time to implement whatever the next stage of his plan was. The rest of his plan was as murky as the pools that occasionally bubbled up with the noxious gas.

As none of them were native to the Wald, Ilaria would have to assume the fish was just as unfamiliar with it its marshy topography as they had been. That left her an advantage. She and Thane had left enough of a trail into the mud to show they had crossed, but had then been helped the rest of the way by Anak. If the Fish had been foolish enough to try the crossing, it would have taken him a long time assuming he didn't get himself stuck in the sludge. There was also the possibility he had been sucked down to his death which was why they hadn't sensed him yet, but that was a remote possibility and Ilaria didn't think her luck ran that good. Besides, if he was dead, they wouldn't know why he was following them in the first place.

One more possibility did occur to the telepath. If he had turned back at the mud, he could have returned to his ship in order to pursue them from the air, but even as she thought it, Ilaria decided that was unlikely. Given the density of the overhanging plant life, a ship's sensors could detect warm-blooded life, but not exact species. In a forest such as this, there was a higher probability of his tracking local fauna than the two aliens he was really after, but he had the direction of the course they had taken and could just indiscriminately eliminate anything that registered on thermal sensors. As the Trees hadn't warned them the man had retreated, she would continue to assume he was still following their original course.

Ilaria had a momentarily elated flush of pleasure when

she realized she would probably see his face when the Fish realized he had walked in a huge circle. She was certain the Fish wanted her dead, just not yet. He needed something from her first and whatever it was, he wasn't going to get it! Ilaria's eyes flashed dangerously as she determined that no matter what happened, she was not going to end up a victim to these Fish and another nameless body dumped in a mass grave on a foreign world. She just had to make sure she knew what he wanted *before* she ended up dead.

Now that she was looking, Ilaria saw the grasses still bent from where they had stood and she could clearly see her own narrow boot marks, Thane's smaller prints and Anak's rather unique stump-like footsteps.

But the fourth set of prints sent chills down her spine. These could only have been made by someone wearing boots— a humanoid both larger and heavier than either she or Thane. This person had paced around their former campsite before following their tracks into the forest towards the bog. She couldn't detect any signs he had finished the circle and returned.

Either unconcerned or unaware that he, too, could be followed, the man had made no attempts to cover his own tracks, but Ilaria was now certain he hadn't returned to his ship. Periodically, she pushed out with her mind, but still couldn't sense him. He could have been out of range, but she was well aware he might know how to block psychic reads the way Dram had. Guessing he'd have more on his mind than concentrating on keeping up a mind-block, Ilaria continued with the assumption she still wasn't close to the Fish to sense him.

After an hour of waiting, Ilaria began to feel a presence and knew the Fish was getting close. For a moment, she wished her empathic reads were as strong as Thane's who could sometimes pick a single individual out of a crowd and tell if they were merely in a bad mood, was angry at a specific thing or simply distracted because his lunch had given him indigestion. For her, trying to read a faraway emotion was like trying to determine a specific color through the fog. She knew he was there, but he was muted the way the trees in the distance were hazy shades of dark and light without definitive form or texture.

Though his mental shape was still unrecognizable, Ilaria's own anger began to rise at the familiarity of his mind. Whoever it was tracking her through the Wald, he was no stranger.

"*Thane,*" Ilaria warned, "*it was as you suspected. He's getting close now.*"

Thane didn't respond, but now that she was sensing the fish, Ilaria cautiously started to edge back to the fala grove. Using the trees and thickets as cover, she darted forward. As she focused on reaching her next hiding place, she had been unaware of the few times she'd needed to traverse the open distances between the thick bushes and undergrowth.

Approaching the fala trees, Ilaria nearly cried out in relief when the small, shadowy form of a Denobian began to take shape in front of her through the mist. He had his back to her and seemed to be so engrossed with what he was doing, Thane was unaware of her approach. What confused her was if his intent was to ambush the Fish, he should have been in hiding.

It wasn't until the man stood up that she realized her mistake. Though his movements were still shrouded by the mist, Ilaria saw now that this wasn't a standing Denobian, but a tall man who had been squatting in order to examine her tracks. At his full height, this person was nearly six-feet tall and was most definitely not a Denobian.

And he clearly wasn't psychic as he still had no idea Ilaria was near. A new wave of panic hit her when she thought the Fish might have been kneeling next to Thane's lifeless body. Pushing out with all of her empathy, a relief hit her like ice water when she felt Thane's life force flickering in her mind like a candle flame glowing defiantly against a breeze. He could very well be unconscious, but at least he wasn't dead.

In as much time as it took her heart to beat thrice, Ilaria analyzed her opponent. From his stance and the tense set of his shoulders, she knew he was a soldier and well trained for combat. His weapon was still holstered on his hip, but his right hand twitched indicating he was ready to draw it at a moment's notice. Outweighing her by more than a hundred pounds, she knew she would have to disarm him quickly if she stood a chance against him in hand to hand combat. In training, she had sparred with opponents as large as this man was, but they had always been her fellow initiates or instructors. Ilaria had no idea what this man's fighting skill was and she couldn't take him with brute force.

Silently, Ilaria gathered three reeds laying on the ground and tied them in a knot at one end. Rocks were nonexistent on this terrain, so the only thing she had that was heavy enough to use as weights were the fala fruit. Lashing one to each of the three free ends of the reeds, she made a makeshift bola, hoping it would entangle him long enough for her to take his gun.

The man had knelt down again to check another track when Ilaria stepped from her hiding place and crept forward to close the distance between them. The fala were heavy and she needed to make sure they hit their mark as she'd only have one shot. If she missed, the advantage would then be his to draw and fire his weapon.

Mimicking the man when he stood to his full height, Ilaria began swinging the bola while aiming for his legs. She didn't think the reeds were long enough to encircle his upper torso and didn't want to aim for his neck and accidentally strangle him. Even a bola could be lethal in the right place and she wanted this Fish alive and questionable.

The man heard the bola as it swooshed through the air, but was too late. Ilaria let the weapon loose and watched it wrap around his lower legs. With a cry of surprise, he fell backwards onto the ground, but still managed to draw his own weapon. Ilaria was shocked to see it was an energy lance! She had only seen those once before at the gala on the *Celest*.

Faster than she knew she could move, Ilaria rushed forward to disarm him just as the Fish used his blade to slice through the strangle vines around his feet. Grabbing his weapon, she twisted the lance from his grasp just as the man landed a blow to her jaw.

Though the hit left her slightly dazed, Ilaria lunged at his midsection with all her weight. Surprised by the ferocity of her unexpected attack, it caught him off guard and off balance, the force knocking him back and into the net of strangle vines. Quickly jumping back, Ilaria watched as he became entangled in the creepers as they wrapped around his body, immobilizing him.

"Damien?" Ilaria was stunned as she leveled his confiscated lance at the Arkellian. Of all the people in the entire universe, he was the last she expected to see and not just because she thought he was dead.

But Rey wasn't out of the fight yet. Reaching into his boot, he pulled out a small dagger. It must have been another plasma blade, because it sliced through the vine net like a shuttle through a cloud bank; he was free almost instantly.

"Shoot him!"

The moment after she heard Thane's order, she heard another voice shout, *"Don't!"*

Ilaria didn't know where the second mental cry came from and for the first time in her life, she hesitated, unable to follow through and pull the trigger. Deep down, she didn't really want to shoot the Arkellian, but the second summons was laced with an urgency which infuriated her. For whatever reason, Damien had followed them to one of the most inaccessible places in the empire with clear intentions kill her so she couldn't fathom why Thane had changed his mind.

Either not realizing that she couldn't seem to take the shot, or gambling that she wouldn't, the Arkellian used her distraction to his own advantage. Kicking her own legs out from under her, Damien hit her with the brute force of his size and weight, knocking her to the ground. Rolling so he was now on top of her, he pinned Ilaria's arms and legs down with his own.

Ilaria had never once yielded a fight. Even if she had been bested in training, she always held her ground until her opponent either relaxed his guard and gave her an opening or her trainers got bored and called the match. But this wasn't a sparring session and there was no chance she would surrender to this Fish in Arkellian skin.

Before she could find a way to wriggle free, Thane swung down from the fala tree on the strangle vines and hit Damien square in the chest with his feet. The force of the blow propelled Rey backwards into the reeds. Ilaria had the immense satisfaction of seeing the once clean-cut and immaculate minister now covered in mud becoming entangled in the strangling vines once more. Wheezing from his painfully bruised ribs, the Arkellian stopped struggling, his eyes full of hate as he glared up at her.

Still in shock that Damien was alive, Ilaria didn't sense Thane's fury until she was hit with the full force of his mental scolding. *"Why the hell didn't you obey me? When I say shoot, shoot!"*

"You told me not to!"

"I told you to shoot him!"

"And then you said 'don't'."

Their argument was cut short when Damien started to laugh. "So, the rumors are true," he said grimly. "You are telepathic."

· CHAPTER 17 ·

Damien's vine bindings seemed to be intact for the moment, but Thane knew he'd have to check them again soon. In Ilaria's absence, he discovered that, alive or dead, the creepers continued to constrict long after detachment from their mother branch. It made them great for nets, but Damien could lose his hands if the vines weren't monitored carefully and the Denobian certainly didn't want them creeping up to the minister's neck and earning their nickname by strangling him. At least not before he got some information out of him.

Glancing up, Thane noticed Ilaria wringing her hands. Reaching over to place his own hand on hers, he sent more gently, *"It's okay. This wasn't your fault."*

"It was," Ilaria said, still shocked that of all the people in the empire, *he* was the one trying to kill her. His mental pattern had been familiar when she'd first sensed it, but after witnessing Rey laying in a pool of his own blood after being shot, Ilaria hadn't been able to make the connection who he was in her mind.

"It was Sarkin's," Thane sent firmly, giving gave her hands a little shake before releasing them. *"His entire counsel*

and *the Empati know your abilities and what he required you to do with it; it was just a matter of time before the information was leaked to his enemies or they figured it out on their own. Forget it for now and let's just see what's on our friend's mind, shall we?"*

Turning his attention to their captive, Thane studied Damien's rage-filled face. On his left temple was a nasty gash still only half-healed. On impulse, Thane tapped Rey's chest and felt the body armor underneath. He must have been wearing it when he was shot, but had knocked himself cold when he fell. Locked in a mind-scan with him, he could fully understand how Ilaria had misinterpreted his death. Thane was certain he would have made the same mistake.

Cocking his head, the empath asked, "Now, why would the Arkellian Prime Minister follow two Psychs all the way to the Wald?"

"You know perfectly well, traitors!"

"*We're* traitors?" Thane asked smoothly. "In what way have we betrayed the empire or our emperor?"

"Not against the empire, but against our sovereignty," Damien spat.

"In that case, in what way have we betrayed Arkell?"

Instead of answering, Damien turned his venomous gaze to Ilaria.

"You are actually blaming me?" Ilaria demanded. Incredulous at his silent accusation, she turned to Thane and said, "I'm a traitor because *he* screwed *me*."

"Don't deny you weren't ordered to sleep with me so you could read my mind!"

"I won't, but as I was ordered to by the emperor, where do you get a conspiracy out of it?"

"You used the information in order to frame me! When you tried to kill me in order to achieve your own goals of bringing down the empire."

"*He thinks we're behind Sarkin's assassination attempt,*" Ilaria sent. "*He honestly thinks that's why he was shot!*"

"You clearly aren't up to date on current events," Thane told Rey with a growl. For your information, Ilaria was nearly killed herself when she tried to save Sarkin."

"She's a mind-raper!" Rey spat. "Your kind manipulates our thoughts to create evidence against us. We had no chance!"

"What do you mean?" Ilaria asked, giving Rey a chance to gloat that the peeks' knowledge wasn't entirely current.

"You set us up to take the fall!" the minister accused.

"Set you up how?" Thane interjected, frustrated that rather than interrogating Rey, they were only talking in circles. "We weren't involved in the attempts on you or Sarkin; in fact, we've been working to find out who was behind it."

"You were working with J'rey!"

The mention of J'rey snapped Ilaria to both mental and physical attention which didn't go unnoticed by either Thane nor Damien Rey.

"You know that name," Rey sneered, vindicated.

Kneeling down to look Damien fully in the face, she asked, "Is he this traitor you believe to have conspired with us?"

"Of course, he is! A traitor from my own House! You were my only lead to find him."

"Why was I your lead?" Ilaria asked. "I learned about him from you."

Damien snorted derisively, "Look, you're a damn peek and I know what your kind can do. I heard his name from you when you violated my mind."

Ilaria began to protest that he hadn't when Thane stopped her. "Ilaria, when did you first learn of J'rey?"

"I don't remember exactly, but it was after we slept together. The name stuck in my head as it was Arkellian."

"And you?" Thane asked Rey. Though the minister didn't respond, the empath knew the answer was the same: a shared mental Push by the Sona.

"Are you understanding any of this?" Ilaria asked.

"Most of it," Thane said, grimly aware what the repercussions of his suspicions would have if people like Damien knew there were peeks with psionic powers more terrifying than just telepathy. Fear over the suspicion of what they could do had led to their enslavement; proof of it could lead to their extinction. "What he knows, he believes with certainty: you slept with him for information that led to him being accused of the assassination attempt on Sarkin."

"Well, that's rubbish!" Ilaria countered. "I actually thought he was dead when he was shot. It had nothing to do with Sarkin."

"Okay, enough!" Thane exclaimed suddenly. "This isn't getting us anywhere. Rey, I'm going to release you, but for your own good, don't try anything. You're unarmed and we're both trained Empati. We'll sense any wrong move the moment you decide to do it."

Carefully testing his resolve, Thane loosened the vines ensnaring the Arkellian. Though Rey continued to glower at the peeks, for the moment he passively accepted the conditions.

"Full disclosure," Thane said told the minister. "Both of us are now In-Valids in the eyes of the empire, so we have nothing to hide. Ilaria, tell him what we know of the attack on the Celest. *But do not mention the augmented serum,*" he added silently.

Feeling the trepidation rise in her mentor, Ilaria sensed Thane's dread didn't revolve entirely around Rey's hatred over the missing J'rey. Something else had sparked the empath into near panic that he couldn't share with her in front of the minister. With a guarded nod, she sat cross-legged on the ground just beyond his reach.

"Okay, full disclosure," Ilaria agreed and proceeded to tell Damien the full extent of her powers. "When I touched you at the Gala, I felt your excitement when I mentioned cybernetics. Sarkin believed there to be a plot against him and ordered me to sleep with you to find out more. While I did sense there was a connection between you and the cyborgs, I wasn't able to determine anything more before you were shot. After I told Sarkin this, that was my extent of my involvement with you."

"Why are you so obsessed with killing Ilaria over this J'rey?" Thane asked. "He's only a name she heard after her night with you. In all honesty and with full disclosure, we assumed he was a former lover of yours."

Damien was bitter. ""Former lover! But you still mentioned him to Sarkin!"

"I did," Ilaria admitted.

"Well, thanks to you and J'rey, I was arrested for conspiring against the empire! His mind-rapers tortured me for information I knew nothing about. They let me go, but not before interrogating my entire House... my mother, my sister! They did the same to them!"

"I am sorry," Ilaria said sincerely. "I didn't know."

Feeling Rey's anger boil once more at Ilaria's ignorance over his own plight, Thane explained, "Once she heard the name, she had no choice but to disclose it to Sarkin. What happens to peeks when the emperor loses confidence in them is far worse than what he does to Citizens. How's your back, by the way?"

"My what?" Rey asked, confused at the sudden change of subject.

"Your back," Thane repeated. "Ilaria said you were shot in the back."

"I was, but I was wearing body armor," Rey said, narrowing his eyes as he confirmed the empath's suspicions over his survival. "I would have been completely unharmed if I hadn't cracked my skull on a rock."

"Smart of you," Thane commented. "Any idea who shot you or why?"

Rey shot at look at Ilaria with narrowed eyes.

"You're a smart man or you wouldn't be Tech's minister, so don't be stupid," Thane said, his annoyance over the Tech's prejudice reaching his limit. "She was standing right next to you."

"*Former* minister," Rey corrected him. "You then."

"That would have been a good trick since I wasn't even onboard," Thane informed him. "Check any manifest you want; I was on the Wald and returned to Prime immediately after. It really bothers you that the emperor ordered Ilaria to sleep with you, doesn't it?"

Thane took Rey's dark glare as his affirmative. "May I

ask who ordered you to sleep with her?"

"What?" Rey exploded. "No one! I'm the victim here, peek!"

"Clearly. Well then, *victim*. If I were you, I'd try to think more on who gave the orders for you to be shot and why then blaming the one you chose to sleep with. What do you know that someone didn't want a telepath finding out because you've got a lot more problems than we do at the moment?"

"And the only time you and I met was on the *Celest*," Ilaria reminded him. "I spoke with you about a cybernetic translation suit that could be used for the V'reem and you were shot after I informed Sarkin's counsel I couldn't discover what that connection was. I believe you know something, even if you are unaware of it, and someone with knowledge of how my telepathy works attempted to eliminate you as a threat."

"It has to be this J'rey," the minister admitted. "If I don't bring him to Sarkin, my entire family will be executed for treason."

"I agree it's most likely him," Ilaria nodded. "Neither of us know who he is as we both believed we heard the name from one another. I can't say if he attempted to assassinate you, but whoever he is, he's clearly important."

"Damien," Thane said suddenly, "have you been to Maelstrom recently?"

"Why would I go there?" Rey snorted his derision at even the mention of the psychic prison.

"Good point; there'd be no reason for you to. How about Haven?"

"I woke up there after I was shot," the minister frowned. "Some doctor said my injury wasn't life threatening; I was released and promptly arrested!"

"I think everyone who was on the *Celest* is being questioned, though I don't think others were treated as unfairly as you were," Thane nodded sympathetically. "Can I ask how you found us? We thought we were hiding pretty well, but you came right to us."

"I don't know," Rey sighed his irritation at the new list of questions. "It was just a feeling."

Turning privately to each other, Thane asked Ilaria, *"What do you think?"*

"He's empty," Ilaria sighed. *"He still hates us for what we are and personally blames me for all his troubles, but he's past wanting to kill me... at least for now. He's more interested in finding J'rey and saving his family. Because of the contraction of the name, he believes that J'rey is a member of his Arkellian House. If he himself doesn't apprehend him, his entire family could be accused of treason and executed."*

"You both heard this name telepathically," Thane said, *"and you both thought it came from one another. Is it possible you're hearing this name from someone else, maybe another telepath?"*

Ilaria considered it carefully before she answered. *"I think it's very possible. Damien isn't psionic, but he 'sensed' the Wald was where he needed to go in order to find J'rey. Yes, I think it's very likely I'm hearing another psychic, and it wouldn't surprise me if it were one of these augmented Fish."*

"Stop there," Thane said. *"Let's finish with Damien before we go down that road."*

Turning back to Damien, Thane said, "Minister, I think we're after the same goal: the people responsible for orchestrating the attack on the *Celest* that nearly killed you and the emperor."

With a nod, Damien agreed. "J'rey was my only lead and I was hoping you could tell me more. Since you don't know any more than I do, I don't know where to start looking now."

"We do," Ilaria smiled. "Thanks to you, we know a little more about J'rey. We suspected him of being Arkellian, but had no idea he was of your House..."

"Or pretending to be of your House," Thane interjected quickly when Damien's eyes darkened again.

"Or pretending," Ilaria amended. "But we have been tracking another set of terrorists we've been calling the Fish."

"Fish? Why Fish?"

"It's how they see themselves," Ilaria said, "as prey fish

taking bites out of smaller bait fish, or in their case, the empire.”

Continuing, Thane said, “We know they are responsible for several murders and a separate attempt on both Ilaria's and my life. The ships that attacked the *Celest* didn't have recognizable signatures. It's not proven yet, but we think these Fish were also behind the attempted assassination on Sarkin.”

“But why frame my House?”

“My theory is that someone is working hard to either discredit you or point the finger away from their own interests. No offense, but I think you just got in the way.”

The loathing descended from Damien, joining the thick fog at their feet. The cloying stench of his distaste caused Ilaria's nausea to return. She hadn't thought much about it while tracking the Arkellian down or during the subsequent fight, but Rey's open hatred made her sick to her stomach. Standing up, she left the two men in order to retrieve her pack.

“Don't judge her too harshly,” Thane told the minister in a low voice. “The punishment had she refused would have been severe.”

“Yes, I know. I just feel so… violated.”

“Yes,” Thane said. “I know what you mean.”

With a dark glare, Damien said, “Do you?”

Even through his lowered voice, there was no way Damien could mistake Thane's fury. “I can't tell you which is worse: having a mind-scan forced upon you or having to be the one to do it. I'm only an empath and can only sense emotion. But as an empath, I *do* know exactly what she felt every time Sarkin gave her over to someone like you to rape. Yes, rape!” Thane insisted when Damien protested the word. “I know you aren't the true rapist as you assumed it was consensual, but just the same, Ilaria didn't sleep with you willingly. This was the emperor's doing and his alone.

“But I can also sense that you still loath her for what she is; a hatred so great you'd still like to literally put your hands around her throat and squeeze the life out her if you ever get the chance again.”

The empath paused a moment for it to sink into Damien

just how accurately he'd sensed the minister's murderous intent before he continued. "So, let me also tell you this: she's my daughter. I couldn't do anything to help her before, but I can now and I will never let someone like you touch her again without her consent. I may only be a peek, but I'm also a trained psi-cop. If I ever sense you near her again with the intent to harm her, I'll break your neck before you even know I'm there."

While Damien Rey wasn't a peek, with every fiber of his being he sensed it wasn't an idle threat.

"You know we're not the traitors you've been looking for," continued Thane, "and you've got your lead. I suggest you go now because there is something else you've miscalculated"

"And what's that?"

"We are not alone."

At that statement, every tree in the area straightened and turned towards the two men. Fear was a rare emotion to the Arkellian and Thane couldn't help but smile when the minister tripped over his own feet as he bolted from the fala, the Trees dispersing into the forest to make sure the minister returned to his ship.

Thane's sigh of relief at Damien's departure burned in his lungs as the Denobian tried to force himself into calmness. He wasn't sure if he wouldn't have strangled Damien then and there if he had to feel his self-righteous loathing for much longer. But feeling Ilaria's dejection more strongly, he went to stand by his surrogate daughter. She was the one bright spot in his life and his heart swelled now that he had openly admitted to another human how deeply his bond with her went.

"Don't let people like him get to you," he told Ilaria comfortingly. "He's a bigot with his own problems to deal with right now. At least he knows you didn't have a choice."

"*It doesn't matter,*" she sent with a gasp as a stabbing pain shot through her abdomen. Sweat that had nothing to do with the swamp humidity beaded on her upper lip as she worked at controlling the ache. It had been growing for a while, but she'd be damned before she let someone like Damien Rey see her like this.

"*The nausea?*" Thane asked in concern.

"*No,*" she answered, taking short breaths in order to control the growing discomfort. "It's something else. Something's very wrong with me!"

Crying out in agony, Ilaria collapsed into Thane's arms.

· CHAPTER 18 ·

Giving Sobek a sound mental cursing for his experimental tampering, Ilaria's pale face made Thane wonder if they were wise to have left Haven after all. His drug had rapidly healed what should have been a fatal wound and had seemed to have continued working when he noticed the gash on her forehead healing over a matter of hours. But when Sobek had mentioned there could be side effects, Thane never for a moment considered something this extreme.

"Food hasn't been appetizing and I've been feeling sick," Ilaria said to her worried mentor. Her mind went into full doctor mode as she listed her symptoms in the hopes that a diagnosis and cure would suddenly appear. The only one that came to her wasn't very appealing.

"Thane, all I can think of is that I might have picked up some kind of parasite when I ate the fala fruit."

"But it scanned green," Thane sent. "I've never heard of a parasite not registering on the scanners."

"Nor have I, but I swear it feels like something is crawling around in my guts. I keep telling myself that it's my imagination, but the pain is growing worse by the minute."

In all the years he had known her, Thane knew Ilaria wasn't one to fantasize an illness. He didn't think it was a parasite; the fala had scanned as safe and he had never read one report of a scan being wrong, but there was always a first time for everything. The empire knew very little about the lifeforms on the Wald. But something was clearly wrong with her. Thane was no doctor, but even he could see it was sucking the life right out of her.

"We've got two choices," he told her. "The first is to make our way to the Pit. Daneb's crew will have medical facilities there and a physician."

"Not ideal," Ilaria said. "What's our second?"

"Rill's main power should have had time to recharge by now. He's not only closer but is equipped with an emergency bio-bed. The problem is if it is parasite, I don't know if he can remove it without a trained surgeon."

Ilaria didn't waste time in contemplation, "I'd rather take my chances with Rill than with the Company."

Thane merely nodded at her decision. "In that case, we go back to our original campsite and rejoin Anak. If he carries you, he will able to get us to Rill faster than we can walk it."

"Why would he do that? We haven't exactly followed through on our promises with him."

"We got shot down; it's not like we weren't trying. And the Akilli did help us get rid of Damien, so I don't think they are the vengeful sort. I admit it's a risk, Ilaria, but I think he will help. I know he has no love for humans, but he doesn't seem to have any ill will towards us personally."

"No, you're right," Ilaria agreed.

With another nod, Thane said, "Then we go to Anak because, truthfully, I don't think you can walk much farther."

As they continued, Thane tried to hide his relief that they were heading back to their ship and he wasn't entirely sure why. The best care for Ilaria was back at the mine, but as she had said, that was also where the Company was. The mining guild may be autonomous, but they were loyal to the empire. He could sense the beginnings of a plan forming in his mind and, while he didn't quite know what form it was taking, he knew it didn't involve them returning Sarkin's clutches.

From the first moment Ilaria had stepped on the Wald, she had been different and Thane liked the changes. It hadn't escaped his notice that she stood straighter and cowered less when confronting Daneb after he had taken Anak to the capital. Ilaria also seemed to be quicker in making decisions that concerned herself. She had just stood up to an Arkellian minister and member of the Senate.

Damien's attitude towards her had been the breaking point. As a soldier, Rey respected obeying orders and the consequences if they weren't followed, but he looked at Ilaria's obedience with disgust. Sarkin, Torquil and the Empati were the ones responsible for her actions, but Normals were more comfortable hating a peek. Thane wasn't sure how the wisdom of letting Rey go would play out, but it was done.

Thane looped his arm around Ilaria's waist to support her and she sagged against him as they walked. They actually made good time back to where Anak was waiting, but every step seemed one too many. As the young woman struggled, Thane wondered how she had been able to track Damien on her own let alone fight him. In all the years he had been her mentor, he had always admired her determination, but never more so than now.

Exiting the forest at the clearing, even Ilaria in her deteriorating condition couldn't help but gasp at the ethereal beauty. Their former campsite was so changed, it was difficult to believe it was the same place. A light fog had gathered in the low-lying area, floating in wisps just above the ground, but higher in the canopy scattered sunbeams broke through the leaves and the bending light caused the mist to radiate a vibrant ocher. The lone tree, its canopy thick with all of its blue leafed insects, was a dark silhouette against the brilliant glow. Only a moment later, mists dissipated and the solitary tree took on more vibrant shades of green and blue.

Thane's heart sank when he saw no sign of Anak and for the first time in his life, he was at a loss in what to do. As Ilaria groaned in pain, he helped her down to the ground while he hunted through his pack for his communicator.

"Rill," he said, trying to keep his voice even, "do you copy?"

"I copy, Thane," the ship answered.

"Glad you're back with us," Thane nearly laughed his relief. "Ilaria's been injured. I need you to trace my communication and pick us up."

"I've located you on my sensors, but I'm afraid I can't make it to you, Thane," Rill responded. "My energy reserves were drained to maximum and have only been replenished to twenty-two percent. I don't have enough power in my thrusters to reach you at this time."

"Thanks, Rill," Thane said dejectedly. "Keep me updated."

Slowly, Thane closed the commlink and looked about the forest edge for any sign of life. Even another Akilli other than Anak would have been welcome at this point, but the Trees were immobile. Thane wasn't sure if this variety of tree even could move. Vibrant green moss grew in thick, undisturbed clumps up the stoic trunks while long strands hung down from the overhead branches. The vines that had draped across the fala trees in the center of the swamp interlaced the upper canopy as if linking the two ecosystems together. If they could walk, they hadn't done so in many years.

"Stay still," he told Ilaria when she tried to get up. "Just let me think a minute."

"It's okay," she said. "I just need to rest for a moment. We'll start back towards Rill and he can meet us half way."

"Okay, half way," Thane agreed, privately thinking she wasn't going to make it that far. Sitting down next to her, he offered her a drink before taking some himself.

"Rill?" Thane asked, activating his comm again.

"Twenty-three percent. Unless you can close the distance, I can't reach you at less than forty-one percent."

Thane hated waiting, but he had no choice, but what was worse than waiting was having very little to occupy his mind except worry. He had been so sure Anak would be here, he had gambled Ilaria's life on it. No, he amended to himself, that wasn't entirely true. He had given Ilaria the choice and this had been her decision.

"Is it time to go?" Ilaria asked when she noticed him watching her.

"Not just yet," he told her, but just then movement at the tree line caught his eye as Anak bounded out from the forest.

"I am sorry I couldn't come to you sooner," the young Akilli said as he greeted them. "Ilaria is sick? She needs to go home?"

"We need to go back to our ship. Anak, can you take us there?"

"Yes, we can," the Tree said as several more Akilli stepped from the woods. Thane never saw them coming which made him wonder how stealthily a Tree could move or if they had been there all along, observing him.

As Anak picked Ilaria up in his arms, another looked down at Thane, offering him his hand. Surprised by the gesture, Thane grabbed hold and the larger, much older Akilli and swung himself up onto the bark-covered shoulders. Two more Trees retrieved their packs and as one, they turned and ran through the humid jungle to the meadow where Rill was still parked.

With the long strides, the Akilli moved quickly. Just as the sun began to dip low on the horizon and they were altering their course to cut the southern edge of the swamp, they heard a sonic boom indicating Damien had made it back to his own ship and left the Wald. For good or ill, Thane was glad he was gone.

"I'm sorry we weren't there," Anak explained at the sound. "The other man didn't head back to his ship after he left you; it took time, but we made sure he did."

"I'm glad you're here now," Thane answered. "If I may ask, what did you do?"

"We blocked his way. When he changed his course away from the direction of the ships, we ensured the only path he could take was back the way he came. I think he was surprised when he kept ending up at the meadow and he finally accepted that he had no choice but to leave."

"I'm sorry I missed it," Thane smiled as he imagined the forest moving to channel the Arkellian in the direction the trees wanted him to go. Though it had been unintentional, the show of power with them being allies with the Wald might go a long way in deterring the minister from pursuing Ilaria any further. And who was he kidding? Thane had sensed Damien's stubborn determination to eliminate whoever had betrayed his house and, even though he knew Ilaria wasn't the traitor he sought, he would still kill her just for the satisfaction of his wounded pride.

By the time the sun had set fully and the larger moon was glowing a crescent in the darkening sky, the Akilli had brought the Empati to the meadow. Rill had been tracking their progress and lowered the ramp in anticipation of their arrival.

Sitting Ilaria down on the lip of the open hatch, the Trees stepped back as Thane jumped from his own Akilli's shoulders and into the ship. Rill had the medical bed prepped as much as he had been able to, sending much of his recovered power to ensure it was fully functional.

Fear gripped Thane when he saw how tightly the Evi-suit stretched across Ilaria's midsection and he jumped back when he saw her belly ripple even through the thick material.

"Cut it off me!" Ilaria said when Thane tried to remove the suit and couldn't. The tension was so great, he wasn't able to get a grip on any of the fasteners.

Taking the plasma knife he only just now realized he hadn't returned to Damien; Thane poked a small hole at her shoulder which was the only place loose enough for him to slice into the suit and not cut Ilaria at the same time. Working his fingers into the slit, he began to work down her front until the suit split open. Ilaria cried out as her freed stomach suddenly protracted several inches.

Thane's eyes bulged when he saw her distorted belly, but quickly pushed his shock aside as he finished removing the remains of her suit and helped her lay down on the bio-bed.

"It's better," she whispered. Bathed in sweat, her pain

began to diminish at her release.

"Just relax while I run the scans," Thane said, stroking her damp hair. "I promise, you'll be just fine."

Nodding, Ilaria closed her eyes to wait while Thane confirmed the worst. All the horror stories from her survival classes flooded through her memory about the gruesome deaths when planetary explorers failed to scan native food. When a food wasn't safe, unknown allergies and bacteria could cause everything from asphyxia to fatal hemorrhaging and, in some documented cases, organs literally exploding. What bothered her the most was that she hadn't been careless; she'd scanned the fala and it had registered as safe.

"How are you feeling?" Thane gently asked later as he sat down beside her.

"A little better now that I'm not moving," she answered stoically, but her chin trembled in fear when she noticed her distended belly. "You can't get it out."

"I'm afraid it's not that simple," Thane hesitated, but quickly added, "No, no, you're fine. You're going to be okay. That I can promise you. *I promise, you're fine.*"

Ilaria nodded at his mental assurance, but he was too worried for her to be fully reassured. "Then what's wrong with me?"

"Rill?" Thane said.

"In short," the ship answered, "what's wrong with you is complications from the Juventas serum. Rest assured, you're not dying."

"Are you saying I'm allergic to this serum?" Ilaria asked.

"Allergic, no, but it is changing you in unexpected ways."

Ilaria wasn't reassured by the ship's evasiveness. "Damn it, Rill! Changing me how?"

With a slight pause as if he couldn't believe it himself, Rill finally said, "It's accelerating the growth of your fetus. Ilaria, you're pregnant."

· CHAPTER 19 ·

Ilaria was too stunned by the news to comprehend the relief that she wasn't dying. "That's not possible. All the Empati are on contraceptives to prevent pregnancies."

"Which can on occasion fail," Rill said. With another pause as if to inhale air into lungs he didn't have, the ship went into detail about the complications Ilaria was experiencing, "As I've told you, I began my research into the Alesium serum soon after I first learned of it. I didn't know it was Sobek conducting these experiments until recently, but I do know now that the serum was used on your mother. I'm sorry to say Jyn didn't survive your birth, but it was because of the serum she was given that you were born empathic and later developed your telepathy. Some of the symptoms you're experiencing now is because you've been given the serum twice: the first time was in vitro when it was injected into your mother and the second was when Sobek gave it to you on the *Celest*."

"I don't understand," Ilaria said. "This is a healing drug. Why would it harm me if I've been given it twice?"

"Because it wasn't designed to heal the sick or injured, but revert aging cells back to their physical peak. Don't forget

Vanth or Zin Tram, both who appeared younger than their actual age. Juventas is a youth serum for the elderly and you weren't old either time it was given to you. As a developing fetus, the serum couldn't revert your cells to their peak because they were already there, so it instead it increased your own fetal development while advancing your psionic abilities. It's the reason you were born empathic. When Sobek gave it to you the second time after you were shot, you were still a young woman. Designed to revert cells to their peak, it healed you from your injuries."

Every bit as shocked as Ilaria, Thane finally found his voice. "What else is doing to her?"

As Rill explained, several diagrams and chemical formulas appeared on his monitors, "I compared the serum Sobek gave you to that from both the Wald victim and your Haven attacker and discovered there are two types of this serum: the original Juventas designed as an anti-aging formula and an augmented version developed from psionic cells. Over the course of Ilaria's life, she's been given both versions."

Thane was sorry for Ilaria. Having been used for years by Sarkin, she now had to come to terms that her entire existence was one of Sobek's science experiments. "Is this the reason she's developed a third and completely unrecorded ability?"

"Possibly," Rill said. "As we know, when Ilaria's mother was given the serum, it altered her own fetal development. What happens to the mother can have a profound effect on the child. As Thane so aptly put it, the reverse can also happen with a mother developing a nut allergy if the infant she's carrying is allergic."

Ilaria wasn't sure she wanted to know what another possibility could be, "So, what is it doing to me now? It's no longer healing me, but making me sick."

"You're not sick, but pregnant. You've never known another pregnant woman before and don't understand that your nausea is connected to the hormonal changes that occur. Your symptoms have been complicated in that your daughter's development has been accelerated by the augmented serum you were given. While you've only just conceived, you're physically entering into your second trimester."

With both his psionic humans too stunned to answer, Rill continued. "Ilaria, I'm sorry to ask you this, but I need to know now if you intend to keep the child. At the rate of development, it would be too dangerous to wait."

Overwhelmed by the news, Ilaria couldn't answer. Rill gave her until morning to decide, but no longer. Rill's medical facilities were basic and a delay would mean they'd need a trained physician to perform the surgery. With the damage to his chassis, the ship couldn't leave the atmosphere leaving the mine the only place on the planet left to them for medical help.

"Unless my undercarriage is repaired, we are stranded here," Rill told them in his matter-of-fact way.

Thane groaned, "The good news is there are replacement parts on this planet…"

"And the bad news is, they're also at the mine," Ilaria finished. "This just gets better and better."

Rill continued, "Part of the good news is that I can still fly within the atmosphere and can get us closer to the mine. If you're careful, you could find the parts I need without being discovered. That would open our options in finding another competent surgeon."

"That's good," Thane said. "Once we get you repaired, I suggest we go to Denobia and hide out in the low-gravity environment buildings. They're designed for offworlders like Ilaria and she won't suffer from the heavy gravity."

"I don't think that's a good idea, Thane," Rill answered. "After Sobek's agents attacked you on Haven, you've become fugitives; In-Valids in the eyes of the empire. We have to stay where no one would look for you. On the Wald, there are only about a thousand people working the gas mines. Even if Daneb is ordered to send every person he can spare, in the millions of square miles of wilderness, it's unlikely they could find us."

"And they will come looking," Ilaria signed. "By now, Vanth Alesium will have reported the attack on his campus to Emperor Sarkin and he'll make sure he knows how we infiltrated his corporation. As peeks, it won't matter that the death of that soldier was a result of defending ourselves."

"Ilaria is correct," said Rill. "You were valuable to him, but now you're enemies of the state. If those agents were Sobek's, and I think we've established that they were, he now knows you've manifested teleportation abilities."

"We should have eliminated them when we had the chance," Thane scowled wondering how badly that miscalculation would haunt them.

"Maybe," Ilaria said softly as she put her hand over Thane's, "but, besides the fact we barely made it off Haven as it was, we aren't killers. It's one thing to kill in a fight, but to murder prisoners we'd already incapacitated? That would have been unthinkable; and for peeks to have murdered Valids would have made it open season on every Psych in the empire."

"They weren't Valids," Thane countered.

"We know that, but no one else does. Not even Sarkin knows about the augments or he would have had me scanning every Valid in the empire."

"Killing them wouldn't have helped our situation," Rill said. "Agents have always worked in pairs. You incapacitated two and a third was killed when Thane shot him. That leaves a fourth who was clearly in hiding and witnessed everything. Sobek will know of Ilaria's new ability. Hopefully, he doesn't know of her pregnancy."

"Could he?" Ilaria asked, shivering as fear suddenly iced her veins.

"It's a possibility," Thane said. "Granted, he was more concerned with saving your life when he injected you with that serum of his, so he wasn't exactly conducting pregnancy tests. But he was monitoring you at that hospital of his. I think we should assume that he does know."

"I believe Thane is correct," said Rill. "As we know from your own birth, in his attempts at creating augmented psychics, Sobek has done this before; it would be foolish to believe he hasn't continued these experiments in others. What we don't know is how advanced these augments are or how many of them are out there."

"Or what his objective is," Thane added.

Both psychics looked at Rill's console, the "face" of their computerized friend for him to supply their answers. Without missing a beat, the AI didn't disappoint. "The facts are that murdered psychics have been turning up on the Wald with the cells that control psionic manipulation surgically removed. Sobek has used the Juventas youth serum created by Vanth Alesium, manipulated it to either enhance psionic abilities in natural psychics, given it to those not born with them, or both. These augmented psychics have attacked you at least twice: once on the *Celest*, and once on Haven. Ilaria has also been injected with the augmented serum which not only healed her from a phaser blast to the chest, but is also enhancing the psychic development of her unborn child. Not quite relevant to this, but the infant is a girl."

Ilaria couldn't help smile. She knew one day she'd be ordered to have a child, but somehow having it happen by accident and not at Sarkin's command pleased her. She didn't have to wait for morning; she'd already made her decision.

"Jyn," she told her friends. "I'm naming my daughter Jyn after my mother so let's stop calling her the 'child' or the 'fetus'."

"Jyn it is. And your theories?" Thane asked, giving Ilaria's hand a pleased squeeze. Having been denied paternity himself, she was the closest he'd ever get. Sensing Ilaria's own thoughts were aligned with his own, Thane swelled with pride that he would soon become a grandfather.

"We know that Sobek is behind the augmentation, but I believe the attack on the *Celest* as well. I admit it's only a theory, but it fits the evidence that we have."

"Still doesn't make it true," Thane tempered, though he believed every word. The healer was the only person he could think of that had the knowledge, resources and the desire to accomplish creating augmented psychics. What had blindsided the Denobian was he apparently, also had the ruthlessness to murder dozens of people to accomplish it.

"Doesn't make it false, either," said Ilaria as she settled herself more comfortably in her chair. "Whatever his plan is, he's been doing this for years. He's got these augmented soldiers doing his bidding and if the *Celest* is any indication, a fleet of fighter ships with pilots the Empati can't psychically detect. How are we going to stop him?"

"Can we even stop him?" Thane asked. "There's only the three of us."

"Or should we stop him?" Rill asked surprising them. "We're not exactly allies of the empire anymore."

Taking a deep breath, Thane's cheeks puffed out as he expelled it. Getting into a ship and leaving the empire had been his childhood fantasy ever since he failed his psychic tests and was sent to the Empati as a peek. After forty years of dreaming about it, he never thought he'd actually do it. All they had was what was with them in the ship: field rations, uniforms and two dead augments. It wasn't exactly the best planned desertion he could have managed.

"We have allies," Thane said. "There are others unhappy with the empire's treatment of us. The problem is we have to stay dark. No one knows where we are or what we've done; hell, we didn't even know what we were doing. For everyone's safety, theirs as well as ours, we're on our own, so could we or should we stop Sobek is the least of our concerns. Thanks to that serum, Ilaria's going to give birth in only a few months and then we'll have a newborn to take care of. We need to plan for ourselves right now."

Frowning, Ilaria said, "It's not true no one knows where we are."

"Oh hell, I forgot about Damien Rey!" Thane huffed. "That's two people we probably should have killed and didn't. That Fish will tell Sobek what you've done and Rey will tell him where we are."

"I don't think so," said Rill. "The Fish... absolutely. There is no doubt that the Big Fish (assuming it is Sobek) knows of your teleportation, but I don't think he's going to tell. For one, Damien Rey isn't a Fish. When they attacked the *Celest*, it was

Rey and Sarkin they attempted to assassinate. Ironically, both their intended targets managed to survive."

"And two," Ilaria said, taking over, "he still wants to kill me. With a damaged ship, we're stuck here. When he finishes his quest to find this J'rey, he knows right where to find us."

Thane leaned forward to rub his face with his hands. It was overwhelming how much had happened to them in such a short amount of time. "We need to decide on what to do and our first decision is whether or not to stay on the Wald... when we get Rill repaired, of course."

Once again, the humans looked to their AI for the answers. The problem was that in Janus territory, there wasn't another planet they could easily get to that could support human life that wasn't already crawling with colonists, scavengers or soldiers.

"But this planet isn't uninhabited," Ilaria reminded them. "The Akilli, the Edu, even the Rebe, whoever they are, live here and they aren't exactly sympathetic to our species."

"No," Rill agreed, "but at least they aren't the ones killing you. Besides, until I'm repaired, we're not going anywhere."

Realizing that Rill was right, they put off deciding what planet they could hide on until after they'd obtained the parts needed to fix him. The ship kept a channel open in order to monitor the interstellar communication frequencies for any mention of the empire's search for the In-Valids while his crew worked on a complete manifest of the items on board.

Rill wanted to bury the bodies of the augments they had on board, but Ilaria said they shouldn't. The natives were unhappy enough when they discovered the burial ground, so they shouldn't antagonize them by doing the same. Once they were back into space, they'd jettison the bodies there. It made her wonder again why Sobek hadn't dumped them in the first place. None of this would have happened if his men had disposed of the evidence properly. Ships had brought the Maelstrom psychics in; why hadn't they taken them away?

If used sparingly, they decided their rations would last

them a month. As they were unsure just how long they'd be on the Wald, Rill set about scanning all the vegetation for available food that wouldn't be toxic. After two days, their campsite felt a little more like home. The bodies had been wrapped to prevent decay and stored in Rill's lowest and least accessible portion of his hold and they found bedding in the "careful not to crash on this planet" emergency kit. Safe, warm and fed for the moment, they were good to go until Ilaria got closer to giving birth when she'd need more help than a medical bio-bed, a computer and a panicking Denobian could provide.

Suddenly, Rill's proximity alarm was triggered indicating someone was near their ship. Looking outside, however, all they saw was the usual forest of static trees which hadn't moved or changed since they'd first touched down in the tiny glen.

"No one," Thane sighed, his shoulders sagging with relief that an animal had somehow managed to trip Rill's sensors. "We're closer than I'd like to be to that mine, though. We'd better find a way to pilfer the stuff we need and get out of here."

"It isn't no one," Ilaria said narrowing her eyes as she scrutinized the forest. "Can't you feel them?"

"Feel who?"

Ilaria shrugged, "I don't know, but someone is out there."

"Damien?"

"No; him we'd both feel."

"Since you've had difficulty reading them, it's a possible it's the augments," Rill suggested.

"They should still show up on your scanners," Thane scowled as he too peered into the dense crop of trees. "Just because they've figured out a way to block themselves from psychic detection, they're still human."

"Could it be the Akilli?" Ilaria asked.

"No," said Rill. "I've taken them into account with my scans; the configuration of the surrounding trees hasn't changed since we landed. The number has remained static and none of them have moved. I believe these trees are not sentient."

"Or they could just be patient," said Thane. "We'd better take a look just to be sure."

"I agree," Ilaria sent. "Let's do a perimeter sweep and hope it's just the local fauna."

Taking hand scanners, the two fugitives cautiously stepped out of the ship. Turning to her left, Ilaria entered the growth of trees. She wasn't an expert in forest growth, but the region both looked and felt old. If these gnarled giants could walk, they hadn't in centuries. The upper canopy was so thick with leaves from their spreading branches, hardly a flicker of sunlight made it to the floor which, without the solar nourishment, was nearly bare of brambles.

Carefully stepping through the thick carpeting of countless seasons of leaf fall, Ilaria examined the area with both her scanner and her mind. The only living thing she could detect was Thane. Even her telepathic sendings to any Akilli in the area hadn't met with a reply. Relieved, she mentally told Thane that they were alone.

"*Thane?*" she sent again, her concern growing when he didn't reply. "*Thane!*"

Grateful her growing belly wasn't large enough to be a hindrance yet, Ilaria sprinted across the meadow to where her senses told her Thane still was.

"Rill, Thane isn't answering my sendings," she said as she ducked under the ship's carriage.

"He's still on my sensors, but he hasn't moved in several minutes," Rill told her. "I don't detect any lifeforms near him."

Realizing she couldn't just blunder into the dense trees, Ilaria forced herself to stop at the forest edge on the other side of the meadow. Putting her back to the trunk of one of the silent giants, she took several deep breaths in order to think more clearly. Thane was close, maybe fifty yards into the forest. Ilaria swallowed the hard fear that he was probably unconscious as he would have answered her telepathically by now if he had been able.

Poking her head around the tree and seeing only the vine-draped forest, Ilaria pushed away her panic before entering the gloom under the shaded canopy. The only sound was her soft footsteps as she carefully stepped on the natural forest litter of fallen leaves; it was so still not even the green foliage of the high branches rustled in the wind.

Slowly, she came to where Thane should be and found no sign of him. As she examined the area, even the dead leaves carpeting the forest floor were undisturbed showing there hadn't been a struggle. Except for the fact that she could sense his presence near her, there was no trace of him. It was as if he'd literally vanished from the surface of the planet.

"*Above you!*" a mental voice that wasn't Thane's suddenly warned her.

The warning came too late. Ilaria looked up in time to see a huge ball of writhing vines before a dozen of the living tendrils shot down from the limbs of the old trees. As they grabbed her arms and torso, the telepath was hoisted high into the canopy where the vines continued to wrap around her like a spider cocooning its meal.

· CHAPTER 20 ·

The vines didn't stop entwining about Ilaria until she could no longer move. Completely helpless, she felt as if she were still in motion and wondered if she were being transported somewhere else or if it was just the motion of the cocoon swaying at the top of the trees. Her natural fear for self-preservation at her capture turned to terror when she realized she couldn't sense Thane at all now and every mental message she sent to her mentor went unanswered.

"I am with you," the strange voice that had warned her not to shoot Damien said.

"Who are you?" Ilaria asked, but the strange telepath didn't reply. She was comforted that she wasn't entirely alone and that her captors weren't the Fish. Though she still didn't recognize who was speaking to her, she didn't sense anything sinister within the communication. She had twice sensed the augmented psychics intention to kill her so they could harvest her psionic cells, so it was unlikely they would have hidden their murderous intent in a telepathic message meant to calm her.

However, there were other ways to subdue her, Ilaria reasoned as she remembered Anak's warning of the carnivorous plants they'd nearly blundered into. With the sentience of most of the plants on the Wald, they could very well have captured Thane in order to lure her into a trap.

Disgusted with herself that she had fallen for it, Ilaria told herself again not to panic. And remembering what she had done on Haven, she knew she was no longer completely helpless. The only question was how? Teleporting to save Thane from the blast aimed at him hadn't been a conscious thought any more than jumping in front of Sarkin to save him had been.

Both Thane and the unborn Jyn needed her help now if they were to survive and Ilaria was invigorated with hope as she struggled to save them. Neither the augments or carnivorous plants were going to harm Thane; they weren't going to kill her and they were most definitely not going to harm her daughter. At least, not while she had anything to say about it. Suddenly, Ilaria couldn't help but laugh. How different her mental attitude was now from only a short time ago when she'd spontaneously reacted to try and end her life!

Pushing her distracting thoughts aside, Ilaria knew she wasn't going to rescue anyone if she couldn't get out of her cage. Ceasing her struggles against the vines, she closed her eyes in order to concentrate her mind completely on her escape. As an empath and a telepath, she used essentially the same mental forces; it was only how she focused her thoughts that caused her to sense the emotions or thoughts projected from those around her. Teleportation had to be just another way to see and use a different kind of energy.

There, just beyond the edge of her conscious mind, was the aura of the forest. The essence wasn't just encasing her in the ivy cocoon; it was everywhere. Above her, the life force stretched far into the depths of space and below her to the Wald's molten core; it was in the air, in the ground and in the plants.

The sensation wasn't much different than when she touched Thane's mind in their unique wavelength of telepathy. Suspended in the surreal balance of between energy and the corporeal, Ilaria felt as if she were swimming through the reeds in the pond on Haven. Moving with their undulating rhythm, she mentally pushed the barriers aside so she could slip through.

According to Thane, she'd successfully teleported several times; she could do it again. Though it took all of her concentration, she suddenly found herself on the other side of her vine cocoon—only to discover a new challenge to her blossoming mental abilities: she'd managed to teleport herself out of her vine prison, but not back down to the ground and gravity didn't give up its prisoners willingly.

Free now from the cocoon, Ilaria would have fallen if her feet hadn't gotten re-tangled in the vines. The humility of swaying twenty feet above the ground dashed all her triumph at successfully manipulating through the ivy at will. She may not be encased in the vines, but she was still trapped.

At least her hands were free, Ilaria sighed and now had access to the plasma knife she'd confiscated from Damien; however, suspended as she was, she decided against using it. Once she cut her feet loose, it would be a long drop head-first to the forest floor. Assuming the fall didn't break her neck, it would be followed by another long climb back into the trees to rescue Thane from his own cocoon dangling nearby. She might be able to teleport again, but wasn't sure if practicing that unreliable talent again was a good idea.

She decided that up was her preferred direction. Bending as best she could, Ilaria managed to grab the vines ensnaring her feet. Using the sturdy ball of her former prison as a base, she unwrapped her legs and shimmied up the supporting vines and into the trees.

With her own escape finally successful, Ilaria listened for any sign of her captors. When she couldn't detect them nearby, she made her way to Thane. Having learned from her own nearly disastrous attempt, Ilaria opened the Denobian's cocoon from the top. As the vines parted, relief flooded through her as his mental voice broke through the barriers.

"*I hear you!*" she called to him. "*Somehow our sendings can't make it through these vines.*"

"*Thank the stars,*" Thane sent sounding just as relieved.

"I was afraid something had happened to you as well when you didn't answer."

"Something did, which I'll tell you about later. Let's get down from here first."

That was far easier for the Denobian, who merely jumped down from the tangle of vines, than it was for Ilaria who had to climb down the nearest trunk. Fortunately for the young woman, the old trees had lots of sturdy branches to hang on to.

"This planet isn't without its challenges," Ilaria said in relief that Thane was alright. *"What now?"*

"Now we talk," a voice answered in their minds. It wasn't the one who had spoken to her earlier stating she wasn't alone, but it was still very familiar to the telepath. The deep resonance reminded her more of the Akilli they met on the tidal flats or the one on the beach. From Thane's expression, he heard it as well.

"Who are you?" the Denobian asked.

"It's the vines," Ilaria said suddenly recognizing the mental image the Trees had given her when she first came to the Wald. *"They are the Rebe."*

Looking around them, Ilaria saw that they were everywhere. Now that she had named them, the vines were suddenly in motion as they uncoiled themselves from the cocoons that had made up their prison and unwound from the branches of the trees.

"We are the Rebe, the voice of the world you call the Wald," the vines confirmed.

"What do you want from us?" Thane asked.

"To hear you."

"When why imprison us?" Ilaria sent as more vines continued to drop down from the canopy. They may have been free of the cocoons, but as the Rebe stretched down from the branches to the forest floor, she realized they were still their captives as they were completely surrounded by the sentient vines.

"To understand you."

"What is it that you want to understand?" Thane asked, turning around to try and see just how many of them there

were. After a moment, he didn't even try to count as numbers didn't matter; there were just too many to either fight or flee from.

"*What makes you different,*" the Rebe answered.

Ilaria found it hard to believe that this was just some kind of science experiment and their capture was an elaborate ruse to test their intelligence. She was getting mighty tired of being someone else's lab rat. Sensing Thane's own indignation at the thought, she began explaining to the Rebe how she and Thane were mammals. "*We look different from one another because we are different genders and Thane is smaller because of the world he was born to.*"

Her explanation seemed to both amuse and offend the Rebe. "*While they are not dominant species on our world, there are mammals here and we know what you are. We recognize both your genus and sexually polymorphic characteristics. By his size and abilities, we also know Thane is native to a planet with a denser gravity field than your own.*"

"Oh!" Ilaria was chagrined at her own childish summery compared to the Rebe's more scientific one. If they were doing experiments on intelligence, she probably just failed. "Sorry about that."

"*Then what is it you want to know about us?*" Thane asked.

"*Why you are different from others of your kind.*"

Though they still weren't sure they were out of danger, the psychics couldn't help relaxing at the Rebe's statement.

"*Well, that is the question, isn't it?*" Thane quipped. "*We're different because we have abilities other humans lack. You've recognized my physical difference coming from Denobia, but both of us are unlike the rest of the empire because of our mental abilities. Correct me if I'm wrong, but what we call mind-speak or telepathy seems to be a natural way of communicating for you. There are very few humans who can do it. Actually, I can't even do it except with Ilaria. I'm an empath and can sense emotion in most people; Ilaria is both an empath and a telepath.*"

"*This is not what makes you different,*" the Rebe

explained. *"You are unlike the others who do not listen when we speak."*

"That's because they can't hear you," Thane said, telling them again about their telepathy. "Most humans can't detect mind-speak."

Coiling their tendrils in what looked like frustration to the psychics, the Rebe went on to explain what they meant. *"They don't hear us because they don't listen. You spoke for us and they still didn't listen."*

"I understand," Ilaria said to Thane. "The Rebe doesn't mean that humans can't hear them speak, they mean that humans, the miners in particular, don't listen because they choose not to."

"And we do?"

"We're listening now, engaging them in a dialogue in order to understand. Compared to the miners, that makes us very different."

"You are different," the Rebe said again, clearly understanding their spoken dialogue. *"You are different from us and you are different from others. We want to know what makes you run."*

"Um, biology?" offered Thane, grabbing Ilaria's hand in order to pull her behind him as if he expected the Rebe to dissect them.

Ilaria was touched by the gesture, however futile it was. Surrounded on all sides by the Rebe, she was only behind her mentor in the direction he was facing. To her back, the wall of vines could still grab her at any moment if they chose to. As Thane's hand closed about her own, she read his trepidation about their questioning still being some sort of experiment in understanding humans. First, they had to escape from their cocoon prisons and now they would have to run through a maze. Their understanding of humans was incomplete if they expected the Denobian to comply.

"Sociology," the Rebe answered. *"You have abandoned your own kind. Why?"*

Stepping forward, Ilaria answered, *"Because, as you say,*

we are different. Humans without our abilities have chosen to exploit this difference and have murdered people with abilities like ours. We chose to run to be free of them."

The Rebe were silent for so long, Ilaria was certain she'd erred in so bluntly declaring their reason for being on the Wald. The sentient plants of this world had their own problems with humans; why would they care about the politics of a species that murdered their own?

"We know that you returned the Akilli that was taken and we thank you. Why are you still here?"

"Our ship was damaged," Ilaria explained. *"Until we are able to make repairs, we're stranded here."*

"And we also have nowhere else to go," Thane admitted. *"We came here because this is the one place we could think of where they wouldn't find us."*

"You mean this is where they won't think to look for Ilaria or her child."

Realizing the Rebe had them under surveillance since the first moment they stepped onto the mud flats, Ilaria wasn't surprised they knew about Jyn. *"That is what we mean. If I go back, they will kill both me and my daughter."*

Even as she said it, she couldn't help but wonder how that sounded to the Rebe. Other psychics were dying, yet she only escaped to save herself and her baby. Psychs like herself had been abused for years by the empire to where she had only recently stepped in front of a phaser blast to end her own misery, but it wasn't until Thane and now her baby had been threatened that she chose to rebel. Either Sobek or Sarkin would kill them if they turned themselves in now. For an entirely different reason, Ilaria knew she'd try to kill herself again before she let them do it.

Suddenly, all but a few of the Rebe tendrils retracted themselves into the canopy of the trees. Ilaria wasn't entirely sure, but it looked as if the vines were letting them go.

"You are more like us than your own kind," the Rebe said. *"You didn't harm the Azula when they took your food; you didn't harm the other human even though he was here to harm you.*

Instead, you spoke with him and then released him. These are traits we admire. If you are willing to help us, we will give you sanctuary on this planet you call the Wald."

"Now that I know what they are, I don't think we've ever actually spoken with the Trees," Ilaria told Thane later as they discussed their changed situation with Rill. Having officially met them, she began to understand her initial sensations of the Rebe as an encompassing idea that surrounded the Akilli and all life on the Wald when she saw the vines were everywhere. "If you remember, these vines were carried on the Akilli when we met with them on the tide flats and the beach."

"And Anak had one with him when Daneb took him to Haven," Thane said, admiring that the intelligent vines hadn't abandoned the child in his terrifying offworld adventure. "Are they listening now?"

Ilaria was confident that they were. "Absolutely. They want to know if we'll help them, but I'm not sure how."

"I do," Thane frowned. "There's only one reason the Indigenous could possibly need our help."

"The mine," Ilaria nodded. "To purge their world of humans. But we're human; what becomes of us after we do this?"

"What becomes of us if we don't? They're offering us sanctuary if we help them. With both Sobek and Sarkin looking for us, it's more than we could have hoped for."

"Good, because I'm not going back," Ilaria said decisively. "Since we found Zin Tram, everything has changed for me, for us. It never occurred to me that there was another way to live, but I will not let them take my child nor will I allow her to be a slave. If the Wald is ready to fight the empire for their freedom; I'm willing to fight for ours."

To Ilaria's surprise, Rill started laughing. "It's about damn time! And with me on your side, we may just stand a chance."

· CHAPTER 21 ·

The psychic Keepers had always known there was more to Rill than he let on, but neither were aware of how unique their aging ship was. They'd always regarded his capacity for independent thought was the result of his advanced Artificial Intelligence and a programmer with a wry sense of humor. No other AI in the fleet offered counter suggestions to the orders of its pilot the way theirs had a tendency to do, but Rill went beyond just offering suggestions. He'd flown himself into a battle and had fired on organics without the direction of his pilot.

Thane had flown the ship for nearly thirty years and hadn't once considered he was missing a bigger and more tragic story than his own. Rill wasn't AI, the ship explained, but sentient cybernetics.

Born on Arkell as Rillian Fischer, the science prodigy had been apprenticed to the Cybernetics Department of Technology and was one of the youngest students ever to be accepted. Even among the senior staff, the young Rillian had been given nicknames like "the Wizard" or his personal favorite, "Techno-mage."

Of course, his life changed after he took his Psych test and was forever labeled a "peek telepath." Shunned by the masters who were now convinced the boy's genius in cybernetics hadn't been natural, but had been stolen from their own minds, Rillian was refused entrance back into Arkellian society after his psionic training was complete.

"Alayne, Sarkin's great-grandmother was empress at this time and recruited many telepaths. As I wasn't an empath, many of my missions were offworld. On one such mission, I was sent back to Arkell into the cybernetics department as a spy. As I was nearly thirty and hadn't been back since I was a child, Alayne thought no one would recognize me; she was wrong. Both my father and uncle were working there and there was no denying the family resemblance. Rather than face any possibility of being labeled peek sympathizers, they blew my cover and turned me in."

"That's awful," Ilaria said.

"In Janus, that's life," the ship answered. "What choice did they have? The stigma of harboring an In-Valid would have fallen on every member of my family and that's if they weren't summarily executed. Alayne took fewer chances than Sarkin on there being any unregistered psychics in her empire."

Once he realized he was no longer safe on Arkell, Rillian stole a ship and fled the planet with three Arkellian fighters on his tail. A blast hit his undercarriage and he crashed into the moon of Sylas.

Right before the crash, Rillian had managed to transmit the data he'd been sent to gather, but they were never received by Control. "I might have been closer to death than you were, Ilaria, and Alayne might have resorted to giving me the Serum had it been available to her. As it was, her only option to try and retrieve the information I'd gathered was to replace my damaged parts with cybernetic limbs and organs. The operation was partially successful. They cyber-surgeons did save my life, but I couldn't remember my mission. They gave me more surgeries and more implants until there was very little of me left. After eight years of trying, they terminated my bodily functions."

"Only you didn't die," Thane said.

"By this time, I was more machine than man, but it was my knowledge of cybernetics that saved me. My implants were attached to the life support systems in the hospital and I instructed the medics to upload the CPU of my brain implants into an AI system. The surgeons just followed the orders they'd been given without knowing where they came from."

"So, you're a living machine," Ilaria said.

"No," Rill replied. "I think what I am now is a sentient computer. I remember Rillian Fischer, but there's nothing organic of him left."

"And you've kept yourself hidden all these years."

"For the same reasons that, as an empath, Thane has kept his telepathic ability to speak with you a secret," Rill explained. "If the empire knew what we are capable of, they would exploit it. Sobek wouldn't stop to consider Thane's mind-speak as a familial bond between father and daughter because you two are not related. If an empath can mentally join with a telepath once, others could do it too. He would have torn Thane's brain apart in order to use it in his augmented serum. To discover my own sentience, Laran would cybernetically implant a thousand people in order to mentally control her fleet."

"You said when you were human, you were a telepath," Thane said. "Are you still?"

"No," the ship responded. "My psionic abilities were established through my organic brain and, once it died, my telepathy died with it."

Frowning at a sudden thought, Ilaria asked, "Rill, you said you transmitted these files on cybernetics, but they were never received. Do you think it's possible they were intercepted by someone else?"

"Absolutely," Rill affirmed. "I've been listening to transmissions for years trying to pick up chatter, but never heard anything directly related. It wasn't until your own report of your scan of Damien Rey and his near execution that confirmed the information had either been found or buried. Ilaria, forgive me for asking, but tell me again what you read during your liaison with Rey?"

"Well," Ilaria said, the question causing her to flush with embarrassment, "I sensed Rey's emotions spike when I asked about his knowledge of cybernetics and how he could use the translation chips to work out a form of communication with the V'reem. He was excited at the prospect of using his technology on a completely alien species, but there was something about cybernetics he didn't want me to discover."

"And he was shot before you could," Rill finished.

"Were the V'reem involved?" Thane asked.

"Not to my knowledge," Rill said. "We weren't aware of them when I first uncovered my own information, but it does strike me as odd they were killed just before the attempts on Sarkin and Rey."

"I think plots within the empire are the least of our concerns right now," interjected Ilaria. "We're homeless and on the run. We need to survive before we can even think about anything else. I know we have little choice, but I want to help the Rebe."

"The question is how?" Thane asked. "The Rebe are smart and we've already seen a lot of what they can do."

"You realize if we do this, we really are talking treason," Ilaria stated.

"Treason or emancipation. We don't wear chains, but the Empati are the slaves of the Empire and if we fail, they won't shoot us."

With a nod, Ilaria acknowledge that she was well aware of the consequences.

"If we are all in agreement," Rill continued, "there is a way. The gas is the single-most precious resource of the empire. While Sarkin and the Company do have other sources such as Maelstrom, on this planet and this planet alone, it is abundant and readily available in its gaseous state. Rebe," the ship said, suddenly addressing the vines, "while I don't have any doubt that you are capable of destroying the mine, it has occurred to me that you haven't done so. After all this time, why not?"

"Because the humans would return," Ilaria translated

for the ship. "We know they have weapons we can't fight against."

"They got that right," said Thane appreciatively. Though they might not use it for technology, there's nothing lacking in the Rebe's intelligence. If the empire ever gave it a thought, Laran could destroy this planet from space without ever setting foot on the surface.

As she listened, Ilaria's tone became grave. "There's more. The Rebe say the humans have opened another mine that's different from the first one. This place spews a yellow smoke into the air that kills anything it touches."

"They're refining the pure crystal," Thane said, "and we've already seen what that does to a planet."

"We can't let that happen here," said Ilaria.

"No, we can't," the ship agreed. "We also can't stop the mining. Rebe, I have a question: if other psions help save your planet, you will offer them sanctuary?"

"They would be welcome as friends," Ilaria translated.

"And to be clear, the humans who help you will be permitted to stay."

"Yes," came the answer. "All friends are welcome."

"Okay," said Rill. "Then I have a plan. If it works, it'll solve not only the Wald's problem, but ours as well. The only tricky part will be to convince the Rebe to not destroy the gas mine; it must remain intact and functional."

· CHAPTER 22 ·

"*W*hat changed for you?*"* Thane privately asked as he watched the tops of the forest blur below them as Rill flew them closer to the mines. Though the Denobian understood what Rill intended, he wasn't sure he agreed with the part of the sentient AI's plan to separate them: Rill was to fly Thane to the gas mine while the sentient Trees escorted Ilaria to where they were mining the crystal.

Ilaria didn't need Thane to clarify his telepathic question; he knew her desire to go to the crystal mine had just as much to do with her own reasons as it did with helping the Rebe. "*What changed is I'm pregnant. Even if Sarkin allows me to carry my child to term, I will never be allowed to be her mother. And because of the serum, we will be experimented on until there's nothing left of either of us. Whatever Sobek is planning by creating these augments, Sarkin will now know of it if he doesn't already. We already know it's enhancing my own abilities, so what is it doing to a growing fetus?*"

"*At the rate she's growing, you'll give birth months earlier than normal. I hate to say it, but Jyn could die of old age before she's ten.*"

"She... could." Ilaria swallowed hard as she acknowledged that horrifying possibility. *"But however long she lives, she'll be one of the strongest psions ever recorded. Either Sarkin, Sobek, or the Fish will harvest both our cells before they are through with us and then they will turn around and continue to do this to other Paths."*

"I know you're right," Thane was thoughtful. *"Tell me again why didn't you shoot Damien when I told you to?"*

"I thought you changed your mind. You told me to shoot, but then I heard you say 'don't'."

Thane smiled, *"I thought that's what happened. Listen, I've had twenty years to think about this, so I'm pretty sure I'm right. You and I are not related, but we are bonded; I am not telepathic, yet I can speak with you. I believe this to be the same with your child. You are telepathically bonded with Jyn and, on some level, she is aware of what is happening to you. You didn't hear me tell you not to shoot Damien, you heard Jyn telling you not to shoot her father."*

Ilaria didn't want to admit it, but she knew Thane was right. If the Jyn was indeed as strong a telepath as they suspected, she would almost certainly be bonded on some level with Damien. No wonder she hadn't been able to pull the trigger!

Continuing, Thane sent, *"I also think on some level, Damien is also aware. He sensed her enough to follow us here and didn't kill us... or at least stopped trying. And you both heard the name J'rey."*

"Yeah, I know," Ilaria sighed, not wanting to admit the truth.

But neither she nor Thane could deny it, either. According to Arkellian customs, Jyn would be called 'J'rey' within the family and both she and Damien telepathically heard the name after Sobek had enhanced her cells. Jyn was bonded, not only with her mother, but her father as well.

After Rill landed in a clearing a couple of miles from the Gas mine, Thane met with four of the Akilli at the edge of the forest near the pit. As he studied the shattered landscape, he knew the region would bear the scars for centuries before time and erosion closed the gaping hole, if it ever did. The area above the mine consisted of flat wetlands stretching for several miles before rising into the foothills of a mountain range where a small river carved its path through the ravines. Even at this distance, Thane could tell from the bleached ring marks in the bedrock that the water level had once been much higher. He guessed that years ago, the water had been diverted after some trees had fallen during the seasonal monsoon storms and created a natural dam forming a lake in the high hills. Once the lake had filled to its capacity, most of the water had diverged from its original path and now carved a different channel to the sea. All that remained of a once mighty river was a mere trickle of a stream.

As he continued to examine the area further, Thane could understand why the Rebe would need a human's help. Severed stumps and the blackened skeletons of once mighty giants had been left to rot in the dead forest above the mine. Flamethrowers and chainsaws kept the flora population cowed under the might of the Gas Company, but to keep the Indigenous away from the mine itself, the humans had gone old-school by salting the ground around the complex. The Trees edged as close as they could to the barren soil, but couldn't advance down into the mine itself.

But while the invaders had their toxic arsenal, with time and patience, the Rebe had powerful, yet underrated weapons. And with their new alliance with the renegade psychics, their patience had paid off; the time of waiting was over.

Keeping himself low to the ground so he wouldn't stand out against the skyline, Thane peered over the edge. The gaping chasm of the mine descended several hundred feet below him. On the pit floor, excavators the size of commercial starships pulverized the rocks as they sifted through the debris and dust for every trace of the rare mineral. There were easily fifty people in plain sight mining the gas from the surface; he mentally doubled that number to be safe. It was going to be tricky for him to get inside.

Allying with the Indigenous had been a godsend the Denobian hadn't planned, but even with the Trees and the element of surprise on their side, what Rill intended wouldn't be easy especially now that they had two separate mines to contend with.

It had taken several hours for them to convince the Rebe Rill's plan was the only way as they had more to contend with than just the mine. While it was to their advantage, they hadn't planned on defecting. Rill had attempted to deflect their intentions, but there were too many in the empire who would be after them to assume the Wald would remain a sanctuary for any of them and, for all their faults, the Royals weren't idiots. The cyborg Niegan would have monitored their movements from the Wald to Maelstrom and from Maelstrom to Haven; Sobek would have been well aware of their failure to go to his hospital. Before they'd liberated Anak and departed from Haven, Rill had informed Thane he'd intercepted several communications regarding updates on Ilaria's status.

Regardless of who was involved with the murdered psychics, the attack on the *Celest*, the serum or their own near capture, the empire was aware that they were missing. If by some miracle no one knew they were on the Wald, that would quickly change once Rill's master plan was put into play. Hopefully by then, they'd have more than just the Indigenous plants on their side.

If the plan should fail and either one of them fell back into the empire's hands, Sarkin's Array would force the truth about Rill from their minds. Maybe it was too anthropomorphic of Thane to think that the ship could actually die, but he'd always thought of Rill as a person long before he knew of his organic past. As far as the Denobian was concerned, if you thought and acted like an organic, it didn't matter what your body was made up of. For all he knew in the advancements of cybernetics, there might be more AIs like Rill out there and that wasn't a comforting thought.

Creeping forward on his stomach in order to look further over the edge of the pit, Thane's situation became more complicated when he saw Daneb down below. After speaking with the foreman at length after Tram's discovery, he was the one miner here who would recognize him on sight and not because of is Denobian heritage.

Turning to the Rebe, Thane said, *"I won't be able to get inside the facility without being seen. Is it possible for your people to create a distraction?"*

After assuring him they could, Thane waited for any noise in the forest that would cause enough alarm to bring the miners up out of the pit. When it came, he was just as surprised as the workers.

Thane had no idea if the Rebe had been down in the pit for years waiting for their moment to strike or simply materialized in response to his request, but suddenly the entire floor was writhing with the sentient vines. At the same moment, all around him the walking Akilli emerged from the skeletal forest as if every tree in the vicinity had suddenly transplanted itself to the edge of the mine.

Before any of the panicked humans below could register their surprise or call for flamethrowers, vines buried under the dirt grabbed Daneb's ankles and pulled his feet from under him. Landing on his back, the force of the impact knocked the air from the foreman's lungs. More vines began wrapping themselves around the knees of his fleeing crew, tripping them as they were sent sprawling into the dirt.

Recognizing his chance, Thane scurried down the steep embankment and into the chaos while half a dozen twenty-foot-tall Akilli latched onto the excavators with their strong limbs and tipped the massive machines over.

Seeing the Trees surrounding the rim of the mine, Daneb finally managed to holler out and order. In response, a group of armed soldiers swarmed out of the complex and took aim at the attacking forest. Thane noticed they weren't armed with flamethrowers, but wicked looking plasma rifles that did their own damage to the natives. Bark and branches exploded from the Akilli sentries while the plasma blast continued burning through their wooden bodies.

Immediately in response to the new weaponry, a cloud of black specks descended on the troops, robbing them of both vision and sound. Disoriented, one of the soldiers blindly fired a round into the attacking swarm of insects, the resulting blast taking down three of his own comrades and two of Daneb's crew who had the misfortune of being in the line of fire. The radiating heat of the shot also fried several dozen of the little midges answering the call of the Rebe that it was time to fight for the Edu, but the death of the bugs went unnoticed as the humans flailed their arms helplessly at the rest of the swarm.

The distraction was more than Thane could have hoped for as both vines and midges had no difficulty identifying friend from foe. The plants didn't cease their attack until Thane had entered the complex unhindered by the chaos outside.

"What about the salt?" Thane asked as he sidestepped a new group exiting the main building. "I thought you couldn't get down into the mine."

"Time and patience," the Rebe sent back. "Though it is poison to us, the salt is soluble and with every rainfall, more of it leached downstream. By keeping up the illusion of a barrier, the humans became complacent. Unfortunately, they won't make that mistake twice and they'll re-salt this entire area."

"Not for a while they won't," Thane told them. "Nobody keeps that much salt on hand. By the way... humans become complacent? Ilaria and I are also human, you know."

"Not to us," the Rebe informed him. "You said yourself that your abilities set you apart from your own kind. To the Edu of the Wald, you are psions."

"Psions, I like the sound of that," Thane smiled. Since the time he took the test, he'd been labeled one thing or another to identify him as something other than human: peek, path, Psych, Empati, In-Valid. But psion had a ring to it that still set them apart from the rest of the empire without making it sound as if they were less. It was still just a label and the Rebe weren't the first to use it, but the empath knew that from then on, that's what they were—psions.

Now that he was in, Thane's next challenge was looking

like he belonged. Fortunately, several things went in his favor, the most important being the distracted miners weren't looking for a two-legged mammal infiltrating their complex as they scurried about trying to assess the damage and understand what had made the formerly placid Indigenous attack.

Another thing was that Thane discovered he wasn't the only Denobian on the premises. It made sense that the mining Company would make use of Citizens able to jump several times their own body length, but it did give the outsider one less obstacle to avoid.

The last one was that the Rebe had done their job well. After the attack, the Trees had retreated back into the forest, becoming invisible to the humans once more. The only evidence of the destruction they had left were pieces of damaged leaves and bark scattered around the pit and three overturned excavators.

Daneb was infuriated when he was told it would take several days for the cranes large enough to right the diggers to be ready. The foreman's mood was so fowl, underlings and management alike kept well out of his way.

Thane could sense Daneb's mood sour even more as he ordered his men to pursue the Trees into the woods. Many of them halted, refusing to venture past the edge of the trees, insisting this forest hadn't been there the day before. This area had all been wet swamplands, full of bugs and mud, but no trees. The ones who did brave the woods found no sign of the Trees that could move. They saw more of the vines high in the canopy, but none of them grabbed their legs or pulled them under.

Making himself appear useful as he joined crews doing busy-work, Thane was amused when the Rebe told him the miners' caution was making them clumsy. As they continued to stare at the vines in the branches above the rim, the underling miners constantly tripped over the scattered equipment and their own feet.

Silently, Thane warned the Rebe not to underestimate them. *"That attack won't make them leave; all we've done is piss them off."*

"It wasn't intended to make them leave," they answered. *"As the humans say, it was just a warning shot letting them know we're here and aren't entirely defenseless."*

"While the distraction worked, is that a good thing? Daneb will get out his flamethrowers and start burning every tree he sees to ash just as soon as he gets his diggers turned upright again."

"He will have other things to think about before that happens," the Rebe told him ominously.

Thane had to pause in order to collect his thoughts. The Rebe sounded confident that Daneb wouldn't get the opportunity to use his fire arsenal, but the empath was well aware that any fire the humans could get started would burn long enough and hot enough that it would be more than a match for wooden people. The water pooled in low-lying pockets leaving the higher ground to form walkable, dry land. On these raised areas of vegetation, the plants were much dryer; it wouldn't take much of a spark to ignite this living tinderbox.

Swallowing his trepidation in order to trust that the Rebe knew what they were doing, Thane reminded himself that in just a few minutes, they'd halted all mining with the humans barely managing to get a shot off. Of course, the humans were taken by surprise today. They were on alert now and wouldn't be surprised again.

Aware they were now under assault; the miners would be indiscriminate killers. With their distraction to get Thane inside, everything that happened from that moment on wouldn't be interpreted just a series of unfortunate events; they were now at war.

The thought that he'd just helped start a war caused the Denobian to pause before his rational mind reassessed their reality. No, Thane reasoned. He hadn't started a war; he merely chosen a side.

· CHAPTER 23 ·

Creeping to the edge of the crystal mine, Ilaria wasn't entirely sure she liked Rill's plan. The Rebe joined her on the ridge overlooking the noxious complex refining the mephitis crystal, so at least their unexpected allies had welcomed them here.

Not without conditions, she reasoned, though she could hardly blame them. With the advent of humans, their lives had been permanently altered and not for the better. They needed the psions' help to rid themselves of the pestilence. For the possibility of a safe place to raise her daughter free of the grip of the empire, it was a chance she'd take.

"Thane," she sent, *"I'm at the crystal mine."*

"Excellent," Thane answered. *"We're nearing the gas mine. What do you see?"*

Unaware she was mimicking her mentor, Ilaria kept herself low to the ground so she wouldn't be visible on the skyline. Though drastically scaled down in size, the mine followed the same configuration as the Maelstrom prison with a network of offices sitting above the refineries, so she knew that underground were the network of caves where workers extracted the mephitis from the rock and separated the impurities before sending the quasi-crystal to be smelted into the precious hyperfuel. Though the Rebe had told her this refinery was only a few years old, the sickly yellow slag had already coated the buildings and nearby stationary forest. Unable to move, these trees were already dead from disease as the acids bore into their wooden trunks.

"A small-scale Maelstrom," Ilaria answered. *"It's already killed anything that can't get out of its way. I don't sense many workers; maybe a hundred."*

"Be cautious," Thane warned her. *"The augments are more difficult for us to sense. You may be looking at a lot more than a hundred."*

"Understood."

Undulating like snakes, six Rebe tendrils slithered from the decaying forest out to where Ilaria lay prone to surveil the mine.

"We are unable to see inside this place," they told her.

When Ilaria didn't understand what they meant, the Rebe informed her that in the larger mine where Thane was, they were *aware*. When the psion still didn't grasp what that meant, the plants explained that ever since the empire had arrived on their world, they'd slowly altered the landscape in order to make the area around the mine more humid. With the increased heat and moisture, edu in the forms of mold and fungus were able to grow inside the building complex and through this, they'd been able to listen. They were *aware* inside the mine.

Incredulous, Ilaria couldn't help but laugh at the Rebe's ingenuity. *"Let me get this straight: you terraformed your own world in order to grow spores inside the mine to use as spies?"*

"Not just spies, but weapons" the plants confirmed. *"But this section is new; we haven't had time to infiltrate this area."*

"Thane, did you get that?" Ilaria asked. *"The Rebe have eyes and ears inside the gas mine, but not inside the smelting plant."*

"I did," the Denobian replied. *"Be extra careful; you don't have the backup I've got here."*

"Thane, we have another problem," Ilaria said, suddenly catching an empathic spike. *"I don't think all of the Maelstrom prisoners were given over to Sobek. I'm sensing at least a quarter of the people here might be psychics... natural ones as I can read them. They're giving off the same pulses of misery I felt at the prison."*

"That's not good," Thane sent. *"Can you confirm this?"*

"Not without telepathically asking them and they'd actually have to be mind-speakers to hear me. The only way I can be sure without giving us up is to go down there and touch someone."

"That's really not good," sent Thane, then mentally went silent as he calculated his private thoughts. *"I'm sorry, but I don't think you have time."*

"I'd be even sorrier if I found out later there were a couple dozen Psychs down there and I didn't help them," Ilaria told him. *"Once this plan of Rill's is set in motion and they evacuate, they won't be taking our kind with them."*

Against his better judgment, Thane had to agree. Valid peeks had some value to the empire, but with an entire Maelstrom prison full of replacements, In-Valids would be as expendable as a forgotten wrench.

Turning to the Rebe, Ilaria asked them if they could get her a set of workman's coveralls and a breathing mask. Assuring her that they could, Ilaria waited while nothing seemed to be happening. She was about to ask if the vines understood that she needed these items right away when two weasel-like edu loped up the hill dragging the affects with them.

"They keep them in a room just inside the main complex," the creatures informed her. As workers were taking them on and off all the time, they didn't even notice when they took them.

As she listened to them excitedly relate the cunning of their theft, Ilaria realized they weren't animals, but an evolved form of flora. It was then that she remembered that fauna, especially mammals, were rare on the Wald. No wonder the edu were all mentally in tune with one another! The plants could communicate on a frequency beyond what even the psionic humans could. The entire world had been made aware of what they were about to do and had joined together for battle.

Thanking the plant-weasels, Ilaria put the coveralls on and was grateful the loose clothing hid her pregnancy. With the serum rapidly accelerating the gestation, she guessed she might only have a few more weeks before she was too heavy to be of help to anyone. Taking a deep breath to focus on what she had to do now, she pushed the worry aside. If all went according to Rill's plan, this would long be over before she was ready to give birth.

Though there wasn't anyone who could possibly recognize her, Ilaria was relieved that the breathing mask the weasels had pilfered covered her entire face. Even up on the ridge, the slag fumes had burned her eyes and she didn't want to breathe in more than she had to. Relaxing in the fact that, not only was no one here was looking for her, this was also the place people tried to break out of rather than into.

Carefully making her way down the slope, she felt off balance as she descended to the floor of the mine. Under her feet, she could feel the slight tremors as borers drilled through the rock below for pockets of the precious crystal.

Sliding down the loose gravel to the pit floor, Ilaria was relieved that the half dozen workers were so intent on finishing their tasks, they were oblivious to her arrival. Nearby were thick pipes stuck deep into the ground which she assumed siphoned gas from the network of caves below them. A young man to her right was struggling to carry several canisters. Seeing him as her best opportunity, Ilaria came around the corner of the refinery and deliberately walked right into him. As the canisters hit the ground in a loud, metallic crash, the other workers merely glanced at the two before going about their business without even offering to help. Such was life at the mine.

"Sorry!" Ilaria said, "I am so sorry. I think there's a leak in my mask. My eyes are burning!"

"That happened to me once," the youth said. It was hard to tell behind his own mask, but he looked to be in his late teens or early twenties at the oldest. "The acids in the air can erode the seals; here," and without another word, he reached to adjust Ilaria's mask. There was an increase in the pressure and she felt the mask tighten to her face.

"Thank you!" she said.

"Even with the tighter fit, if your eyes are stinging, you should go inside and rinse them. People have gone blind working the gas."

"I will," Ilaria promised, "but first let me help you with these. None of us want to be out here longer than we have to."

She sensed that the boy was about to protest her help, but then gratefully changed his mind. Since this idiot greenhorn had caused the mess in the first place, he'd be inside in double time once she helped restack the canisters

Ilaria was just as pleased to help. With the young miner rattling on to a sympathetic ear about everything someone new to the mine should know, including the essentials of protecting your eyes against the toxic fumes, the telepath had several opportunities to read him during the casual contact as their hands touched while they stacked the empty containers.

"These will be filled tomorrow," he was telling her. "Of course, since we only have a small refinery, these are only collected once a month. The cargo at the big mine goes out every week."

Now that they were "friends", Ilaria found it was harder to get his flow of information to stop. With their job finished, he was walking back into the complex, fully expecting Ilaria to follow.

Touching the worker confirmed that she'd been right in that Psychs brought in from Maelstrom were being forced to labor in the deep mines. Determined not to abandon them, Ilaria glanced up at the ridge before following the youth inside.

But the Rebe had the last word. As Ilaria stepped through the door, she felt a tendril of the sentient vine wrap around her ankle.

· CHAPTER 24 ·

Now that he was in, Thane was able to observe Daneb from a unique perspective he never expected as he ranted to any person unfortunate enough to be within earshot. The recent outrage right outside his doors caused the foreman to nurse his former grievances. Apparently, Daneb was still livid about being dragged not once, but twice by those damn tree people. And then he had to stand there and take orders from a peek Denobian!

By Daneb's definition, all Denobians projected a superior smugness because of their low-gravity agility. Oh, being able to jump twenty to thirty feet in a go would be a handy skill to have, especially trying to get around the Pit and through the caves, but not at the way the planet's gravity had squashed its inhabitants down to half the size of a normal person. They were like toads compared to normal humans.

He'd always been wary of the mind-speak peeks like the one that short empath had called in. Those telepaths were real peeks and not just hoodoo psychics that read someone's emotions expressions like some kind of living lie detector. Once she had shown up, (unescorted and in her own shuttle!) not one of those Keepers, peek or Normal, had bothered with his account of the body or his humiliation at being carted off like a bag of dirty laundry.

That woman had also been the one on Haven when he brought that tree person in for questioning. Once again, she did her little mind trick and no one cared that he, *he!* had discovered more bodies *and* brought them a witness.

Amused that he was hiding out right under Daneb's nose, Thane's enjoyment soured quickly when he learned Torquil was also on the premises. According to the miner's monotonous monologues, even the emperor had had enough of these two renegade peeks who, apparently, had gone missing along with the tree-man Daneb had personally brought to Sarkin for questioning. Suspecting they'd take him to the Wald, Sarkin had sent Torquil himself along with a garrison of Keeper troops to recover them. Thane quickly sent a telepathic message to Ilaria while the Rebe tendril tucked discretely under his jacket sent the same warning to the plants to be on the alert for humans searching the woods.

"They are aware," his vine told him, adding that the Trees will keep them away from Rill.

At least the Rebe knew, Thane thought as he slipped into the miners' control room. Trying to hold back his concern that Ilaria hadn't answered his warning, he reasoned that other things were holding her attention and panicking at her silence wouldn't do either of them any good.

Making his way inside the control room, Thane learned that all was not well between the miners and the additional Keepers as each blamed the other for the recent attack by the plants. The mining crew were insisting it had been due to the arrival of the garrison as they'd never had trouble with the natives before while Torquil had the audacity to lay the blame solely on Daneb. Had it not been for his incompetence, the trees wouldn't have entered into the pit in the first place. The controllers became incensed as Daneb had been out there with them and nearly dragged underground by those damn tree roots while Torquil remained safe inside while his supposedly highly trained troopers only managed to shoot their own soldiers while simultaneously taking out half of Daneb's men.

Technically, they were both right, Thane decided. Intent on finding fault with anyone but themselves, neither side noticed the Denobian log into a computer to send his message. And the Rebe were correct as well. The humans had been caught off guard, but now they were ready and armed with not only weapons, but with new orders allowing them to shoot on sight. Daneb didn't care that Torquil wanted the AWOL peeks captured alive. His own men were ready to burn down the forest with flamethrowers if he had to and if the damned peeks, or Torquil's troops were in the way, then that was just too bad. They didn't have to deal with either the Company or Admiral Laran when hyper-fuel deliveries were late or under quota.

Despite the high anxiety of so many people around him, Thane still felt Daneb. He was close by, probably sitting at his desk in his office. The foreman, tapping into the gut instincts most creatures had when it came to self-preservation, was acutely aware the attack wasn't over. The empath sensed Daneb slowly relax as he assured himself that he alone was in control on this alien world; after all, humans had been a presence on the Wald for more than eighty years and their flamethrowers had extinguished the first and only rebellion these flora-evolved *plantoids* had dared raise against them. The attack today had been a surprise, but what could these trees really do when the flesh and blood wielded their only mortal enemy?

As Thane began working his way back to the exit, he noticed that now that the crisis was over and everyone was relaxing, he was beginning to get noticed. As large as the gas operation was, it was small enough for the workers to become suspicious that Thane didn't belong. Even if they didn't know the names or shared after hours drinks with their crewmates, faces became familiar and Thane's wasn't one they saw day in and day out every single day. He had to get out and soon.

There was another flurry of activity. No one was running or screaming as they had been when the Rebe overturned their equipment, but Thane could feel the growing agitation like the sensation of beachcombers mesmerized by the building wave of an incoming tsunami—they were terrified of something ominous, but unable to react it swept over them.

"Sir!"

Thane turned as a man entered Daneb's office. His tone clearly signaling it was the tsunami: don't panic, but flee for your life!

"What now?" Thane heard the foreman's dangerous growl.

"Sir, you need to come and see this."

Swept along in a new wave when the miners poured out of their work areas to see what the new catastrophe was, Thane had no choice but to ride the flow of people into the kitchens with them. The agitated man showed Daneb an area strewn with cans and packages. Half a dozen cooks were hauling food out of the storage rooms onto tables so others could examine them with hand-held safety scanners.

"We noticed an unnatural odor from the first package we opened and just thought it had spoiled. It doesn't happen often, but it does happen so that wasn't unusual. But everything we've opened in storage is contaminated. Old supplies, fresh, it doesn't matter. As soon as it hits the air, it seems to rot before our eyes."

"Check the water," Daneb ordered through clinched teeth.

The nearest worker to the water tank ran his scanner over the casing, his shoulders sagging with relief as the lights lit up green. "It's clean!"

Unsatisfied, Daneb narrowed his eyes and barked, "Fill a glass and check again!"

The workman's mouth opened in horror as the lights now winked red.

"It's in the air," Daneb growled. "Scan what you have already opened and identify it. It's probably a spore or fungus. Once you've found it, sterilize this room. Nobody eats anything until they've scanned it first; no one drinks anything until it's been filtered. Is that understood?"

"Yes, sir!" the kitchen crew responded simultaneously while bumping into each other to obey.

"Sir!" a new worker panted as he entered the kitchen. Whether he was out of breath from running from his post or trying to navigate through the tide of panicked onlookers, Thane wasn't sure.

"What?" Daneb demanded.

"It's the Trees, sir… they're back."

Daneb had no trouble making his way through the crowded hall as every person flattened himself against the wall to give the furious foreman room to pass. Relieved they were heading in the direction he wanted to go, Thane followed in the flow of the mob. Once outside, the Denobian easily slipped away and jumped to the lip of the mine in two leaps. With one last jump, he was in the canopy of the Trees just as the informant was pointing to the ring of Akilli surrounding the edge of the mine.

From his vantage point, Thane saw the extent of the damage the vines had done. One digger had been flipped completely onto its roof while two others rested on their sides. It would take them a while to get them righted before production could resume at full capacity and even longer now that Daneb also had to contend with the food spoilage in the kitchens. Without food or water, humans wouldn't be here for long.

"Something's wrong," Thane sent to the vines. "Daneb should be more concerned about the attack… that little sneak!"

"What is it?" the Rebe wanted to know.

"It's the second mine," he told the vines. "He doesn't want to inform the Company of the attack because he doesn't want to risk them discovering the crystal mine. He's been building that on his own!"

"We don't understand the significance."

"I expect not," Thane said. "According to the empire, the Company has the rights to any gas they mine, which they sell for hyper-fuel throughout the realm with Laran and the Stellar Navy getting the largest portion of the contract. It's a technicality, but *by refining the crystal, Daneb is essentially stealing from the Company, but doing it this way, he can pass psychic honesty scans when they ask about gas mine productions. He did it the same thing to us when I sensed he was truthful that Zin Tram didn't disappear from here."*

Thane stopped explaining when the Rebe clearly didn't understand, but he made a mental note to make sure they kept a closer eye on the shrewd foreman. The man could not only embezzle raw crystal, but also refine it while avoiding mental evaluations from the Company and two of the strongest psychics the Empati. In another few years, Daneb would've rotated out of the Wald mine and retired from the Company with enough of his own hyper-fuel to live like a king. Now that the Indigenous were sabotaging his plans, he was going to be a very dangerous man.

When Daneb eyed the indigenous Trees ringing the lip of his dig, Thane sensed the foreman wasn't going down without a fight. The flamethrowers he had on hand would make the natives retreat back into the mud quick enough and he'd place an order for salt... lots of salt. Enough to make sure not even a weed could take root up within a hundred yards of the mine for the next century.

But he wasn't just looking at the Trees; Daneb was scrutinizing the entire area surrounding the mine and coming to the realization that the plants really were smarter than he'd given them credit for. The area had always been a muddy swamp in the five years since he'd been foreman, but the records of his predecessors made no mention of having to drain water whenever they expanded the Pit. He'd assumed the area had probably been flooded by some water rodent backing up a local stream, but he hadn't as yet been able to find the source. Thane knew that draining this stinking swamp had just been added to his list of showing this world who was boss. When he was finished, only the humans would be alive... once he had his fortune in refined gas, he really didn't care if they survived, either.

Though Thane could feel Daneb's outrage, it wasn't until

the foreman went back inside that he knew he'd been spotted.

"*Get me out of here,*" he warned the Rebe as emotions spiked again inside the complex. Only this time, it wasn't the fear or panic of a new wave of attack from the sentient plants, but the contained excitement of a pack of hunters stalking their prey.

Immediately, the Akilli complied as they bolted into the forest with the armed Keepers following as quickly as they could. The trained soldiers didn't have nearly as much difficulty with the terrain as the miners and quickly scaled the steep walls of the pit to follow the retreating Trees into the dense woods.

The advantage of the Trees was the humans couldn't tell the difference between the sentient Akilli and the unmoving foliage whose roots gripped down into the earth for hundreds of feet. Their disadvantage was that the soldiers didn't care what their weapons burned when they spewed tongues of flame over everything that lived.

Even if the sentients survived the fire, once the flames charred the forest to ash, all the humans would be able to spot anything that moved for miles.

· CHAPTER 25 ·

No sooner than the peeks were gone, Daneb turned with renewed fury to his men.

"I gave orders that Denobian was to be shot on sight!"

"We tried to, sir, but all our weapons wouldn't fire."

"Not all of them," Daneb seethed as the air above the mine began to reflect the orange mixture of both flames and smoke.

"No, sir. The flamethrowers the Keepers brought with them didn't malfunction. Everything else has been choked with some kind of mold."

"This has gone far enough," Daneb growled. "I want every weapon cleaned and inspected. Use that disinfectant we put on the walls; kill everything that can grow in this humidity. That's how they're getting in. Sterilize this place from top to bottom; I don't want to find a single spore in the air. Move it!"

Like rats abandoning an exposed nest, workers scattered to obey. The mold was everywhere, but mostly along the joins of the walls and floors, almost invisible and never growing in noticeable locations. Every habitable location in the complex was infected with mildew, except each area seemed to be inhabited with a different variety. Daneb could only assume each was an attempt at a different form of sabotage.

Once he had made sure there wouldn't be a single square inch of the complex unscoured, Daneb demanded to know where Torquil was.

With knowledge that would only have infuriated the mining foreman even more, the Peace-Keepers hadn't been as unaware of their compromised weapons as they had discovered the growing mold during their routine morning inspection. The blasters were immediately cleaned and Torquil's Keepers had reported the mold had begun to grow back again. Without knowing the exact solution to kill the virulent spores, the guns would have to be cleaned right before they were intended to be used and then they might only get one or two shots off before they were too corroded to fire properly. Having no other option, Torquil ordered his men to stand down and observe the renegade peeks when they came. Everyone had a weakness and he would surly find theirs.

"Torquil!" Daneb shouted as he entered the room.

"Yes?" the Admiral said calmly as he turned to acknowledge the foreman's entry.

"Where the hell were your troops? So far, the only damage you've managed to inflict is on our own people and on top of that, your peeks got away!"

"Calm yourself, Daneb. We noticed the mold during our morning inspection, something your own men would have discovered had they followed proper weapons protocol."

"Don't you dare put this on me," said Daneb, his eyes flashing dangerously. "If you had kept better watch on your peeks, they wouldn't be here in the first place. What's the idea of letting them gallivant across the galaxy unchecked anyway? If my understanding is correct, these two even have their own ship!"

It was Torquil's turn to become dangerous. "Be careful you don't overstep yourself, *foreman*, or your corporation might become aware of the raw crystals in the caverns below us."

"Are you threatening me?" Daneb demanded, but he

couldn't help a spasmodic swallow.

"Not at all," Torquil said giving Daneb a placid smile. "Just letting you know where we both stand. For your information, the two Empati were here on orders and crashed due to damage after an attack. Not exactly negligence on the part of the Keepers. It is what happened after we lost contact with them that concerns us."

"Oh? And what was that?"

"That doesn't concern you. What does concern you is this facility and how you intend to resist their next attack. These Indigenous florae are more intelligent and resourceful than you anticipated and have clearly been planning this for a while."

"I think your peeks need the majority of the blame. None of this happened until they riled up the natives."

"Nonsense. Take a look at this area. Only a few years ago, this ecosystem was both dryer and cooler; now it's a hot, humid environment most conductive for molds and fungus. The Indigenous infiltrated your complex ages ago and were biding their time for the right moment. Admittedly, I believe Thane and Ilaria were their moment and we'll deal with them in time, but time is the one thing you've underestimated here. Most flora-evolved species are long-lived compared to humans. They have both time and patience on their side."

"Time to do what?"

"My dear, Daneb, haven't you been listening? Time to terraform their own world in order to eradicate the invading vermin... that would be us, by the way. In just over a day they have spoiled your food, contaminated your water, and destroyed your equipment. If I were you, I'd be worried about what they intend for tomorrow."

"We're already working on it."

"With your flamethrowers? Considering what happened today, I wish you luck with that. And in case you hadn't yet noticed, they've already put the fire out."

"At least we're doing something," Daneb spat. "We've checked the equipment and it's clean. What have you been doing?"

"We're already doing it. These 'peeks', as you call them, have tracking devices embedded in their communication implants. They have a lair nearby and my men are already working at locating it."

"Well, good luck with that."

"Thank you," said Torquil. Giving the foreman a serene smile, he turned his back on the outraged miner.

· CHAPTER 26 ·

s this going to work?" Thane asked Strom, the tree he was hiding in.

"It already has worked," came the answer. *"They're following the track we left and the Akilli will lead them in one big circle right back to where they started. They've been changing positions so they won't realize they've passed a place more than once until they're back at the mine."*

"Isn't this the same move you used on Damien?"

"Indeed, it is. Simple plans are often the best."

"Good lord!" Thane exclaimed suddenly. *"That's Meeka. Last time I saw her was two years ago."*

"We don't know who that is," Strom said.

"She's just someone I've worked with in the past," Thane shrugged as he remembered the efficient, if unimaginative young woman. Meeka didn't have a psychic cell in her body but had been good at asking excellent questions that had allowed the empath to sift through conflicting emotions in order to uncover the truth. Watching her pass beneath his Tree, Thane wondered how she ended up with an assignment on the Wald. His mind entertained the scenario that she probably slept with

the boss' daughter. No, that didn't fit, Thane countered to himself as Torquil wouldn't care. Maybe the boss then. Torquil did prefer to keep his lovers at a distance.

But that didn't fit, either. Thane was almost sure he'd seen the Commander when he infiltrated the mine. He frowned as Meeka disappeared into the forest, sensing her spark dwindle the farther away she moved. He'd *seen* Torquil, but the empath hadn't *sensed* him. Torquil was a normal human; there should be *something* that registered with his psionic abilities. It nagged him that there was an ever growing number of people he couldn't detect psychically: the augmented psychics, Laran... Sobek. There was something about them that blocked his abilities, but Thane couldn't quite place his finger on it.

Thane was interrupted from his musings when he sensed the Keepers backtracking to his location.

"We thought they were returning to the Pit, but then they separated," the Rebe told him apologetically. *"Half are determined to return here; the others are heading north towards the crystal mine."*

Alarmed, Thane replied *"They know we're here! Somehow they're tracking us."*

In a graceful backflip, Thane leapt from the limb he was hiding on and onto an adjacent Akilli waiting nearby. As soon as the Denobian landed, the tree took off running deeper into the swamp where it would be harder for the Keepers to follow.

All of the soldiers turned when the Akilli ran into the marsh and gave chase. Though the humans couldn't match the speed of the fleeing Tree, they persisted in maintaining the same direction. The Akilli did their best to block their path or tripping the Keepers with their roots as they passed and, even when the Trees aligned so close together they formed a wall so tightly packed the Keepers couldn't pass between them, it didn't deter them.

Meeka raised her arm. At her signal, one of the Keepers raised his weapon, the flames igniting the bark of the Akilli barricade. With their trunks on fire, the Trees had no choice but to scatter into the forest in search of the standing pools that would extinguish the agonizing blaze. Now that their path was open, Meeka glanced at a small machine and motioned the Keepers through the open gap.

"The Akilli failed to stop them," the Rebe told the Denobian. "They have a machine which tells them where you are."

"It's a scanner," Thane informed the Rebe, "but I don't know what it's reading. Maybe my body heat. Rebe, I don't want to put your people in danger, but are there any other warm-blooded animals in the area that might be able to distract them? If the devices are registering heat, they won't be able to distinguish me from other mammals."

After assuring him there were, Thane waited, but the attempt failed as they held their course. Either the animals were too small to fool the humans or their machines were reading something else. Thane was still ahead of the Keepers, but without further help from the Trees, it was only a matter of time before they caught up to him.

One way for his heat signature to be blocked would be for the vines to encase him in another cocoon, but Thane didn't suggest it; he'd rather fight them.

The Rebe had other ideas. As if anticipating his thoughts, the reacted by joining together in the branches with him, the thick woody tendrils shielding him from anything who could see him from the ground. "We've made sure they can't see you," the Rebe told him.

"Thank you, but they still know I'm here," Thane sent only to sense the Keepers getting closer. "That device they're holding is still tracking me."

"You've been on our world for several days now," the vines commented. "Why haven't they tried to locate you before now?"

"That is an excellent question," Thane said. "Either they didn't try or were biding their time. Can you destroy the box that one is carrying?"

"The female you called Meeka?" the vines answered. "Of course, but would it not be better to confiscate it so you can know what it is that makes it find you?"

Shaking his head, Thane chuckled at his odd companions. *"Yes, that would be much better."*

Immediately, the vines swung down and grabbed the machine, lifting it high into the canopy before the surprised Keepers could react. As soon as it was in Thane's hands, his Akilli took off once more into the swamp leaving the stunned humans behind. Drawing machetes, they attacked the vines holding them back from following, but by the time the Rebe made their own strategic retreat, the Keeper's true quarry was beyond the range they could pursue.

Thane and Strom waited until the Rebe confirmed the humans had returned to the gas mine before the Denobian asked the Tree to take him back to Rill. He needed to know how the Keepers had been tracking him, but his concern now was for Ilaria. Since she reached the crystal mine, she hadn't replied to any of his telepathic sendings.

· CHAPTER 27 ·

There is definitely a signal emanating from your communicator chip," Rill told Thane after he analyzed the device the Rebe had taken from the Keepers. "It is so subtle, only someone who knows what to scan for could find it."

"Can you deactivate it?" he asked, subconsciously putting his hand to his ear. The empathic ex-Keeper didn't know anyone who didn't have the small implant; without them, working offworld was nearly impossible. Even when people spoke in the Common language of the empire, lingual shifts along with regional accents and idioms always occurred making communication range in the spectrum from frustrating to impossible. Adding to that, many of the indigenous species on the colonized worlds continued to use their own native tongues which made the translation devices crucial to interstellar business and trade. Occasionally, species such as the Akilli and the Rebe were unable to use the chips due to either their physiology or lingual complexity and in those rare times, telepaths like Ilaria were required. A necessity that had brought her to the Wald in the first place, he noted.

"I believe so," Rill answered. "The signal is merged with

the translation circuitry, but deactivating the one shouldn't render the chip useless for translation."

"So, this was how Torquil knew Ilaria had traveled to the Wald the day of the Gala," Thane mused. "I knew he was angry that she left the *Celest*, but it hadn't occurred to me until now that he already knew exactly where she'd gone."

"Yes," the ship agreed. "I cannot say for certain it was Torquil, but this would also explain why you both were attacked on Haven when you were alone and without backup."

"Niegan also knew we were going to both locations," Thane suggested. "It's part of his job to monitor travel activities."

"I agree, but as an operative within Control, his function is to manage the traffic through the Gates, not individuals. I would recommend we analyze who's behind tracking the signal at a later date. I assume you would like your chip deactivated?"

"You're right on all accounts, as always," said Thane, never gladder of the ship's capacity for independent reasoning. "How quickly can you do it?"

Rill hesitated only a few seconds as his circuits did the calculations. "Five minutes to prep and ten to scan the circuitry so I can shut down the tracking signals while still leaving the unit viable for language translations."

"Good," he said with a single nod. "Once you've found the signals, can you jam Ilaria's tracker remotely?"

"No, but I can give you a hand device that will work. You'd need to place it over her chip, but it could shut it down completely."

"Due to the nature of Ilaria's telepathy and her linguistic abilities, I don't think that would be much of a problem for her," Thane said. "Do you have an update on her? She hasn't been responding to my sendings."

"I lost contact with Ilaria nearly a half hour ago," the ship informed him. "It is my assumption she is inside the mine. I don't know if she entered willingly."

"*She went in willingly,*" the Rebe informed them. "*It was her intention to find psions inside the facility. Do you wish us to stop the attack?"*

"No," Thane sighed. *"It's vital now that we keep to the plan. We'll have to trust she knows what she's doing."*

Without anything to do while Rill worked on his chip, Thane had more than enough worry to occupy his time. The fact that Torquil had been tracking them for years was obvious. Even after all the poking and prodding during his decades of training and conditioning, Thane had never felt more like a rat in a maze than he did now. But despite the new knowledge of the trackers, he was grateful to his new friends.

Before they had befriended the Edu of the Wald, they'd been nothing but peeks without Citizenship, social standing or even money. There hadn't been a world in all of Janus where they wouldn't have been rebels or pariahs. Without the Rebe, he and Ilaria were homeless, worldless, and friendless; if they were ever caught and returned to the clutches of the empire, they would be forced to endure either hard labor at Maelstrom or madness with the Sona. Thane had no doubt Sarkin would gut the entire Keep of psions to teach the next generation the folly of disobedience. This new violation only added to Thane's increasing hatred of the empire and the empath vowed that once they were able, he'd find a way to help all the psions enslaved by Sarkin.

· CHAPTER 28 ·

Unlike Maelstrom, most of the crystal refinery was built inside a large, natural cavern. Thick pipes vanished through the cave ceiling to spew the acrid Mephitis slag into the outer Walden atmosphere; however, escaping slag vapors had already slickened the once grey rock of the interior with a dirty yellow grit.

Upon entering the complex, Ilaria stood on a catwalk high above the cavern floor where miners labored with the arduous task of pulverizing the raw crystal carved from the rock in the subterranean labyrinths below. Watching them work, she sensed something was very wrong.

No, that wasn't quite it, Ilaria amended. Workers scurrying to secure a load of gas canisters seemed to hunch their shoulders, almost flinching as if they were anticipating either pain or punishment. But looking around, she couldn't see the cause of their alarm... it was just the *sensation,* an ominous expectation of what might be coming. They knew of the attack on the other mine; expecting the same to happen here, the mounting paranoia seeped through them like the oozing, noxious vapors of gas.

"*Ilaria, you shouldn't be in here,*" the Rebe tendril. Entwining itself through her thick hair so it wouldn't be noticed, the vine made the danger she was in abundantly clear. "*It is too late to stop the attack.*"

"*I understand,*" she answered as she heard the deep thrum emanating from the engines of a large ship descending outside the mine. Familiar with the different sounds various starships made, Ilaria recognized it as an industrial cargo hauler. Above her, the ceiling opened to admit a tether lowered from the hovering cargo ship. The workers scrambled to secure a shipment of the refined gas to the line and then stood back as the ship engaged its engines. Rising into the Walden sky, the craft broke free from the jungle world's gravity before the ceiling doors blocked her view.

It dawned on Ilaria that if they were evacuating the hyper-fuel, Daneb wasn't taking any chances of losing his embezzled gas. If he expected an attack here, it wouldn't be long before the mining crew evacuated.

Another rumble reached her, only this time the shield doors didn't open to admit another shuttle. Miners looked around in alarm, but couldn't identify the cause of the tremors.

"*Ilaria, leave now!*" the Rebe said, but it was too late; the attack had begun as the walls began to crumble inward.

The middle supports of the catwalk collapsed causing Ilaria to slide down the unstable path to the center of the cavern. Though she was still suspended in midair, workmen all around the crumbling cave grabbed hold of anything sturdy they could find that might support their weight as the shaking continued. One man screamed as he was hit in the face by a jet of gas hissing from a broken pipe. His exposed skin blistered from the acidic gas, but his agony didn't last long as the ground directly under his feet give way and his terrified cries were swallowed by the abyss. Other vents opened across the crumbling cavern floor, engulfing humans and equipment alike.

Above her, the ceiling shield doors buckled under the weight of the collapsing mine. The twisting metal of the damaged catwalk groaned and Ilaria felt the sickening pull of gravity as she tasted the choking dirt in her mouth. Loamy soil rained past her through the maw opening in the roof, but before she was sucked in with the falling earth and buried under tons of debris, she felt roots twist about her flailing arms as the sentient plants stopped her fall.

Coughing up the dust before it could turn to mud in her lungs, Ilaria blinked the gritty dust from her eyes. Dangling from the roots nearly twenty feet above the cavern floor, she discovered her predicament was no better than if she had fallen down to the bottom to join the broken carcasses of workers and equipment.

Old vines and roots hung like vipers from the broken ceiling; the only sound was the occasional clanging echo as loosened rocks ricocheted off the exposed pipes.

"Ilaria!" she heard the Rebe call out as a new slide of fresh rubble fell into the chamber. *"Watch out! The ceiling is unstable."*

"Yes, I noticed," Ilaria answered through another spasm of coughing before thanking the quick-acting plants.

"Are you okay?" they asked her as more vines snaked into the hole to support her weight.

"Battered and bruised, but I'll live," Ilaria answered. *"You weren't kidding when you said you were going to wipe out the mine."*

"More is coming," the Rebe warned her.

"The gas?"

"No, the dam. We've been jamming the rivers for years with logs and the water has already been released. We cannot stop it now; it'll flood everything here. We'll pull you up."

"No, don't!" Ilaria sent. *"There are psions below in the deep caverns. When the humans evacuate, they'll leave them to die. I can't allow that."*

The Rebe seemed to understand her determination and Ilaria felt the grip on her arm loosen, but not enough to let her fall. Unable to climb up, her only other option would have to be down. The fresh sunlight spilling in through the hole in the cavern ceiling illuminated the ancient chamber and Ilaria decided the framework for the metal ladders that had been pounded into the wall was her best option if reach them.

Bracing themselves against the hole, the roots helped support Ilaria's weight as she carefully climbed up the angling ramp of the catwalk. Twice, portions of the ceiling gave way and covered her in a fresh shower of dirt and debris, but she managed to make it to the solid stone wall without sliding into the cavernous pit.

Once there, Ilaria used the handholds to scale the rest of the way to a ladder that took her down to a platform. Originally, the ledge joined another catwalk spanning the length of the cavern, but falling boulders had twisted it into a shapeless mass of swaying wreckage.

Only after she was safe on the platform did she realize she could have saved both time and energy by teleporting. If the vines hadn't stopped her fall, she probably would have done so by instinct, but it hadn't even occurred to her after she was dangling from the ceiling. Grumbling to herself, she wondered what the point was at having a new ability if she didn't use it?

Thane's anxious voice interrupted her self-admonition. *"Ilaria, thank god! I thought something had happened to you."*

"Something did," she answered, quickly, explaining what had happened when the mine collapsed.

"Ilaria, make your way to the processing plant; the Rebe can get you out from there."

"No, I'm going down for the prisoners. I can sense them trapped below me."

"No, Ilaria," Thane mentally growled at her stubbornness. *"I want to save them, too, but there isn't time! Don't kill yourself."*

"I have to do this," Ilaria sent while mentally pushing through her determination. *"They're like us, Thane; they're psions."*

Thane didn't want to admit that a portion of his mind had been aware there were psychics from the moment he'd learned of them. Now that he was aware, his mind sensed the terror they felt as they mentally called for help, something they were certainly not going to get from their human overlords. To the empire, they were peeks and not worth saving.

"*I know,*" Thane sighed in anguish. "*Is there anything we can do to help?*""

"*Yes! The Rebe's roots go down deep all over this world. See if they know of another exit to these caves and I'll try to lead the psions to there.*"

"*There is,*" he said, explaining that the Keepers had turned back to the gas mine. "*The edu say the two caverns join together; they plan to cut off your escape from below. Good luck, Ilaria.*"

"*See you on the other side, Thane.*"

Ending the mental contact, Ilaria began climbing down the ladder again. Now that the landslide had ceased and the finest particles of dust slowly drifted to settle on the cavern floor, she realized not everything in the chamber was dead. Soft moans of pain mingled with faint cries for help. In the gathering silence as their minds winked out one by one, Ilaria understood that help didn't always come for normal humans, either.

The imprisoned psions were far and below in the caves under her feet, but Ilaria knew she was headed in the right direction as their terror solidified at the entrance to one of the tunnels branching out from the central chamber. Ilaria flared with anger when she saw the heavy, metal gate welded into the walls of the narrow passage. Even if the mine had naturally collapsed or if the toxic gasses permeated through the narrow chambers through an industrial accident, these prisoners would never be able to leave without permission from their masters.

Well, gates needed keys, Ilaria reasoned... and prisoners needed guards. To her left she saw what could only be a monitoring a room, its windows facing the giant chamber gave an unimpeded view of both the cavern and the barred passage. Her senses told her there were two people in the room. Ducking to the side of the entry, she waited until one of them was just on the other side of the open door. In a fast jab, Ilaria hit the man full in the throat before he could shout a warning and then just as quickly, put her hand to his face, cracking his skull as she slammed it against the stone wall. The second guard was already on the ground, bleeding from where ceiling debris had crushed his body. He was alive, but wouldn't be for long and was in no condition to sound an alarm. Not taking any chances, she grabbed a rifle and hit him with the butt, knocking him completely unconscious.

Neither men wore a set of keys, but now armed with a laser rifle, Ilaria no longer needed them. With no one left to raise a warning, she returned to the gate and kept firing the weapon into the key lock until the melting metal dripped to the floor in chunks and she was able to kick the gate open.

She paled as a new and sinister rumble reached her. Rushing back to the lip of the main cavern she saw that the river released from the shattered dam in the hills had reached the crystal mine. Thousands of gallons of water began pouring through the broken ceiling doors, filling the chamber. The force of the flood was eroding the fragile ceiling even further; the hole grew steadily wider as the volume of water increased.

Sprinting down the corridor, she shouted for help to anyone who could hear her. Expecting to aid injured miners, two guards responded only to be shot as Ilaria rushed by still searching for the psions. Ilaria felt the passage descend deeper underground. It was rough, as if a work crew had merely widened a natural fissure enough for people to enter with a pack of tools or to exit with a load of ore. Finally, the passage opened into the most stunning cathedral Ilaria had ever seen. The room was made entirely of living crystal, some growing so large, three people could have walked across the hexagonal beams and still have room to let another pass. The gems refracted a prism of light from the glow of a single lantern.

"The cavern's been flooded!" Ilaria impulsively shouted telepathically to them, stunning the empaths who'd never before heard the mind of another. *"We have to leave now!"*

"Too late!" a natural telepath answered pointing to the passage as water gushed into the crystal chamber.

Leaping out of the way, Ilaria landed on the giant crystal shaft. Using it as a bridge, she crossed the cavern to the imprisoned psions, gratefully accepting a hand as they helped her the rest of the way. Looking back, the water poured over the edge of the chamber, disappearing in a frothy mass into the chasm below. In the black distance, they could hear the pitch of the waterfall change as the cascade began to pool and slowly rise. It wouldn't be long before this chamber was also flooded, leaving nowhere for them to go.

· CHAPTER 29 ·

Thane," Rill said opening a compartment in his console, "I've disabled your chip so the Keepers can't track you, but Ilaria's is still active."

"Yes, I'm aware of that," Thane said grimly, glancing at the cylindrical object Rill gave him. "What's this?"

"It's a dampener which should block transmissions emanating from her chip until I can disable the signals permanently."

"Fantastic! How does it work?"

"You will have to place it directly over her implant in order to deactivate it; however, once the signal has been blocked, the circuitry will reboot."

"How long will I have?"

"The dampener will block the signal for ten minutes and has enough power for two hits."

"Great," said Thane, jumping out of the ship. "Twenty minutes should be more than enough."

The Denobian didn't get far as a curtain of the Rebe dropped down to block his way. Several of the nearby Akilli shifted from foot to foot in what seemed to be human mannerisms of agitation.

Unable to hear the telepathic vines, Rill asked, "What is it?"

"They tell me that Ilaria has entered the crystal mine in order to rescue the psions she sensed inside."

"We knew that, so what's the problem?" Rill asked, picking up the panicked tonal changes in Thane's voice.

"For decades, the Akilli have been forming a log jam upriver which has collected into a substantial lake. They say they released the water before Ilaria entered. The flood's heading right for the refinery."

But before the Denobian could act, the Rebe spoke again and Thane translated, "There's more; it has to do with the humans who were tracking me before. They knew of Ilaria's location from their instruments, but they didn't go to the refinery. They returned to the gas mine and the Akilli say they are going inside."

Thane heard a chime as the data he gave the ship finished computing. "The two caves most likely join somewhere underground. The Keepers know the water is coming and plan to reach Ilaria through the interconnecting cave system. What are they saying now?"

Listening, Thane said, "There are cave dwelling creatures called *Caecilian Edu* who live in the subterranean rivers. They say you are correct that it is all one system, but the paths between the caverns wind around for miles before they do."

"Either they have found a way through or they're going to create one," Rill said. "Thane, you need to go to the gas mine and stop them. If they intend to blow the walls in the caverns, it could bring the entire ceiling down on top of Ilaria."

Covering more ground with low-gravity leaps, Thane bounded away towards the pit with several of the Akilli and Rebe close on his heals. The lush jungle parted when he passed so they wouldn't impede his race back.

"Ilaria, the Keepers know where you are!" he sent. *"They can track us through our communication chips."*

"Damn Rey!" Ilaria cursed back. *"I knew he was holding*

something back about his cybernetics programs. Maybe we should have killed him when we had the chance."

"Maybe, but you were right: we're not killers. Besides that, Sarkin already knew we were here; we'd only have given them more reason to hunt us. Rill deactivated my chip, but they are coming for you. The Akilli have released the water for the flood and it's too late to stop it. You've got to get out of there!"

"I can't," she answered, her mental voice resigned to the inevitable. "The water has already reached us. I'm going to have to find another way out. I was right, though, Thane. There are psions here, but I don't know if they're from Maelstrom or Sobek's rejects."

"I know."

Sweating from both his exertion and the humidity, Thane lay down on the blackened scar where the Keepers had flamed his wooden friends and cautiously peered over the lip of the pit. Miners scurried to secure canisters of gas while attempting to avoid the unit of Keepers lined in rows as they awaited their orders.

"Ilaria," he sent to his daughter, "the Keepers are armed with alternating weapons."

"I understand," Ilaria sent back.

"No, you don't! They mean to take you alive, but they will kill you rather than allow you to escape again. If it comes down to it, I want you to teleport out. You have your daughter to think about now."

"I will, Thane, I promise. If I can, I will."

"What do you mean 'if you can'?"

"I mean just that, Thane. For starters, I'm not entirely sure how it works. Every time I've done it, I was both out in the open and operating on instinct. The only time I've done it on purpose took a lot of concentration. Right now, I'm surrounded by rock and water. I might jump myself right into the cavern walls!"

Ilaria would choose now to get all logical on him, but Thane also knew she was right. Unless she didn't have another choice, now wasn't the time to experiment with how far she could use her power to mentally travel or through what substance. Another thought struck him and he asked the Akilli if they could dig her out.

"*We cannot,*" came their answer. "*The area above them is covered with water, but even if it was dry, our roots can't go down that far or through the rock. We could dig, but it would take time and the cavern could collapse and bury them.*"

Having no other choice, Thane had to stick to the main plan and try to stop them from laying the charges. At least from this side, he could let Ilaria know where they were. Scooching over to the edge, the Keepers had turned on their heels and were marching into a wide hanger that undoubted led into the lower portions of the mine.

Thane quickly ducked as one of the soldiers paused and looked in his direction. He sighed in relief when the alarm wasn't raised.

"*Wait,*" the Rebe said when Thane moved to see if it was clear. It wasn't until the man turned and joined the other troops before the vines told him it was okay to move. "*What do you intend to do?*"

"I've got to follow them, but I didn't see any other Denobians with them. They'll notice me immediately."

"*Go in the way you did before. The Edu are inside and we can guide you.*"

It's good to have friends in high places, Thane thought to himself as one of the Rebe slithered up the sleeve of his uniform. With a jump, he landed a third of the way down the embankment, but his second wasn't as graceful. Landing hard on his still tender ankle, he pressed himself against the wall which then collapse a portion of dirt over him. Grateful that no one had heard his involuntary cry of pain, or could have over the shouts and grinding of machinery, Thane gingerly stepped forward to peer over the edge.

Intent on their jobs, no one gave the Denobian a second look. It made him nervous that he could enter a place on high alert like this twice and unchallenged. Both Daneb and Torquil knew he was here and he was almost certain that one of the Keepers had spotted him, but maybe not by sight. That would make him their embedded Empati.

Shaking the dust out of his hair, Thane made his way into the facility well aware that this time, the enemy knew he was there. Paranoia battled with his empathic senses when everyone he passed eyed the Denobian. He didn't relax his guard even though all of them barely glanced at him as he walked down the hall.

Thane reminded himself to project confidence as if he belonged here. Walking purposefully like he knew exactly where he was going, Thane followed the voice of the whispering Rebe when they told him to turn left and then take an immediate right.

When Thane reached the middle of the next hallway, he felt an anxious presence turn the corner behind him and then suddenly relax when he caught sight of his quarry.

"I've been spotted," Thane told the Rebe.

"How can we help you?" they asked.

"I'm not sure. He's an empath and is mentally following me. I need to lose him in a crowd of people, but not ones who might recognize me."

"We know a place; turn left."

Thane obeyed them, but wasn't sure this was what he had in mind when he entered into the dining hall and nearly three dozen people angrily milling around eyed him. The psion couldn't help taking a step backward at the force of their fury, but quickly ducked into the crowd when he sensed he wasn't the one they were interested in. All of their agitation was directed towards the kitchens from which emanated the same range of anger and frustration.

Of course, Thane thought. No one here had eaten or drank anything since the Rebe had poisoned their supplies. Daneb only had two choices to combat it: let the Company and the empire know they were losing control on the Wald and evacuate their workers or try and sterilize the mold. Clearly, the foreman didn't want to risk the emperor discovering his failure, so his crew was forced to go hungry.

Everyone turned along with Thane when another man

entered the dining hall, but only the empath knew he wasn't here to commiserate with his fellow sufferers. Thane was about to step deeper into the crowd in the hopes that he wouldn't be spotted when the Rebe spoke up.

"Go get some water."

"Isn't it contaminated?" he asked.

"Not yet," they told him, *"and we won't poison you."*

Trusting his new friends knew what they were doing, Thane did as they told him. After pouring himself a glass, he filtered it twice to ensure there were none of the spores were present. When it scanned green, he raised a toast to himself before drinking it all.

The entire room held their breath as they waited for him to either double over with agonizing stomach cramps or just die. Thane was just as relieved as they were when he did neither.

"It's okay," he smiled, handing his glass to a woman next to him. "It's clean!"

Still with fear in her eyes, the woman took a tentative sip and then greedily began sucking the water to alleviate her dehydrated body.

"Easy; drink it slowly," Thane said, gently pulling the liquid away from her parched lips, but it was already too late. Like a wildfire spreading through dry grass, the desperate people clamored around him to quench the drought in their parched throats. The mob quickly escalated into a riot as they all wanted their share first.

Their hero didn't escape unscathed. Ducking into the kitchens, Thane discovered he'd been cut on his left forearm, though from whom and what, he had no idea.

"Leave quickly," the Rebe said.

With a glance at the stunned cooks who were becoming aware of the melee in the other room, Thane ducked out the far doors just as the cries of triumph turned into curses as the miners began to vomit up the now contaminated water.

What a bioweapon the Rebe had! They could not only turn it on and off at will, but direct it only at their enemies. As he entered into a stairwell, he wondered why the Rebe waited so long to use it. With such a powerful resource, did they really need his or Ilaria's help?

"We need you," they answered. *"Without you, they would only return and burn our world to the core. Take the steps down; you are still being followed."*

Thane knew the Rebe were correct when he sensed his pursuer enter the stairwell a couple floors above him. He was about to go down another flight when, smiling, he noticed a sign that indicated he was on the medical wing.

Getting through the kitchens without being noticed had been tricky... getting into medical, on the other hand was going to be very, very easy.

"Good lord, what happened to you?" a nurse demanded as she rushed to stop the flow of blood dripping from Thane's slashed arm.

"There was a riot in the dining hall for fresh water," the Denobian answered, wincing as the nurse applied a compress and pressure to his gash.

"Idiots!" she snapped as she lifted the towel to glance at the wound. "Told them a thousand times that water was scanning safe, but they wouldn't touch it. I guess thirst finally got the better of them. This isn't too bad; deep enough to bleed a river, but you won't need stitches. How did you get involved?"

"Well," Thane slowly admitted, feigning ignorance that the water wasn't safe anymore, "I was sort of the one who drank first and got mobbed for it."

"Good lord!" the nurse said again, tutting sympathetically. Slopping on some antiseptic cream, the medic wrapped his arm and then bustled away muttering that there would be more of the idiots coming in soon and they probably would need stitches and serve those fools right!

The medic had no idea how right she was. Any moment the riot was about to arrive on her doorstep.

"Thank you," the empath called after him before giving himself a sly smile. Yup... easy.

Slipping off the gurney the nurse had put him on for his treatment, Thane silently cursed when he sensed nearby minds suddenly flair into panic. His psion tail must have figured out he was there and had raised the alarm! Thane only had moments to get through medical before guards crashed through the door. It had taken them long enough, he thought, but then humans never seem to lack the capacity to underestimate a psion.

With a frown, Thane realized something else was wrong. Leaning his ear against the door, he heard people swarming down the medical hall, but they were coming from below him where the mines were and not from the direction of the dining rooms. Cautiously cracking the door, he saw about half a dozen people stumbling through the corridor as they blindly tried to make their way into the main medical bay; their eyes were nearly swollen shut and their lungs wheezed as they tried to breathe.

"What happened?" Thane asked.

"Gas!" a worker gasped as she tried to inhale so she could speak. "Gas lines ruptured!"

"Coincidence?" Thane asked his Rebe companions.

"*Hardly,*" they replied as the man exited the med-bay and tried to navigate the growing crowd clamoring into the hospital wing. "*This is our latest attack. We thought you could use another distraction.*"

"*You have no idea!*" Thane exclaimed relieved.

The panic from the workers was nearly mind-numbing to the empath as those with injuries clamored through the halls for medical attention while the uninjured attempted to crush their way past in order to escape outside and into fresh air. Those unfortunate souls were met by the retching crew crowding the other stairwell in their escape from the dining hall.

In the chaos, the Denobian's smaller size wasn't an advantage; he could barely move as the exits became more packed with people. Ducking into a storage room, Thane waited for most of the terrified miners to pass before trying to make his way out. It wouldn't do for him to be seen going in the opposite direction as everyone else. Forewarned by the few gagging stragglers he passed, Thane found an abandoned gas mask in the stairwell and donned it before entering the lowest region of the mine.

It was easy to follow the Keepers now; theirs were the only calm minds in the entire complex. They were also the only minds moving away from him and not towards. What he couldn't sense in the chaos was if he himself was still being followed. Focusing his mind forward, Thane gave a low-gravity leap and jumped into the cavernous void.

· CHAPTER 30 ·

When the frothing water pouring into the crystal chamber reached her boots, Ilaria stepped higher on the giant Mephitis spear. With the gushing cascade spurting from the channel leading back to the main refinery, none of the twenty psions were getting out the same way she came in.

"Thank you for the attempt," the telepath said as he helped her to a more secure location, footholds that were rapidly shrinking as the desperate people scrambled to latch onto anything that would stop them from getting swept away.

"We're not done for yet," Ilaria told him. "I'm here with friends."

"Will they be able to reach us in time?"

"Not likely," Ilaria admitted as she watched the ink-black water roil below them. The Rebe and Akilli were on the other side of hundreds of feet of solid rock currently being scoured by the flash flood. "I'm afraid this is the worst rescue attempt in the history of rescues."

"We appreciate you trying," the man said. "We sensed the miners' panic, but figured we were safe down here from whatever was up there. Without them opening the gate, we couldn't leave here anyway. I'm Tarn; if we are to die here, I'd like to know your name, friend."

"Ilaria," she answered, stepping even higher.

"Keep climbing!" Tarn ordered everyone. "Don't swim unless you have no other choice. There might be eddies that could suck you down."

It had been a useless order as the psions had already been scrambling to keep themselves out of the water, but Ilaria sensed they were used to obeying Tarn. Whether through a subconscious instinct to follow the dominant member or because of a vote, the telepath was this group's leader.

"Jess!"

At the cry, Ilaria looked just in time to see a middle-aged woman slide down a shard of crystal and disappear into the roiling flood, but her attending Rebe was faster. Before Ilaria could react, the vine lanced down and coiled about her flailing arms. But even as the vines stopped Jess' fall, the salvation was brief. Stretched to its limit against the force of the rushing water, the tendril snapped and Jess was left at the mercy of the raging torrent.

"She's still alive," Ilaria whispered even as it dawned on her that the vine which had accompanied her wasn't. The mental connection she'd had with the tendril had been severed and, as a consequence, to the rest of the Rebe on the surface as well.

"I'm going after her!" she told Tarn and, to the psion's astonishment, Ilaria vanished before his eyes.

Feeling Jess' panicked essence dim as the woman was swept away from them, Ilaria, reacting on the instinct of her new abilities, knew she could reach her. It wasn't all that different from when she saved Thane from the plasma blast on Haven; she *wanted* to get to her as soon as possible and her psionic mind obeyed.

The moment Ilaria reappeared in the world, she began choking, unable to take a breath against the raging water. Her own ability to battle against the force of the current were hindered when the panicked Jess grabbed hold her rescuer with an iron grip that threatened to drown Ilaria as well. With her arms pinned, both women plummeted towards a waterfall as the cavern channeled the flood into a chasm. When Ilaria felt herself falling over the edge, she teleported again, this time taking Jess with her.

There was no time to contemplate that she'd not only used her new power on command, but had taken someone else with her. Forcing the terrified woman's hands apart, Ilaria looked around. The new chamber wasn't large and the torrent was filling this cavern as well, but it was better than the crystal chamber and would give them a few more minutes to live.

"Tarn, we're alive!" she sent to the telepath. *"I think we're maybe thirty meters below you. The water is filling a pool, but I believe it's deep enough that you won't be crushed."*

Whether realizing their own survival depended on Ilaria's leap of faith or because they were used to following Tarn's commands, the empaths allowed themselves to be swept away in the flood. The force of the water didn't leave the psions unscathed when the currents bashed several of them into boulders. As Ilaria and Tarn helped the sputtering empaths out of the water, they discovered the leap wasn't without more serious casualties. One of Tarn's men had taken a blow to the head against the cavern walls; unconscious, he'd drowned before they could haul him out of the growing pool to safety.

"I'm so sorry," Ilaria told them.

"He died free," Jess said. "As I would have if you hadn't saved me."

"Ilaria, what happened?" Thane sent suddenly panicked. He'd been aware of her growing agitation since the Rebe informed him the flood had reached the refinery and felt her sudden spike of panic. Then, for an instant when he hadn't been able to sense her at all, Thane was certain she'd drowned. He couldn't help stagger in relief when her mind winked back into existence as full of life as ever.

The empath was astounded that he could now sense another mind along with Ilaria's; he could feel Jyn!

"We're okay," Ilaria answered. *"I had to teleport, but we're okay. We lost the Rebe and another empath."*

"Where are you?"

"Safe for the moment, but I'm not sure for how long. The caverns are still flooding."

"What are you doing here?" a verbal voice demanded, breaking Thane's mental contact.

Cursing that his concentration on Ilaria had brought him to Daneb's attention, Thane evaded with his version of the truth. "I saw you heading into the caverns with the Keepers. I thought maybe you could use a Denobian."

Thane was relieved that the foreman hadn't recognized him behind his breathing mask, but, whether it was his opinions on Denobians in general or his previous encounters with them, it was clear Daneb thought little of the offer. "What makes you think I'd have use for you?"

"Because I'm a Denobian," Thane stated the obvious. "I can jump higher than any of you and can fit into smaller places."

Apparently accepting the short man, Daneb turned on his heel, but Thane knew he wasn't in the clear. There was still an augment on his tail and Torquil was farther in the caverns with the Keepers. Even behind a mask, Thane doubted the head of the Empati would fail to recognize him.

Keeping himself at the rear of the troupe, Thane followed them down into a massive cavern. Great stalactites hung down from the ceiling from the like fangs from the maw of a rock monster after eons of water seeping down from the swamplands far above them. The stunted canines were scattered about the damp floor as, drip by calcified drip, they slowly rose to close the cavernous jaws around their prey.

Stepping around the stalagmites, the Keepers entered a long, round tunnel. Thane realized all the chambers must have been carved by ancient lava flows, but the cold volcano had been dead for eons. The liquid rock that had once flowed through these passages in rivers had long ago settled on the floor, creating an almost smooth path that advanced down into the deeper bowls of the cave.

Thane wasn't sure how far they had marched in an almost straight line before the tunnel opened into another massive magma chamber, the contents having drained before the volcano went cold.

"Here!" Daneb said to Torquil as he pointed to the far wall. "The tunnels snake around for miles, but this chamber abuts another that leads to the crystal mine."

"Too bad you didn't blast a hole through it before now," Torquil sneered.

"There wasn't a need before now," Daneb retorted back.

"Not to worry; we'll get through it soon enough," the head Keeper smile before turning around to his men. "Won't we, Thane?"

The Denobian wasn't sure which sensation was worse: that every Keeper turned in unison to level their weapons at him or that he hadn't for one moment sensed it coming. He wasn't being followed by an augment; he was surrounded by them!

Ilaria and Tarn helped some of the injured psions onto a higher ledge as the waters continued to rise in their new prison. While they could see eddies swirling into passages at the far end of the cavern, it was clear the chamber was filling faster than it was draining. Though they were still alive, they had only managed to delay the inevitable. The only passages out of this cave were narrow and under water.

All of the trapped psions gasped at once as they were suddenly struck blind. Suddenly paralyzed in the blackness, Ilaria hadn't realized they shouldn't have been able to see at all in their rocky tomb until the lights went out.

If not for the minds and terrified moans of those around her, Ilaria would have thought she were utterly alone in the overwhelming dark. No matter how hard she strained, there wasn't even a glimmer her useless eyes could focus on.

At least she could still hear. Grateful she wasn't bereft of all her senses, Ilaria listened to her pounding heart beat with the rhythm of the waterfall that still roared as the flood continued to fill the chamber. And she could still sense the psions still alive around her as they flailed blindly to feel the warmth of a human and not the chill of wet, ancient rock.

"Look," Ilaria said in an almost reverent whisper. Though the ceiling of the cave was only a few feet above them, the single pinprick of light made it look as if it were thousands of miles away.

The tiny dot was a cold light without heat or radiating glow, but to the sightless, it was the most beautiful thing in the universe. The dot was joined by another and then by another as other bioluminescent cave dwellers began to shine in the encompassing dark. Though the blindness had felt like an eternity, in reality only a few minutes had passed.

Distracted in the gratitude that their sight had been restored, the trapped psions momentarily forgot the chill from their wet clothes and the certainty that death was rising up to meet them. It was as if the universe had gathered across the ceiling. Awed, they stared at the beauty of the cave edu.

"We must have startled them," Tarn said, "to make them go off all at once."

Ilaria agreed as individual creatures began winking on and off. More of them blinked their light until all of them flashed across the ceiling in a unified wave. The lights seemed to begin just above the psions' heads and over to the edge of the ledge they were clinging to. Over and over they pulsed in the same direction. The only change the creatures made in their pattern was an increase in the tempo as the waves flowed faster and faster.

"It can't be!" Ilaria smiled as she shook her head.

"What is it?" Tarn asked.

Ilaria didn't answer, but slowly crept along the wall to where the flashing pulses ended. Only they didn't end!

"Salvation!" Ilaria said. "Everyone, come up here quickly. The edu are showing us a way out!"

Following her, Tarn saw the tunnel illuminated by clusters of tiny glowworms wriggling across the ceiling.

"The edu are some of the lifeforms on this world," Ilaria explained as she helped Jess into the tunnel. "I lost contact with them when the Rebe died, but they've found another way to help us."

Though she could sense Tarn and the others bursting with curiosity as they had no idea what either edu or Rebe were, her new friends didn't waste time in satisfying it. Though the small passage was a tight squeeze for the battered refugees, they quickly followed Ilaria's order and shimmied through the hole as fast as they could.

The glowing worms never abandoned them with their light again and Ilaria presumed the darkness from before was to get their attention. Though Ilaria's growing belly was more of a hindrance than she was used to in the small tunnel, her pregnancy didn't slow her down.

The passage emptied into a wide chamber with a low ceiling where sunlight spilled through a natural opening. Though the mouth was only a few yards above them, reaching it, however, was going to be an entirely new challenge.

Torquil bent down on one knee so he could look Thane in the eye; he didn't want to miss a moment of the stunned expression on the Denobian's face. With a smirk, he asked, "Have you told Ilaria we're here yet? No? I thought you two told each other everything."

Thane kept his silence as the two men carefully studied each other. Stretching his mental abilities to the fullest, this close the empath should have been able to read Torquil clearly, but he couldn't. It was as if everything emanating from the commander had been drowned in tepid water; fear, hate, anger... it all blended together until one feeling was indistinguishable from the other. Thane realized that was how Torquil masked his emotions: he allowed himself to feel all of his emotions, he just made sure nothing surged to where he felt things passionately. He killed and made love with the same indifference he gave to his next meal.

"Ah... now you know," Torquil said, widening his humorless smile, but he wasn't referring to his ability at hiding dampened emotions from an empath. "I haven't worked most of my life around you damn peeks without recognizing when telepaths are talking. I admit, it took a while because you weren't a tele, but the signs were too obvious. Of course, no one cared until now, but I'm afraid that as a telepathic empath, you've caught the attention of some very powerful people."

"Sobek," Thane stated flatly.

"Perhaps." Torquil seemed amused behind his frozen smile. "But it hardly matters now. You've become quite a problem for us, drawing Sarkin's attention to what we were doing on this world. Thanks to you, more Valids have become aware of our activities. Valids can too easily become In-Valids and we'd rather not waste our time quashing a revolution right now."

The augmented Keepers turned their heads towards Thane when they sensed his startled reaction to Torquil's choice of words. That was what Ilaria had mentally read from their attacker on Haven, that it was time for their revolution. He didn't have time to question whether it was the Valids or the augments planning to rebel.

"I am thankful that you're here to help us fix this mess," Torquil continued. "You're absolutely right that we need someone like you. Meeka, Shenzi! Tie him up! Good and tight so he can't get away, but give him a long leash. There's no sense having a Denobian who can't jump."

Thane didn't resist when his former friends bound thick ropes around his middle, leaving his arms free so he could perform whatever task Torquil had in mind for his prisoner. His mind raced as he took in everything the commander had said. There wasn't any doubt in Thane's mind that Sobek had been behind the killings of almost two hundred psions in his research to augment their powers, but if he wasn't the one behind it, the healer had to be working with Laran. She was the only person who would gain from it. With Sarkin dead, she'd become empress and with an army of psychics loyal to her, there wasn't anyone who could stand against her if she ascended to the throne through assassinating her brother. She'd even launched an offensive against her own attack on the *Celest* in order to deflect suspicion away from her murderous activities!

But whatever Laran's goal, she desperately needed Ilaria to complete her plans. Since the Admiral needed empaths and telepaths for Sobek to create his augmented serum, they must know the double dose to Ilaria had manifested, perhaps even mutated, into teleportation.

Now the question was: did they know about Jyn? Ilaria's daughter would be born a second-generation augment. Even in the womb, she was empathic, telepathic and most likely a teleporter. Since Ilaria had developed a second ability when she reached maturity, it stood to reason that Jyn would, too. What if they gave Jyn yet another dose the way they had to her mother and grandmother before her? There was no telling how powerful the child could become. Certainly, strong enough to take over Janus; an army of Jyns could very well take over the galaxy.

"Sir," one of the Keepers interrupted, "she's moving again. They must have found another passage out."

"What?" Torquil exclaimed, his surprise briefly spiking his fury before his mental control reasserted itself. "They don't have lanterns, so how could they find a passage in total darkness?" he asked looking shrewdly at Thane. "You could find out, of course, but I doubt you'd tell us."

Smirking again in his half-hidden amusement, Torquil took Thane's silence as confirmation that he wouldn't betray his surrogate daughter. But as the commander's smug demeanor intensified, Thane realized he'd have no choice but to do just that when the tall man gave a signal to his subordinates. Stepping forward, three Keepers wearing satchels over their shoulders pushed the Denobian roughly towards the back wall.

Stumbling forward, the light attached to his breather glinted off the damp boulders piled at the base of the once smooth wall. The area was littered with rubble after eons of erosion had brought portions of the ceiling down.

"*Thane,*" the Rebe tendril hidden inside his uniform said, "*we are working to get you free.*"

Thane didn't answer as the tug against his midsection reminded him the Keepers were watching. Meeka reached into her satchel and handed the ex-Empati a small, round object.

Thane was too experienced not to recognize it as an explosive. Carefully shielding his horror, he took the charge and jumped midway up the boulders. Tiny rivulets of water were seeping between the stones before flowing into the calcium rich pool in the center of the chamber.

"Thank you," he told the vines now that his face was turned away from his captors, *"but we have a bigger problem. What I'm holding is a bomb. When it goes off, it will shatter this wall. It'll kill me as well as you leaving Torquil an open passage to reach Ilaria."*

"We can no longer hear her. The Rebe who was with her has perished."

"I'm sorry to hear that. I've already told her what the Keepers are up to. The edu have shown her a tunnel that leads out. Ilaria is safe for now."

"Do you want the spores to attack their breathers?" the Rebe asked.

Jumping down for another charge, Thane considered that option. *"No. If they start choking, they'll shoot me before escaping up the passage. I have something else in mind, but I'm going to need your help. Do you think you can get me one of their guns?"*

Ilaria was entranced as she looked up at the hole in cavern ceiling. Shafts of sunlight poured through the meter-wide opening creating a miniature forest of bright green moss and dainty trees wherever the beam of energy warmed the cold stones. She recognized the species as varieties from the surface, but the conditions of their micro world had left them stunted. The diminutive trees were too fragile for them to climb to the opening

"What do we do now?" Jess asked, ignoring the overwhelming beauty of the cavern diminished as she pointed out that they were still trapped.

"We wait for rescue," Ilaria said.

"You realize our rescue is going to come at the hands of the Keepers," Tarn said privately, not taking his eyes from the

freedom that was just out of reach.

"Snakes!" Jess' shout caused several of the trapped psions to scan the floor desperately looking for creatures slithering near their feet, but the serpents weren't on the cave floor. Looking to where Jess was pointing, the ceiling was suddenly writhing with dark, muddy creepers. Clods of loamy soil rained down as they shattered through the hole, their undulating tentacles coming through the gaping maw and into the cavern.

The dirty tendrils coiled about the screaming Jess who was then hauled up through the hole. Others began screaming, scattering through the small grotto in their attempt to avoid the new threat from above.

"No!" Ilaria cried to the frightened people. "These are the Akilli and the Rebe. They are indigenous to this world and are our friends!"

To prove it, Ilaria rushed to be directly under the bright doorway and stretched her arms up and waited to be taken. "I'm fine!" she hollered back into the hole after the Akilli set her back down on the surface. After the flood and the crawl through the caverns, it took a while for her reassurances to calm the panicked psions, but eventually, the last one allowed the roots to take them. Safe on the surface, Ilaria was finally able to introduce her new friends to one another.

Gently, the Rebe made contact with the refugee empaths, though not all of them enjoyed hearing the plant's telepathic link with their minds.

Suddenly, the ground rocked violently beneath them, the force knocking all of the psions who were standing off their feet. "That wasn't a quake!" Tarn stated as he felt the wave dissipate as it continued to spread away from the epicenter.

Ilaria's face was ashen when she realized the aged telepath was right. The tremor had been almost directly under their feet and far too massive to have been a natural event. With dread rising in her gut, she knew the explosives had gone off. Through the layers of rock and the rising panic of every other human in the vicinity of the Wald mine, there were too many minds for her to sense the one she sought to hear the most.

· CHAPTER 31 ·

When Thane jumped back onto the boulders to set the third charge, the Rebe told him he was right about the Keepers. The moment his back was turned and his attention on the explosive, Meeka stepped forward and secured her end of his tether to an enormous stalagmite before following her retreating comrades to a more secure location in an adjoining lava tube.

"Nothing personal," she told him as her barking laughter echoed off the calcified walls. "No, of course it's personal, but you already knew that."

Thane wondered what Meeka's response would've been if she knew almost half of the soldiers with her were augmented humans with the same powers he had. Though it was unlikely it would have changed her mind about sacrificing him, he'd have placed a good bet she'd join them if Sobek ever gave her the opportunity. Meeka was a Keeper who hated the Empati not for what they were, but for what she wasn't. That would have soured the moment her Citizenship was revoked, but it gave the empath pause to wonder what Sobek had offered those he changed. However many he'd already altered with his serum, he clearly had their loyalty against the natural-born psychics.

The moment they were out of sight, Thane jumped down to the floor, his bonds falling away having been loosened by the Rebe. With only seconds before the charges detonated, he hesitated, unsure which way to go. There was only one passage out and it was currently occupied by Torquil who wouldn't waste time shooting him now that the heavy labor was over.

"Get away from the center!" the vines told him. *"Against the wall and as high as you can."*

Instantly obeying, Thane jumped again, ducking behind a massive column of conjoined stalagmites as the blast rocked through the cavern. Stalactites crashed around him as portions of the chamber ceiling collapsed, but that wasn't the only danger in the damaged cave. Dislodged from their moorings, the shattered wall couldn't withstand the pressure of the flood building behind. Billions of tons of water from the adjacent chamber poured through the widening gap.

To Thane's immense delight, he sensed Keepers and augments alike mentally scream as their escape route was overrun with the gushing rapids. For all their planning, they hadn't anticipated the flood was filling the adjacent chamber! Several of their minds winked out when they were overtaken by the raging water, but not all fell victim to the torrent. That passage opened into the first magma chamber they had entered and those who survived could escape back into the main cavern of the gas mine before the giant chasm could fill.

None of the Keepers were concentrating on mental blocks now as they struggled against the raging water. Thane wasn't sure about Daneb, but the empath knew that Torquil was one who made it out.

With the floods raging below him and Keepers up above, Thane was now just as trapped as Ilaria had been.

"Need a hand?"

Startled as Ilaria suddenly materialized beside him, Thane couldn't help but cry out in surprise. "What the hell are you doing here?" he demanded. "I told you not to teleport unless it was absolutely necessary."

With a wry smile, Ilaria looked around the flooded chamber, "It seemed to be necessary, or would you rather stay?"

"It's not like I can go anywhere."

"Well, I learned a neat trick," Ilaria said. With another smile, she wrapped her arms around her father in a tight embrace and teleported him back to the surface near the rescued psions.

Blinking against the brightness as light suddenly stabbed his dilated eyes, Thane was unable to focus properly. The empath tensed when people rushed to their side before he realized they had no intention to harm him.

"Quickly," the Denobian ordered after greeting the group of psions, "we don't have any time to waste. Rebe," he added addressing the vines, "were you able to get that gun?"

"Yes; in fact, we got one for Ilaria as well."

"Fantastic! Let's go, psions. The Wald isn't ours yet."

With the Akilli aiding the injured, the psions made their way back through the jungle to the gas mine. Both Thane and Ilaria were surprised at how far they had traveled in the underground tunnels from the pit. Along the way, Thane explained how the lake the Akilli had dammed had scoured the crystal mine down to its foundations. The inner chambers of the caverns had been so flooded, it would take special equipment to make it operational again. The expense far outweighed the advantages of the crystal to make such an effort worthwhile… even for someone as greedy as Daneb.

"If he survived," Thane added before signaling to the psions they were nearing the pit.

"What is your plan, Thane?" Tarn asked when they looked over the edge of the gas mine. "I'm grateful for what you and Ilaria have done, but I don't see how we've gained an advantage. Two peeks with guns aren't going to stand a chance against a hundred of armed Keepers."

"It's not just us," Thane replied, "but all of us. Do you want your freedom, Tarn?"

"Of course, I do. We all do, but we also don't want to die. This is suicide."

"It isn't," Ilaria promised. "We have a plan. Rebe, are the edu ready?"

"*We are ready!*" Ilaria wasn't sure, but the vines sounded almost giddy.

"*Then let them have it!*" Thane sent and to all of the psions astonishment, they heard the joined command with the Rebe.

But as they waited on the rise above the mine, nothing happened. Tarn looked accusingly at Thane, but before he could rebuff the empath for his failed coup, Thane told him to wait.

They waited again. The empaths felt the faint panic slowly rise through the mining complex before bursting through every exit. Every human who had been underground clawed his way through the people jamming doors. Having spent years growing in the humid facility, the edu knew where the invaders were vulnerable.

"What happened?" Tarn asked in astonishment.

"The edu happened," Ilaria answered him. "They've been growing their spoors in the complex waiting for the right moment to attack and expel the humans from their world. They've lost their food and water... and now they no longer have air. This final attack opened the gas pipes fully and flooded the mines with Mephitis."

"But they have breathers."

"Also sabotaged," she smiled as together they watched as even more people scrambled through the doors. Doubled over as they tried to expel the toxins from their lungs, not even the augments were aware of the psions observing up above.

"Now, Jax," Thane said into his comm.

Immediately, a siren alarm mounted on a tall post blared, signaling a factory-wide evacuation. Whether they expected it or had just had enough, those who hadn't already been stumbling towards the emergency shuttles began running. New fights began as the miners rioted for space on the departing vessels.

"That won't get rid of them all," Tarn warned.

"No," Thane agreed. "We knew they didn't have enough ships for a total evacuation at once, so Jax is in space ready to collect any stragglers. Ready, Ilaria? Stun anyone who doesn't look like they're going to go willingly. There can't be a single human left."

"But we're humans!"

Thane paused before following Ilaria down the hill. With a smile, he informed Tarn, "Not anymore, psion. I suggest anyone who's not with us jump on a shuttle because there's no going back. But those you who do stay, the Indigenous have promised us sanctuary and freedom from the tyranny of the empire!"

It wasn't the most impressive rebellion Thane could have hoped for, but to their credit, none of the refugee psions surrendered. Those without injuries followed Thane down into the pit while the others were lifted into the top branches of the Akilli to keep watch and inform the fighters of trouble through their connection with the Rebe.

It helped that very few of the retreating miners had enough energy to fight. Herded by hundreds of walking Trees, most of the hungry and battered humans didn't even try to resist.

"Did Torquil leave?" Ilaria asked after stunning one of the augments Thane had followed into the caverns. She waited for an Akilli to carry his unconscious body to the landing pads.

"I haven't seen him," Thane frowned. "I'll have Rill scan the area once Jax has taken the last group offworld."

"That was your idea to call Jax?" Ilaria smiled at her father's guile.

"It was Rill's idea, but yes," Thane answered. "Daneb would never have sounded an evacuation, so Rill hacked into the system and did it for him. I sent a message to Jax to bring more ships."

"Well done, Thane!" Tarn said, his tone a mixture of praise and consternation. Stepping over one of the bodies, the elderly telepath wasn't sure if the prone man had been one of the casualties or had merely been stunned. "Though I must admit, I still don't see what we have gained. They'll be back with more firepower than the few of us can withstand. They will destroy us."

"Tarn's right," Ilaria agreed. "They won't stay gone."

"That's why we have to be ready before Laran and the Company return. Psions, Akilli, Rebe and Edu!" Thane shouted to all the lifeforms on the Wald. "Today we are family; today we are all Edu of the Wald! Let's make sure we stay this way."

It was three days before the Company returned with Laran's fleet, which was two and a half days longer than most of the psions had expected to live. To Thane's immense relief, Sarkin and his siblings agreed to meet before they used their ships to annihilate them from space. On the other hand, he reasoned, it was in their best interest to do so. Destroying them would destroy the mining facility and set gas production back for years.

As the Denobian watched troops of Laran's soldiers march off transport ships along with Keepers and the Empati, Thane knew they wanted to round up the rebels with as minimal damage as possible to the remaining mine. As there were only twenty-one psions against a thousand soldiers, the humans were confident the rebellion was already over.

Joining the soldiers was Sarkin's Array. The four telepaths spread out in an arc around the renegade psions so they could use their combined powers to scan more of the rebels. With an air of arrogant confidence that barely masked his fury, Sarkin walked to where Thane was waiting. In an attempt to use his size and mass as a show of power to intimidate, the emperor straightened to his full height and took one step closer to the shorter man than was necessary.

His pompous show of strength had the opposite effect as Thane recognized Sarkin hadn't dealt with many Denobians. Having always been the smallest adult in the room, Thane was far more confident; his own strengths didn't necessitate how far a man's feet were from his head.

As he studied them, Thane saw that all three siblings now wore the headband and not just Laran. He understood the golden bands, glinting like angelic halos in the Walden sun, were not fashion accessories, but sensory blocking devices and clearly a product of Arkellian technology. The empath was amused again at the lengths the three of them went in trying to gain an advantage. Even though he couldn't sense it, he already knew every emotion they were hiding.

"You look well, Thane," Sarkin began, "but I don't see Ilaria anywhere."

Out of the corner of his eye, Thane saw the closest member of the Array shake his head slightly at the emperor. So, Sarkin thought he'd have the better hand if his psychics could read the emotional state of the rebels while their halos muted what could be sensed from them. As Thane had raised Ilaria as a daughter and his mind didn't even flicker with sadness, he couldn't pretend she was dead.

"She had other duties to attend to," Thane answered truthfully. He didn't add that those duties were solely to keep herself out of sight. Even in workman's coveralls, her accelerated pregnancy could no longer be hidden, especially from a doctor with Sobek's experience.

"And what would those be? Practicing teleportation?"

At a signal from his listening Array, Sarkin knew Thane wasn't surprised the emperor was aware of her power. Continuing, Sarkin said, "I admit, that she caught us off guard when she vanished from our trackers. Give her back and we'll forget all about your rebellion."

"No," Thane said simply.

"What do you mean 'no'?" Unaccustomed at being denied anything, Sarkin's anger flared. "I don't think you understand how precarious your situation is. I don't intend to place her back with the whores. A teleporter would be of far better use with Laran's soldiers."

"That's all we are to you is tools. No more. From now on, we choose our destiny and our lives. And our situation isn't as precarious as you would believe."

"You mean these walking Trees?" Sarkin let out a short bark of laughter. "Keep defying me and we'll burn every plant on this world to ashes."

"No, you won't," Thane said. "Not if you intend to mine another molecule of gas from this planet. The reason Mephitis is so abundant on this world is the unique chemical structure and the evolution of its Indigenous lifeforms. As their own dead are buried and decay, their cells break down and become the very crystal you need, but it is the wet nature of this world that dissolves the Mephitis and turns it into the gas you so covet. If you destroy the environment of this planet, you will destroy the gas forever."

"You lie!"

"Your Array will tell you that I'm not," the Denobian stated flatly. "And if you kill us, you will have to contend with the Indigenous. In just a few days, they have obliterated your crystal mine, poisoned your food and sabotaged your air masks. They know how to deal with invaders now and you won't get a second chance to mine crystal anywhere on this planet."

Thane had chosen his words carefully. Though he couldn't sense anything through the dampening halo, Sarkin's reaction made it clear he didn't know about the second mine. If Daneb survived, he wouldn't be alive once Sarkin was through with him, but the foreman's fate wasn't his current concern.

"Emperor Sarkin," Thane continued, lifting his chin in defiance of the emperor, "consider this mine under new management."

Before Sarkin could rage his contempt at being spoken to in such a manner from a peek, Thane gestured to the neatly piled stack of cylinders on the loading dock. "Here is your entire quota of Mephitis Gas. Leave this world now and all future shipments will continue in full and on schedule. The contract and payment that is currently held by the Company will be signed over to us, the Psions of Janus. Refuse and the Indigenous will continue to sabotage this facility until the invaders die of asphyxiation or starve from lack of food. But I warn you: if you destroy us, you will lose the gas forever."

To Sarkin's credit, he actually considered his options rather than letting his indignation make the choice. "Very well, *psion*. Mine the gas yourself, but if I'm ever short a single canister, consider yourself in breach of contract."

At the emperor's signal, the army turned and marched back into their shuttles. Most of the soldiers were disappointed that after coming all the way to the Wald, there wouldn't be a fight. Though Sobek kept his silence as he also obeyed his brother, the dark glare he gave Thane told the psion it wasn't over. He would be back for Ilaria.

As Tarn stood by Thane's side to watch the ships leave, the Denobian sensed it also wasn't over for the aging telepath. Tarn had made it clear he didn't agree with the psions taking over the mine. In his opinion, the only change he'd made in their lives was to evict their overlords. And Tarn wasn't wrong; the Company might be gone, but the psions were still mining the gas as slaves of the empire.

"He'll get his gas, Thane, but don't think for a moment he'll actually leave us in peace."

"I didn't expect him to," Thane answered.

"Even with the help of the Trees, Thane, how do you expect twenty-one of us to mine the gas when the Company had nearly a thousand here to meet the quota?"

"Once Jax returns with the In-Valids from Maelstrom, we'll have more than enough people to meet the quota and with the help of the Akilli and the Rebe, we won't even have to dig. The edu can detect the pockets of gas collecting on the surface and all we'll have to do is siphon it. Your days of chiseling rock underground are over, my friend."

Thane could tell Tarn would need a few months of the psions actually meeting their quota before he was convinced Sarkin wouldn't obliterate them on principal. The empath actually held out some small hope that the emperor would ignore the insult they'd given him by rebelling when he realized the new arrangement was in his favor. With the Wald providing everything the psions needed to survive, there was practically no overhead in mining the gas except for the canisters and tools needed to ship it.

But Tarn wasn't quite finished. "However tenuous this is, Thane, you've liberated us and it appears you've also liberated the peek prison." Gesturing as he spoke, Tarn pointed to a shuttle angling down through the atmosphere to land on the docking platform.

At Thane's suggestion, Jax had told the Maelstrom's warden he had orders from Torquil that all of the remaining prisoners were to be transferred to the Wald. Though Drell was surprised that all of them were to be released to Jax's authority at once, he'd fulfilled his transfer of peeks for so long, he didn't question it; in fact, he was relieved. With such a large bonus, he'd be able to retire and live out his few remaining years with his family. Jax was relieved he wouldn't be there when the warden discovered the transfer had been forged.

Of the hundred and forty-two empathic and telepathic prisoners debarking from the shuttle, thirty of them needed immediate medical care after the harsh conditions of Maelstrom and eighteen of them were not expected to recover. The others needed plenty of food and rest before they had strength enough to be of use in siphoning the gas. It wasn't the most auspicious start Thane could have hoped for. The Denobian had gotten them out of prison only to send them to a penal colony.

But in time, Thane would change that, too. He had a plan; he always had a plan.

· EPILOGUE ·

Over the next couple of months, the small colony of psions did better than Thane could have hoped. While they weren't exactly thriving yet, both psions and edu worked hard. Twelve of the prisoners succumbed to the harsh conditions they'd endured on Maelstrom, but thanks to the abandoned medical facility in the mine, six survived despite the odds against them. While the psions recognized they were still technically slaves of the empire, life on the Wald was so much better than what they had before, none of them complained. Food was an abundant resource in the forest and, with the help of the Akilli, those who could still work found the labor both easy and enjoyable.

Anak had finally been reunited with his parents who informed everyone he was the only Akilli they'd ever known to become an adult without first having his *improva*. While the seemingly emotionless Trees didn't laugh, everyone knew the youngster was being teased when they said he'd still have to wait for the breeding season.

And none of them, Rebe and psions alike, could contain their excitement for the first baby to be born when Ilaria went into labor. As not one of the psions had any experience with a birth, Ilaria was moved into Rill's medical bed so the AI could take over the duties as doctor. Thane was so anxious; he was next to useless as he sensed both his daughter's physical and mental distress during each contraction. After making the Denobian give the young woman an injection the ship said would help ease her discomfort, Rill finally ordered Thane out of his bay so Jess could take over as midwife. When the evicted empath wouldn't stop hovering at the door and asking if everything was alright each time Ilaria cried out, the ship finally had to shut his doors on the worried man.

It may have stopped him hearing her cries through the metal walls, but it didn't stop the empath from sensing her. All Thane could do was pace tracks around Rill's exterior until the doors finally opened to the sounds of Jyn's tiny cries.

With an exalted look of joy at his fellow refugees, Thane darted up the ramp before slamming to a halt at the opened hatch as if he were suddenly fearful of disturbing the precious cargo inside.

"Come in," Ilaria smiled weakly at him. "Come meet your granddaughter."

Exhausted from her entry into the world, Jyn had fallen asleep in her mother's arms. Looking at her own drooping eyelids as Ilaria passed the tiny bundle into Thane's arms, he knew his own daughter soon be asleep herself.

"She's perfect," Thane said, too awed by the wonder of holding the newborn to notice the baby hadn't been in the world long enough to look like Ilaria had the first time he'd held her. Though Jess had cleaned the infant, Jyn's skin was mottled and wrinkled as if she'd been born too soon.

Four and a half months too soon, Thane reasoned, though Rill insisted the early birth was due to the serum and not because Jyn was premature. Even as he watched, the odd-colored flesh was slowly turning a healthier shade.

Giving Ilaria another tender smile, he said again, "She's perfect."

Smiling her serenity as she looked at two of the people most precious to her, Ilaria sighed and closed her eyes.

Feeling her mind drift away, Thane snuggled the sleeping Jyn even closer as he studied the tiny baby. Her hands had worked themselves free of the blanket, framing the round little face with half-relaxed fists.

Focused on his granddaughter, Thane wasn't aware anything was wrong until an alarm startled him from his contentment.

"Rill, what is it?" Thane demanded, unconsciously passing Jyn over to Jess when the sudden panic inside Rill caused every psion in the camp to bolt upright and turn their attention to the ship.

"I've lost her heartbeat," the AI said, infuriatingly calm.

A panel near the bio-bed opened. No longer the anxious grandparent waiting the birth of a child, Thane was now the laser-focused Keeper trained to act. Grabbing the offered defibrillators, Thane waited for the charge and shocked Ilaria to restart her heart.

"No response," Rill informed. "Defibs ready in three, two, one... now."

Ilaria's body jolted under the electricity before her lifeless body collapsed once more on the bed.

"Again!" Thane screamed after tensely waiting for the monitor line to pulse.

"Wait," Rill said, opening another compartment to reveal a syringe with a wicked looking needle. "Inject this directly into her heart."

Instantly, Thane obeyed by plunging the dagger deep into Ilaria's chest. Anguish nearly overwhelmed him when the still body didn't answer his frantic mental sendings. Throwing the paddles to the side, Thane climbed onto the table and began CPR. Counting out chest compressions, the small man covered Ilaria's mouth with his in order to breath his air into her lungs.

"Charge them again!" Thane ordered the ship as he retrieved the defibrillators. "I said charge them!"

"No," Rill said, sadness filling his computerized voice. "I'm sorry, Thane; she's gone."

"She can't be," Thane whispered. "The serum was

healing her. She'll heal!"

"Not this time," Rill told him. "The dose she was given has been exhausted. It healed her from being shot through the chest, but the rest... went into Jyn. I'm sorry, Thane. There's nothing we can do."

With tears streaming down his face, Thane took the baby back from Jess before stepping out to introduce his granddaughter to the other psions. With their joy shattered, Thane vowed he'd make Sobek pay, not only for Ilaria, but for every psion he'd killed.

With the dusk gathering around him, Anak reached into Rill's interior and gathered Ilaria's body into his branch-like hands. Cradling her close, the youth walked away from the camp and into the darkening forest. Pausing only to make sure he wasn't being followed, the Akilli continued, only stopping when he saw the shuttle in a clearing far enough from the psions' settlement that no one had seen it land.

"Thank you, my friend," Jax said, cupping his hand over Ilaria's still face.

"This isn't right," Anak told him. "This isn't our way and it isn't yours."

"It has to be our way now. Sobek is beginning the next phase of his plan; we need Ilaria now more than ever."

Anak waited as Jax put Ilaria into the hold of his shuttle. About to leave, the young Tree suddenly turned back. "What about Jyn?"

Jax hesitated. With a sudden shake of his head, he pushed a button to close the ramp door. "Nothing for now," he answered. "It was all I could do to plant the suggestion about J'rey and that Damien Rey is her father. I'll have to meet my daughter another time."

Anak stood in the clearing until the shuttle was out of sight. Once he was alone, the young Akilli turned and headed back to camp.

The psion revolution was over; their evolution was only just beginning.